MY SERVANT CALEB

My Servant Caleb

A Jewish boy
A Gentile girl
A world at war

Kerstin Sheldrake

MONARCH
BOOKS
Oxford, UK, & Grand Rapids, Michigan, USA

First published in the UK 2004 by Monarch Books
(a publishing imprint of Lion Hudson plc), Mayfield House,
256 Banbury Road, Oxford OX2 7DH.
Tel: +44 (0) 1865 302750 Fax: +44 (0) 1865 302757
Email: monarch@lionhudson.com
www.lionhudson.com

Reprinted 2005

UK ISBN-10: 1-85424-647-X
UK ISBN-13: 978-1-85424-647-9
US ISBN -10: 0-8254-6057-3
US ISBN -13: 978-0-8254-6057-9

Distributed by:
UK: Marston Book Services Ltd, PO Box 269,
Abingdon, Oxon OX14 4YN;
USA: Kregel Publications, PO Box 2607,
Grand Rapids, Michigan 49501.

Scripture quotations are taken from the following:
The Jewish Jerusalem Bible, Koren Publishers Jerusalem Ltd,
1998; The NKJV, New King James Version. Copyright © 1979,
1980, 1982 by Thomas Nelson, Inc. Used by permission.
All rights reserved.

British Library Cataloguing Data
A catalogue record for this book is available
from the British Library.

Printed in Great Britain.

Dedicated to Israel's Remnant

Contents

Note of Thanks

"It was one of those crystal clear mornings in early summer, when the rain of the previous night had washed the air clean enough to let the sun shine like a glistening diamond from a deep blue sky."

This was the first line of the first draft. My husband, Andrew, loved it, so I promised him that, should my novel ever reach publication, it would appear in the Acknowledgements as a personal "thank you" from me for him. So here it is. It is a "thank you" for the many hours he spent teaching me the ABC of computer use and retrieving files lost in the depths of the hard drive. Most important of all, he endlessly and patiently discussed with me all the various shades of Messianic Jewish and Christian theology and understanding.

A very special "thank you" goes to my Christian friend, Tim Chapman, who substantially edited the draft version. His professionalism, expertise, unwavering commitment over many months of time-consuming work, and, above all, his wonderful sense of humour and continuous encouragement helped me many times when I felt stuck. *Todah rabah, chaver.*

I also wish to express my thanks to Tony Collins of Monarch Books UK. He decided to publish what I believe to be one of the first completely Messianic Jewish novels ever written. For that "risk" taken, I am grateful.

But, above all, I want to thank the God of Avraham, Yitzchak and Ya'acov, and Father of our Lord Yeshua the Messiah. He inspired me without failing, page by page, and led me to the right material, sources and people at the right time. Many times I stood amazed. I feel I have walked a long path from the "crystal clear morning" to the "homeland". But, holding on to our Father's hand, I'd gladly do it all over again.

Kerstin Sheldrake,
Norwich, September 2003

Glossary

H. = Hebrew, Y. = Yiddish, F. = French

Ashkenazim (H.), German, Russian and Polish Jews

Bar-Torah (H.), synonym for the Messiah

Baruch HaShem! (H.), Praise the Lord!

Beit Din (H.), Jewish court of judgement

Brachah (H.), blessing

Ça va pas, non? (F.), That's not acceptable, is it?

Gefilte fish (Y.), traditional Ashkenazi fish dish

Chaver, Chaverim (H.), friend, friends

Chutzpah (H.), nerve, as in "He's got a nerve!" or "He's got a cheek!"

Da-i! (H.), Enough!

Frumm (Y.), pious

Gadna The youth organisation of the Haganah. Its members received military training in the guise of Boy and Girl Scouts

Goyah (H.), non-Jewess

Goy (H.), non-Jew

Haganah (H.), "Defence"; umbrella underground organisation for most of the Israeli armed groups that formed the basis for the future Israeli army

Ishah Anglia (H.), Englishwoman

Kippah (H.), head covering for Jewish men

Mais c'est terrible! (F.), But that's terrible!

Ma pauvre chérie (F. fem.), My poor darling

Mensh (Y.), a person who is reliable

Meshugge (H.), crazy, mad

11

Meshumad (H.), traitor; convert to Christianity

Mezusah, pl. Mezusot (H.), case containing a scroll with Hebrew verses (Deuteronomy 6:4–9) affixed to every doorpost

Mishpocha (H.), family

Moshe Rabbenu (H.), Moses our Teacher

Niddah (H.), term for ritual uncleanness during menses

Noachide Laws From a Jewish point of view, for a non-Jew to qualify for rewards in the Afterlife, he need only observe the Seven Noachide Laws:

1. To behave equitably in all relationships, and to establish courts of justice
2. To refrain from blaspheming God's name
3. To refrain from practising idolatry
4. To avoid immoral practices, specifically incest
5. To avoid shedding the blood of one's fellow man
6. To refrain from robbing one's fellow man
7. To refrain from eating a limb torn from a live animal.

Olam Hazeh (H.), lit. "This World", in contrast to *Olam Haba*, "The World to Come", life after death

Oy gevalt! (Y.), expression for an unpleasant surprise

Palmach (H.), "Strike Companies"; full-time military force set up by the Haganah in May 1941. Elite of the Haganah. Many *Palmachniks* received commando training from the British during WWII

Palmachnik Member of the Palmach

Quand même (F.), Even so

Quelle catastrophe! (F.), What a disaster!

Sephardim (H.), Spanish or Portuguese Jews

Shlepp (Y.), to carry a heavy load

Shobbes (Y.), Shabbat

Shiksah (H.), derogative for non-Jewish girl or woman

Shnorrer (Y.), leech

Shul (Y.), synagogue

Stetl (Y.), Jewish ghetto settlement

Succah (H.), temporary shelter erected to celebrate Succot
(Feast of Tabernacles); Leviticus 23:42
Tollis, Tollises (Ashkenazi Hebrew), Jewish prayer shawl
t'shuv (H.), someone who returns to Orthodox Judaism
Tzitzis, tzitziot (Ashkenazi Hebrew), tassels at the four corners
of the garment; Numbers 15:38, Zechariah 8:23, Luke 8:44
Tu peux imaginer (F.), You can imagine

~ 1 ~

Norfolk, England, 26th June 1936

The overnight rain had cleared the air and the sun had risen to reveal a beautiful morning. The clock had barely struck half past eight and golden sunshine was streaming through the open doors of the breakfast room.

Three men were enjoying a nourishing breakfast. As lord of Bleckham Manor, Sir Arthur Hornby, a man just past his prime, was at the head of the table. Since the death of his wife he had remained single, even though childless. Without a natural successor, Alistair, his nephew, was next in line. And Alistair was very fond of his uncle.

Alistair was visiting. This time he had not come to rural Norfolk alone but had brought a friend of the same age, like Alistair, an Oxford law graduate. Before starting his articles with a leading firm of London solicitors, he was allowing himself the luxury of a last long holiday. Although he didn't know it yet, he was about to be introduced to someone Alistair had long wanted him to meet.

"Well, I don't know where the young lady is this morning. I have to go in a few minutes . . . don't want to miss my train." Sir Arthur wiped his mouth on his blossom-white napkin of starched damask. "She usually arrives for breakfast with the lark," adding, "and with the appetite of a cuckoo chick."

He had barely finished speaking when a voice in the hall heralded the arrival of a young woman. She was evidently very much at home. Propelled as by a whirlwind, the door to the dining room burst open. The men's tranquil circle was irretrievably broken. To Sir Arthur's consternation, a bridle was flung across the nearest Regency chair. The young woman, dressed in riding gear, paid no attention to his guests. She rushed past them and gave Sir Arthur an enthusiastic hug. If Alistair was the son he had never had, this young lady was undoubtedly the daughter. Sir Arthur's love for her was plain to see.

She picked up the newspaper from the sideboard, leafed hastily through it and pushed a page under Sir Arthur's nose. She pointed to an article. "Uncle Arthur, look! Here! He's going. Satin will be going to Berlin. One of *our* horses is competing in the Olympic Games for Britain!"

Sir Arthur took the paper and read the good news for himself.

With flushed cheeks and sparkling eyes, Celia folded her arms and looked triumphantly at Alistair.

Alistair smiled back at her. An entrance like this was nothing new. It was good that some things in life never changed. The lack of formality made him feel more like a brother. He put down his knife and fork carefully.

"Well, what can I say? I stand in complete awe of the equine athletes you are breeding here. Congratulations! And when you've finished your sports report, maybe I could introduce you to my friend?" he teased. "By the way, this is Celia." He raised an eyebrow at his friend, who had looked up from his plate in puzzled amazement.

Celia looked at Alistair first, and then, like someone who had forgotten to post a letter of vital importance, at the young gentleman opposite her. The visitor pushed back his chair and rose politely, revealing himself to be of no more than average height.

"Oh! I am so sorry. I do apologise for my inexcusable behaviour." She stretched out her hand. "Hello. And welcome to Bleckham Manor!"

"Celia, this is Mr Levine, an old friend of mine who was hoping to relax for a while in our peaceful corner of Norfolk. Caleb, may I present Lady Celia? She's certainly her usual self this morning."

Mr Levine made a hint of a bow to the young lady. As they shook hands, he was surprised by her firm grip. "I am pleased to make your acquaintance, Lady Celia." He gave her a little smile, showing slightly irregular teeth.

The moment Celia became conscious of Caleb Levine she had only one thought: "Goodness, he doesn't go with the wallpaper at all!" With all the goodwill she could muster, Celia could not shake her initial impression: Caleb Levine simply did not fit into the surroundings. He looked outlandish, even a little foreign, with those high cheekbones, deep-set brown eyes and curly, unbrilliantined hair. Yes, it was the unruly hair that caught Celia's attention. Also the high forehead and receding hairline. They gave him an air of refinement. Her eyes passed over his superbly sculptured, slightly curved nose – how unfortunate – and a mouth surrounded by well-delineated lips, underlined by an assertive chin.

"Well, Mr Levine, I hope you enjoy your stay and don't get too bored. The social life here is, I'm afraid, not worth mentioning. Unless you like the company of cows, wheat and sugar beet."

With this encouraging remark and a teasing smile, Celia turned her attention to the breakfast buffet. It offered a generous selection of sausages, bacon, mushrooms, fried bread, grilled kidneys, black pudding and egg dishes.

As Sir Arthur rose to leave he remembered something. "Cosgrove should be calling later this morning. He needs to go through some accounts with you, Celia."

"Of course."

"Jolly good. I'll be off then. See you Sunday evening. And do take good care of these young chaps, won't you?" He patted her shoulder lightly and left Celia to enjoy her breakfast.

Sitting down opposite Mr Levine, she watched him from the corner of her eye as he chatted to Alistair. She noticed the way he ate his toast and scrambled eggs; the determination and vigour with which he cut up his food. How different from Alistair, who exhibited the calm superiority of a true gentleman – even in the way his knife discreetly pressed, rather than cut, his bacon. Suddenly, without warning, Caleb Levine glanced at her. His look bore the audacity of someone who was entirely unimpressed by the honour of sitting at Sir Arthur's table!

Thoroughly vexed, Celia attacked her breakfast with gusto, her man-sized helpings astonishing the guest. Alistair tried, chivalrously, to draw her into the conversation, knowing that social small talk had never been one of her strengths. Nor was it Caleb's.

"Celia, if you've a moment today, would it put you out terribly to give us a guided tour of the estate? It would be most kind."

"With pleasure." Very casually, she added, "Do you ride, Mr Levine?"

"I'm afraid not."

That was the death knell for any future friendship between them. In Celia's opinion, a man who could not ride was not worth a moment's notice.

"Well, maybe a little," corrected Mr Levine. It was a crucial afterthought.

"I'm sure we'll find a gentle hack for you. Riding makes showing the estate so much easier. It's rather large, you know." Celia changed the subject. "Alistair told me you're from London."

"Yes."

"And your family? Do they live there, too?"

"In London, yes. My parents and my younger sister, that

18

is. My older sister lives abroad." Mr Levine sounded a little reticent.

"How very interesting. Anywhere nice?"

"Esther is a doctor at the British Hospital in Jerusalem. Judy, my younger sister, is training to be a nurse at the Great Ormond Street Hospital in London."

"Alistair told me your father is a well-known surgeon; a famous specialist in his field. Why did you take up law?" Celia was working hard to keep the conversation flowing.

"It's in the blood. No, actually, I can't bear the idea of cutting people up, dead or alive."

"He can't stand blood; that's what he's really saying," Celia thought. But before she could make a glib comment, the estate manager arrived. She excused herself and followed Cosgrove from the room.

"She works with the estate manager?" Caleb showed his surprise.

"My dear friend, Celia lives and breathes Bleckham Manor. My uncle has taken her across the fields and farms of the estate since she was a little girl. I dare say she knows every sheep by name. She is dreadfully keen to learn everything she can about farming and estate management. Strange fancy, don't you think?"

Cecil Court, Celia's own home and birthplace was not a happy place. Lady Norah, Celia's mother, had never forgiven her husband, Henry, Earl of Besthorpe. He had been quite unable to fulfil her adolescent dreams of a lifestyle and position she still believed was her due.

When the children were born, Lady Norah placed her surviving hopes on them. Francis, however, Celia's brother and seven years her senior, showed no inclination or taste for the life expected of an aristocrat.

"I'd rather join the Labour Party," he told his parents.

Not long after his graduation from Oxford, he had

embarked on an Orwellian lifestyle. Unkind friends and relatives called it Bohemian.

So Cecilia, as her mother called her, became the earthly embodiment and resting place of all of Lady Norah's remaining aspirations. The investments she had made to prepare her daughter for a life in "Society", maybe even to become the future Princess of Wales, had paid no dividend. Two years ago, when Lady Cecilia had stayed with her grandmother in London and formally "come out" into well-bred society, it had briefly looked as if she might hook and land the son of a wealthy and influential industrialist. He had certainly shown all the signs of being attracted to her, but Cecilia had given him the cold shoulder. The whole affair had ended in a minor scandal when the spurned lover had turned up at a ball, angry and unacceptably drunk.

Feeling used and abused, Celia had rebelled. To Lady Norah's fury, she had packed her bags and returned to the safety of the Lancastrian country estate, her true home. Since then Cecilia had buried herself in these provincial back-waters, near a dreadful little market town, in a damp old house that was falling apart, delighting in cows and sheep. To make matters worse, she was now wasting her precious youth on the neighbouring estate of a man old enough to be her father. He was not even of high birth. If only Henry would make some effort to talk a bit of sense into his daughter. It might make all the difference. Just one word of command, delivered with gruff paternal authority, and Cecilia would be forced back into society and made to follow her mother's sensible advice. She might then have the chance of making at least a *reasonable* match. But instead of acting as he should, the Earl simply saw his daughter as natural, un-affected and equipped with an enviable dose of common sense. How much more humiliation could Lady Norah take? Why could Cecilia not be like her friend, Lady Georgina? She was so exquisite, so charming and so amusing. She attracted admirers as a buddleia drew butterflies. And then there was Sebastian, Georgina's brother, a frightfully handsome, delightful and most sought after bachelor. Oh, why could she not have had children like these?

But, instead of being like Georgina, her daughter had grown into a source of persistent embarrassment. Especially when she was entertaining high-born company. With socially useful people the girl seemed bored, stiff and forever watchful and guarded. Fearing the disapproval of her mother, she felt it safest to say and do as little as possible in such situations. By now she had developed a reputation for being rigid, tedious and supercilious – which only stoked the fires of Lady Norah's bitterness and criticism.

Mr Levine had managed the hack across the estate tolerably well. In fact, he had managed better than Celia had expected, given the initial clumsiness with which he had mounted the reliable old mare. He had even gone so far as to jump the occasional fallen tree trunk, but he lacked the inbred elegance of a true horseman. During their ride, he gave the impression of being a rather private person with a mind of his own. When he spoke he looked straight at her, weighing her up as much as she was trying to weigh him. This cat-and-mouse game amused Celia. Soon she was smiling at Mr Levine in a way that seemed to say, "I know just what you are up to, and I find it most entertaining." Yet throughout, the young lady had sensed that he was wary and careful. And, while he measured every word before speaking, his evident self-assurance showed a surprising absence of arrogance. Celia found him a rather intriguing character.

This early impression was enhanced next day when she heard the piano being played in the music room. Assuming it was Alistair, she was surprised to see Mr Levine sitting at the piano. He acknowledged her entrance with a nod, but carried on unperturbed, caught up in his music. As his fingers glided over the keys, Celia listened to the foreign-sounding piece he was playing, with growing interest. When he stopped, Celia encouraged him to carry on.

"Please, do continue. It sounds so lovely."

His face brightened. "You liked it?" The pianist vacated his seat. "It's your turn now."

But his invitation was not taken up. Celia shook her head. "I don't play."

"You don't play the piano?"

"I have no musical talent at all, I'm afraid."

His smile disappeared. "I don't believe it! Everybody has some musical gifting."

"Then I must be the exception that proves the rule." Celia turned to go.

"Nonsense! I insist – please."

Celia glared at the grand piano. That big black monster had been the cause of many tears over the years. But Mr Levine had spoken with such a pleasant, calm voice that she allowed herself to be persuaded. His face was so open and boyish, and showed no ill intent or desire to humiliate. Her fingers stumbled over the keys a few times and then she played a simple piece from memory. It was mechanical and clumsy. Before long she hit a wrong chord, and her fingers jumped off the keys as if they had touched hot coals.

"Did your piano teacher slam the lid on your fingers?" Caleb had recognised her instinctive reaction.

"No, she used a cane."

"No wonder you don't like the piano."

"It's not just that. I've always been a keen rider, and riding stiffens your fingers terribly. My friend Annabel had to give up riding altogether when she began to play the cello seriously."

Caleb chuckled. "That must be why I am such a bad horseman."

"But with music you can give pleasure to lots of people. You don't bring joy to anyone by riding except yourself."

"Then allow me to teach you a little song. If you liked the other pieces I was playing, you'll certainly like this one." He started a new melody and before long she found herself tapping her foot in time to it. Caleb grinned.

"I love it. What's it called?"

Instead of answering, Caleb moved over and motioned her to sit next to him. "It's quite easy to learn. Look." He gave another demonstration. "It's a traditional Hebrew song."

"You know Hebrew songs?" Celia exclaimed. "How extraordinary."

"Not when you are a Hebrew," Caleb replied, without elaborating.

"That's where you're hiding." Alistair called, approaching them. Recognising the tune he added, "Not the *Hava Nagila* again? Celia, once you've heard this song it'll be dancing round your head for the rest of the day."

With a twinkle in his eyes, Caleb Levine played the song again, this time adding the words. Alistair joined him and together they sang a beautiful round. As the song gathered speed and momentum, Alistair tried to outsing his friend. Celia laughed. Caleb noted she had a very infectious laugh. When the men had sung themselves to a standstill, exhausted and laughing, Celia clapped and asked what the words meant.

Caleb translated: "*Come, let us be glad and rejoice. Arise, brothers, with a joyful heart.*"

"Oh. Do you sing much, Mr Levine?" Celia found his voice rather attractive.

"You should hear him when he plays with Esther." Alistair interjected.

"Does your sister play as well as you do?"

"Better."

"Esther plays the piano and Caleb the violin."

"I'd like to hear you on the violin." Celia dropped an undisguised hint.

"Maybe. In the meantime you need to practise. I'd like to hear you playing this."

In the evening Celia played the song at home from memory, but kept hitting wrong chords and stumbling over the tempo. But she was determined to master it. As she played, she recalled the provocative twinkle in Caleb Levine's eyes.

"Oh, Cecilia. Please, do stop or at least close the door and windows. Your playing has not improved one bit since your last attempt."

Lady Norah shut the door noisily to underline her point. Stubbornly, Celia went on practising.

Next day, she felt sufficiently confident to play it, albeit shyly, in Sir Arthur's music room. Caleb, who had come into the adjoining library to fetch a book, surprised her by singing along.

"Well done. Now play it again and I'll accompany you on the violin." He strode into the music room.

On her next attempt Celia made a mess of the song. Blushing with embarrassment, she stopped.

"What's the matter? Why stop? Ah, you are just nervous. Let's try again. Just relax and pretend I'm not here. Would it help if you sang along?"

"I can't sing."

"That's what you said about playing the piano. It's just a matter of practice. Don't you sing at home?"

"At home I have nothing to sing about," Celia snapped. She bit her lip.

"I do apologise," Caleb said softly after an embarrassed pause. "I've taken too many liberties and was too presumptuous, Lady Celia. Do please forgive me."

Sensing that he had upset her, he picked up a sheet of music and excused himself.

~ 2 ~

Bleckham Manor, 28th June 1936

Caleb returned to his comfortable guest room. He needed to bathe and change before lunch. The sun had moved to the front of the house, leaving his room in shade. From his window he looked out over the terrace with its steps leading down to a formal garden laid out round a weathered fountain. Beyond that, an invisible ha-ha kept the grazing cows in the meadow out of the garden. A dark green line of woodland in the distance completed the picture. How peaceful and relaxed it was. He liked being here.

He thought back to how he and Alistair had met at boarding school, where his troubles had started as soon as his peers discovered that a "Jew-Boy" was in their midst. Name-calling was the least of his problems. He had been the butt of verbal abuse and even physical attacks for as long he could remember. But he had drawn the line at pigs' ears in his satchel and a cross in his games kit. Challenging his tormentors had only made matters worse: he was then considered a troublemaker by the school authorities. The headmaster sighed. Letting Jews into the school always created problems, even when the parents professed to be Christians. The wisest thing was to turn a blind eye to the bullying that was going on and give Caleb "six of the best" whenever he stepped out of line. Caleb received many beatings but, gritting his teeth and clenching his fists, he never shed a tear. At least not in public. He was determined that the Goyim – the non-Jews – would never see him cry. Never.

He rejected both the old ghetto mentality, that of silently accepting suffering and humiliation, and his parent's exhortations to "turn the other cheek". Surely, in the 20th century, the appointed time to fight back had arrived? But his lone battle was not always successful.

It was on one such occasion that he had first noticed Alistair. A gang had crowded in on Caleb to settle a score. As they started to push him around, a timid but determined voice was heard above the shouts. "You cowards! It's ten against one!"

"And that's how many Gentiles it takes to beat down one Jew," Caleb shouted back, before he had an arm pushed against his throat to silence him.

"Teacher coming." A guard sounded the alarm.

"We'll deal with you later, Jew-Boy. And you, Jew-lover!" snarled the pack leader as he ran off.

The group dispersed quickly and Alistair picked up Caleb's cap, which had been knocked off in the scuffle. With a shy smile he handed it back. "I'm really sorry about that," he said.

"Why? What's it to you? Why did you interfere anyway?" Caleb snapped back at him, and snatched his cap from Alistair's hand.

"They weren't being fair and I hate bullying. They used to pick on me before you came; now they've turned on you. I owe you one, I suppose. Anyway, why shouldn't I help you? Aren't you one of God's 'Chosen People'?"

"Am I? And chosen for what? To be everyone's scapegoat and whipping boy?"

Alistair felt hurt at this rebuttal, but he was sensitive enough to make allowances for another's feelings. Caleb turned and stalked off without another word.

This was the first time Alistair had met a Jew, and he was intrigued. He had read about them in the Bible, but knew no one who could tell him anything about them.

Neither God nor religion was of any relevance or interest to his parents. But God mattered a lot to Alistair. Especially Jesus. The Sermon on the Mount was one of his favourite passages in the New Testament. Alistair knew that Jesus loved the poor and meek and was their friend. His parents had told him many, many times that he was a failure and inadequate. And he believed them. So, he concluded, as one of the poor and weak, maybe Jesus loved him too. Once – he would never forget that moment – he had been sent to bed without tea for crying during a "blooding" after a hunt. The desperately unhappy child had prayed, "Please, Lord Jesus, forgive me for being a coward and useless, and be my friend." Then he had begun to read the Bible, secretly so as not to be laughed at. It was then that he had started to discover the wonderfully comforting words Jesus had spoken. Even sermons in church began to make sense.

By the time he was sent to boarding school, Alistair had a pretty good understanding of what the Christian faith was about. And he tried to live it out. But because he stood up for his religious convictions, and was small for his age, he soon became the target of ridicule and bullying. Then a Jew had appeared on the scene. This had taken the pressure off him. It seemed odd to Alistair that they had singled out a Jew for bullying, while at the same time making fun of *him* for being a Christian. Who could explain it?

The school chaplain said that God loathed the Jews because of their wickedness and for killing the Messiah. He explained that the church was now Israel, a new Spiritual Israel. Well, he ought to know, being a man of the cloth. Yet there was one thing Alistair still was not happy with. As he saw it, if God could break His promise and end His eternal covenant with the Jews, what would stop Him doing the same thing again and cancelling the new covenant He had made with the church? Wouldn't Christians then be

27

condemned to eternal damnation if they too sinned, just as the Jews were? And where did that leave Master Alistair Hornby? It was all so irrational. Such was the state of Alistair's private theology when he encountered Caleb. But Caleb was in no mood to befriend a Christian, and Alistair did not approach the Hebrew boy again.

Caleb, meanwhile, had learned fast – the hard way – how to keep young upper class Gentiles at a safe distance. But he noticed that this Christian boy was an outsider like himself, and that he spent most of his free time in the library. Caleb loved to study too, but was also brilliant at sport. Before long he emerged as a natural leader on the playing field. Because he was both fast on his feet and able to think quickly in tactical play, he was a much sought-after member of the rugby team. But even when he was made team captain, the abuse did not stop.

"The Jew-Boy is a fast runner because that's what Jews are best at: running!" One teammate, Edward Gordon, had once mocked him in the changing rooms. Gordon was two years Caleb's senior and stood a few inches taller.

Caleb had calmly walked up to him, stared him in the eyes, and said, "Have you ever heard of Aharon David Gordon, a famous agricultural reformer in Palestine? He's a good Jew. And do you want to know how many Jewish Gordons there are in this country? The Gordons are the only Scottish clan that did not originate in Scotland."

Edward Gordon was speechless and felt humiliated in the presence of his peers. Later that day Caleb was ordered into the headmaster's office for calling Gordon a Jew-Boy.

But, in the end, Jew-Boy or not, what really mattered was winning. So, Caleb rose gradually to a status of despised popularity. This may have made life easier for Caleb, but Alistair lacked his gifting. He remained isolated and alone.

One day during his first summer at the school, some errand had taken Caleb to the library, where he found

Alistair reading. "Aren't you going out to play?" The boy shook his head. "What are you reading that's so interesting, then?"

"I don't think you'd like it," said Alistair.

"I didn't ask whether I'd like it; I asked you what you were reading." He grabbed the book and looked at the title. "*Growth of a soul* by Hudson Taylor. You must be desperate."

"Don't you ever ask yourself why we are alive? Why we feel and think? And what we're supposed to do with our lives?" asked Alistair.

Caleb was quite unprepared for such profound questions. "Gosh, you are intense, aren't you? Who cares about the meaning of life and the universe on a sunny afternoon?" He looked at the cover. "Anyway, all you live for is to die, and in between you suffer pain and disappointment."

"So you *have* considered these things before." Alistair hoped he had found a kindred spirit. "You don't think there's any reason for life, then?"

Caleb became uncomfortable whenever these questions cropped up. He preferred to bury them conveniently under the pile of hurt, rebellion and rejection that littered his heart. Having hidden his hurts, they would sometimes resurface in uncontrollable waves of self-pity. At such moments, he would end up wallowing morosely in the simple, unhappy fact that he was a Jew.

"Listen, I didn't come here to debate the meaning of life with you. And if you intend to convert me to Christianity, then you're barking up the wrong tree." Caleb turned to go.

"Please, don't be offended. You are quite right. I always bore people with my questions."

Caleb looked back over his shoulder. The poor chap did look forlorn. He changed his mind and sat down on a pile of Alistair's books. They began to chat and talk but kept to less contentious subjects, such as Caleb's current battle with

English literature. Shakespeare's *Merchant of Venice*, to be precise.

When the boys parted, Caleb was surprised that he had found the Goy – the non-Jew – a surprisingly agreeable companion. But why did he make life so complicated for himself? Goyshe boys had no reason for it; they were meant to be simple and straightforward. It was a Jewish prerogative to be rejected, despised and persecuted, and the prime target for mockery. A wealthy young Goy ought to be deliriously happy. Why? For not being born into a Semitic cradle; for not having to live, day in and day out, with the awareness that they were different; for not being dispossessed of their land, their dignity and – he sometimes felt – their hope, too.

This chance meeting was the beginning of a peculiar friendship. Caleb had, quite unintentionally, won himself a Gentile ally. Then, the same year, Alistair's parents had decided to go to the Continent during the school holidays. They thought it would be rather tiresome to take a painfully shy lad with them, so they had arranged for him to stay at school for the holidays. Caleb was outraged: he could not believe that any parents – even Goyshe parents – could be that cruel. He therefore told himself that it was only an act of charity – and a reluctant one – to offer to take care of someone unfortunate enough to have a Goyshe mother. On the spot, he invited Alistair to spend the holiday with his family.

Since that first invitation to stay with the Levines, many more visits had followed. Alistair's kind, accommodating nature had quickly won their hearts and he was soon accepted as a member of the family. Moreover, as Caleb's parents and sisters had converted to Christianity, they were able to answer many of Alistair's questions.

This aroused a fierce anger in the young Caleb. He eventually drew a firm line in the sand: either Alistair dropped the subject of religion in his company once and for all, or he would drop their friendship. "Let's get one thing straight, Al. Don't even think about preaching to me about your gospel or Jesus. I hate that name more than any other. As long as you remember that, we'll get along just fine."

Valuing Caleb's friendship, Alistair did not raise the subject in his friend's presence again. But he was deeply puzzled. If his parents, whom he obviously loved and respected, were such warm and sincere Christians, why should Caleb be so angry and vehemently opposed to Jesus and the faith He had founded? Then Mrs Levine took him aside and shared a vital piece of family history with him. That did much to explain Caleb's behaviour. But when he broached the subject with his friend, all Alistair got was, "Well, now you know, so leave it there."

Once Caleb's ban on religion had been accepted, their friendship flourished. Alistair remained strongly drawn to the lively Levine household, and their gentle warmth rubbed off on him. At first, Mr and Mrs Hornby, Alistair's parents, had voiced strong objections to this friendship. Then they started to notice the positive changes taking place in their son, of whom they had almost given up hope. So they grudgingly allowed the friendship to continue. They also watched Caleb growing into a young English gentleman of impeccable manners and strong character. When Alistair at long last asked to ride to hounds, without any prompting, his parents breathed a sigh of relief. They had to admit that, while their threats and punishments had availed nothing, the little Jew's friendship, inspiration and reassurance had worked wonders. For his part, Caleb was well aware that the Hornbys never granted him more than grudging toleration. But their opinions mattered little to him. He shrugged off their rejection as easily as picking a hair off a suit. After all, he, the despised Jew, rode their horses, shot their pheasants, ate at their table, and made use of their servants and stately home. He cheerfully admitted to himself that he used them as much as they were using him.

* * *

Celia's bedroom had shiny, dark floorboards, oak panelling and heavy beams supporting the low ceiling. Her pride and joy was the four-poster bed, which filled most of the room. It left space only for two armchairs in front of the fireplace and her dressing table, which doubled up as her writing desk, by the window. There were no unnecessary fripperies in the room and only a few ornaments: a handful of personal belongings each preserving a special memory.

The oak door creaked a little as she entered. Celia kicked off her jodhpur boots with a sigh of relief. It had been a busy day and a pleasant tiredness was seeping through her. She welcomed it. She would far rather spend her days outdoors in wind and rain, with freezing hands and feet, than live the life of a salon poodle. The memory of her year in London made her shudder. She had hated the endless receptions and fastidious rituals, the compulsory attendance at interminable social events and essential balls. She had loathed the fatuous picture magazines filled with posing debutantes and the fashionable clothes no one could possibly wear. And she had felt trapped by the utter impossibility of declining yet another invitation to take tea with a dowager duchess. That year had nearly broken her.

Celia turned to the window and looked at the same sky Caleb had admired earlier that day. The chestnut tree outside was so close she could almost touch its leaves. The glowing sun was playing with the foliage, and flooding the countryside with its orange-golden evening light. Her heart was full of wonder and thankfulness: no painter could mix his colours so brilliantly, no sculptor carve the intricate tracery of a mature tree, and no man compose the beauty of a dawn chorus, or the whisper of the wind in the heights of the poplars. Celia smiled at her old friend waiting patiently outside her window.

"And how are your leaves today?" she enquired.

Feeling spoilt and relaxed after a long and self-indulgent bath, she sat down at the dressing table with her wet hair bundled up in a towel. She examined herself critically in the mirror. It should have reflected the dignified expression, the fine classical lines, and the air of serene confidence of one of her class. She sighed. She had none of these. Indeed, she did not even consider herself pretty, let alone beautiful. Her face was just too square. And then there were these freckles! No true lady had freckles, a charge repeatedly impressed on her by her mother. Goodness knows what Celia had not done in order to be rid of them. She had tried lotions, sunhats and parasols but nothing could prevent them from returning each summer like migrating swallows. Who could possibly fall in love with anyone who looked like her? Nor was poor Celia a dab hand with make-up. While moderately confident in her use of scent, her dressing table had no place for powder and lipstick. But then, who cared about make-up in the stable yard? And what on earth was she to do with her hair? Those long, frizzy, strawberry-blond curls had a wild will of their own and resisted every effort to tame them. Once, as a child, Celia had even tried to straighten them with a hot iron. She knew she would never have Georgina's chic good looks, or the *je ne sais quoi* of Annabel's Paris finishing-school charm and wit. Celia sighed again. She was not like her friends and doubted she ever would be.

She loosened her towel and the long, curly strands slithered down her neck and settled on her shoulders. "Maybe Mummy is right. Maybe there really *is* something wrong with me," she thought.

33

Celia had never expected much from life. What she longed for was a flowing stream of steadfastness, a life unshaken by tumultuous events, a quiet and unassuming existence. She just wanted to be left alone; disturbing no one and being disturbed by no one. But instead of the calm fulfilment she longed for, an abyss had opened up before her, in the form of the empty and aimless life of her class. Would she ever escape it? How many people lived like that, seeking to fill their empty lives by chasing after love, power, riches or fame? But she didn't allow herself to be deceived. She knew, deep down, that they were simply searching for a meaning to their futile, silly existences. They were just chasing dancing chimeras along the bars standing between them and eternity. To stop and think about the path they were rushing down would be an act of reckless insanity. So they kept on hunting and struggling, loving and playing, occupied but never content, desperately trying to fill the vacuum in their souls with transient nothingness. And like them, or perhaps because of them, Celia found she was being sucked into the same whirlpool of senseless busy-ness in a frantic attempt to give her life some depth. Hard work was becoming her escape into meaningfulness and self-esteem. And whenever the unanswerable questions welled up inside her, she would bury them in yet more activity. Then she would be fine, she told herself. But, in her heart, she doubted this new answer to the riddle of her life.

Forcing these thoughts from her mind, Celia busied herself with dressing for dinner. She was almost ready when there was a knock on the door. Lady Norah entered and carefully closed the door. "Ah, you're here, dear. There was a telephone call for you. Annabel has heard that Alistair is at Bleckham and she's invited you both over for tea. Isn't that nice of her?"

Her mother sat down, brushing the jodhpur boots aside. "It'll do you good to mix with some people of your own kind and age for once." Lady Norah seemed in a bright mood. She watched her daughter getting ready. "That dress is horribly out of fashion, you know."

Celia chose to ignore the barbed comment. "Tea with Annie would be lovely, but I don't know whether Al will be able to come. His friend arrived only three days ago."

"I'm sure Annabel won't mind extending her invitation to include him. Is he nice?"

Celia's thoughts had wandered. "Who?"

"Alistair's friend, of course. Did you talk to him?"

"We were introduced over breakfast and went for a hack around the estate. He's nice but no one out of the ordinary, really."

"Do you think we ought to invite him to tea? Alistair is such a pleasant young man; his friend must surely be the same."

Celia frowned at the thought of Mr Levine sipping tea in the drawing room. "Mummy, he's Al's friend, not mine. I don't know him. Please do stop trying to invite eligible men to tea on my behalf!"

"Well, I'm just doing my best. When I was your age I had more suitors than fingers on my hand, but ended up with your father." She pressed her lips together. "But never mind that now."

"I know, Mummy. I know. I promise I'll call Annie."

"I wonder if she's invited Sebastian. Now *he's* a wonderful young man. Good pedigree too. If you married him you'd want for nothing. Just imagine yourself as mistress of Lenkham Hall. Don't you like him – at least a little? He's called so many times lately, but all you ever do is tease him!"

"With all due respect, Mummy, he's been teasing me ever since I was little. It's not that I don't like him; it's just that he's more like a brother than a potential husband. And he thinks every woman should fall at his feet and worship at the altar of his wit, intelligence and dashing good looks. And I don't want to give him that satisfaction. Anyway, he needs to take some of his own medicine."

"One day a girl with her head screwed on straight will come along and marry him. I only hope it's you."

"Mummy . . ."

"Cecilia Eleanor, I'm at a loss to know exactly what you're looking for in a husband. I have always maintained that a young lady ought to pretend to be hard to get – but you're making it impossible. And don't forget you're not as pretty or well-off as all that."

"And you make jolly sure I won't ever forget it. I believe that, when the right man comes along, I will know it's him."

"And just how do you think you'll know that? Are you expecting to hear a voice from heaven?"

"I don't want to go looking for a husband as if I were writing a wish-list for Christmas. If I did, I might end up with someone like Daddy."

"That was a bit below the belt," said Lady Norah, thoroughly piqued. "You will call Annabel then?"

"Yes, Mummy."

~ 3 ~

Bleckham Manor, 30th June 1936

Celia and Caleb met again under less pleasant circumstances. She was kneeling in one of the brood mares' boxes doing her best to bottle-feed a newborn foal. To wish the young woman a good morning seemed inappropriate, so Caleb just leant over the stable door and said quietly, "I'm very sorry about what happened."

Celia looked up. "Oh, good morning. You've heard then?"

"Sir Arthur mentioned the new arrival. And that you'd lost a mare." Caleb seemed in no particular hurry.

"Yes, it's a crying shame. Now I'm trying to get this little fellow onto the bottle before we find him a surrogate mother."

"Any success yet?"

"Not since I got here."

"And when was that?"

"Six-thirty."

"Good gracious. Are you always up that early?"

"There's no quieter time than the early morning. Mind you, the farmers are out long before that."

"You're not a farmer," reminded Caleb with a smile.

The foal kept refusing and Celia, looking miserable, brushed away a stubborn strand of hair that kept falling into her eyes.

"Shall I give it a try?" Caleb came into the box and Celia passed him the bottle.

37

"The vet had to deliver him by Caesarean, but it was too late for the mother. She died soon afterwards."

Caleb glanced up at her quickly. He noticed for the first time that she had firm, clear features and a perfect, natural complexion. To have added make-up would have been ludicrous. He spoke soothingly to the little colt.

"There you are," he said when it eventually decided to take the teat and suck hungrily.

A smile of relief broke over their faces and they exchanged pleased glances. Caleb continued feeding the foal, while Celia got up and stretched her legs. As she leant against the stable wall, watching the peaceful scene, a strange, sweet sensation crept over her. He was caressing his little charge tenderly as if he could understand its feelings of loss and shock. He continued to talk to it, softly, almost whispering, as if they were quite alone. He forgot Celia's presence, his world shrinking to only himself and a needy creature. But here she was, watching an unassuming man she barely knew pour out his love and tenderness on a tiny foal. She suddenly, irrationally, felt jealous of the foal. She shook her head impatiently, scolding herself. She did not like these uncomfortable, invasive emotions. She thought she had dealt with that side of her nature long ago.

Caleb gave the colt's short back a last stroke with his bony hand. "Finished. We can't bring back the mare, but at least we've saved the little one." He handed the empty bottle to Celia.

She rewarded him with a crooked smile. "So far so good, Mr Levine." She hid her turbulent emotions behind a slight stiffening. "We still have to find a foster mare and that'll be difficult. Mares only accept their own foals. Even if their own has just died, they won't readily take an orphan in its place."

Celia had a look on her face that Caleb recognised. Her words had been spoken as a *fait accompli* – an unalterable fact – but he sensed her underlying pain. Caleb hated that look. It made him feel helpless and reminded him of his father.

Dealing with death and disease may have been Professor Levine's daily lot, as it was for every doctor, but he had never been able to accept it clinically. He had never managed to dissociate his medical mind from his compassionate heart, and could not stop himself from sharing in his patients' suffering. He always battled against feelings of hopelessness and defeat. At times he would bring his feelings home with him from the hospital.

Caleb felt that he needed to say something. "What you say may be true, but miracles do happen. Anyway, it's time for a cup of tea. That'll make things look brighter." The moment it was said, he knew that he had waffled platitudes, and felt silly.

They walked back to the house together and the butler brought them tea. They did not talk much; words didn't seem to be needed. Each knew what the other was thinking. Then Caleb smiled. "Tea. That famous English cure-all. My grandmother would have served us chicken soup." Celia did not understand this allusion and looked at him questioningly. "In Jewish homes, chicken soup is the equivalent of a cup of tea," he explained.

"Oh," was all Celia could say.

She knew no Jews and nothing about Judaism. And she had other things on her mind at that moment.

The next day, Celia arrived at the stables earlier than usual. She wanted to help with one of the many feeds the newborn foal needed. When she asked where the bottle was, a stable hand informed her that Mr Levine was already giving the little lad a drink.

"Is he indeed?" asked Celia with mixed feelings.

Whatever her opinion of Mr Levine, he was not going to take over the running of the yard. That was her responsibility. Nevertheless, she entered the stable quietly so as not to

39

startle the foal. She could hear Caleb talking softly the way he had the day before. Leaning over the door of the loose box, she watched the foal taking its milk greedily. There was such a feeling of family here that her initial crossness evaporated.

"May I offer you the job of wet-nurse, Mr Levine?"

Caleb had just become aware of her presence, and turned around. "You're offering me a second career? What's the pay like?"

"Dreadful. And the hours are terrible."

There it was again, that feeling of nearness, the total absence of any need for pretence.

"Have you found a foster mare yet?"

"No, but I know our vet will do his best. He's most likely to be the first to hear if anything suitable comes up." She pointed at the colt. "For the time being he's doing well, but he really needs proper mare's milk before he'll get any stronger. Bottle-feeding is only a temporary solution."

"I'm sure everything will work out fine. And please do call me Caleb. 'Mr Levine' sounds dreadfully formal."

He shot Celia a quick glance. He had made an offer of closer friendship and did not quite know how she would respond.

"I accept, but only if you stop calling me Lady Celia. My name is Celia." She steered the subject back to safer ground. "You really do love horses, don't you?"

"'Love' would be too strong a word, I think; 'like' or 'fond' would be more accurate." As soon as Caleb sensed her shocked disappointment, he wanted to make amends. "What I mean to say is that I know of no other animal as noble and gracious as a horse. If a horse were only aware of its strength and capabilities, where would mankind be? Consider your horse: he could so easily make it plain that he was refusing you his services by simply throwing you off. Instead, if you treat him kindly and with understanding, he'll faithfully carry you to the ends of the earth."

"You believe in showing kindness and compassion to animals, don't you?"

"Is there any other way to treat a fellow creature, whether man or beast?" Having checked his watch he handed her the empty bottle. "I'd completely forgotten I've to be somewhere else in half an hour." He smiled at her and added, "I'll see you again. Soon, I hope."

Celia followed him out. She stood watching him until he disappeared from view.

Her daily routine was about to begin. Working with horses is a rather solitary occupation. You don't need to be a team player. Many horsemen and women are deeply private individuals with little need or desire for human company. It is so much easier to relate to an animal than a human being. Animals make few demands on your life and emotions and never challenge your attitudes. They docilely do all you ask of them, happy to do their best. They never complain. You can choose to talk to them or remain silent, and they never bother you. They never tire you with endless questions, unpredictable tempers, burdensome demands and unmet emotional needs. Once you have finished with them, they are content to be left alone provided they have a full belly and adequate shelter. In short, a dumb animal makes a far better companion than most people. It is much easier to deal with, and is often more grateful for your company.

Not surprisingly, perhaps, Celia preferred the company of animals to that of people. People were too complicated. Not only could they hurt her physically, they could also – and frequently did – bruise her emotionally. A physical bruise was easily forgotten, but who could heal a broken heart?

One day, perhaps inevitably, she had reached that breaking point. The constant nagging of Lady Norah had ignited yet another dispute between mother and daughter. Celia could not remember what had sparked it off or what was said. The only thing she now recalled was that, on that day, her feelings had died. She, Celia, all by herself, had voluntarily decided to kill them off. As a compassionate person would quickly kill a wounded animal to release it from pain, so Celia, at that moment, humanely put to death all feelings of love, hope, joy and trust in anyone or anything. If she could not die physically, then at least she would die to disappointment, betrayal, tears and despair.

From now on she would accept, serenely and uncomplainingly, all that fate would throw at her. She would obediently and silently bow under its mighty hand. She knew that she had finally surrendered and succumbed. From now on, she conditioned herself to accept neither joy, her fickle friend, nor pain. She cloaked herself and numbed her senses in a quiet semblance of contentment, erecting an impregnable fortress to defend her heart against hope, hurt and happiness. And in her fortress she would reign supreme as Queen Untouchable.

~ *4* ~

Holt, on the Norfolk coast, 6th July 1936

The vet found a suitable mare on the Saturday of Annabel's tea party, which had by now grown into an all-day affair. Celia felt it was her duty to introduce the colt to his new mother, so she had warned Annabel she might have to miss the luncheon. To her relief all went much better than expected and the mare, whose foal had been stillborn, accepted the little orphan without any fuss. By the time Celia left the farm, her colt was busily sucking proper mare's milk from the mother's painfully stretched udder.

Celia eventually turned up at Annabel's family home at four o'clock. She was greeted by her friend with an affectionate hug. "It's lovely you could make it after all. You are just in time for a glass of champagne."

Arm in arm, the young ladies walked round to the back of the house. A laughing crowd of young people were lounging in the sunshine chatting.

"Al and his friend have come too. Isn't that jolly of them? They must be around somewhere. How handsome Al has become."

"I must admit I haven't noticed. I've known him for so long now, I just think of him as family. There's no point asking a sister if her brother's handsome, is there?" Celia replied.

The only person who looked uncomfortable was Caleb Levine. Dark-haired and in a white linen suit, he stood to one side, gazing out over the lake, looking a bit alien and lost.

Celia walked across to him. She knew what it was like to have no gift for small talk. Caleb was clearly pleased to see a face he knew and Celia told him the exciting news about their little charge. When she had finished she said, "Anyway, I'm here now. Are you enjoying yourself?"

"Well, we had a sumptuous buffet lunch followed by a poetry reading." In a stage whisper he added, "I'm not a great one for poetry, I'm afraid. For the life of me, I can't understand why people should want to express themselves in riddles and rhymes instead of plain English."

Celia smiled. She shared that sentiment. "Well, Annie is likely to give us another reading tonight after dinner. If you don't like it, you'll need a good excuse to escape now. I recommend a toothache. Headaches are a bit too obvious."

Caleb chuckled. Their innocent conspiracy was drawing them closer.

"You'll find that my lovely friend has a highly developed sense of beautiful things: music, paintings, poetry, literature . . . that sort of thing. And she has a rare gift for spotting the less obviously beautiful. I lack this kind of, well . . ." she searched for the right word, ". . . awareness of the finer things in life."

"I can tell you're very fond of her. And I'm sure you're a good observer of beauty in your own way."

Celia noticed his compliment but continued by telling him about Annabel's family and holidays she had spent here. Celia's musings tinkled on pleasantly as they strolled across the lawn, sipping champagne. There was something he really liked about her. Was it her straightforwardness or the way she talked? Or was it the total absence of that pretension so common in people of her class?

Annabel made the rounds to ensure that all her guests were being well looked after. She eventually reached the young couple. Celia smiled at her.

"I've just been telling Caleb what a very attentive hostess you are. We've also talked about your mother's paintings. Do you think we could see them?"

"Oh, I'm afraid not. Mummy isn't here and she doesn't like my going into her studio when she's not there. She's most particular about that."

"What a shame . . . but never mind. Maybe we can see them another time," said Celia. "I like her paintings, particularly her watercolours. They are so vibrant and alive. I wish I could paint like her. My own pictures look like the work of a dilettante. I just haven't got the gift, I suppose. It's so frustrating."

"Oh, you mustn't compare yourself to her. Mummy went to art school and has had to work really hard to overcome her shortcomings and find her own style. It took her years. Yet look at her now. People have at last started to recognise her work. But not everyone. They argue most horridly over art, and no two critics seem able to agree on what good art is. Anyway, Mummy's taste in art isn't very conventional."

A friendly voice interposed, "Hello there."

"Gina! Darling!" The girls squealed and gave their old friend a peck on the cheek.

"It's been so long since we last saw you! How are you?"

Caleb was formally introduced to Lady Georgina Holsworth-Leigh. Then the three young ladies excused themselves and hurried off to a quiet corner to press Georgina for her news.

"Gina, we've started to hear the most exciting rumours about Stuart and you. You're being seen together in public too often . . ."

"I'll tell you on one condition only: that you swear on your honour to keep it a secret." She waited till the girls had promised, letting the tension build up. "The truth is . . ." She paused again for dramatic effect. "Stuart has proposed. And I've accepted him. My parents are delighted. We'll be announcing the engagement formally next week, and then we'll have such a party to celebrate." She looked expectantly at her friends. "You will both come, won't you?"

"Of course. How could we possibly miss your most important day?" said Annabel.

"You're the first of our little group to get married and leave us." Celia felt suddenly sad as this new reality hit home. "Engaged to be married. That would make me feel so old. I'm not at all ready for such a serious step. We're only twenty, you know."

"Well, we all have to grow up some time. Our childhood can't last for ever," Gina said with a sigh. She looked terribly mature.

She was the first of them to get engaged. And, naturally, to a well-to-do, socially respectable young heir with both wealth and character. Some things were just too predictable.

Celia hugged her friend and wished her all the luck in the world. They emerged giggling from round the corner of the laurel hedge like little girls with a naughty secret, which wasn't too far from the truth.

By the early evening, Celia had had enough of company. She disappeared discreetly into the park for a stroll around the small lake, keeping a lookout for birds, bats and other wildlife. She returned to one of her favourite spots and sat down. A marble terrace and balustrade separated the formal lawn behind the house from the steep, sloping meadow that led down to clumps of wild rhododendrons and beech trees surrounding the artificial lake. She sat down with her back against the pedestal of an urn overflowing with geraniums.

She let her thoughts ramble. They rose to the tops of the trees and were soon high in the clouds, painted golden-pink by the brushstrokes of the setting sun. The day had been a complete success, the evening was breathtakingly beautiful, and Celia's heart was full of gratitude. She felt like singing to the God she did not know, for, surely, only a wonderful God could have created everything so well. That the world had popped up out of nothing was something Celia could not believe. To her mind, evolution was too great a leap of faith.

Far away, lost in her private thoughts, she did not notice the figure emerging from a rhododendron tunnel. Caleb was already halfway up the slope before Celia spotted him.

"Am I disturbing you?" he asked.

"By no means. No." She invited him to sit down beside her. "There are times when I just want to be on my own. Too many people in one place . . . even if I really like them . . . make me feel trapped. I'm afraid I'm rather notorious for that."

"I've just taken a little walk around the lake myself."

There followed a silence. Neither of them felt awkward, nor did they feel under any pressure to fill the void with words. Then, out of the blue, Celia asked, "Do you believe in God?"

She had continued her train of thought where she had left off. And nothing seemed more natural than to put the question to Caleb, as if they had been pondering the same thing at the same time like kindred minds.

Caleb thought hard for a moment. He did not think the question odd. "You may be asking the wrong question. Whether I believe in God or not is irrelevant. You might as well have asked if I believed that red is yellow and yellow is blue. The fact is that red is red, yellow is yellow, blue is blue, and God is God. Your question should rather have been, 'Does God exist?'"

"I wish you wouldn't analyse everything I say. It makes life so complicated."

Caleb could not help smiling. "We Jews are called the 'People of the Book'; so what do you expect?" He shrugged his shoulders in the comical way that was unique to his people and culture. "The first thing a little Jewish boy is taught is how to ask questions. Who but the Jews could pick

47

on one night in the year and ask themselves 'Why is this night different from all other nights?'"

Celia struggled with his answer, which, once again, seemed both evasive and impenetrable.

Sensing her frustration, he said, "Let me put it like this: I'm a Jew; I've been brought up in the presence of God; and there has never been any doubt that God exists. Our knowledge of God is hereditary. If it weren't for God's eternal covenant with us and His protection, we would have ceased to exist long ago. After all, we seem to attract trouble as honey attracts bears."

"Do you also believe," she hesitated, "that all the miracles in the Bible are true?"

"God parted the Reed [Red] Sea to deliver the Children of Israel from Pharaoh and slavery in Egypt. If they had just marched across a submerged sandbank, as some theologians want us to believe, then the whole Egyptian army drowned in three feet of water. But that would be a miracle, too, wouldn't it?"

They laughed.

"Are you very religious?" asked Celia.

She knew it was very important for her to remain on this God-focused path. Also, she had never spoken to a non-Christian before. Because the Jews were mentioned in the Bible, her curiosity was aroused. It was a bit like being given the chance to talk to a fossil.

"I used to be. We call it being 'observant'. But I'm not any more." He picked up a stick and played with it, distracting himself, feeling the tension rising inside him.

"Why not?"

"It's a long story."

"Please, I don't want to pry but if . . . I mean . . . if you would like to talk about it, I am interested. Truly."

The invitation had slipped out unmasked. To cover her sudden embarrassment at this unpardonable breach of good manners, Celia looked at her toes and wiggled them in her sandals. Silly goose. Why should a man she barely knew turn out the drawers of his private life for her? Perhaps he would now think she was no more than a snooping social gossip-columnist after a juicy story to spread around. Perhaps she had just blown everything.

Caleb might be mistaken, but could Celia be reaching out to him because she too wanted to share what burdened her? He would have to wait and see. He didn't wait long.

Blushing, Celia blurted out, "Oh, I'm sorry. You see, I'm not quite what you might think. My family is ruined financially, my mother detests me, and my father couldn't care less whether I live or die."

Celia was shocked at herself. Without obvious rhyme or reason, here she was, spilling out her squalid family secrets to a total stranger. Was she mad? But, far from recoiling from her frankness, Caleb embraced it. He spoke, far away, as if talking to himself, gently searching for exactly the right words to frame his question. "Which do you believe is harder: to lose a precious possession or chase after a dream?"

She had no idea what he meant. "What do you mean?"

"When I was twelve, my grandfather pronounced me officially dead."

"What?" Celia wondered if she had heard right.

"I was the great Rabbi Mendel Levine's favourite grandson, the best loved of nine boys. I could recite the Sh'ma, our holiest declaration of faith, almost before I could say 'Mama' and 'Papa'. I was top of the cheder class and my grasp of Torah was excellent, if I say so myself. Everyone expected me to become a student at a religious school and to prepare for the Rabbinate; that is, to become a Rabbi."

Celia's eyebrows shot up. She could hardly believe it. This quiet English gentleman . . . a Rabbi?

Caleb looked at her. "Do you know anything about Judaism? No? Let me explain. Did you know that the worst crime a Jew can commit is to become a Christian? It means denying our faith, our heritage, our traditions, our people, in fact, our very God. It means exchanging the Almighty God of Israel, Adonai, for three gods called father, son and holy spirit. It happened six months before my formal rite of passage to manhood, my Bar Mitzvah. My parents told the family that they had accepted Jesus Christ as the promised Messiah of Israel, that they had converted to Christianity. You can't imagine the explosion it caused. They had already braced themselves for being cut off from the family on the spot, but my grandfather gave them an ultimatum: if they would repent and recant within three days, he would be merciful. I'll never forget those dreadful three days. I tried everything I could, as a twelve-year-old lad, to persuade my father to turn from his heresy. He refused. After the time was up, my grandfather came to our house. He was accompanied by three members of the synagogue. But he refused to cross the threshold. He asked, coldly and formally, "Are you ready to repent and recant?" My father replied that he couldn't. At this my grandfather gave an anguished wail and ripped the collar of his coat. Then he formally pronounced us all dead. From that moment, we were totally cut off – excommunicated – from every member of our own family, as well as the whole, close-knit Jewish community in which we had always lived. My father went to plead with him the next day, but did not even get as far as grandfather's house before he was spat at and abused by people in the street. Then they staged a mock funeral to make the message absolutely clear: a Jew who converts to Christianity is as untouchable as a corpse."

Celia stared at Caleb in horror and utter disbelief. "But, that's not possible! It's unbelievably cruel."

"Not when you're a Jew. To an Orthodox Jew it's both logical and necessary." Caleb seemed to accept such draconian reprisals quite calmly. "You see, apart from outright persecution, our worst enemy is assimilation into the Gentile world. Whenever someone assimilates, we die a little as a people."

"But must the preventative measures be so drastic? Is it really so overwhelmingly important to you?"

"You don't know what it means to be a Jew," Caleb said with a sad smile. "After what had happened, we couldn't stay in the area any longer. The friends we used to play with were forbidden to talk to us. My mother, who was chiefly blamed for the conversion, was spat at in the street. Our butcher and greengrocer refused to sell anything to us. It felt insanely unfair. As a boy, the Christian children beat me up for being a Jew; now the whole Jewish community hated us for being Christians." He picked up a stone and, with a bitter laugh, threw it angrily out over the lake. "I suppose I'm a sort of ghost now; undead, yet not alive."

"Please, don't say that. It's simply not true." Celia was hurting for him and wanted to draw close to him to take his mind off the pain. "I honestly don't know if I'm a real Christian. At least not 'real' in the sense I think the church and Bible mean it."

Caleb looked up, surprised. "You don't know? Surely you've been christened and confirmed, and go to church on Sunday and so on?"

"Yes, but what I want to say is that I'm not a real Christian . . . not like Al."

"Ah, I know what you mean." His voice had a hint of a sneer. "You mean 'born again' like my parents and younger sister say they are. So, if you're not a real Christian, what kind of Christian are you, then?"

Caleb braced himself for the kind of ridiculous nonsense he had met at university. He had had many arguments with opinionated, pseudo-intellectual, would-be philosophers who lacked even the vaguest notion of the nature of God.

To his surprise she just said, "I know I believe there is a God, and that He's good. But you're a long way ahead of me.

You seem to know who your God is; that He is great and awesome and watches over you. Your God must be a much bigger and better god than mine."

Suddenly Caleb was overcome by pity. "Lacking Torah, these Gentiles are without any direction in their lives," he thought. "They do not even know which god to worship. No wonder they don't know their left from their right spiritually. How on earth did they manage to survive this long?" He could not remember a time when he had not acknowledged the existence of the Almighty.

"But you have your Jesus." He felt himself choke on the name.

"Yes, but is He God? I believe that he was a good man; someone very religious and terribly strict. But I'm always sad and a bit frightened when I think of Him on the cross. There's no hope or encouragement in that, is there? It just glorifies austerity and martyrdom. Who wants to worship a dead man, anyway? And my most profound memories of practical Christianity are interminable sermons in a freezing church." Celia shivered.

"So you don't even believe that Jesus rose from the dead?" Caleb wanted to be sure.

"I've been told that he did and I know I should believe it, but I've never been able to convince myself it actually happened. And how could it possibly have any relevance for me today?"

Caleb looked penetratingly at her. Before he could say anything, however, Georgina came gliding across the well-kept lawn.

"There you two are! Will you rejoin the human race now . . . or are you planning to spend the night under the stars?"

Celia and Caleb felt disappointed that their time of intimacy had come to so abrupt an end, but good manners required that they follow Georgina. Celia shivered again and rubbed her bare arms. Light and laughter drifted across the lawn from the house. Reluctantly, Caleb and Celia got up and obediently returned to the party.

The fun and chatter of their friends were in stark contrast to the quiet, close relationship they had enjoyed on the terrace. Celia found it hard to concentrate on the party games. Sebastian sat down next to her on the settee, and looked enquiringly at her.

"You look deep in thought." He glanced across the room at Caleb, who was miles away, lost in a serious discussion.

Celia followed his look and felt irritated. "I was engaged in a most interesting conversation with a gentleman who actually says something when he opens his mouth. Quite a rare species, wouldn't you agree?"

Sebastian pretended to be upset by her piqued reply. "I apologise unreservedly for being such a bore." He changed the subject. "How's Francis?"

"I had a letter from Berlin last week. He says it's an interesting city. I'd so like to visit him."

"Really? Did you know that compulsory military service was reintroduced last March? And that Mr Hitler can't bear the Jews? He'd love to get rid of the whole lot of them." Then, teasing her, "I wonder what your Jewish friend makes of it all."

"I don't know. We don't talk about religion."

"Celia, dear. This has nothing to do with religion; it's just bad politics and good economics." Although Sebastian looked like a fop, he took the *The Times* and what it said seriously. "And it'll probably turn out to be jolly grim for the Jews. Anyway, a Jew is a Jew, after all, whether his name is Isaac Cohen or John Bull. Or Fritz Doppeldorf. Let's move on to a more amusing topic, shall we?"

~ 5 ~

Norwich, 9th July 1936

Despite the confidential exchanges of the weekend, Caleb maintained a certain distance between himself and Celia. After all, he thought, what has an English aristocrat in common with a Jew, and a Jew in common with a Gentile? Nothing. So, however favourable a view he might now have of Lady Celia, he must remember to keep his feelings under strict control. His attitude towards her must at all times be wholly correct. Human feelings were not to be toyed with, and nor were any false hopes to be entertained. They could talk to each other, exchange views and ideas, and laugh together – yet still remain worlds apart. Celia might not understand this, but Caleb knew it as an everyday living reality. He knew that, as a Jew, he was different. What was more, he was determined to stay that way. He intended to prove that his Christian family's prayers for his conversion were futile. He had once boldly declared that, if their Jesus was indeed the Messiah, then He Himself must divinely find a way to convert him. To this day Caleb was still waiting – triumphantly: Nothing had happened yet. As he had confidently expected.

Occasionally Celia ventured into Norwich to meet her friends and acquaintances. They would take tea or coffee in their favourite tea rooms opposite the market before going shopping. From there they could enjoy watching the world pass by. Celia wondered about the people hurrying past, each one clutching his own joys and sorrows to his chest. For her, watching people was a fascinating pastime: their different faces, their unique ways of walking, what they carried and what they wore. How astonishing it was, that no two human beings were the same; not even their fingerprints, even though there were millions of people living on planet earth. Each one was a unique individual; there were no duplicates, no identical copies.

Celia saw Gina winding her way through the half-past-ten coffee crowd and waved.

"Have you been waiting long?" Gina asked.

"No. I've only just got here myself. Look at them. Aren't people amazing creatures?"

Gina was not sure what to make of this observation. "Most likely. Why do you say that?"

"I was just thinking out loud. Coffee?"

"Please. Oh, Celia, I'm so excited. We must have the wedding gown designed and made at once. I want you to be one of the bridesmaids. Do say yes."

"It would be a wonderful honour."

Celia committed herself, her mind already busy on the cost of her dress. No doubt, the Holsworth-Leighs would choose a dreadfully expensive design but, after all, it was her best friend's wedding. She could not possibly refuse.

After tea they strolled around the shops. Celia admired the things she could not afford, and Gina bought whatever caught her fancy.

They met Caleb by chance in London Street. He raised his hat slightly. "Lady Georgina, Lady Celia . . ."

He was amazed when he saw Celia. She looked every inch a lady, transformed by her formal town outfit and her smart broad-brimmed hat. She must look simply stunning in a ball gown, he thought, amongst her own kind, surrounded by admirers.

He suddenly thought of little Rivka Leibkowitz. He had been twelve and she was ten. The little Orthodox girl had worshipped the ground he walked on, but he had been too proud to pay her any attention. He had to study; he wanted to become a famous Rabbi, a great teacher. In the street, he had had no eyes for the diminutive girl with her two long black plaits. Once she had dared to write him a note: "Caleb, one day I want to light your Shobbes candles." Deeply offended by her forwardness, he had crumpled up the piece of paper. He determined to take the very next opportunity to lecture her on the impropriety of a Jewish girl making such advances. It was the job of her parents and the matchmaker to find her a suitable spouse, not hers. She had replied, very meekly, with "Yes, Caleb, as you say" and had slunk away. He had been a true "Caleb" then, bold and impetuous, but he had been forced to swallow his pride after his expulsion from the Jewish community. Once he had basked in the glory of being the favourite grandson of Rabbi Mendel Levine; now, amongst the Gentiles, he was a nobody, indeed less than a nobody: he was a Jew.

Now, in front of this beautifully dressed Gentile girl, he was confused and lost for words. He felt shy; betrayed, yet again, by his inability to conjure up witty small talk when required. Celia, too, felt awkward to see Mr Levine so smartly dressed in his dark city suit. He was so clearly the handsome gentleman of great self-assurance and intellectual distinction that she imagined him to be. No doubt he had a classy young lady waiting for him back in London. By contrast, she was just a childish, awkward country girl. No wonder he had nothing to say to her now. Georgina never had such confusing thoughts. Her world was orderly, neat and proper – one where everyone had his place. To her, Mr Levine was a gentleman from a background very different from hers and, therefore, inappropriate for her. Social intercourse between them was hardly likely. One does not mix socially with those of a different class but, if obliged to do so, one behaves as a lady should. Despite Georgina's instinct to keep Caleb slightly at arm's length, her natural kindness and upbringing required her to be gracious, polite and courteous. And this she was, being the first to break the brittle silence.

"Mr Levine, how do you do? What a pleasure to see you again. It's not London, but I trust our dear provincial capital meets with your approval."

"Very well, thank you. Oh, it's very nice, very pretty. I thought I'd take the opportunity to do some sightseeing today." Caleb suddenly felt self-conscious, realising that he had been staring at Celia.

"Celia and I would love to show you round, if you'd like that."

"That would be most kind of you. Yes, I'd appreciate it greatly."

Gina thought it best to start with Tombland and the cathedral, so the young people strolled up London Street. Gina walked next to Mr Levine, while Celia, because of the narrow pavement, trailed behind them. Gina chatted easily to him in a light and friendly way.

"Will you be visiting the Show, then?" she enquired.

"Which Show would that be?"

"The Royal Norfolk Show, of course. Celia," she pretended to be shocked, "haven't you told Mr Levine about the Show?"

Celia was jerked out of her lonely reverie. "No, I haven't, now you come to mention it. I didn't expect a Londoner to be interested in it. It's the event of the year in our local agricultural community. Gina's father has pioneered many new farming techniques; it's a passion that has been running in the family for generations. And he and Sir Arthur are friendly rivals. Between them I'm sure they'll carry off most of the trophies again this year. The Duke is as enthusiastic about his sheep as Sir Arthur is about his sugar beet," explained Celia.

"I must admit I've never been to a country fair before."

Caleb's innocent reply immediately provoked a loud protest from the ladies.

"Country fair?" the two young ladies chorused. "It's the white-hot furnace in which a farmer's performance over the past year is tested. There, for all to see, will be revealed whether he's made good use of new farming methods, or whether his experiments have been a disaster; whether he's succeeded in improving his herd, or whether he should slaughter his breeding stock and start from scratch. Country fair, indeed!"

It was dawning on Caleb that he had probably said the wrong thing. "It seems that I've no choice but to go. My shameful ignorance has been exposed. I hardly dare ask, but will you be going as well?"

The truth was, he did not care whether Gina was going or not. His real concern was for her friend.

Celia jumped in with a reply before Gina could open her mouth. "Certainly. For the past six years I've been presenting Sir Arthur's horses, or at least some of them. Gina, do you remember when Foxtrot was first in the lightweight hunter class?" Celia was recalling past glories with an enthusiastic immodesty that Caleb found amusing. "This year I'll be showing four Suffolk mares and their foals, as well as some hunters I've broken in."

By now they had reached the cathedral and were admiring its soaring spires.

"Shall we go in?" Celia looked at Caleb who nodded.

As the three of them entered the building, a small guided tour was just getting under way, so they joined it unobtrusively.

It was a typical cathedral tour, led by an elderly clergyman. He referred to names and places that meant nothing to Caleb, and not much more to Celia and Gina. Eventually they came to a small plaque.

". . . and this commemorates Saint William of Norwich. History records that the twelve-year-old William disappeared on Good Friday, 1144. He was last seen delivering a cloak to a Jew's house but on Easter morning, he was found dead in the local Thorpe woods. The Jews were accused of ritual murder and an obscene mockery of our Lord's Passion. As a result of this, a severe and bloody persecution of the Jews began here, which quickly spread to York and Lincoln. So it was in Norwich that the 'blood libel' was revived, and from here it spread throughout Europe . . ."

The old man allowed a touch of pride to creep into his voice. Caleb had heard quite enough. For centuries these "blood libel" stories had circulated in Medieval Europe. Even when they had been exposed as vicious lies, they had rarely failed to fan the smouldering embers of anti-Semitism into blood-red flame. "There's no smoke without fire," people would say. "Anyway, what's the harm in a little Jew-baiting?" Why, Caleb fumed, if it was now proved to be a total fabrication, did no one remove the disgusting plaque? Oh no, it was part of Norwich's sacred history after all; poor little St William had to be commemorated. At that time, Norwich had needed a new saint: saints meant pilgrims, and pilgrims meant money. This in turn provided the finances to build the cathedral. So, in a sense, Caleb's ancestors had paid with their lives to build this magnificent monument to Christianity.

The young Jew turned abruptly and, pushing his way through the small crowd, walked briskly out of the cathedral. Celia grasped what had caused his angry reaction and followed him. They waited by the gate for Gina, who arrived a few moments later. She was terribly apologetic.

"I must say, Mr Levine, I'm most dreadfully sorry. If I'd only known I'd never have exposed you to that. It was all too beastly."

Gina hated upsetting anyone. Whether she was concerned because she had found the content of the discourse shocking, or because it was simply bad manners to upset anyone, was unclear to Caleb. He suspected the latter and was, in large measure, right. "Please, don't trouble yourself on my account, Lady Georgina. I know it was never your intention. It's just the way things are. In any case, I must be going. Please excuse me. Goodbye."

He lifted his hat and went. The friends were left standing in the courtyard. "What a thoroughly unpleasant thing. And so sudden. How can I ever make it up to him?" Gina was struggling to regain her composure.

"Stop fretting, Gina. I'm sure he knows you meant no harm."

Nevertheless, she began to think about the reactions of her friends and family to Caleb. Sebastian had mentioned Hitler and her mother had cooled remarkably towards him once she knew he was a Jew. She had not mentioned inviting him for tea again. What was so distasteful about Caleb Levine, she wondered?

"Do you know why people react with such antipathy towards Jews?" she asked her companion.

"To be perfectly honest, I've never thought about it. Maybe it's their strange lifestyle and alien religious rites; they're a different cultural species and all that. I mean, they've got no Christian values, have they? Perhaps it's just as well to be a little wary of them."

"Gina, don't say such things! Mr Levine is not strange or alien. How many Jews do you know anyway?"

"Well . . . For all I know, Mr Levine may be the first I've ever met, apart from the Rothschilds. And I've got nothing against him personally. Anyway, I didn't mean *all* Jews; there have got to be exceptions. Mr Levine is probably one of them. Do you think I should invite him to our garden party to make up for what happened?"

The annual garden party of the Holsworth-Leighs was legendary and lavish.

"You could try. After all, he didn't disgrace himself at Annabel's party." Celia was surprised at the note of sarcasm in her voice.

~ 6 ~

Bleckham Manor, 10th July 1936

Caleb was handed an envelope at breakfast the following day. It contained a formal invitation to a grand garden party at Lenkham Hall the following week. There was also a neat, handwritten footnote, which read: "I am sorry but I cannot accept no for an answer. Georgina H.-L."

Caleb put the letter to one side. He knew the flattering formalities demanded by etiquette and could read the expectation between the lines. The note had the feel of an order rather than an invitation. How could anyone dare to disobey her command? But he knew he was free – if he had the *chutzpah* – to turn it down. He was not one of them and he did not feel bound by their rules. But to turn down her invitation? Could he lower himself to indulge in such petty revenge? So he procrastinated for a couple of days, unsure what answer to give.

"I'm not sure, Celia. I'm not really a party-goer."

"Oh, but you must go," protested Celia. "If you don't want to go for Gina's sake, then come simply to see the splendour of Lenkham Hall. It's magnificent. It's a palace by the coast with a private beach. Although the exterior isn't much, the interior is outstanding. Why don't we go a day earlier and stay the night? I always take Foxtrot. He loves a gallop along the beach." Celia's eyes lit up at the prospect.

Caleb looked at her and imagined the beautiful picture she would make by the edge of the sea, her hair tossed by the wind. But he felt uncomfortable. He knew that if he did go it would be solely for Celia's company. He had never in the past done anything simply to impress a lady and, he told himself, he had no intention of starting now. But on the other hand . . .

"Very well then, I'll go. There doesn't seem to be any way out of it." He was sorry as soon as he had said it. He disliked parties intensely.

A week later they arrived at Lenkham Hall in time to change for dinner. Then Georgina gave them a tour of the house, which was as impressive as Caleb had been promised. Built in the 1700s by a wealthy East India Company nabob-turned-landowner, the house was the epitome of stately luxury. It was resplendent with the finest inlaid furniture, breathtaking ceilings, marble staircases, silken wall coverings, precious porcelains and many, many exquisite paintings and sculptures. Celia loved it.

"Every time I come, I discover something new," she exclaimed. "Even rainy days can never be boring here."

"Don't bet on it," Georgina sighed.

"And this all belongs to your family?" Caleb was admiring a painting high up on the wall, his hands clasped behind his back.

"Yes."

The answer was casual and matter of fact, as if it were the most natural thing in the world for the Holsworth-Leighs to live in such a place.

"I still find it strange that one family should own so much," Caleb remarked, without taking his eyes off the painting in its intricately carved and gilded frame.

Georgina looked at her friend, who just shrugged. "You aren't by any chance a socialist, are you, Mr Levine?"

He knew she was teasing him, but sensed the steel under the velvet glove. His reply was a nebulous smile.

Everybody had retired, but Caleb's mind refused to go to bed. The thought that Celia was sleeping a few doors away stirred up the most fanciful of fantasies. His imagination was working overtime and he struggled to divert his thoughts to more sober subjects, but with little success.

All was quiet.

Then he heard a shuffling close by, the squeaking of floor-boards in the corridor, and a door being closed. He got up to investigate. If necessary, he could pretend he needed the bathroom.

He opened his door and peered out, spotting a familiar figure creeping along the poorly lit corridor. It turned round, sensing someone watching.

"Celia! What are you doing up in the middle of the night?" he whispered.

"I can't sleep," she whispered back. "Besides, one can't miss a night like this. Have you seen all the stars? I'm going for a walk."

"A walk? Now? It's well past midnight!"

"What of it?" The young lady was determined to have her romantic moonlight excursion.

"Wait. I'll come with you," said a slightly irritated Caleb.

He closed his door long enough to slip into a shirt and trousers. This was utterly ridiculous. Why on earth did he feel compelled to go along with this kind of folly? They went downstairs together. Celia grabbed an apple as she passed a fruit bowl and led him out through the French doors. "Provisions for night hikers," she said and bit into it.

Walking on the damp lawn to avoid crunching the gravel, they left the garden and followed a path down to the shallow lake. It had only recently been created and looked a little bare and sad. But they sat down nevertheless and admired the stars reflected in the still water.

"Have you ever been swimming at night?" the girl asked.

Caleb felt a sudden rush of heat in every part of his body.

He was a good Jewish boy and wished he were back in the safety of his room. With the door firmly shut.

"No."

"Neither have I."

Caleb prayed silently but fervently against any more unusual ideas.

"What a glorious night," she said in an awe-stricken voice. Above them the heavens expanded with a billion stars. "This is no night for sleeping, it's a time to . . ." She broke off in mid-sentence.

Caleb followed her gaze with the same wonder. "To do what?"

"I wish I knew. You look at all this and you think, there must be a Creator."

"And God said, 'Let there be lights in the firmament of heaven to divide the day from the night; and let them be for signs, and for seasons, and for days, and years.'" Caleb recited from memory.

His words sounded beautiful and Celia looked at him admiringly. "I'm a terrible pagan, aren't I?" She felt a stab of guilt. "Here I sit, admiring all this natural beauty and I don't even know the One who made it."

"In Judaism there's a blessing for everything. We bless God for bread and wine, when we discover the first blossom in spring, and when we plant a tree. We even bless Him for choosing us to keep His commandments."

Celia felt poor and ashamed. She could not bring to mind a single prayer, having paid no attention to them in school or church. Now she felt she was standing, shame-faced, silent and empty-handed, before God.

"Would you like to thank God for the beauty of this night?" Caleb spoke with great gentleness as if he had read her thoughts. "You could say something like: 'Blessed are You, O Lord our God, King of the universe, who has given us the lights of the firmament'."

Celia was quiet for a moment, then opened her mouth. "Blessed are You . . ." she stammered, feeling pathetically shy and self-conscious. She stopped.

Caleb led her through the blessing a phrase at a time. Afterwards he said, with a pleased smile, "You see, it didn't hurt at all. For us, blessing is a way of life and reminds us of God's presence. Every time you see something beautiful, or want to thank God for something, that's how you start: 'Blessed are You, O Lord, our God, King of the universe,' and then you just tack on what you want to say."

"It's so embarrassing."

"Why?"

"I'm not at all religious."

"If you said thank you to your parents for something they'd done for you, would that be religious? How much more then should we thank the One to whom we owe our very life."

Caleb spoke of his God so naturally that Celia wished she too might know the God of the Jews. The way Caleb explained it, prayer sounded so simple and logical; it suddenly seemed relevant to the ordinary things of life. She realised that she did not know whom she liked the most: the young man next to her, or his God. Or did she like them both?

"I wish I were like you," she sighed.

Caleb laughed and shook his head. "Oh no you don't. The last thing you really want is to become a Jew. Judaism is a dangerous religion. Every Rabbi will tell you that! Why not become a Christian? That would be a more obvious choice for you."

"Al has tried to convert me lots of times – but so far without success."

"Do you have a particular problem with Christianity?"

"I can't see any relevant connection between the Bible, the church, society and home. The Bible is a book I can't understand; it's full of endless and pointless old genealogies and prophesies. I do understand Jesus' parables, but I think they are based on common sense anyway. The Book of Revelation is – well, I don't even begin to understand it. And the church is simply a place you go on Sundays, Christmas and Easter. I've even stopped doing that now. What's the point? You leave the building as bad or miserable as you went in. And what good has Christianity done the world anyway? I have seen people doing horrid things to one another and then they troop off to church and sing hymns. Christianity is just so much loveless hypocrisy. And then there is our Al, bless him, with his air of intimidating holiness. He just spreads a frightening aroma of saintliness wherever he goes. Just to see him leave for church every Sunday morning makes me feel guilty."

"I don't go to church on Sundays, and I don't feel guilty at all," Caleb said and shrugged. They laughed. "How about 'Love your neighbour as yourself'?" Caleb suggested.

"I thought you didn't believe in Jesus."

"I don't. That's a quotation from the Torah."

"Oh, I always thought . . . I'm sorry. I'm very stupid."

"Not at all. Most people think that loving God and your neighbour is a Christian invention." There was a hint of sarcasm in the Jew's voice.

The chill of the midnight air made them shiver and the conversation drew to a natural close. They got up to go.

"Well," Caleb said, "that was an unexpected end to the day."

Together they returned to the house.

Over breakfast, in the bright light of day, their night's walk seemed far away and a bit surreal. But Celia could not help thinking about their conversation. Caleb did not refer to it again, and mingled normally with the company. The girl was disappointed that he was not paying her any special attention. She kicked herself; silly little fool, what had she expected anyway?

But appearances can be deceptive. While Caleb was avoiding any obvious contact with Celia, he knew now that he was falling in love with her. When he was with her he could be himself. When they talked he knew that deep was meeting deep. She understood him and in her company everything was possible: He could speak or keep silent, eat apples in the moonlight and praise Adonai for His greatness. He wanted her to understand and know that there was no artificial separation between God, religion and everyday life. Each was complementary and each supported the other. Only when all three were integrated did they have meaning and reality. He had to smile at the thought that they might one day find themselves discussing his beliefs and God while mucking out the stables. He wondered if she was starting to see the living Creator's hand in everything, as he did. How could anyone confine God to a church service or a book?

In Celia, he sensed he had found a soul mate. She never laughed at or belittled the Jewish traditions and religious observances he told her about. Instead, she listened seriously and asked him more questions than he had answers for. One day he could not avoid laughing out loud because she kept up a steady flow of "Why? Why?"s like a four-year-old. She was becoming a proper little religious Yeshiva student, and he loved every minute of it. He also had to admit that it fed his pride and latent sense of superiority over the Gentiles. But at last he could share the things that really mattered to him. Celia was so different. She was sensitive towards him; she honoured what he honoured and abhorred what he abhorred; she was searching and seeking things stored deep in his heart. His affection for her was growing steadily. He recalled that first sweet tender feeling when he saw her running upstairs, two steps at a time, as if she had no time for so mundane a thing as her dignity. Or that time she walked in shoeless because she had left her muddy boots in the porch and could find no other footwear.

The day of the garden party did not start very promisingly. It had rained in the early hours and now, hounded by a wild westerly wind, herds of thick clouds were stampeding across the grey sky. Regardless of the threat of rain, the six young people decided to hack along the beach. Foxtrot, smelling the change from sweet meadows to salty sea air, was tense and excited. Anticipating the gallop, he danced, rather than walked, down the long drive to the road and beach. By the time the group had reached the first soft sand, Celia could barely hold him back. After crossing the road, the path narrowed and forced the disorderly bunch of riders to proceed in pairs, side by side. So, purely by chance, Celia and Caleb found themselves together again, leading the way along the pine-lined track to the beach. He could not stop himself glancing sideways at her. It was the freckles he found so enchanting. They gave her an air of freshness and spontaneity; a lovely natural non-conformity. He wondered if she felt about her freckles as he did about his nose. There, it had happened again. Whenever he was in her company his thoughts darted off in directions that were entirely their own.

Celia was tiring of Foxtrot's antics. "Are you in for a gallop?"

Caleb smiled and nodded. Celia turned in her saddle and called to the others, "I just need to release my steed's surplus energy. Hope that's all right with you. I'll beat you to that first big dune, Caleb," Celia challenged her riding partner. "Are you ready?"

"Whenever you are."

The horses shot off, leaving the remaining riders to manage their bolting mounts as best as they could. Foxtrot's racing blood showed and he settled quickly into a rhythmic, powerful gallop, his hooves pounding the firm damp sand of the wide beach. His neck stretched forward, pumping the fresh sea air into his heaving lungs. He covered the distance fast and effortlessly. He was not the only one enjoying himself. These were the moments when Celia could forget her cares and give herself completely to the intoxicating sensuality of the moment. She was alive to the rush of the wind in her ears, its caressing touch on her cheeks, the speed, and the numbing cadence of the hooves.

She bridled her horse at the dune, then turned to Caleb. Throwing back her head she gave a shout of joy and victory. Caleb delighted in watching his beloved, and her cry sent a shiver of excitement down his spine.

Her laugh sank to a happy chuckle. She patted her restless horse exuberantly and embraced him. Caleb turned in the saddle to look for the rest of the party. They were far behind. "Are you desperate for company?" Caleb asked.

Celia, still catching her breath, just shook her head.

"Neither am I."

They trotted off to the sea's edge to calm their horses, then slowed to a gentle walk. No words were needed. The only sound was the foam-crowned ripples of the quiet sea lapping at the horses' feet. The riders stopped to take in the dramatic view of the overcast sky and grey sea and listened to her ancient song. The hot climax of the race now behind them; they strolled along the shore. Time became a meaningless inconsequence.

"I wonder why people are so mesmerised by the sea. I have yet to find a person who was never struck by the mystery of the sound of water," mused Caleb.

"The sea may be gentle or cruel, but she'll still be here, unchanging, when we're all long gone. Maybe that's its mystery: the eternal clockwork reliability of its wet tick-tock: wave on wave and tide on tide. At least the sea is one certainty in our precarious existence."

How typical it was of a Gentile, Caleb thought, to look to the sea for comfort and meaning, to a mere created thing. And how alien it was for a Jew: "And the Divine Presence hovered upon the surface of the waters." Could she not see that?

"Are you seriously looking for God?" he asked.

"Am I looking for God? Who knows? And how should I find Him, anyway? I've yet to meet anyone who said, 'I'm looking for God. Are you coming with me?' But that's not your problem: you have a God you know already. For you Jews, God seems to come as an attachment to your birth certificate."

"Circumcision actually," said Caleb with a faint smile. "You may think everything is straightforward and clear to me, but it's not. I know God exists, but . . . I am down here, and He is up there in His highest heavens, and nothing and no one can reach across the gap. I was brought up to be extremely *frumm* – observant, that is – and I felt at home in my religion. In the Jewish area where I lived nearly everyone is *frumm*. It's not a conscious decision you have to make. It's a way of life; it's your identity. Once we were forced to leave the Jewish community, and were thrown out into the big, bad world, it became very difficult to be *frumm*. So I became weaned from it. Did that make any difference to what I thought about God? Of course it did. My parents talk about faith. Once out of the familiar Jewish environment, I lost my faith – if I really had any in the first place."

"No. I don't believe that," contradicted Celia.

"You're very kind, but don't be fooled by the fact that I can quote a few Bible verses."

A long silence followed. Then Celia said, with startling insight, "You're suffering from a bereavement."

Bereavement. The idea struck Caleb with force. He was unprepared for the sudden intrusion of this fact – this death – into the depth of his soul. It was something that he had refused to accept for years, pretending it was not there. He was at the same time both amazed and shocked at the ease with which Celia had seen into him. Yet the allegory fell short of the whole truth. In natural death, the tragedy is final, the beloved enters the Hereafter never to return, and the funeral rites provide a last farewell. We know the departed's final resting place, the grave, a fact that plays a key role in the grieving process. Some talk to the dead while visiting the grave, others put flowers next to their pictures. We talk about the deceased, remembering their quirks, and receive the condolences of family and friends. We relive treasured memories while the bitter ones gradually fade away. Time heals death's wounds.

But Caleb had experienced none of this. Mama and Papa had made every effort to explain why things had happened and why other people had reacted as they had. But they had no answers to the young boy's deepest and unspoken needs, nor could they provide him with any real comfort. Night after night he had lain in bed, reliving his immense tragedy, questions turning over and over in his mind. What was Grandfather doing at exactly this moment? Were they already home from the Shabbat service? How many new Yeshiva students did Grandfather have this year? Were they doing well? How he missed the animated debates as young minds searched for truth. But the biggest, most terrifying question of all was: did Grandfather miss Caleb as much as he missed his grandfather? Or had he really been able to kill his natural love, and purge his living grandson from his heart? Caleb had often wondered if that were really possible for any person.

Sensing his deep grief, his mother had asked him to turn his back on the incurable past and look forward to a more promising future. "The Rabbi's decision was final. It really was, and you have to believe it. Please don't keep bringing it up; it's too painful for us all, especially your father."

So Caleb, while still a child, learned the art of burying his hurt in his heart.

They heard the sound of a cantering horse close behind them. "May one join the élite group?" Sebastian bridled his gelding alongside Celia's. "Caleb," he said jovially, "I hope you're making the most of our marvellous scenery while you're here. Do you know, ever since she was little Celia's been coming here with her pony. Do you remember the time when you climbed to the top of the highest dune over there?" Sebastian pointed to a landmark in the near distance.

"How could I possibly forget? We used to play Cowboys and Indians – the boys chasing the girls of course. Who used to be with us?" Celia thought for a second. "I remember: you, me, Gina, Annabel and sometimes Alistair and others. Those were happy days, weren't they?"

"Anyway . . ." Sebastian insisted on telling his story, ". . . we were chasing Celia and eventually surrounded her at the top of that dune, thinking she'd have to surrender. But Oh no! Not Celia. She just made her pony jump off the top of the dune. The poor creature lost his balance and just about somersaulted down. Celia got tossed over its neck and we all thought the pony was going to squash her."

"We never told anyone, did we? We were afraid they wouldn't let us come here again." Celia laughed.

Unknown to her, her laugh had a hidden barb that stung Caleb. That was another difference between him and her: while she had frolicked on private beaches with her childhood friends, he had been sweating it out in London studying Torah and Talmud. Coming home after school, doing his homework, then trotting off to Grandfather for more study. Before his parents' conversion to Christianity, every weekend was saturated in Judaism. After the Shabbat meal they would go to the Friday evening service. On Shabbat morning, they had the Torah service, then went home for lunch. The afternoon service was next, followed by tea and then the closing Saturday evening service. And every Sunday morning there were Hebrew classes.

On bright spring days his mother had sometimes pulled the books out from under his nose and elbows. "Enough of all this learning," she would say. "The world will not come to an end because you can't recite the Ethics of the Fathers backwards. You're ruining your eyes. Go and play with your friends. Do something different for once."

Of course, there were no friends around because they were all at home studying. No amount of pleading could change his mother's mind. He would feel so embarrassed, not knowing what to do with himself out in the street. And if he chanced to run into someone from the synagogue, they would scold him. "*Oy*, Calvele. Not at home studying?"

The young boy would blush and shuffle his feet, embarrassed. "Mama says I need some fresh air and too much studying is bad for the eyes."

"What Jewish mother would keep her son from studying Torah?" Mrs Sharp's concerned voice would ring with horror.

The matter would be reported to Grandfather. Then another argument would erupt at home, with Mama and Grandfather shouting at each other. Papa would try to negotiate a peace settlement between the warring parties. Papa understood how his father felt, but could also see his wife's point of view. At the time, little Caleb could not understand how he, and the religion that totally filled his life, could so upset his mother. She had been brought up in an assimilated German-Jewish family from Berlin and had not at all fitted into her husband's Orthodox one. Papa was deeply in love with her and had even risked being cut off by his own father in order to marry her.

Now, years later, he could sympathise with the struggle – the pain and agony – she had gone through. He knew she was an outstanding woman with tremendous personal integrity and courage. But to denounce Judaism and convert to Christianity . . . that he could not forgive.

Ach, Mama.

~ 7 ~

Lenkham Hall, 18th July 1936

The weather did not hold. By early afternoon, the low-flying clouds that had filled the morning with foreboding began to unload their watery cargo as a light drizzle. Maids and servants rushed to bring in the tables and chairs, flower arrangements and cold buffet. The first garden party guests began to arrive. Despite the ill-concealed chaos, Sebastian was as optimistic and enthusiastic as ever.

"Just as well we've got such a jolly big house. We'll have a wonderful time indoors. Pity, though, we've had splendid weather most years."

By now some sixty couples had arrived. Young ladies emerged butterfly-like in beautiful dresses, after changing out of their travelling clothes. Caleb sighed. Celia was still not among them. He watched and listened, with rising irritation, as the rich and noble passed by. Of the many faces present, there were only a sprinkling that Caleb recognised.

"Charles, darling," chirped a well-built, middle-aged woman as she gave Georgina's father a peck on the cheek.

Celia's lateness was caused by the temporary disappearance of an earring, but she appeared at last in a long, sea-green dress of raw silk. Her hair was neatly brushed and tied into a knot to reveal her bare shoulders. Caleb was lost for words when he saw her. And everything about her made it clear where she belonged. She smiled appreciatively as she scanned the grand room with its familiar faces. Her eyes took in the people she knew, the friends who made up the world she called "home". A small palm-court orchestra had been hired from Norwich. They were playing dance pieces in an adjoining room and a young man invited Celia to dance. She hesitated, and then rose, giving him a quick smile; she was not quite sure if they had been introduced before. Caleb kicked himself for not anticipating this; he could have secured her promise for this dance long ago. How could he possibly have assumed that Lady Celia Lancaster was not going to be eagerly sought after by those of her own class? His heart sank as he felt himself starting to slide into anxiety, introversion and depression. The splendour and sumptuousness of the party did nothing to raise his spirits; if anything they had the opposite effect. He fought off an impulse to slip away altogether, away from the voices and the music, away from the stress of having to be impeccably agreeable, charming and correct at all times.

"You seem most unaccountably glum, my friend," cried a happy Sebastian as he came up to Caleb. He raised his champagne glass to acknowledge an acquaintance across the room. "It's a brilliant party, despite the dreadful weather, isn't it? Have a glass of bubbly and ask one of the many lovely ladies for a dance. That'll cheer you up."

"I'm no dancer, I'm afraid."

"Oh dear. Well, join me for a round in the billiard room. If we're lucky, our absence will go unnoticed." Sebastian was a natural and relaxing host.

"I'm sure mine will," thought Caleb morosely.

The men walked through a number of staterooms before reaching high doors that Sebastian opened for Caleb with a hint of a bow.

The billiard room was elaborately decorated with an exotic theme. The walls were covered with green silk printed with golden pineapples and pomegranates. The plasterwork on the ceiling sprouted images of palm trees; stuffed heads of antelopes and rhinos looked down on the players. They witnessed to the bravery of the hunters who had shot them from a safe distance. It oozed wealth and good taste.

Outside, the light rain had matured into a full-blown thunderstorm, almost eclipsing the light. In the gloom, the strong lights above the billiard table were lit, and the intimate and slightly sinister atmosphere of a gambling den invaded the room. Two men had already sought sanctuary there, whisky glasses in hand, and Sebastian introduced Caleb to them. They negotiated the polite introductory small talk as they picked their cues from the rack. No sooner had they placed the balls on the green baize when another party of male refugees from the ballroom arrived. The two young men concentrated on their game in the bright pool of jade at the centre of the room. They were vaguely aware of a discussion taking place in the shadows about the situation in South Africa. An indignant voice could be heard above the murmur. "Well, what do you think about this damn-fool idea of giving the Blacks their own Council? Utterly ridiculous, if you ask me. If we do that, they'll be wanting equal rights before long."

"Bah!" responded another voice, obviously in full agreement, "Those jungle bunnies will never be able to run their own country. They need strong leadership, and where can they get it but from us? Look at the Transvaal: for centuries the tribal chiefs were sitting on vast gold reserves, but did they mine them? The Boer wasn't much better, was he? Good fighter, mind, but it took a war to knock some sense into him. And now they've got the gall to complain that we're robbing them of their wealth. My brother owns a farm down there. Built a school for his natives, and you know what? They now think they've got the right to higher education. Next they'll want to go to university, like the Indians and half-caste cheechees. No, no, I say. We need order in society and that means everyone being in the place God put them. And we all know where He's put the Blacks: closer to the monkeys than us. Try to change that and you'll just be making trouble for yourself. They were perfectly content and happy up to now – until those Jew-Boy socialist troublemakers came along telling them otherwise."

A murmur of "hear, hear"s showed that this summary of the situation was agreed with by the majority here present. Caleb was concentrating on the game, sensing the drift of the discussion but shutting his ears to it. But he was not surprised when he heard another voice from the darkness say quietly, "Mr Levine? It is Mr Levine, isn't it? What do you think? What's your opinion on this subject?" The elderly gentleman spoke from deep within his armchair.

Caleb knew from his university days that this was the opening prelude to a quarrel, the polite invitation to the Jew to enter a discussion. They knew he was likely to hold views different from the imperialist British world view. Today he felt uninvolved and dispassionate and tried to avoid getting drawn in. He concentrated overly hard on chalking his cue and replied deprecatingly, "My personal views are, I'm sure you'll agree, far too unimportant to make it worth your while listening to them." He smiled politely, refusing to rise to the bait.

The gentleman angler chose not to hear the rebuff; instead he chose another fly and cast again. "Don't be silly, man. Every gentleman's opinion is important. We live in a democracy, don't you know?"

Caleb wandered around the table to find the best position for his next shot, eventually leaning over the baize and sighting the ball. Very quietly he rose to the fly and took it with a sigh, knowing that good manners left him no option. "I don't believe it is right to stop any man from trying to improve himself or his life – whatever his race, colour or religion. As far as it is possible within the constraints of society, each man should be in control of his own destiny."

The ball plopped into a side pocket.

"So you believe in the equality of all men?" a new voice asked from the gloom. Although the voice was calm and correct, a bright shaft of coldness sliced through the room.

"All men are equal before God. And righteousness exalts a nation."

Caleb knew immediately that his words had come out a touch too sharply. He turned to his next shot. Everybody knew that horns had been locked now.

"Isn't that a bit strong . . . coming from a Jew?" It was out in the open now. "You claim that God has elevated you above the rest of us because of the – what do you call it – the Torah? And aren't you notorious for riding on the backs of others through financial and political corruption and manipulation? Do you really think you can teach us anything about equality and fair play?"

"God chose us for a unique and specific task. And haven't we been made to pay for God's choice ever since?"

"Gentlemen, gentlemen! We came here to enjoy a quiet game of billiards, not to argue."

As a good host, Sebastian was trying to stem the rising tension before it ended in a serious argument. He was totally ignored.

"I think you are trying to say that the white man has elevated himself over the Blacks and that this is both immoral and ungodly. But I think you'll find you are mistaken. If you care to read your Bible you'll find that the Almighty Himself ordained that Ham, the black man, was to serve the white Japheth. Besides, isn't your position a bit hypocritical? Wasn't Joseph sold into slavery by his own brothers? Didn't slavery thrive under Judaism? And who put a stop to the slave trade anyway? The British."

Caleb, whose mood had already been soured by Celia's lack of interest in him, had had enough. He knew it wouldn't make any difference to the outcome but he wanted to make one last statement before the inevitable end. Now he spoke fast and sharply, wanting the truth to strike home. He didn't care about the consequences, knowing that they were not under his control anyway.

"Slavery is not God's invention, and He never treats any human being as anything less than fully human. All men are made in His image – irrespective of race, creed and colour – and His mercy extends equally to all men. I think you'll find that Christianity teaches the same."

Caleb's reference to Christianity had the effect of a spark in a powder keg. The old man exploded from his chair in rage. "This is intolerable. I don't have to take that from you, you ill-mannered young whippersnapper. I have been going to church all my life and now you, a Jew of all people, have the effrontery to lecture a Christian gentleman on God and Truth. In a different age I would demand satisfaction and see you go to hell." He paused for a second, breathing heavily. "But you're not worth the cost of a bullet."

There was a murmuring and clearing of throats – the baying of the pack – and a new voice joined in, quietly, teasingly. "If it hadn't been for white missionaries and Christianity, the millions of natives would still be running around naked, like the savages they are, without any education, law or medical care. And still in chains to superstition and witchcraft!"

Caleb's temper frayed. "So, instead of being in bondage to the witch doctor, he's now a peasant slave serving the white man. How has his lot really improved? He's just changed masters."

The old gentleman was now trembling with rage, spluttering with indignation. "Never have I been spoken to in this manner before. Who are you, anyway? And what right have you to be here where you don't belong? The ghetto, that's the only place for you and your like."

His white moustache was set against a shiny, crimson-flushed face. Lord Purley stormed out of the room, his indignant huffing and loud footsteps following him into the ballroom. Then there was more shuffling of feet and another clearing of throats.

Sebastian was the first to react. "Oh dear, I think you seriously upset the old chap." He spoke in a low voice. Seeking to lighten the atmosphere, he added with a grin, more loudly, "Actually, I think you're to be congratulated. You are one of the very few who have ever dared stand up to old Purley. Anyone like to join me in drinking to that?" He put his hand on Caleb's shoulder in a friendly gesture. Lifting the champagne bottle from its cooler, he held it up and laughed. No one responded.

"If you'll excuse me . . ." Caleb put the cue back on the rack and walked past him.

He left the witnesses to the hostile exchange to make what they would of it. While it was of course true that a gentleman must never give way to anger and rudeness, but remain cool and detached at all times, there were justified limits. Those who took Lord Purley's side closed ranks and muttered amongst themselves. The others drifted out of the room. Sebastian, left on his own, felt embarrassed for his silly and ineffective efforts to make light of what had happened.

Caleb emerged from the semi-darkness into the brightness and noise of the ballroom. Feeling empty and alien, he worked his way through the happy crowd towards the garden. The rain had stopped. Couples and small groups had ventured out into the cool of the early evening and were watching the sunset as they chatted.

Was this really the 20th century? Had mankind learnt nothing? Events on an international level, and even in this gracious home, indicated plainly that one race would desire to oppress another, one nation another, until the end of time.

And tonight Caleb had, once again, been on the receiving end of British anti-Semitism. In Germany, Hitler had ratified the Nuremberg Laws. How many British supported his views and applauded his actions, even if they might not say so? Would Oswald Mosley gain sufficient votes at the next election to force the government to adopt any of his policies? Caleb clenched his fists, his fingernails digging into the palm of his hand. The pain caused him a perverse satisfaction: as long as he could feel pain, he felt alive. He determined never to be lulled into the meek moderation and social passivity that might allow tradition and power to triumph over truth and justice.

Celia appeared by his side. "I've been looking for you." She stood close to him but did not look at him. "There is some gossip going around that involves you." There was a ring of disappointment, if not of disapproval, in her tone.

"That didn't take long," sneered Caleb. He was not unduly bothered by what had happened, except that he now felt so distant from Celia. She had taken their side, not his . . . naturally. These were her people; this was her world. How else could it be?

"Won't you tell me what happened?"

"Would it make any difference?"

"Does truth make a difference? Can truth make a difference? To me it does. I need to hear the truth . . . from you."

Caleb smiled, as much at Celia's attempt at philosophy as at her encouraging words. Her gentleness melted his frostiness. "I am very sorry if I've caused you any embarrassment. Just remember, wherever there's a Jew there will be trouble. It might as well be the eleventh commandment."

"I wish I had your courage. Keeping silent is not always the right thing, is it?"

"You come from a long line of civilised people who have glorified tradition and mastered the art of not rocking the boat. For that you have a remarkable talent. As for me, I've had a lot of experience of the opposite. I'll never 'fit in' for the sake of it, and I usually don't want to anyway. For a Jew, a craving for social acceptance means spiritual death."

~ *8* ~

Cecil Court, 20th July 1936

"I shall certainly speak to my daughter most sternly. I had no idea . . . I'm so very grateful you came to tell me . . . A most unpleasant task you had the kindness to undertake . . ."

Lady Norah did her best to appease her elderly guest, who sat in her chair, very upright, resting on her walking stick. She was well satisfied with the outcome of her mission. Then the door was flung open and Celia raced into the drawing room. At the sight of the Duchess of Garnbrook her heart sank. The Duchess had never liked Celia and had caused many heated arguments between mother and daughter. She thought Celia a wild and wilful child and her entrance at this moment confirmed the aristocrat's view.

"Your Grace . . ." She curtsied in the Duchess's direction.

Celia hoped she would be able to make a swift escape and grabbed a book – the reason why she had come – from a table.

"Cecilia, the Duchess has just told me about a most unpleasant incident at the garden party." Lady Norah's words caught Celia as if by the ear, rendering escape impossible. "Were you aware that Lord Purley was gravely insulted by . . . Mr Levine, wasn't it?" The Duchess nodded, closing her eyes theatrically. "It is my wish," Lady Norah continued, "that you cease all contact with that person at once." This was the correct thing to do.

"That won't be possible, I'm afraid, Mummy. He is Alistair's guest and his sister will be joining them soon.

They've asked me to keep her company while she's here and I've already committed myself. I'm sure you wouldn't want me to break my word."

The two older women exchanged meaningful looks. Lady Norah felt humiliated by her daughter's disobedience. She bit her tongue, determining to deal with her later.

"I can assure you, your Grace, that this . . . er . . . disagreeable person will certainly not be allowed into this house."

"Mummy, Mr Levine is not a disagreeable person; he was goaded into this unfortunate exchange of words. It is certainly not entirely his fault," defended Celia. "And it was not correct to threaten a Jew with the ghetto. Especially now, with all that's going on in Germany. And I'm quite sure the honourable Lord Purley wouldn't want his distinguished name mentioned in the same breath as the National Socialists and Blackshirts."

The Duchess took a breath, audibly. "I'm shocked that you would take the side of a Jew against Lord Purley. You meet one Jew and all at once you consider yourself an expert on German politics and good manners." She made a dismissive gesture. "Anyway, you're far too young to have an opinion on these things. It is pointless talking to such a self-opinionated creature as you." She turned to Lady Norah pointedly, changing the subject. "Lady Georgina was so delightful at the party. So graceful and accomplished. What a pity that you weren't able to come, Lady Norah."

With these words, Celia was dismissed. The peace she had felt had vanished, to be replaced by a simmering anger. Everyone treated her like a child. Was she not old enough to have her own opinions and convictions? Did they think she was an imbecile? She felt hurt and humiliated. Gina would never have been treated like that. But then Gina had presence and never put a foot wrong. She had to face reality: she was just as much of a misfit as Caleb.

Caleb too was in turmoil: he was now sure that he had fallen in love with a Goyah, a Gentile girl. He needed time and space to think, to consider and weigh both sides of the argument. His confusion showed itself in his sullen withdrawal. He felt lonely and isolated, hiding in an inner place where no one could reach him.

Fallen in love? No, "grown" was much better. As a seed falling to the ground grows roots to nourish the young plant, so the seed of love had fallen into the fertile ground of Caleb's heart, where it grew steadily. And it had already established much deeper roots than he dared admit. This love was not like a cut flower: beautiful and lush today, but wilted and dead tomorrow. His love was living and growing, very much alive. How had he failed to notice what was happening until it was too late? Now a day without Celia was a day without sunshine. That lovely girl who carried feed buckets with the sweetest smile, who listened seriously to his Jewish jokes – which he usually had to explain. It didn't matter. He realised that he loved her, not just for her naturalness and sense of humour, but for her whole attitude towards life and creation. But was this empathy between them mere coincidence? She was, after all, just a Goyah.

There was also another problem. Out here, in the fields or stable, or under the trees and stars, she was a normal human being, a person he could relate to. In the ballroom, among her peers, she was the aristocratic daughter of the Earl of Besthorpe, untouchable. He must not deceive himself; the gulf that separated them might be invisible now, but it would soon become all too tangible. Celia was innocent and she knew him only in these sheltered surroundings. What would happen when they encountered the wider world? The unpleasant incident at the Hall had been a mere foretaste.

When Celia had come up to him to ask about what had happened, he had been painfully aware of the divide that separated them.

How could she possibly identify with the real him? Until a few weeks ago, she had hardly even heard of Judaism. She might have an unusual and keen interest in things Jewish, but how could she comprehend the 4,000 year history that had moulded and forged him and all his unique and very peculiar people? What did she know about the Torah and Talmud, about Halachah and the ancient traditions of Israel, about persecution, hate and fear? Were they not the very essence of his being, the yearnings that drove him? It would be easy for Celia to reject her weak and corrupted religion and lightly embrace another because she was in love. But it was out of the question that she should convert to Judaism simply to please him. How could he expect her to commit herself to something he was no longer certain of himself? He was far from leading the life of a devout Jew himself, so how could he insist that she convert to Orthodoxy? How could he ask her to adopt a lifestyle he had largely rejected because of its stern, unyielding rigidity, which squeezed out even innocent pleasures? It would make them both hypocrites; and God hated hypocrisy.

Could he marry an unconverted Gentile then? How far could he turn his back on his people and all they stood for without surrendering his Jewishness? In the Jewish community he knew the words "Marrying out" were pronounced like a curse. You did not talk about family members who had married out: they were cut off; they had ceased to be. This attitude and practice had been engraved on Caleb's heart. And how could he ever come to terms with it, when he felt guilty even at the thought of marrying out? He and Celia were not equals; they were utterly and irreconcilably different. Caleb could not bear to think about it.

But what were his chances with a good Jewish girl? Would he even be allowed over the threshold of her house? In his mind he imagined her parents whispering together. "His parents converted to Christianity." They would have no choice: they would have to end the relationship before it had a chance to blossom.

He recalled his university days. He had hoped to find life easier and less complicated away from home, and that he might feel less isolated. Maybe he would join the Jewish Students' Society. But at the Society's meetings he never talked much about his home or family life and this soon became noticeable. While other students might look forward to celebrating the High Holy Days with their families, Caleb could not.

"Will you be going home for Passover?" a fellow student asked him one evening over dinner.

"No." Caleb pretended to be preoccupied with his meal, too busy to give a fuller reply.

"Why not? Too many memories of family quarrels around the table?" He grinned.

Caleb pushed away his plate and looked the other student straight in the eyes. "My parents have converted to Christianity. There are no Pesach or Chag haMatzot, Shavuot or Succoth celebrations in our house, not even Yom Kippur." The words seemed as bitter in his mouth as they were in his heart.

Visibly baffled, his friend opened big eyes. "Not even Yom Kippur? And I thought you were just a lapsed *frummer.*"

Once the shameful secret was out – that Caleb Levine's parents were disciples of the heretic from Nazareth – his relationship with the other Jewish students cooled. If his father and mother were Christians, even though he was not, might not the rot already have infected him? Better keep a bit of a distance, just in case. And, while rejecting him, they kept on pretending to be good Englishmen, even trying at times to be more English than the English.

Shunned by his own people, Caleb had to make do with Gentile company. But they regarded him with equal suspicion. Whichever way the young Jew turned, his personal integrity was questioned by both Jew and Gentile. Now at last, as if by a miracle of God, he had found one person – just one in all the world – who did not care about his parentage. But, by a cruel twist of fate, she turned out to be an untouchable heathen. He made a decision: he must disappear from Celia's life before it was too late. From now on he would keep her at arm's length, both inwardly and outwardly. There was no hope for them; the divide that separated them was too broad, too deep for them ever to cross in their own strength. The very fact that his heart was still desperately searching for ways to continue this strange and wonderful relationship proved that it had gone too far already. Another ten days and it would all be over. He would return to London and Celia could continue her quiet, calm life until the right suitor came along and swept her off her feet. He was suddenly ambushed by the image of her in someone else's arms and felt a blind hatred for that unknown man.

There was a narrow terrace alongside the white drawing room, which overlooked the secluded garden flanked by mature chestnut trees. It was a lovely place to sit and one of Celia's favourite spots, especially as the heat was waning on a summer evening.

The day had been very hot and Lady Norah had withdrawn to this cool, dapple-shaded place. The day's farewell light streamed through the lush foliage of the trees.

"Good evening, Mummy." Celia greeted her politely. "Hasn't it been hot today?" She poured herself a glass of iced lemonade from an elegant jug standing on a silver tray.

"Yes, but it's nice now, here in the shade." Lady Norah dropped her needlework into her lap to look out over the garden. She was making something for the Christmas bazaar. For once she looked relaxed. "Did you have a nice day?" She took up her work again.

"Nothing out of the ordinary."

"Did you speak to Mr Levine?" asked Lady Norah casually.

"No. He's gone sailing with Alistair."

"Maybe he's hiding because of the incident at Lenkham Hall?" Celia did not respond. "Really, Cecilia, think rationally for a moment." Lady Norah tried to get through to her again. She didn't look up from her sewing. "It's so important to be careful about whom you see, and whom you are seen with. You do realise it will greatly affect your chances of making a good match. Who is going to marry a girl of dubious reputation, even if she does come from one of the best of families? You have duties and obligations, you know."

"Mummy! You're talking as if I haven't heard all this a thousand times before. I am not an heiress and you know it."

"Well, no, but you know the state Cecil Court is in. Even if your suitor isn't titled, which I naturally hope he will be, he must at least have money. Don't you understand? The drains need urgent attention, and that costs money."

"So, if it were up to you, you would give your daughter away to some cruel man if that would get the drains repaired?"

Celia could see the funny side and laughed. Lady Norah became bolder in her approach. "Be serious, child. What are you going to do with your life? At your age I was married." She stitched away for a while, planning the best way to make her point. "Jews can't be trusted, you know. That's a fact. Oh, yes, the clever ones come out and try to marry into our circle, but underneath their English-gentlemen exteriors they are

91

still just Jews. Centuries of financial malpractice and extortion are inbred. Even with the nicest of them, it's still there."

"What are you trying to say, Mummy?"

"All I want to say is, 'Do be careful'. You are so very naïve and trusting."

"Mummy, did you know that if there are 99 scoundrels and one righteous beggar, you are to give to all of them for the sake of the one who is righteous?"

Lady Norah looked up as if she had been slapped. "Who taught you that? The Jew? I told you they were smart. How typical. Tricking us with innocent-sounding proverbs just to make us feel guilty for not welcoming them with open arms. The Jews know how to use the financial system to line their own pockets and keep everyone else poor. Your father once had dealings with them and had the devil's own job to get out of their clutches. You ask him."

"But that can't make them all bad . . ."

"Don't you believe it. One rotten apple in the barrel . . . But I can see you are refusing to listen to me. Very well then, but don't say I haven't done my duty and warned you."

Her mother had, on the whole, spoken to her in a caring and kindly way and, to please her, and out of gratitude, Celia had listened to her attentively. But by the time she was ready to come indoors, her mother's words had begun to trouble her.

The product of her upbringing, Celia could not rid herself instantly of the values and ways of thinking into which she had been born. What if her mother were right? Was she really being tempted to believe an artful, foxy deceiver? She had genuinely trusted Caleb; to her he was simply the Caleb she knew, truthful and honest. Now tiny seeds of doubt began to take root. Was Caleb playing with her feelings, cynically and cruelly, just to take advantage of her? Could she be so mistaken? Celia felt lower and more wretched than she had for some time. How had she drifted into this state again? What had upset her carefully maintained equilibrium? She had subdued her hopes and mastered her dreams; she had fought so hard to overcome her insecurities and achieve her detached peace of mind. But for the past month an inner restlessness had been creeping up on her and had now taken hold. It was as if she were waiting for something to happen, but did not yet have the slightest idea what it might be. Her mind, which had earlier been like a calm river, began to be buffeted by turbulent undercurrents welling up from deep beneath the surface.

～ 9 ～

Bleckham Manor, 25th July 1936

"Why don't you talk to her?"

"I'm sorry, what were you saying?" Caleb turned the pages of *The Manchester Guardian* carefully, glancing over the morning's headlines. He skim-read a few articles.

"You should call her or, better still, *see* her," repeated Alistair, forking some bread round his breakfast plate.

"Who?" A pair of eyes appeared over the top of the paper and looked at Alistair absent-mindedly.

"You know exactly whom I'm talking about. You two were almost like Siamese twins. Then, suddenly, you're sulking and miserable and it's deadly quiet between you. I may be stupid, but I'm not blind. You and Celia were inseparable."

"That's ridiculous. It's just your imagination." Caleb lied to himself as much as to Alistair. Without lowering the paper, he pointed at the cold, shrivelled bacon rind on Alistair's plate. "It comes from eating that stuff." He returned to his reading with a sour expression.

"Come on, old chum. Whom are you trying to fool? I thought you were in one of your morose moods, except that you've agreed to come sailing with me. Last time we went out you were ill the whole time. I'm starting to think you find sea-sickness better than being love-sick."

"Even if I were in love, which I'm not, it would be none of your business. I don't make any comments about you and Judy." As soon as he had said it, he regretted his outburst.

Alistair and Judy were very discreet about their feelings for one another. Their long-standing affection had stood the test of years and was no sudden passionate fling. He had no right to cheapen it. But being in love had caught Caleb unawares; he felt alone and vulnerable and had no idea what to do. This insecurity just made him feel worse. "I'm sorry. I shouldn't have said that," he mumbled.

"How much do you know?" Alistair asked. The pain in his voice was obvious.

"Nothing. It just slipped out."

"No, I insist."

"Al, you and Judy have been sweethearts since the day I first brought you home! Even Mama and Papa realise it, I think, but they love you enough to pretend otherwise."

Alistair looked like a spaniel caught with a stolen delicacy. Caleb felt he needed to make some amends for his rash words. Without really thinking he blurted out, "I love her. I can't find any words to describe what I really feel. You are perhaps the only person I know who can understand what all this means for me." He was tired, wrung out emotionally. He wiped his hand across his face as if to ease away the confusion and pain in his heart. "Now you know. I don't want to discuss the matter further."

Alistair understood exactly what he meant and felt truly sorry for his friend. As a Christian he could imagine the struggle Caleb was going through. He thanked God that Judy was a Christian too, sharing his faith. But what if Alistair had fallen in love with someone who did not share his most precious, life-giving beliefs? What if Judy had been an outright pagan or a Jewess? And to Caleb that was what Celia was: an untouchable pagan girl. She could never be the "Daughter of the Covenant" chosen by God to be his wife.

"I understand your predicament, but, however you feel, you still have to behave like a gentleman. Have you told her about your feelings?"

"No," assured Caleb.

"Even so, you can't keep on ignoring her. When did you realise you had fallen for her?"

"During that wretched weekend at Lenkham Hall. But I mustn't love her; she's forbidden fruit."

"I wish I could suggest what you should do. Couldn't you explain your feelings and predicament by letter?" suggested Alistair.

Caleb shook his head. "If you don't hit exactly the right tone, I find letters just make things worse. An unfortunate choice of words, an inappropriate sentiment, even a word carelessly omitted . . . No, I must go and talk to her."

Caleb might be stubborn and pig-headed sometimes, but he never shied away from unpleasant realities and responsibilities.

Rather late that evening, Caleb went to Cecil Court, his heart and self-confidence in tatters. He had no idea what to say to Celia or how to say it, but he was determined to bring the whole affair to a close tonight. One way or another. A wild, theatrical conversation echoed through Caleb's mind as he drove to the Lancaster estate:

"Celia, I love you with all my heart but I'm not allowed to because, to us Jews, you are unclean. I'm frightfully sorry."

"Oh, Mr Levine, that's awfully nice of you, but, actually, I couldn't care less. What a preposterous idea anyway, for you to imagine I could possibly feel the same way about you. Perhaps you've forgotten I'm an aristocrat and you're just a Jew, one of the most despised people on earth."

Celia was at home, alone. She had settled in the white drawing room, nestling into the settee with a cup of tea, and was engrossed in a book.

The weather had deteriorated, releasing a brooding yellow light. Thunder rumbled in the distance. She looked out at the encroaching darkness, revelling in the mystery of the moment. What could be more enigmatic, earthy and sensual than a summer storm? She felt secure between the four walls of this gracious room – in the safety of her home. The bricks and mortar reflected the solid certainties of her ancient lineage and traditions. What could disturb or unsettle her in her own home? Who could touch her in this last bastion of security? She remembered the ancient trees of the estate that had watched over so many generations of her family like faithful and familiar retainers. She wondered what joys and tragedies they might reveal if they had eyes to see and mouths to talk.

"I'm bound to this land," she thought. "This is where I belong . . . where my roots are. Nothing will ever change my feelings towards this soil."

Her gaze wandered over the parched and dry, storm-darkened garden. Celia tucked her feet under her and covered them with her skirt. Before she could get comfortable, a maid slipped quietly into the room and handed her a card.

"Thank you, Molly. A visitor this late?"

"Mr Levine is waiting in the hall, m'lady."

First, he gave her the cold shoulder by going sailing without even telling her. Now he was calling, out of the blue, at this late hour. Celia frowned and hesitated, her fingers toying with the visiting card.

"Show him in, please, Molly," she said, shifting her position on the sofa. She must adopt a more correct and formal pose.

"Good evening, Celia. I apologise for calling at this hour. I hope it's not too late?" Caleb's greeting was relaxed but formal, his manner perfect, correct, revealing nothing of his inner turmoil. The confidential bond that had existed between them seemed forgotten.

"Good evening. This is rather unexpected. Please, do sit

down. Can I offer you a sherry? Or a long drink: a glass of elderflower soda maybe? Or something stronger?"

Celia slipped into her role as hostess, covering her own nervousness. There were occasions when she was glad to have been at a finishing school. They had trained her to build a convenient, protective shield to hide behind when threatened.

"No, thank you. I'm fine." Caleb looked around, waiting for the curious parlourmaid to disappear.

When she realised she had been noticed she slipped out unobtrusively.

"Well, how are you?" Celia opened the conversation with a hint of social distance, even polite indifference. It was like a stab to Caleb's heart. This was not how he remembered her. For an instant he was tempted to hit back. But he restrained himself.

"I've come to apologise for my attitude over the past few days, and for deliberately avoiding your company." He wanted to come straight to the point. He knew that, as a gentleman, his discourteous behaviour to a lady demanded an unreserved apology.

"Why?" Celia asked, pouring tea into her cup, although it had not needed topping up.

Caleb was confused. "Why have I come to apologise?"

"No, why did you stay away from me? I thought we were friends." Her heart had spoken before her tongue could check it.

"Friends." He savoured the word. "It's no light matter to call someone 'friend'," he said.

"I am quite aware of the meaning of the word, thank you. And I'm not so naïve that I'd use it lightly. But, very well, maybe I did speak hastily. I have very few real friends. Just forget that I said it." Her hand moved in a dismissive gesture.

Caleb spoke as if he had missed the last exchange. "I'm

sorry, I'm not used to . . ." He groped for the right word to express his thoughts.

". . . Being treated as a normal person?" Celia completed his sentence for him. "What's the matter, Caleb?"

Her searching look met his. He now had to choose between making his escape or confiding his true feelings to her. To give himself time, he walked across to the French doors and watched the first gentle rain running down the panes. The garden lay in complete darkness now. Caleb folded his arms, his back to Celia. How could he make her understand the forces tearing at him, one moment in this direction, the next in the opposite? There was a long silence. Celia sensed his inner conflict but was powerless to come to his rescue.

She was not what one might call a sensitive creature, nor was she particularly delicate in the way she related to people. She used brashness as a defence, adopting the "don't-come-too-close" attitude of a badly treated horse, which would bite before giving you the chance to stroke it. Her approach had its advantages. She could shrug off disappointment and keep her eyes dry at all times, but she paid a high price for the privilege. All true passion, commitment and trust had, of necessity, to be locked away in the dungeon of her soul. It could never be exposed to the mocking light of day. It was because of her own emotional barrenness that she so loved Annabel's company: with her ebullient spirit, her ability to articulate and communicate her feelings, she could carry Celia to inaccessible places of inner beauty, revealing to her the hidden secrets of the human heart.

Who else but Annabel could have said: "Whenever you express yourself in art, you have to give a little of your self away – open up some of your precious sensitivities to others – so that you can draw them into your world. You can learn to be a good painter – to excel technically – but you can't learn to be truly great. For that you must be able to sow a grain of yourself into each work, to impart a unique, distinguishing seed of originality. Without this, your work is nothing more than a brilliant photograph of reality; brilliant, but still just a copy. I believe it is art that sets us apart from the rest of creation. A bird will build an identical nest each year; only humans are truly creative. I want to be a painter, paint my life with my own colours, be an original, not a brilliant copy of other people's masterpieces. I want to choose the colours and the theme of my own life."

Celia recalled this conversation many times. It blessed her, inspired her, and gave her courage. "You haven't yet decided either the colours or the theme of your life, have you?"

"I'm sorry?"

Caleb stirred out of his own thoughts and Celia repeated her question.

"What do you mean?"

"You don't know whether you want to give your life Jewish or Gentile colours. You know you'll have to paint on that awesome blank canvas of your life one day, but you don't know where or how to start. You don't know if you want to copy an old masterpiece, or be bold and innovative, creating your own unique style of life, daring to run the risk of being misunderstood and rejected."

He was turning her allegory around in his mind, trying to fit it to his situation without raising too many carefully hidden fears. Then he spoke: "I suppose I've two colours on my palette, but they won't mix, or only very badly. It would spoil the picture to try to work with them both." He spoke with the utmost sincerity, addressing himself more than her.

Their mood changed again, making room for another long silence. Caleb's heart was yearning to entrust his feelings to her. He felt spellbound in her presence, unable either to bid a simple goodbye and go, or to talk freely. But his head knew that to continue this relationship would only repeat the tragedy of his family history. It would have been better if he had never come to Norfolk. He would return to London and put this doomed affair behind him. He sighed involuntarily.

Celia was full of pity as she looked at him. Within two days his face had changed from open to lonely, from confident to troubled. She dredged through the debris of what she had learnt at Mme Trousseau's Swiss finishing school about keeping a conversation flowing, but nothing surfaced. She lacked wit and anything worthwhile to contribute to a conversation: this had always been her weakest skill. As so often happened, she would have to leave the young man to his own devices, trying to work out where this situation might lead him. Caleb remained an enigma to her. Kind and softly spoken, she had felt so at ease with him. He could laugh with her and share her passion for nature. She had felt safe, confident he would not be offended by her outspoken ways and liberal, naïve attitudes. But tonight she felt on tenterhooks and was confused in his company. Why had he come so late in the evening? Could a simple apology not have waited until the following morning? He was clearly burdened with something more than embarrassment over a pardonable breach of good manners.

She tried to think of ways to make it easy for him to confide in her, but this had not been included in Mme Trousseau's curriculum. To ease another's heartaches did not feature in the traditional education of grand people. To probe the things of the heart was prying. All spontaneous, warm and compassionate impulses must be mastered and subdued; they must be channelled into acceptable and more delicate social intercourse. People solved their problems in the seclusion of their private chambers and let others do the same. One did not reach out for help through pleading or tears. How many times had little Cecilia been told, "Don't make a scene, dear. It is not becoming for a lady. No man will look twice at a woman who is prone to hysterical outbursts."

"Mummy will be furious if she finds you here," said Celia.

Without meaning to, she had wrenched Caleb out of his dark brooding. "I'm terribly sorry for putting you in this predicament. You should have told me my visit was unwelcome. I shall leave at once."

"No, I want you to stay. Besides, I've already fallen from grace once today. Mummy noticed my scratched hands at breakfast and couldn't resist scolding me."

The state of Celia's hands had not escaped Caleb's notice but it had seemed inappropriate to mention it. Now that she had touched on the subject, he asked, "What did you do to them?"

"I've been gooseberry picking." Celia stretched out her arms and showed him the back of her hands.

"And is that so terrible?"

"It is when Lord Sebastian Holsworth-Leigh has just sent you 20 red roses because you won a showjumping competition. Mummy is praying that he'll make me an offer of marriage before too long."

"Well, he seems nice enough. Wouldn't you accept?"

The young woman looked disappointed. "Would you really expect me to? Buzzy and I grew up together; we were playmates. I just can't think of him as a husband."

Caleb concentrated hard; he must not allow any compromising comments to escape his lips. Struggling inwardly, standing in front of the unlit fireplace, he was a picture of unhappy indecision.

"Please, do sit down," she said gently. Then, forgetting herself, "I won't have you running away from Mummy."

"What turned her against me?" he asked. "Yes. Let me guess: she heard what happened at Lenkham Hall."

"The Duchess called on her the very next day to tell all: a dark tale of dastardly wrongs . . . but not necessarily a true tale. Anyway, Mummy has made up her mind that you were rude and are, therefore, unsuitable company for me."

She faltered, letting Caleb ask, "That wasn't the only reason, was it?"

"She also said Jews can't be trusted, that they're always trying to worm their way into our circles, that they are full of guile and deceit. She said all sorts of horrible things."

She could have added, "Of course I don't believe a word," which would have belied her true feelings, but she did not. Instead, she waited for his response, thereby admitting the doubts her mother had planted in her mind. She looked at him with the questioning eyes of a child asking for the truth about Father Christmas. Caleb was pleased with her openness.

"Celia, there are good people and bad people all mixed together. Some of my people may not always be the most upright of citizens, but I'm not going to apologise for them. Everyone in this world is allowed to make mistakes – except the Jew. This is one of the first lessons a Jewish child is taught. Please try to see it from a Jewish point of view. How often have my people been massacred without justice, rhyme or reason? How many people see nothing wrong with insulting and mistreating, even murdering, a Jew on the sole grounds that he *is* a Jew? But they take great offence if he should defend himself. And when we try to better ourselves, society accuses us instantly of subversion. It works both ways. Two thousand years amongst your enemies is a long time." Here Caleb saw an opportunity to tell Celia what was really troubling him. "Look, we belong to two different peoples, and our upbringing is totally different. We use the same words but we often mean and understand quite different things." Then, switching to the abstract again, he continued, "There is great mistrust and dislike on both sides of the camp. You must try to understand this."

Celia became very subdued by what she had heard. So there really was a rift between them. They were divided. This revelation affected her more than she was able to admit. She had so enjoyed Caleb's company; his presence had changed her days, not dramatically but steadily, and deeply. He had answers to her questions about life and, with his explanations, so many things had at last begun to make sense. When she shared her doubts that any of her feeble efforts made the slightest difference, he had a comforting reply for that too:

"There are flowers which blossom high in the mountains. No human eye will ever see or find pleasure in them. But do you think their efforts are wasted just because you and I won't ever see them? God delights in them, and the world was created for His pleasure. It is man's arrogance, his self-centredness, his belief that everything revolves around him, that deprives his efforts of meaning and denies him a grateful heart. You are God's creation, and He delights in your little ways, however insignificant they may seem to you. And if He cares about them, what does it matter if no one else does? In Judaism, even the tiniest deed has significance to God and doesn't go unnoticed."

Celia loved his gentleness and wisdom. She had felt close to him on many occasions and realised she had grown very fond of him. But now a line had been drawn in the sand. "Can nothing be done to change this mistrust and dislike between your people and mine?" Celia put her question softly, with a mixture of timidity and vexation.

"You tell me how. I'm very open to suggestions."

"I . . . Oh, never mind . . . It's getting rather late." She hesitated, not wanting to go on down this frightening road, but not wanting to let him walk off alone. "Will I see you tomorrow?"

"Yes, of course. My sister arrives in the afternoon."

"Thank you for reminding me. It had slipped my mind."

Celia retired to bed but her feelings stayed up in a state of confusion. Caleb had called to apologise for his attitude, so he really was concerned about her opinion of him. Did it matter to her if they were friends? She knew she did not want to be ignored by the young Jew, but why was this so important to her? He had made it abundantly clear that there was no common ground between them. Their different backgrounds made any union of mind and spirit impossible. Any genuine belonging together was out of the question. Maybe he was right. She had sensed that he felt uncomfortable in her world. He had not wanted to mix with her kind, and her class had no desire or need for a Jewish presence. So why did she care? Did her heart not beat faster each time she saw Caleb? She could not help responding with tenderness to the care and respect he showed every living thing – herself included. She felt good, almost intelligent, when he took her views seriously. And he had a beautiful way of bringing out the best in others, teaching them to grow as individuals. He did not simply insist that she unquestioningly learn, understand and regurgitate facts. Yes, she admitted to herself, she did have tender feelings towards him but, if necessary, they could still be mastered and smothered by her upbringing, self-control and natural reserve.

Or could they?

~ 10 ~

Bleckham Manor, 26th July 1936

She heard wheels on the gravel, followed by the sound of car doors, footsteps and voices. Celia looked through the window. She saw Alistair walking towards the front door, a young lady by his side.

"This must be her." She checked herself in the mirror, turned and brushed her dress with her hands. She felt a strange, tense sensation at the thought of meeting Judy. "For goodness' sake," she scolded herself, "she's only his sister! What could her approval possibly mean to me? She's here today and gone tomorrow." She took a final critical look at herself in the mirror. "Well, that ought to do," she thought and went downstairs.

Caleb and Sir Arthur were already greeting the new arrival. Celia took a deep breath and joined them.

"May I introduce Miss Judy Levine?" said Alistair with a beaming smile. "Judy, this is Celia."

Celia, who usually ignored her title, felt a little piqued at the brevity and familiarity of this first encounter, but her reservations were met with the sweetest, frankest smile. "I am so pleased to meet you," said the young woman.

Celia noted that she was not yet in her twenties.

"Come, let's all sit out on the veranda and have a cup of tea as soon as the young lady has refreshed herself and feels a little more comfortable," suggested Sir Arthur good-humouredly.

"That would be lovely." Judy had a light, mellow voice.

Celia heard herself offering to show her up to her room. A

defensive aloofness crept over her as she led the guest up the staircase. Celia felt both threatened by Judy Levine and jealous of her. She was not used to seeing other women at Bleckham Manor and immediately assumed that Judy might well carve out a place for herself in Sir Arthur's heart. At first sight Judy was the picture of perfect gentility. Modest and sociable, with a humble self-assurance, she seemed quite unaware of the instant charming effect she had on others. She was, in short, the model of a perfect, well-bred lady, a modern Jane Austen. Celia knew she fell short of this high ideal, and this always made her short and abrupt with such sweet and innocent angels.

Celia opened a door and put on a welcoming smile. "This is your bedroom. I hope you'll find it comfortable. If there's anything we can do, please do let me know."

"Oh, it's beautiful. And what a lovely view!" Judy exclaimed and took a long look out of the window.

"Well, I'll meet you downstairs then. Just as soon as you're ready," said Celia lamely.

"Won't you wait for me? I won't be long. I'm not really used to such big houses and may not find my way around. I would hate to end up in the wrong rooms."

Celia had to smile. "This isn't Versailles, you know. But if you'd like me to stay . . . of course I will."

While Judy was freshening up, Celia weighed her up mentally. She and Caleb were quite alike, although Judy was very petite and he was rather lean and athletic. The Jewess's complexion was pale, almost transparent, and lacked that full, healthy colour which made Celia's face so glowing. She had long brown hair, grey-blue eyes, and a delicately shaped face with a pretty, unassuming nose peeping out over full lips.

"Like a little grey mouse," Celia thought, and then felt ashamed of herself.

"You actually want to go out with Judy?" Celia said, rather sarcastically. She had overheard Caleb asking his sister if she would like to come with him to see an art exhibition in Norwich. "Most of the time you leave Alistair to look after her."

He was aware he had been ticked off. "I suppose she prefers his company to mine."

"Why should she do that?" asked Celia, dismounting and patting Foxtrot.

"Has it occurred to you that she might not have come here for the sole purpose of visiting her brother?"

"You mean . . .?" Celia could hardly believe it. "You mean Al and Judy?" She found it quite incredible, if not downright funny, that quiet Alistair might be romantically involved.

"They wanted to meet here so she and Sir Arthur could get to know one another. They're banking on his support."

Celia felt immediately threatened by this sudden change of circumstances. She beckoned a groom to take her mount to the stables. If Judy and Al's friendship was really serious, it could totally change her position and influence at Bleckham Manor. She was always uncomfortable when confronted with the possibility of change; her inner peace depended in large measure on the securities around her.

"I believe they are already . . . engaged secretly," Caleb confided. "My parents will be delighted, but I suspect Al's will be furious."

"No! Why should they be? Judy is perfectly lovely. What objections could they possibly have to her as a daughter-in-law?" protested Celia, despite being preoccupied by worrying thoughts of her own.

"Because she is Jewish, of course."

Celia shook her head. "But you said yourself, she's converted to Christianity. Surely . . ."

"You haven't seen her birth certificate. Her real name is 'Yehudit Levine'."

"I confess it doesn't sound very English, but . . ."

"Al's parents will be outraged. Imagine them at the marriage ceremony as the names are being read out. 'Wilt thou, Yehudit Levine, etc., etc.' I can see their faces now. If they only just manage to tolerate me as a necessary evil, how do you think they'll react to her?"

"They might see her in a better light when she actually becomes their daughter-in-law," said Celia naïvely.

"You just do not understand, do you?" Caleb emphasised every word. "They do not want any Jews in their family, however sweet she is – and however often she converts."

The thought flashed through his mind that no observant Jew would ever truly welcome a proselyte into their family either. Even if she were the most observant *frummer* in the *stetl*. There would always be whispers and suspicion: "She isn't really one of us, you know . . ." The doubts would then be passed on to her children: "And he's the son of a proselyte . . ." Thanks to his own Jewish sense of self-preservation, he could understand the Hornbys' reservations. But now his sister's happiness was the only thing that really mattered to him.

"Oh, do stop your whinging and self-pity," cried Celia impatiently. She was irritated, both by her own fear of losing her position as the First Lady at Bleckham Manor, and by Caleb's obsessive fixation with his Jewish social disadvantage. "You always assume the worst. Why can't you just leave the past behind and look to the future? Do you know what your problem is? You're always thinking someone's about to get you. I'm sure the Hornbys will come round to love and accept her in time."

For a second, Caleb was left speechless by her offensive reply. She was so naïve, so trusting. "Love covers a multitude of sins," he supposed cynically. "Right! Then imagine this: would your parents agree to you becoming Lady Celia

Levine? Maybe you should take another look at what's happening in Germany."

As soon as he realised what he had said he blushed deeply and turned away. But Celia was in a fighting mood and wasn't going to back down.

"They might object, but I wouldn't care. And this is England, not beastly Germany," she said vehemently.

"Ah, precious England, this Sceptred Isle." Caleb rolled his eyes skywards. "Even as you speak, Oswald Mosley and his Blackshirts are rallying the British upper classes to his policies. And these include – as those who are evenly moderately well informed should know – a 'No room for Jews' clause. As for Al, he's not like you. He certainly does care what his parents might say and do."

"Have you finished?" demanded Celia, red-faced, her eyes burning with indignation.

"For today, yes!"

"Fine! You may or may not see me at tea." She huffed and strode away. Her plait bounced in time with her brisk step.

Caleb smiled: "There goes someone who can give as good as she takes." He had never met anyone English who had argued as passionately and with such a wonderful spark of anger. He felt quite at home. If her appearance reflected her character, a girl like her – with her straight shoulders, narrow waist and strong hips and legs – would not yield easily to a husband. Nor would she surrender her ideals and her individuality, and become a submissive and bloodless little housewife. She would need someone with a strong character to care for her; preferably someone with the experience of living with a forceful, opinionated older sister . . . like Esther.

Who would have thought that quiet, open Alistair would have a romance going on the sly? Well, it certainly explained the worry lines on his forehead and his absent-mindedness. Celia imagined that he and Judy would be like each other –

overflowing in indecisiveness. She imagined them together, each trying to outdo the other in consideration:

"Would you like one or two lumps of sugar in your tea, dear?"

"I don't mind, darling."

"No, really, whatever you prefer, sweetheart."

"I prefer it just the way you do it . . ."

Celia shuddered at her caricature of young Hornby domestic bliss.

Something else irritated her. It was her mother's words: "The Jews are cunning and will try to marry into our circle." And here was pretty little Judy Levine trying to get her claws into Alistair Hornby. Was Mummy right after all? But on what did she base her strong opinions? Did she know anything about Jews or Judaism? Her only source of information was hearsay. Mud sticks: "There's no smoke without fire, is there?" But could so many upright and worldly people all be wrong? Was sweet and gentle Judy really a cunning vixen? Judy Levine couldn't harm a fly – let alone the British aristocracy.

"Have you got a moment . . . in private?" Celia asked Alistair later that day.

"Of course."

They went to the library and Celia closed the door. This bought her a little time; she did not really know how to phrase so delicate a question. Alistair sat down in an easy chair and stretched out his long legs. He was happily relaxed and at home here.

"Al, you and I have been friends for years. I'd appreciate your honesty."

"I heard you and Cal had an argument today," he teased, amused at the thought of what might be coming.

Celia did not allow herself to be diverted and looked resolute. It was most unusual for her to ask him anything. Normally Celia knew all she wanted to know already. "Oh

111

ho! Methinks the lady relenteth!" He smiled his broad, boyish grin, showing beautiful white teeth. Miss Know-it-all had to come to him for once.

"I'm currently somewhat confused, because I'm getting mixed signals," she began. Her finger moved over a table surface, as if to check on the maid. "Are Jews trustworthy?"

Alistair was mildly shocked at her question, but Celia silenced him with a movement of her hand before he could answer. "I don't know what to think, and I've no experience in these matters. It all started at Lenkham Hall, remember? That silly quarrel between Caleb and Lord Purley. Well, Mummy was told about it, and has warned me not to have anything to do with Jews, and all that. And now, well, there are discreet innuendoes circulating about Judy and you. And I can't forget what Mummy said about Jews always wanting to worm their way into the gentry and nobility; that it's all a sort of Machiavellian plot to undermine Britain. Goodness knows what else she's blaming the Jews for. And Caleb can be so oversensitive and prickly. He mentioned Judy and your parents, and got really silly and angry when I tried to be encouraging about it. All I said was that it might all work out well, despite his dark forebodings. I can't make head or tail of him. He seems so different lately. And I can't see him as Caleb any more, the person I like and respect. Now he's just 'Caleb the Jew'. All my innocence seems to have gone." While Celia had begun rather coolly and calmly, she had steadily gained in passion and spontaneity. "And then I lost my temper and accused him of paranoia," she added with the voice of a child caught out lying.

"Ouch!" exclaimed Alistair and winced. "Maybe that wasn't such a good thing to say." He got up and scratched behind an ear. "How can I explain his behaviour? It must seem jolly puzzling to you." He scratched the other ear for a moment. "First, let me put your mind at rest. Caleb Levine is one of the most honest, upright and decent people I've ever met. The most terrible crime he could commit would be to dishonour his God. So you can trust him as far as you can trust any human being. As regards the other . . ." He rubbed his neck. "How can I possibly describe, in a few simple words, the mind of someone who is carrying 4,000 years of turbulent history on his back? Someone whose heart is a mosaic of antiquity, persecution, threats of extinction, and of hopes of freedom in the face of failure? How can we know the collective conscience of a people who have been wrestling with their Maker since the Bronze Age? I have known Caleb for nine years now. For the best part of that time, I've been trying to understand him. But even now he's a closed book to me at times. I believe there are moments when he doesn't even understand himself. Then he gets confused and goes all quiet and withdrawn. I know about some aspects of his family history that also have a bearing on your question. But, forgive me, I can't share them with you. They're very personal."

"I know that his grandfather disowned the family because his parents became Christians."

Alistair looked surprised. "He told you that? He's a very private man, especially about that. It's like a terrible family secret. I can't explain it in a few minutes. To really understand the issues involved, you'd have to sit down and study Judaism and Christianity. By the way, how did you come to know about Judy and me?" he asked, suddenly serious and enquiring.

"I told Caleb he ought to spend more time with his sister instead of leaving her alone with you all the time. He replied that she wasn't here to see him." She smiled, happy to be restoring the old equilibrium in their relationship.

"Well, for the time being you must jolly well keep it to yourself. And I mean it. Do you promise?"

The weather held beautifully and Judy was enjoying her stay. She loved the walks, gentle hacks, swimming and archery. She was getting lots of fruit and vegetables from the kitchen garden, fresh dairy products and sound sleep. Within a few days, the pale city girl was transformed into a much healthier-looking woman. Her cheeks glowed with the fresh air and physical exercise, and her face shone with love and affection.

It was late afternoon, and the young people were strolling towards the lake behind the manor house. Poppies, cornflowers, corncockles and corn marigolds stood coquettishly amongst the grain, dotting the fields with lively specks of colour. Celia was sorry for the farmers: this year was particularly bad for poppies and corncockles.

Caleb was telling Celia about his sister. "When she was born she was so tiny that the midwife didn't expect her to live. But Mama didn't give up hope. Many times during her childhood, Judy was very ill."

Judy was walking in front of them, just within earshot. She was chatting away to Alistair and delighting in the wild flowers waving at them from both sides of the path. She turned back and took her brother's arm affectionately, having overheard his last remark. "Caleb used to look after me. As soon as he came home from school he would make sure I was all right. He carried me around when I cried, let me ride on his knees until I laughed, and tickled me till I begged for mercy. And he repaired my dollies. Do you remember when Esther played doctor with my favourite doll?" Judy chirped. "She had amputated one of her arms and removed all her 'intestines'. You had to make her well again."

He chuckled. "If Mama hadn't intervened I would have amputated Esther's arm in turn. I remember she was preparing dumplings when she heard Esther's yell. As soon as she saw what was happening, she threw a dumpling at me. I ducked and it hit a photo of our grandparents hanging on the wall. The glass shattered into a thousand pieces."

They both giggled at the memory. Their listeners laughed with them. Celia said, "It sounds as if you had a very happy childhood, Judy. You seem so full of wonderful stories. The Levines seem to have a vast treasure chest of happy and mischievous anecdotes."

"Oh, yes, vast!" exclaimed Judy.

She caught her brother's eye and her smile froze at his glance. She and her brother saw things very differently. Judy had a sunny nature and seemed able to recall only the happy times. In any case, she had been much too young to remember the old Jewish way of life. For Caleb, the joys and pains of the past were ever-present, mixed like a drop of gall in a jar of honey.

"Do you have any stories to tell us, Celia?"

Now it was Celia's smile that withered. "No."

She turned to the fields and tested the ripeness of the wheat between her fingers. The joy of the walk had been spoilt and it was a rather downcast Judy who rejoined Alistair. She felt responsible for the sudden change of mood. Celia fell behind, brooding over the loneliness and bitterness of her life. How often had she envied her friends' homes, feeling that anything had to be better than her own family life? She stood still, looking at the fields but not seeing them. Caleb also stopped, watching the countryside rolling by . . . and Celia. He waited for a while. If only he could sketch: she wore a light, summery cotton-print skirt and a white v-necked blouse. Her plait flowed down from a straw hat.

The biblical story of Ruth and Boaz drifted though Caleb's mind. Did Boaz look at the young woman from Moab as she gleaned in his field in just the same way? Was not Celia gleaning in his Jewish fields, picking up the small morsels of wisdom he let drop for her? Did it make him feel superior to graciously pick out grains of truth for her to scavenge eagerly? "Here are a few titbits from my banqueting table, little Gentile, but only those I decide you shall have. The rest is all mine." But were one or two Jewish crumbs really enough for the poor Gentiles?

Discussions with his father returned from long ago to haunt him. Caleb now had a deeper revelation of what his father had tried so hard to help him understand. "We Jews were called to be a light to the nations, but we failed in our mission because of our stubbornness and sin. So God went to the non-Jews. They repented and received forgiveness so, from then on, they became His ambassadors of the way of salvation."

Caleb was furious. "That's blasphemy, Papa. As if God would or could revoke His sacred Covenant with Israel. And how can you belittle the righteous deeds of our sages just because they didn't believe in your Gentile Messiah? Keeping Torah is what matters, not just believing in love and forgiveness . . . and then marching out to slaughter Jews – and other innocents – in His name. Look at Christian history! It's full of bloody and murderous crusades, inquisitors and pogroms . . . all in His name."

His father was not convinced. "Look at our own history first. All truly righteous people put their trust in the Messiah, because He is our righteousness. It is God who is our ultimate righteousness, not our own good deeds. Besides, the righteous patriarchs and prophets of old knew about the coming of Messiah long before He was manifest in Jesus Christ." How the father had pleaded with his son!

"You are equating Christ with God," screamed Caleb. "That's an even greater blasphemy! And the way you argue shows clearly that you think the Torah is now obsolete. According to you, righteous deeds are now worthless in the sight of God. So, you believe in Christ in order to be 'saved', and throw the Torah out of the window. Well, *ani ma'anim be'emunah shlema b'viat HaMashiach:* I too believe that Messiah will come with all my heart. So I too am 'saved'. But

116

I believe in a Jewish Messiah and King – HaMashiach Malkenu – not a pagan fake."

Still, his father's insistence that the Jews had been chosen to bring the heathens to God niggled at him. His only answer to this was: "God gave the Goyim the *Noachide Laws*, what else do they need? They have only to keep these laws and they too could be saved, like us Jews. But let them have their Jesus if they want Him – only leave us to get on with our lives unmolested."

"But the Rabbis are wrong, Caleb, don't you see? No one can attain salvation through keeping laws, whether the Torah or the Noachide Laws. Not even our forefathers. It's only by trusting in God's supreme act of deliverance from sin that anyone can be saved from eternal death."

"That's exactly my point. We keep our Torah, and the Goyim their Noachide Laws. Ultimately we all have to fall back on trusting God's grace, for salvation. When Messiah comes He will explain everything, and, if I'm wrong, I'll admit my faults, repent and change. Until then I'll hold to my views."

Now these words were returning to haunt him. Celia kept some of the Noachide Laws, but were these really sufficient? Her spiritual life was a terrible muddle; she did not know a single prayer of blessing, let alone anything about the character of God. Could he turn his back on her, leaving her to find her own deliverance? Could he pretend that the non-Jews would be all right while they went on worshipping other gods? And if they weren't all right after all, who would teach them the truth? So responsibility for the deliverance of mankind remained with the Jews. Was that not what his father had really meant? Only the Jews could teach people like Celia about God and Torah. How else could they be made acceptable to Him? But this conclusion went against everything he had ever been taught. Judaism was not an outward-looking, evangelistic religion. A good Jew stayed inside his community and tried – if he tried at all – to persuade lapsed Jews to return to Judaism. You never bothered with the Gentiles; too many of his people had burnt their fingers with them – and often much more than their fingers.

So Celia must convert to Judaism. But which form of Judaism? There were as many as there were Christian denominations. There were the black-frocked Chassidim. They were too exclusive and even denied many Jews the right to call themselves Jews. Why? Just because they were not *frumm* enough, according to the Chassidic Rabbis. And what about Orthodoxy? Or Reform? Oy! Caleb would not be seen dead in any of their synagogues. They questioned – even denied – that Torah was given by God in person at Mount Sinai. They had already gone much too far down the slippery road of liberalism to be considered kosher. Questions, questions and still more questions. What was the point? How could he lead Celia to God if he didn't know the way himself? His life was such a mess, with thousands of loose ends he still couldn't tie up. "Do you always have to analyse and question everything; take everything apart and make problems for yourself where there are none?" Mama had said more than once. But that was an integral part of being Jewish.

Celia turned to resume the walk and was startled to see Caleb standing close by. The expression on her face told him everything. He knew she would need time to compose and gather herself, to become once again the pleasant and attractive person she really was. Alistair and Judy had continued walking and were now almost lost in the hazy distance. On an impulse, Caleb took Celia's arm and gently put it over his. He wanted to let her know he was available if she needed him. But she remained quite passive; neither rejecting him nor drawing closer. It was as if she hadn't noticed his gesture. The only outward sign she gave was an almost imperceptible tensing of her whole body.

Inwardly her mind was racing and she could feel her heart beating faster. Many young men had gallantly offered her their arms in the past, and she had accepted them without thinking twice about it. Not so now; this offer was different. For the first time in her life, she found herself walking, arm in arm, next to a man who really meant something to her. And she was all tense and uptight and had no idea what to say or do.

"What were you thinking about?" Caleb asked gently.

They had walked along side by side for a little while. Her hand was still resting passively on his arm where he had put it.

"Oh, nothing in particular . . ." she replied. Caleb knew she was lying. To give her lie more credibility she added, "The corn needs more rain; these last few years have been unusually dry." There were so many things she wanted to say, but she was tongue-tied and her mouth stayed closed.

He did not press her to continue.

~ 11 ~

Bleckham Manor, 4th August 1936

"I have taken the liberty of inviting a few neighbours and friends for tomorrow evening," said Sir Arthur at the dinner table. "Nothing grand. Just a little dance and a cold buffet, something for us all to remember when you go home. Does that sound like a good idea?"

He smiled in Alistair and Judy's direction. They understood him. This was Sir Arthur's way of giving his blessing on their secret engagement. His grin was as wide as his moustache and his eyes sparkled. It was a joy for him to give a little happiness to those he loved.

Judy was delighted. "I love dancing!" she exclaimed.

"Thank you very much, Uncle." Alistair nodded in a man-to-mannish way. He had understood the unspoken message of encouragement.

Caleb did not feel too happy about the idea: the ghost of Lenkham Hall was still hovering over him. He looked across the table at Celia, who was cutting up her chicken as if she had not heard. The excitement about the prospective wedding in the Hornby family reminded her that she was not one of their kin. She was just the neighbour's daughter, nothing more. Alistair and Judy would take centre stage more and more at Bleckham Manor, and she must fade into the background. Especially once children arrived; Sir Arthur loved children. This young family would soon become the focus of his time and attention, which was only natural. Celia felt suddenly tearful.

"Are you all right, dear? You don't look very well." Sir Arthur knew she loved his informal dances and her quietness was out of character.

"I feel tired, and would like to go home. I think I'll skip the pudding, if you don't mind." She folded her napkin and Caleb jumped up to offer her a lift home in his friend's car. "Thanks," she said without looking at him, "but I came on Foxtrot. I must take him home."

Caleb felt snubbed. He sat down again.

Sir Arthur rose. "I will see you out, Celia dear."

"Poor girl," he thought. "A loveless home and a heavy heart."

On her return to Cecil Court, Celia went straight to bed but could not sleep. The moon was full and, through a gap in the velvet curtains, a wide beam of silvery light illuminated her room. She lay there, staring at the oak panels, while silent tears ran onto her pillow. Why was she crying? Why did she feel so empty and miserable? She wanted to be pleased for Alistair and Judy's sake. Engagements were happy occasions, but instead she was lying here bemoaning her own fate. This was not how she wanted to be, full of self-pity and selfishly jealous of her friends' good fortune. But who could change her heart? Tomorrow was the dance and then the Levines and Al would go back to London. And her life would return to normal. But would it? The departure of her friends would leave a gaping void. Her days would be empty; she would have nothing to look forward to.

Her thoughts returned to Caleb. When he was around, she felt happy and relaxed. She could share her immature and rambling thoughts with him without feeling ridiculed or misunderstood. He had a wonderful ability to pick them up like windfall apples, mull them over, give them shape and form, and re-present them, cleaned up, bright and polished. In him, she had found a gifted mentor, one who was able to sort out and interpret her garbled ideas. "That's exactly what I meant," she would exclaim, delighted to discover that her thoughts were not half as foolish as she had imagined. Then Caleb would lead her on to the next step and, by teaching her to ask the right questions, discover the answer to her own riddles. This both sharpened her mind and opened up a whole new and exciting world that had enriched her life. Now that she could articulate clearly what she had previously just sensed intuitively, she seemed less frustrated and rebellious. What a shame he could not stay. She knew she would miss him a lot.

"Oh, Cal! You're not ready yet. You're absolutely impossible." Judy was cross with her brother. He was sitting at the desk, writing a letter, as if there was nothing in the world more important. "The guests have all arrived and we're just about to start the first dance."

He turned to face her, his arm on the back of his chair. "I've already presented my apologies to Al and Sir Arthur. Big social gatherings are just not my forte. And I want to avoid another social disaster."

"I think it's very rude of you. Sir Arthur organised this little event especially for Al and me. And I'm your sister. I just won't have it. You're the best brother in the world and I want you to come. Please?"

"Unfortunately the rest of the world doesn't think so. You go ahead, I'll be fine." Caleb turned to his letter again, but Judy was persistent. "You can write that another time."

"No, I can't. It's to Esther. It's the last one before I go. It has all my travel plans. It should have gone yesterday."

"Then promise you'll come down once you've finished."
No reply.

"Please!" Judy persisted, applying a liberal dose of emotional pressure to make him change his mind. "Tomorrow we're all off to London. Sir Arthur has worked so hard to make our last evening special. And I don't want you to spoil it for him – or me."

"I'll see what I can do." He stubbornly refused to commit himself. Judy knew she could only push Caleb so far and would have to make do with this half-hearted assurance.

He did not like standing around mindlessly with a glass of punch, and really had no intention of attending. But, once the envelope was sealed, there was little else for him to do. He could just hear the band and eventually an interesting violin solo – almost Klezmer-like in its speed and complexity – tempted him down to join the party.

The event was in full swing by the time Caleb appeared. He stood at the entrance to the dining room, which had become the ballroom for the evening. Some ladies next to him were enjoying a lively conversation.

The violinist Caleb had heard upstairs started again, impressing him with his virtuosity. His fingers were nimble and firm, and he hit every note with precision. Moreover, there was genuine feeling in the way he played. He had that special gift which transformed an accomplished performer into a true artist. Caleb's foot began tapping to the beat of the music while he looked over the crowd. He could make out Sir Arthur talking to someone. Alistair and Judy were dancing, starry-eyed. Their love for each other was clear for all to see and he could not help but smile when he saw them. He could not remember Judy ever looking more radiant than tonight . . . Alistair led her swiftly and lightly to the cadences of a Viennese waltz.

He spotted Celia, almost hidden by a big lady he didn't know. Celia did not look like someone in love, or even happy. There was no smile on her face and she seemed to be paying little attention to the small talk around her. A gentleman addressed her. Celia looked embarrassed and he repeated the question. Caleb took a deep breath and politely pushed his way through the guests.

"Good evening," he whispered in her ear.

She turned around and, like a sunburst after a downpour, a lovely smile spread across her face.

"I thought you didn't want to come," she said with a hint of gentle reproach.

"Your local violinist intrigued me," he teased. Celia looked disappointed and he added quickly, "and a little bird told me that you needed company."

"And you are it?"

"Any competition?"

"No."

"You look very beautiful, even more so than at Lenkham Hall."

Celia blushed. "Do you really think so? Mummy finds this dress too plain."

"Why do you always judge yourself by your mother's taste or style? You keep doing that, you know. You must stop it. And it's not the dress I'm referring to; it's you."

Celia changed the subject abruptly. "Do you dance?" She just did not know how to receive his sincere compliments.

"No. I'm sorry. I don't seem able to get any pleasure out of ballroom dancing."

"Oh," said Celia, disappointed. "What about country dancing? It's very easy to learn and great fun."

"I don't think tonight is a good time to learn it."

Celia searched for another excuse to keep them together. "Have you been to the buffet yet?"

"No, but we could do something about that."

Though neither of them was hungry, they worked their way through the crowd to the buffet. On two occasions Caleb's arm accidentally brushed against hers, and this stirred up strange sensations in her.

Once at the buffet table, they had to make do with what the swarming locusts had left. They carried their plates into the garden, where filigree-style garden furniture had been set out for the diners. Small groups of people were everywhere, enjoying the fine weather, food and entertainment. Silver cutlery chimed on fine china, creating an exotic melody against a subtle counterpoint of laughter and the ring of crystal glasses. Celia and Caleb found a table at the far corner of the lawn. For a moment they sat in silence.

"So what will you be doing once you are back in London?" Celia enquired, without looking up. She poked at her salad.

"I'll repack my cases and then go off to Palestine. I hope everything will go smoothly. My sister wrote saying she would meet me at Haifa. Then it's only a short run up to Jerusalem, but there is the constant threat of Arab ambushes along the road. In the latest incident, they burnt down an entire orchard." He shook his head. "Such a pointless act of destruction."

Celia looked up anxiously. "Why do you insist on wanting to go to Palestine?" Caleb had mentioned this to her some time earlier. "There are much nicer places to go to if you must travel. Greece, for example, or Turkey if you're really ambitious. The papers are full of reports about Arab riots erupting everywhere in Palestine. I've read the articles myself." She lowered her head. "It'll be dangerous."

Caleb noted her anxious frown. He tried to catch her eye. "Don't worry. I'll be fine. This may be my last chance to travel extensively. After that a solicitor's office and the courtroom will be my furthest horizon." He paused for a moment, thinking. "I must go, and it must be Palestine," he said, quietly but with determination. "I don't quite know myself why but, with every letter my sister has sent me, the urge has got stronger. Maybe it's my Jewish blood after all." He shrugged. "Who knows?" Changing the subject, he asked, "May I write to you?"

Celia's eyes lit up. "Yes, I'd like that very much."

Renewed silence. Comfort and yet discomfort in each other's company.

"Look, Celia . . ." Caleb began.

Then Alistair came strolling across the lawn, invading their world.

"Ah, here you are. I was looking for you everywhere. Are you enjoying the evening?" He beamed at them happily. "I wondered whether Celia would give me the honour of a dance? I know you're not likely to ask her, old chum."

"Has your bride deserted you already?" he asked, wanting to get his own back. Caleb had to work hard to conceal his annoyance at Alistair's interruption.

Alistair was obviously excited by the evening's brilliant success and Caleb's jibe passed harmlessly over his head. Everywhere, guests had commented on Judy's charm and loveliness. She had become a much-sought-after dance partner. Celia just wanted to stay with Caleb but felt she could not refuse Alistair's invitation without appearing rude. So, against her will, she followed him indoors. By the time she returned to their table, Caleb had left.

Tonight events were out of her control and she was being swept along like driftwood on the waves of her irrationality.

"Has anyone seen Celia? We've got to leave soon." Caleb looked at his watch nervously.

The under-butler brought the suitcases down and lined them up in the hall. Judy was checking them.

"Why? Haven't you said goodbye yet?"

"No. One moment she's here, the next she's gone." He raised his arms exasperatedly and let them fall back again.

"Well, she said partings upset her. That's why she said goodbye to Al and me after lunch. Didn't she come over to see you?"

"No."

Caleb was angry and tired of these cat-and-mouse games. He just wanted to get things out into the open now. He blamed himself for being so indecisive. He should have told her the truth last night. He had resisted this moment with all his strength but now his defences had yielded; he knew the battle was lost. He had to tell her that he loved her, regardless of the outcome.

"Did she say where she was going?"

"No." Judy was surprised at Celia's bad manners; she really should not have gone off on her own without saying goodbye.

"I'll see if I can find her." He left the house hurriedly, leaving Judy to fret about catching the train.

Caleb found her in the tack room, absorbed in cleaning a bridle. He knocked quietly on the doorframe so as not to startle her.

"May I come in?" he said, but did not wait for a reply.

Celia glanced at him and nodded.

"You didn't come to say goodbye," he said with gentle reproach.

Celia carried on with her work without looking at him. "Well, I'm just not very good at it, that's all."

Caleb didn't reply. He just stood there, with his hands in his trouser pockets, looking at the floor and then at Celia who continued to scrub at invisible spots. She concentrated all her senses on the tinkling of the bridle bit, the whispered clank of buckles hitting against each other, and the scent of clean leather and horses. Caleb's presence hung heavily over her. The atmosphere in the tack room changed radically to something she had never experienced before. Their emotions hovered in the air, almost tangible. Her hands began to tremble. The saddle soap escaped from her fingers and jumped to the floor. She picked it up quickly, irritated at her clumsiness. She felt the bitterness of rising tears at the back of her mouth.

She turned away to put the bridle back in its place but, as she turned, the skylight betrayed her. Caleb had seen the silvery path a tear had left on her cheek. In an instant he was by her side and drew her tenderly into his arms, holding her close while long suppressed and uncontrollable sobs burst out of her.

"Please don't leave me. I am so afraid." It didn't matter any more if she made a fool of herself. For once in her life she wanted to release all her pent-up anguish and heartbreak with someone she felt close to. She had no choice but to surrender to her weakness, to be an ordinary human being with normal human feelings. She had to stop behaving like a well trained dog. And, with this abject capitulation to her true emotions, a new Celia – the hidden Celia – was born: a Celia who felt she belonged wholeheartedly to another person, who could receive genuine warmth and devotion from another; someone who gave her his affections and attentions freely, and not out of politeness or duty alone. The complete trust she now had in this other person, this stranger – was this what was called love? This revelation transformed Celia's tears of desolation into tears of joy.

"I have come home," she sighed. To feel his arms firmly around her, the warmth of his body, her head resting against a shoulder stronger than hers, feeling his heartbeat . . . This was Home. Gradually the sobs subsided and the girl, trembling like a little bird in a man's hand, recovered from the sudden shock of love revealed. Caleb stood quietly and patiently with eyes closed, savouring the moment, resting his cheek against her hair, from time to time touching it with his lips. How tortured their unacknowledged love had been, unaware of its intensity until this moment. But there is no sure instruction for first love in untried hearts.

Celia lifted her face so naturally, so trustingly, to receive her first, timid kiss. Her heart beat violently. She could not help marvelling that a good and upright man like Caleb Levine had chosen her, Celia, above all the Annabels and Georginas of this world. While she relaxed, secure in the arms of love, Caleb was in temporary free-fall. As he felt the warmth and softness of Celia's lips, his world abandoned itself to reckless and unrestrained chaos. Religious upbringing, personal principles and good resolutions collapsed under the onslaught of his overwhelming feelings for the young pagan, his heart joined to hers in a forbidden embrace. He, Caleb Levine, of the best Jewish and Rabbinic stock, was kissing the lips of the Gentile woman he loved in the discreet privacy of a tack room! His soul was being battered by cursing self-condemnation, while simultaneously delighting in the thrill of that very first kiss. His conscience was crying out in despair, while his heart danced for joy.

"How long have you known?" Caleb asked, tenderly.

"I didn't really know until I thought about your leaving . . . I just couldn't even bear to think about it."

"My sweet, sweet love."

This was all Caleb could utter, overwhelmed by the sweet infinity of her love. She held him as tightly as her trembling arms would allow.

Where else could he have found a heart so pure and innocent? He felt humbled. Then he loosened her hold, taking her hands into his. There were things he had to say, things that must not be swept away by their passion.

"Celia, I love you more than you can imagine; if it were not so I'd not be saying this." He took a deep breath and caressed her hands nervously with his thumbs. The words tumbled out. "You know I'm a Jew. Nothing in the world will change that fact: not for me and not for you. You must always remember this."

"But it makes no difference to me," she pleaded. "I don't care whether people accept or reject you, least of all my family. I love you and I'll grow to love your God as much as you do. You must teach me about Judaism. I'll convert . . ."

Caleb stroked her hair and shook his head slowly. "My own sweet darling, how can I make you understand?" His soft brown eyes, full of love and tenderness, looked into the dear face. He could see in her eyes that she was anxious about what he might say. "It's not really your family and friends I'm concerned about. It's my own people. For me to be united" – he carefully avoided the word "marriage" so as not to arouse false expectations – "to someone outside the Jewish faith is utterly and totally forbidden. My Jewish relatives would never approve of it. I might as well be marrying a Hottentot. I've seen it happen before – a young couple cut off from their family because one of them was not a Jew. I approved of it then . . . and now . . .? My whole world has been turned upside down. And I can't ask you to convert, because I've still got so many unanswered questions about Judaism myself. I can't ask you to commit to something I'm not sure of myself. And I certainly wouldn't let you do it just for my sake. Remember what I first told you? Judaism is a dangerous religion. You'd even be putting your very life at risk. I've loved you with all my heart since that evening at Lenkham Hall, when we sat under the stars. But I couldn't be sure then . . . for precisely these reasons. Even now we can't be united. I say this because I love you and want to protect you. I know what it means to be a Jew. You don't. Should your feelings for me ever change, I want you to know that you are under no obligation to me. Whatever decisions you might have to make in the future, I will fully understand."

Celia became as serious as Caleb. "But we love each other. Why must it all be so complicated, so impossible?" Her brow furrowed, but he smoothed her worries away with another kiss.

Very tenderly, Caleb asked her, "Are you able to say goodbye to me now?"

In response, Celia buried her face in his shoulder once more.

"Thank goodness! There you are at last. We were about to send out a search party for you. We've got to go," Judy said as he returned to the house. "Did you find Celia?"
"Yes."

Caleb was quiet on the journey back to London. Judy suspected her brother was in one of his dark moods, but Alistair guessed that he and Celia had said more than just goodbye. Since his friend was clearly unwilling to say anything, Alistair did not press him to speak.

When Caleb thought about his situation more calmly – from the eye of the storm of his emotions – he still wondered whether he had done the right thing. A Jew could not marry anyone outside the Jewish community; it was something that was simply not done. It was utterly impossible, *verboten*. He watched Alistair and Judy sitting opposite him in the carriage, contentedly holding hands. Yehudit had chosen to marry out and he knew she would never raise her children as Jews. Torah meant very little to her; she had only known the teachings of the carpenter from Nazareth. Of course her children could still be considered of Jewish descent, but would they have Jewish hearts? Would they have a heart for the people of their mother, and for the Torah and the traditions? Or would they grow up just feeling they were English? He felt sad for his people. In Germany, the Jews and their heritage were being systematically and publicly exposed, humiliated and crushed by the Nazis. Here in Britain, they were choosing an easier route to extinction: spiritual suicide through conversion, assimilation and . . . marrying out.

~ 12 ~

Haifa, British-ruled Palestine, 4th September 1936

The quay was teeming with people. There was scuffling and pushing, and mothers were holding their children tightly. With much angry shouting, boxes and cases were being pushed and heaved about with little thought for others. On board, a forest of waving hands, hats and newspapers tried to attract the attention of those on the quay. A Chassidic family was attempting the perilous descent of the gangplank: the father went first, carrying a toddler, and the mother followed with a newborn baby in her arms. The oldest boy was doing his best to keep his five siblings in line. Further down the quay, disembarked British troops had collapsed limply against a wall, their canvas bags at their feet. A staff car full of starched British officers pushed and hooted its way through the crowd. Caleb smiled – Eretz Yisrael! Baruch HaShem! The Land of Israel! Praise the Lord!

His blessing was cut short by a suitcase being banged painfully into his shin without a word of apology. Soon he too was preoccupied with shuffling his own luggage towards the gangplank. His cases were impossibly heavy. Why had he ever given in to Mama? She had insisted he take jars of homemade jam, as if Esther were living in famine conditions in Jerusalem.

"But Esther always loves my jams. And who knows what they'll be giving you to eat!" She tucked another jar into his bulging bag.

And the heat! Although it was only ten o'clock in the

morning, the temperature was soaring with devastating effect. Those fresh out from England, including the pale Tommies, were suffering most under the early September heat.

Safely down on the quay, Caleb wiped his forehead and pulled his Panama down over his eyes. Suddenly, a few yards away from him, an accordion started to wail joyfully. A group of young German immigrants had spontaneously burst into song in Hebrew. Their arms on one another's shoulders, the crowds pushed aside, they were trying to dance the Hora. In this heat? Caleb's smile widened damply as he breathed in the noise, heat and atmosphere. He worked his way slowly towards the customs shed. A tall woman with a rolled-up magazine was waving frantically. "Caleb! Caleb! Over here!"

Esther had spotted him first. She was still as thin as he remembered her, but now also very suntanned. She was wearing a yellow summer dress, a small white hat and a huge smile, beaming with delight at seeing him. After more shoving and pushing, he eventually reached his sister. He put down his cases and they embraced warmly. He stood back to get another good look at her. It had been two years since she had left England.

"You look so well. Palestine seems to do you good," he said.

Esther turned to the serious-looking man standing beside her. "Leon, this is my brother, Caleb." Then to Caleb: "Leon Brann is a friend of mine. He had to come to Haifa today and has offered us a lift up to Jerusalem. Otherwise we'd have to take the bus. We're being spoilt; the buses are horribly over-crowded. Come on, let's get out of here."

Caleb passed through the customs and passport check without any difficulty. His British passport had no doubt helped him. Many of the confused and scruffy new immigrants were less fortunate.

Esther's companion helped him with the heavy cases. "Did you have a good journey?" Leon asked, his look still surly. He tossed the luggage into the car. Caleb was not sure whether he was genuinely interested or just being polite. The dark-haired man with the facial features of eastern European Jewry had not smiled once.

They climbed into the vehicle and worked their way, slowly and erratically, through the Middle Eastern city traffic. With hooting and yelling all around them, normal conversation was impossible. The car picked up speed as they reached the outskirts and the rushing wind through the open windows cooled and revived Caleb a little. Leon caught his eye in the rear mirror. "Do you know how to use a rifle?"

An interesting opening gambit, Caleb thought. "Well, I used to shoot clay pigeons and the odd pheasant . . ."

"Here we don't shoot pheasants; here we shoot Arabs," Leon said.

Caleb did not know how to respond, and noticed Esther signalling Leon to keep quiet. She turned and tried to talk to Caleb but, with the noise of the vehicle and rushing wind, soon gave up.

Some miles out of Haifa, they drove past a burnt out bus. A military vehicle was parked beside it. Three British military policemen were examining the wreck and taking notes. Leon nodded in their direction.

"Arab ambush. Early this morning. One child dead, five passengers wounded. Welcome to the Jewish homeland."

"Would you mind dropping us off at the Demskys'?" Esther asked. Then, turning to her brother: "I found you lodgings with a nice Jewish family with six children. They're observant, so you'll like it."

Caleb was relaxed. "Don't worry, I'll be fine anywhere."

The car stopped in a narrow side street near the centre of Jerusalem. Esther helped them unload.

"Goodness! Have you got guns in your cases?" she groaned.

"No." Caleb laughed. "Just tons of strawberry jam."

"You're not serious? Mama made you shlepp jam out here? I *hate* strawberry jam." Then, for Leon's sake: "Every summer Mama makes vast quantities of the stuff and then forces us all to eat it."

Something vaguely resembling a smile flickered across Leon's face. "Right, this should be it. I'll see you later."

The Levines thanked their grim chauffeur and he roared off as the door of the house behind them opened. A stout little lady in a dark dress and lily-white apron emerged from the dark interior. She was speaking fast in excited Yiddish. Beckoning them in, she led them through the hall and sat Caleb down at the kitchen table. She invited Esther to stay too, but she declined. "I'm sorry, Mrs Demsky, but I've got to get back to the hospital. Thank you for being kind enough to take in my brother." Turning to Caleb, she added: "I'll try to come this evening, Cal. In the meantime, Mrs Demsky will tell you all you need to know. I'm sure you need a rest anyway." She bade them goodbye and left.

Caleb was surprised to hear how fluent Esther's Yiddish was. His was very rusty now. Mrs Demsky poured some tea and offered him fresh raisin cakes, which he accepted gladly. He had been too excited to eat anything since the previous night and was very thirsty after the drive. She smiled happily when Caleb praised her cakes and sat down to keep her new lodger company. "You finish your tea and then I'll show you your room."

Caleb struggled: the tea was very hot, very strong and very milk free. "Have you been living in Palestine long?" he asked.

"Almost twenty years."

"My sister told me you have six children."

"Nu, the oldest, is married and expects her first baby

soon. Chava, number two, gets married next month. Then there are Taliah and Shimshon. Avraham will become a Bar Mitzvah soon. And little Rachel, of course." She counted them on her fingers with motherly pride as she named them. "You must come to the wedding and Bar Mitzvah!"

After he had unpacked, Mrs Demsky explained the daily household routine. He would now have to adapt again: not mixing meat and dairy dishes, respectfully touching the mezusot each time he went through a door – the usual Orthodox observances. It was good to be back amongst Jews again.

Mr Demsky came home at dusk, delighted to have a young man staying in his house. "We must pray together, and I'll take you to the Western Wall. The Goyim call it the Wailing Wall, but why wail?" He hitched up his shoulders and turned his palms skyward. "The captives are returning to Zion!" He stood looking sideways at Caleb. "You're a strong young man, you are!"

Taliah and Rachel giggled.

Caleb settled in very quickly. He felt happy in a way he had not done for a long, long time. He wanted Celia to be able to share in his happiness and decided that he had now seen enough of Jerusalem to be able to write a letter that would be truly interesting. Ever since he had left her, he had wanted to write. Of course they had spoken on the telephone a few times before he set sail for Palestine, but he knew there were things he could say only by letter. He had kept a diary during the passage out. In it he had logged his love, his turbulent emotions and his thoughts about their future together, however it might work out. That was in the hands of the Almighty; only He could resolve all the conflicts, differences and difficulties.

But now, as he sat in his little room, his pen poised to

write, he was shy of telling her all that was in his heart. What had happened in the tack room so long ago – or so it seemed – was like an unreal intrusion into the reality of his life. It was all so new, so unexpected, so impossible, so uncharted. How could he begin to say these things and still be himself to her? She only knew him as Caleb the Clever, Caleb the Comforter, Caleb the English gentleman. She hardly knew him as Caleb the Man, Caleb the Lover, Caleb the Passionate Jew. And as he procrastinated and argued with himself, his determination to pen the letter he wanted to write evaporated. And, so he wrote a letter that carefully replaced his love for Celia with his love of Jerusalem, the warmth in his heart with the warmth of the climate, and the beauty of his dreams with the beauty of the Promised Land. As he finished the letter, Mrs Demsky called to announce the evening meal. So, leaving his heart in Norfolk, Caleb rose and went downstairs – across a million cultural miles – to resume the normality of life in an Orthodox Jewish home in Jerusalem.

Esther kept her promise as well as she could. She spent all her free time with her brother, showing him Jerusalem and telling him about life in the Land. The impression she gave was that it consisted of little more than relentless fighting and struggle; no rest, no shalom anywhere. Sometimes Leon joined them. One warm evening, the three were sitting outside a cafe on Ben Yehuda Street enjoying a cool drink and watching the crowds. Caleb had invited them and was telling them about the kindness he had received from the Demsky family. He was sharing his happiness at being back in an Orthodox family again. At first Leon was sullen and silent, but then he joined in the discussion.

"Religion is no help in the fight for a Jewish national home. Quite the opposite. Pious hope alone has achieved nothing in the past two thousand years." Leon was a passionate atheist Zionist and argued his case forcibly. "The

League of Nations promised us a homeland under the British Mandate. And what did the British do? They took our land away from us. By 1921 they had given 70 per cent of what we were given – Trans-Jordan – straight back to the Arabs. Now, when German Jews desperately need a place of refuge, your precious Brits are refusing to raise the immigration quota. Just to appease the Arabs. Do they think we want to live as despised and persecuted exiles among the Goyim for ever?"

"No. The prophets say that if we turn to God, He'll restore the Land to us." Caleb too could argue with the characteristic vehemence of debating Jews.

Esther sighed and Leon made a dismissive gesture. "If you're so convinced of that, why not do something practical to help instead of just talking and praying? It's harvest time and we need all the hands we can get. Could you join us on the kibbutz for a couple of weeks?"

So Caleb found himself committed to a spell of heavy manual work. The Demskys were disappointed, especially Taliah, but Caleb promised to return for family celebrations and the High Holy Days. Leon was on the management committee of the kibbutz and things happened fast. Two days later, Caleb was assigned a clean, airy kibbutz guest room with its own tap and washbasin. "That's for visitors only. Those who live here use the communal washroom," said Leon. His tone indicated his disapproval of such small personal luxuries – even for guests.

The day started when the comrade cock crowed. By sunrise, the whole community was at breakfast in the canteen, discussing the daily work rotas. The head kibbutznik allocated the work to the different work parties: "Elkanah, you and your team will be in charge of the new fences. And you, Siegfried, will continue drilling for water."

Caleb turned to his neighbour with an amused smile. "Siegfried?"

"That's my husband," said a voice behind him.

He turned round and saw a woman with a friendly face and a milk jug. "Everyone smiles when they hear his name for the first time. Then they discover how hard he can work. My name is Mahle. Mahle Finkelstein." She reached out her hand in greeting. "Welcome to our community. You must be the gentleman from England."

"I am. Caleb, Caleb Levine." He rose politely. "Have you lived here long?"

"Since '33. After the Nazis won the election we could see the writing on the wall for members of the wrong race and political party." Mahle's voice was full of scorn.

A little boy tugged at her apron. "Bye-bye, Mama," he chirped in Hebrew.

Mahle put the milk jug on the table and lifted him up. She gave him a kiss and a big hug. "Have a good day, Ezra, and behave yourself." She put him down and turned to Caleb. "Our son, Ezra."

The kibbutzniks began to move out of the canteen to start their day's work. Caleb had been assigned to work on the well-drilling project and Siegfried came over to fetch him.

The work was heavy, hot and seemingly never-ending. After three days, Caleb found he was falling asleep over his evening meal. And every muscle in his body ached terribly. But he didn't complain; no one else did. He was amazed, humbled and deeply impressed by the determination, sheer hard work and commitment of these people. They were living out their dream of a Jewish national home. However hard, exhausting and discouraging their circumstances might be, they never gave up. What a shame that they're not at least a little bit observant, Caleb thought. Otherwise he would have felt in his own Jewish heaven.

It was two o'clock on Friday afternoon and the kibbutz bell announced the end of the working week. Wearily, the kibbutzniks collected their tools and returned to the settlement.

"I thought you didn't believe in keeping Shabbat?" Caleb remarked to a fellow worker.

"We don't, but old habits die hard. The Russian communists tried to abolish the seven-day weekly cycle and failed miserably. We don't want to make the same mistake."

The tools were returned and refreshments provided. Most of the kibbutzniks were passing the afternoon under the olive trees that shaded the compound, resting in their rooms or queuing at the washrooms. Caleb slid down against a mottled trunk with a glass of water in his blistered hand. He closed his eyes and relished, with blissful satisfaction, the end of a week of hard work. Never had the approach of Shabbat seemed so sweet, so welcoming. The voices around him began to fade as he drifted into a shalom-filled half sleep.

"Congratulations, you survived your first week. I must admit, looking at you, at times I thought you wouldn't last the course. But I knew you'd be all right if you were half the man your sister is." For the first time since they had met, Leon gave him a warm smile. "Do you want to go back to Jerusalem for the weekend?"

"I must," said Caleb rubbing his eyes. "I promised the Demskys I'd come. It's one of their sons' Bar Mitzvah."

"Ah, they may be religious, but they're basically all right." He laughed. "Just like you."

The men exchanged smiles, each knowing what the other was thinking: "I may not agree with your values, but I respect your sincerity." Leon sat down next to Caleb and relaxed. He was less fidgety and tense than usual, his well-earned tiredness bringing him peace. Maybe, Caleb thought, there is a limit to even his strength and determination.

"Only two or three more days and the harvest will be safely in. This is the first year since the founding of the settlement that we've grown big enough to make a profit," Leon said proudly.

The two men were quiet, occupied with their own thoughts. Then Caleb spoke again. "Do you go up to Jerusalem for the High Holy Days?"

"I told you, I am not religious." Leon's reply was categoric.

"What made you reject Judaism?"

"Ach," he said with a dismissive gesture, "my parents only went to the synagogue for Yom Kippur. For the rest of the year, apart from keeping a few traditions, being Jewish made little difference to the way we lived. Once my Bar Mitzvah was out of the way, I stopped going to *shul* altogether. To be honest, even my Bar Mitzvah was a fake. I didn't believe a word I was saying. I only did it because of family pressure, to fulfil the old saying, 'You have been circumcised, and you will also be a Bar Mitzvah'. It's all hypocrisy, and no child should be reared as a hypocrite. It's detestable!" Leon was getting agitated again. "Let's be honest, religion is about power over people. The Rabbis controlled us with the Torah and Talmud like the Christians and Muslems ruled us with the ghetto and the sword. But here we're building a homeland where we can be free. And that means free from Torah and the Rabbis too. No, I won't have anything to do with religion."

"I'd have loved becoming a Bar Mitzvah, a Son of the Commandments." Caleb sighed with a heavy heart and thought about his "ifs" and "onlys". If his parents had kept quiet about their conversion for only another six months, he would have become a Bar Mitzvah and a member of the synagogue in his own right. Then Grandfather would have cut off Mama and Papa without any dire consequences for him. And now he was sitting under an olive tree listening to a fellow Jew tell him that Torah was a meaningless and oppressive burden. "Why did you come to Eretz Yisrael if you feel like this?" he asked.

"Thanks to Herr Hitler and his Brownshirt thugs, I knew there was no future for me in Germany. I was a member of the *Po'alei Zion* Zionist Organisation and believed that much of what the Communist Party thought and did was right. I came here, largely ridiculed by my family, with more idealism than common sense, but now I see clearly that it was the right thing to do, and that I'd come at the right time. There are more and more Jews leaving Germany now, arriving here with tales of ever increasing Nazi intimidation and brutality. I know for sure that we have to establish a Jewish homeland here. It's the only place where we Jews will ever have a chance of long-term safety and peace. I just wish the wretched Brits would pull out. They give us nothing but grief. Somehow, they manage to blame us for every incident. An Arab rapes and murders a Jewish girl and they decide it was the Jew's fault. It's obvious that war is brewing in Europe and I understand the Brits want to keep their Arab oil pipelines open. But don't they understand they're selling Jewish lives to buy their precious oil? Jews need to escape the Nazis and come here – to the only legally constituted place of refuge they have – and the British government won't let them."

Before Caleb had a chance to respond, they saw Siegfried and Mahle coming towards them, with little Ezra in tow. Siegfried was still bent and weary after his week's work. "My wife has cashed in a promise I made to take her for a coffee on Ben Yehuda Street. If you'd like a lift to Tel Aviv, Cal, you'd better get yourself ready before I change my mind."

Caleb had been given a spare key to the Demsky home. He unlocked the front door and walked into the tiny, refreshingly cool hall. "Hello? Is anyone at home?"

He put the key on the dresser. There was a clatter from the kitchen. Taliah was preparing *challah* bread for Shabbat, and had just broken off a small piece of dough to throw it into the fire. Putting his bag on a kitchen chair he felt compelled to ask, "Do you know why you are doing this?"

It was a silly question. Of course the girl would know why; she was Orthodox, after all.

"Yes, yes, the Temple sacrifices and all that."

"No, it's not 'and all that'! It's to remind us of God's instructions," said Caleb with a hint of the nose-in-the-air attitude of an older brother teaching his siblings.

"Please, spare me." Taliah groaned and rolled her eyes. "I hear this all day long."

"Taliah, what are you saying?" Caleb was genuinely shocked.

"What I'm saying," Taliah sighed despondently, "is that I don't believe in all this stuff. I'm sorry, but I'm not like my parents." She carried on kneading.

"How can you say such a thing?" Caleb exclaimed.

During his time with the Demskys he had been watching the girl, and not without a little personal interest. She was a pert and pretty little thing. And Taliah, in her budding womanhood, had noticed his glances. She enjoyed his casual compliments, and had made every effort to attract his attention. She took note of his little habits and needs and was quick to attend to them. She would always offer him the largest piece of cake, and bring him a glass of water when he came in. She had even done her best to catch and hold his eye at her sister's wedding. Flattered and amused, Caleb submitted to her efforts to attract him. And who could blame him? He was as susceptible as any other to a little flirtation. And who did not enjoy being made to feel special? Moreover, it was happening in a good Jewish home and with a real Jewish girl. He too was aware of Taliah's ways of doing things: her special way of laying the Shabbat table, the care with which she kept the meat and milk separate, the way she spoke, and her special gestures. Everything she did reminded him of his childhood. She would soon grow into a virtuous woman and would make a fine wife. Her husband would feel well looked after and proud of her. He would not have to worry about neglected observances. Now she had suddenly revealed her true feelings about Judaism.

"But Taliah, we're Jewish. These things must mean something to you."

Taliah looked up and fixed him with large, dark eyes, her small hands covered in flour.

"I didn't say our traditions mean nothing to me. After all it's our lifestyle that makes us Jewish and separates us from the Goyim. I'm proud I'm not a heathen. I keep the traditions because that's what you do as a Jew. You and I have been brought up like this, haven't we? How could we possibly live differently?" She continued her work, wondering whether she had been too honest with him.

"But isn't it also a question of religion? It's God who has commanded us to live like this. If we do His will, He'll bless us. Without believing that, what's the point of being Jewish or *frumm*?"

"Ach, Caleb, you talk like my father." She smiled at him with amused tenderness. "It's fine to be pious if that's what you like. But I don't think you have to be pious to be a Jew. It's our lifestyle that's important, not belief in God."

Caleb could not believe his ears. How could anyone subject himself to such a rigid and disciplined lifestyle without believing that it served any meaningful spiritual purpose? "Taliah. Tell me truthfully: Do you believe in God?"

The girl hesitated, but not for long. She shrugged her shoulders and shook her head. "No, not really. Does it matter?"

Caleb's bubble of self-delusion burst with a bang. He stared at Taliah, wide-eyed. Now the girl really knew she had made a mistake.

"You won't tell anyone, will you?" she asked, alarmed.

"Why should I?" he replied, "That a young Jewess, for whom the Almighty slew every firstborn in Egypt, does not even acknowledge her Maker? Why should I tell anyone?"

He turned and left the kitchen, and went to his room. He flopped down on his bed, tired and disillusioned. To be a Zionist political activist and honestly and openly reject observance and the existence of God was one thing. Not a good thing, but understandable. But it was quite another to make others think you believed in God by outward deeds, while your heart was empty and hard. That smacked of deception and hypocrisy. Esther was different again; undecided about what she believed. She would never have chosen to be a Jewess, which was evident from her Gentile behaviour and lifestyle, but she had never gone so far as to deny the existence of God. He simply could not get over what he had just heard: little Taliah, a true, observant Jewess by word and deed, had no more faith than a pagan. How could she do it? Did not the very survival of the Jewish people, the return to this Land, the Western Wall, and the Tombs of the Fathers compel her to believe in their God? And if she was like that in her heart, what might other Jews be like?

He wondered what the Almighty, blessed be He, might be thinking as He examined each heart – including his own. And what about Celia? He had almost forgotten her out here. Each day brought so many fresh challenges and took all his time and attention. Celia knew virtually nothing about the God of his Fathers, or Judaism, or the Jewish way of life. But had she not, in her own poor, wretched heathenism, hung on every word he had spoken as if they were pearls of truth and life? Did she not long to offer praise to the God of Israel whom she now considered better than her pagan gods? Was she not, in fact, a truer Jew than Taliah?

He lay on his bed, his arms folded behind his head, watching the curtains moving in the breeze. He was feeling very sleepy. As he dropped off, he was wondering what was wrong with his people. What would it take to turn this rebellious, contradictory people back to their God and King, the Almighty, blessed be He?

~ *13* ~

K'far Altermann, 27th September 1936

Another week had passed and the kibbutzniks were delighted. It had been their best week in a good but challenging year. They were now offloading and stacking the last sacks of wheat in the barn. So, to the accompaniment of loud clapping and cheering, and much laughter and rejoicing, the last of the harvest was brought in.

The settlement's elected president, Sammy Blum, climbed up onto a tractor. "*Chalutzim*, pioneers. We'll make a good profit this year. At last we'll be able to do something we've wanted to do for a long time: establish a beef herd." He was interrupted by loud cheering. "Tonight, for those with enough strength left," he continued with pride, "we shall all celebrate. Join me by the campfire. It's time for roast meat, music and dancing." More cheers. Caleb, who was helping to unload, wiped his brow.

"Do you want to celebrate with us tonight or return to Jerusalem?" Siegfried asked. He put the last sack on Caleb's shoulder. The rough Hessian pricked through his shirt and hurt his raw shoulders.

"You'd like that, wouldn't you? Make me work like a slave in Egypt and then send me away when it's time for food and dancing. You can bet I'm staying."

It was a wonderful night. The sky was bright with stars and the air was refreshingly cold after the heat of day. The large campfire crackled and there was dancing to the music of the kibbutz band. The musicians took turns to play and eat. Jewish jokes and the latest anti-British ones made the rounds. There was much laughter around the campfire. Leon turned to Caleb triumphantly. "At least you can't say it needs the blessing of the Rabbis for people to be happy."

"That I admit." Caleb waved a lamb chop under Leon's nose. He was in a debating mood. "But you might as well bless God for it. After all, He made us with a built-in need to celebrate."

"Ach, you *frummer*!" Leon grunted good-humouredly, and pulled a face. He got up and called for quiet. "*Chaverim*," he said loudly, "as you all know, we've had a greenhorn staying with us these last two weeks, who has been working very hard indeed. I think we should, in the spirit of Zionist brotherhood, acknowledge his contribution to the harvest with a little farewell present. So, in recognition of your willing efforts to rebuild the Jewish homeland, we present you, Mr Caleb Levine, with your own spade!" Leon ceremoniously handed him the instrument of toil. Caleb bowed in mock formality and accepted the accolade proudly.

"Speech, speech!"

"Well, I'd like to thank you all for welcoming me in your midst with open arms and for making me feel so much at home."

This was greeted with shouts of "Hear, hear!" and "Make it yours as well, Cal!"

"You've given me a lot to think about," Caleb continued, "and I will make you a promise: my mother always says that if you want to return to a place, leave something behind to reclaim at a later date. So I'm leaving my spade with you as a pledge that I'll return one day and collect it. And whenever you look at it – say a blessing for me."

"Awww," Siegfried patted Caleb on the shoulder. "We'll make a good Zionist of you yet."

He could not tell how long he had been asleep when he was woken by shots, banging and bright flashes. As he came to, his door was flung open and someone – it must have been Leon – threw a rifle onto his bed.

"It's clay-pigeon shooting time," he shouted, and disappeared. Caleb was in his shirt and trousers in a moment. He checked that his weapon was loaded and rushed outside.

"Arab raid!" a settler shouted.

Everyone in the tiny community was rushing about trying to see where the enemy was and what he was up to. All around him was utter confusion and a bitter exchange of fire. Caleb knew that under no circumstances was he going to shoot another human being, Arab or not. Mahle came running across the compound and jumped into the makeshift trench next to him. Her nightdress was tucked into her trousers and she had a revolver in her hand.

"Have you seen Elkanah?" she gasped.

"No."

"We need more people on the other side. I can't stay. Give me cover."

"You're not going back into that!"

Caleb tried to grab her, but it was too late. Mahle was starting her dash back to the other side of the settlement, through the crossfire. Terrified for his friend and forgetting his vow of a few minutes earlier, Caleb targeted a shape in the far bushes and snatched at the trigger.

It was all happening so fast that time went into slow motion: Mahle running, head low, jerked upright, arms thrown up, weapon dropping, body arching backwards, crumpling to the ground.

Violent anger exploded in him: aiming, shooting, reloading, fast, automatically, mind sharp, clear, consciousness bypassed, Caleb, very slowly, deliberately, breathed in – hold, sight, steady – squeezed.

The shape in the bushes disappeared.

Suddenly there was a whoosh and a bright orange flame shot high into the night. Then there was crackling, more shouting, screaming, running, car engines, revving, tyres skidding, shouts in Arabic, German and Hebrew, and finally the noise receding.

The barn had been dynamited and set alight. Having achieved their goal, the Arabs left as quickly as they had come and vanished into the darkness. Everyone rushed to extinguish the fire, to save what they could of the precious harvest and prevent the fire from spreading. Caleb ran over to Mahle, who lay motionless, and gently turned her over. She was unconscious and barely alive.

"Someone find Siegfried, quickly!" he shouted, bending over her. Her nightdress was soaked with blood.

Siegfried arrived. "Mahle is wounded," Caleb said, standing up. He felt . . . he did not know how he felt.

He left Mahle to the privacy of her husband's grief while the stars in the sky silently watched over their catastrophe. Then lights in the nearest houses were snapped on, obliterating the darkness and spotlighting the couple huddled in the dust. Caleb tried to think what he should do next. After the shock and horror of the minutes of mayhem, cold logic was re-establishing its right to rule over him.

With the fire out and the wounded patched up with the little first-aid material available, it was time to take stock of the situation. The attack was a terrible setback for the kibbutz. Half of the harvest was smoky or burnt, and the remainder was water-damaged. Once again the future of the kibbutz hung in the balance. Much more tragic was the human loss: Mahle had been killed and five other kibbutzniks wounded, two of them seriously. They must take the wounded to hospital at first light. Opinions differed about what to do with the wounded Arabs.

"The Brits can fetch them if they like."

"We can't just leave them."

"No? You tell that to Siegfried and Ezra," protested an older woman, her face bitter.

Some of the kibbutzniks grumbled as the dead and wounded Arabs were lifted into the lorry, already full of bleeding bodies. "If there are snipers out there, let's use them as shields," someone suggested.

"As if they'd give a toss even about their own wounded. They'd shoot them and say they were murdered by us. Why not just leave them here to die?"

No one could imagine how Caleb felt at that moment. Impenetrable darkness began to overwhelm his soul. He had fired on a living human being with intent to kill. There had been murder in his heart. Two key commandments had been drummed into him since he was a toddler: "Do not worship other gods" and "Do not murder". Everything else might be subject to interpretation, but not those two. Caleb stared into the abyss of his own heart. What else was there in him that he was not aware of? Theft? Rape? Even idolatry? "Adonai, have mercy," he cried silently to his invisible God.

Even if it should cost him the friendship of his brothers, he had to do something to atone for what he had done. He was terrified. No more blood must ever again be attributed to his hands. He felt compelled to defend the wounded Arabs. "Hatred isn't going to help or comfort anyone. Letting them die won't bring back Mahle. Any man can kill, but it takes a better man to show mercy. If we want to establish righteousness and justice in the Land, then we have to prove that we're morally better than the Arabs, whatever they do to us. We mustn't stoop to their level; our teachings, our traditions, are different, higher, better. We've always valued human life. Murdering a person is destroying the image of God. We can't retaliate like that. We must defend the moral high ground we've claimed and proclaimed throughout our history. Don't let the good you're striving for, and your wonderful ideals, be destroyed by blind animal violence."

All Caleb reaped from his well-intentioned moral posturing was angry looks.

"We've to do to others as we'd like others to do to us . . ." he faltered, toppled from his soapbox by their indifference and hostility, and fell silent. He could not believe he had really said all that.

Caleb was in the back of the lorry with the wounded. The drive to the hospital in Jerusalem passed without incident. Esther was on duty that day and saw to their wounds, fast and efficiently. By eight o'clock she had finished, and withdrew to her office for a short break. Caleb followed her into the small room. It was cramped and filled with a desk smothered in papers, two chairs and filing cabinets. The room was dark, a tiny window its only source of light.

"Coffee?" Esther reached for a pack of cigarettes and took one out. She offered the pack to her brother.

"Please. Thanks. Since when do you smoke?" Caleb lit his cigarette and took the proffered mug of coffee.

"Three weeks after I got here," Esther replied, blowing the smoke through her nose. "After I was called to the scene of a particularly gruesome Arab ambush. Five girls, or rather what was left of them. Gang-raped and then stabbed to death. It wasn't very nice. Sit down if you like."

Esther flicked through some files on her desk, scratching her forehead without letting go of the cigarette. While she did this, his clammy hands clasping and unclasping the hot mug, Caleb searched for a way to unburden his conscience. "Esther, I almost murdered a man last night."

His sister looked up. "Could you elaborate?"

It was a relief for Caleb to talk about it at last. His sister did not lose her composure once, nor raise so much as an eyebrow. When he had finished, she stubbed out her cigarette and observed coolly, "You acted in self-defence. A perfectly understandable response."

"Weren't you listening? I shot at a man with intent to kill.

152

I'm a murderer." He was looking for a soul mate who could relate to his guilt and self-reproach, someone to come alongside him in his quest for forgiveness.

Esther was neither impressed nor moved. "How are the mighty fallen. I never thought I'd live to see the day when my perfect, holier-than-thou brother might need forgiveness."

"What do you mean?"

Esther leant back in her chair and could not suppress a sneer. "You always found fault with me because I was never like you. You always tried to make me feel wretched and unworthy. You knew nothing of my struggles when you judged me and heaped condemnation on me. Just because I didn't want to live the life of a good little Jewish wife and mother, tied to the hearth, with ten children crawling around me – you saw me as some kind of monster. Judgmentalism grows like a weed. If we don't hate it and root it out of our hearts, it just spreads and overwhelms us. That's what's happened to you. Do you remember when I told you I wanted to become a doctor? You just criticised and scolded me for choosing a profession that would require me to work on Shabbat. All I wanted was to be like Papa, to leave the world a better place than I'd found it. Now I am saving lives, while you're agonising over your precious guilty conscience. Do you want me to absolve you of killing a fellow man? I can't, it's not within my power, because you haven't wronged *me*. And if you're looking for something more spiritual from me, well, I'm sorry, you'll just have to wait till Yom Kippur."

For the first time in his life, Caleb was looking into the dreaded mirror that reflects the soul of man, the mirror Christians had once told him about. When our eyes are opened, we see the naked ugliness and corruption of the human psyche. Only when we know the depravity of our own dark nature – our failures, weaknesses and darkest thoughts – can true compassion be liberated. A moral lifestyle and religious knowledge can never do this. Caleb had at last reached this point of self-knowing. It is a traumatic experience, and was hard to come to terms with.

Esther's eyes had long been opened. She had learned to accept it and live with it. By rubbing shoulders with a cruel, harsh world, sullying her hands with blood and filth, she had learned the meaning of natural grace and love. Her Hippocratic Oath forced her to respond to the enemy's plea for help, although her feelings pulled her in the opposite direction. She had seen enough of the hidden depths of her own nature to empathise with her fellow man. She now understood the need for mercy, even though she might hide her own compassionate nature under a brash and cynical exterior. Seeing him sitting there, like a lost and frightened child, stirred kinder feelings in her.

In a much softer tone she said, "It's not very nice to receive the revelation of your own . . . well, let's call it sinfulness, shall we? But you'll be better for it. I'm not cross with you. Just one thing, though: be very careful what you tell the British. They'll almost certainly interview you. Maintain that you acted only in self-defence. Otherwise things could get a bit complicated for you."

Esther had barely finished when there was a knock on the door. A tall, sun-bleached blond British officer entered. He seemed to be no stranger. "Good morning, Dr Levine."

"Good morning, Lieutenant." Esther seemed more irritated than surprised by his appearance.

"I suppose you know why I'm here."

"More enquiries. By the way, this is my brother, Caleb. He was at the kibbutz last night and is an eyewitness."

"Oh, splendid. Would you mind telling me exactly what happened last night, Mr Levine? Of course, I'll also be questioning the others."

For the second time that morning, Caleb recounted the harrowing events of the night.

154

"And you fired a gun?"

"Well . . . yes . . . everyone who had a gun was defending . . ."

"Of course, of course," nodded the officer. "You didn't happen to notice, by pure chance of course, whether you killed anyone?" He concentrated on stuffing his pipe. There was a silence. He looked at Caleb, then at Esther who had turned back to her papers, then back at Caleb. Caleb looked to his sister for help but got none.

"It was dark . . . there was a lot of confusion and shouting. And shooting . . ."

"I understand, I understand. So now I find myself with one dead Jew and two dead Arabs on my hands, not including all the wounded. And no one is responsible for the killings. The dead just seem to fall from the sky around here." He turned to go. "I'll see you again later, Dr Levine."

"Make that two dead Jews, Lieutenant," Esther added, without looking up. "Mahle Finkelstein was four months pregnant."

~ 14 ~

Jerusalem, 28th September 1936

After leaving Esther's office, Caleb roamed the streets aimlessly. He was too overwhelmed by what had happened to find rest and peace. Eventually he wandered through the Old City to the Western Wall, where the pious had met for the early afternoon prayers. Exhausted, he sat down, watching the worshippers from the back of the square.

"Jerusalem, Jerusalem, how often I have wanted to gather your children together, as a hen gathers her chicks under her wings, but you were not willing. Your house is left to you desolate." Why should these lines come to mind now? And where had he heard them before? He had memorised large portions of Torah; he had been well trained. Maybe it was from one of the Prophets? Jerusalem, Jerusalem, City of Peace. Yet peace seemed so far off. Her people were divided and the Land polluted with hatred and murder. He found he was weeping silently for Jerusalem, the strife-torn city God had intended as a source of joy for the whole earth.

"Oh, it's you. I wasn't sure you'd come." Esther opened the door to her flat and let Caleb in. "Make yourself comfortable. Food will be ready in a few minutes. I cooked in hope."

She returned to the tiny kitchen while Caleb sat down on the settee in the living room. His thoughts were with Siegfried and Ezra: tonight they would sit down to eat without wife and mother. Esther chopped cucumbers, chatting to alleviate her brother's heaviness. He did not say anything. What was there to talk about? Noting his silence, she popped her head round the kitchen door to make sure he was still there. He looked terrible.

"You look terrible," she said, leaning against the door-frame. "Did you get some sleep during the day?"

Caleb looked up with dark shadows under his eyes. "Sleep? How could I possibly sleep? I tried to rest, but my mind was much too agitated." He leant back and closed his eyes; he badly needed a little peace.

"I could give you something."

He shook his head and she returned to the kitchen. "You must look to the future," she continued. "If you look only at what's going on around you, you'll get thoroughly depressed. As I did when I first arrived here. But now I believe passionately in the future of our nation."

They had both been brought up to believe that only the Messiah could re-establish the Jewish nation in her home-land. But it was now overwhelmingly obvious to Caleb that his people needed a haven right now. They must have a place they could call their own, a home. And no other place would do except Palestine, their ancestral homeland, Eretz Yisrael. No one could force God's hand, but Hitler was forcing Jewish hands.

Esther returned with a bowl of salad and put it on the dining table. She decided to try to snap him out of his despair. "Come on, you're the *frummer* here. Especially now you must remember the words of the Prophets. They said there would be an ingathering and a restoration. And if I can build on that, so should you – if your faith is up to it."

Esther's words achieved their target. "God is always greater than our circumstances, isn't He? Are you, too, able to draw strength from our faith?" Caleb asked her.

"I don't know. Two days after I arrived, I just wanted to go home again. I thought I'd made a terrible mistake taking up a post in such a quarrelsome, Godforsaken place. But then things began to change. I don't know what did it. Who knows, I thought, I've always been a lousy Christian, maybe I'll make a better Jew after all?"

"You have renounced Christianity?"

"How can I renounce something I never believed in? My conversion was a way to make things easier for me at university, remember? I believe Jesus was a good Jew, but whether He is the Messiah . . ." She shrugged and set out the cutlery. "Who can tell? I don't even know if the Messiah is a real person, or just a conceptual ideal in all of us we should strive for."

"But, Esther, how can you be so vague about this?"

Esther smiled. "There you go again. Just as you did when you were a boy. I'm glad some things never change." She sat down, ready to eat, and waited. "Aren't you going to say a blessing?"

"You want me to?"

"Well, that's what one does in Jewish homes, isn't it? If the Arabs want to kill us because we're Jews, we might as well give them a reason."

Caleb obliged. He remembered one occasion when he had snatched a glass of grape juice out of Esther's hand – she had forgotten to say a blessing before drinking it – and in the ensuing struggle spilled it all down her dress. She had hit him for it, and Mama had been furious over the spoilt dress.

Esther ate her dinner hurriedly as she always did; she lived her whole life as if she had a last train to catch. "Did you like the food?" she asked, wiping her mouth.

"Yes, thanks."

"Speaking of cooking . . . Is there anyone special in your life yet?"

Caleb hesitated, wary. "Maybe."

Esther's eyes lit up mischievously. The thought of her pious brother being romantically attached was too funny. "Let me guess . . ." Esther followed up the scent. "A lovely little Chassidic girl who just hangs on your every word? Or have the Demskys been trying to arrange a match with Taliah?"

Caleb rolled his eyes. "I think I avoided that by the skin of my teeth. Mr Demsky eventually took the hint that I had other plans."

"Someone in London?"

How much dared he tell her? "No. In the country."

"There aren't many Jewish girls in the country."

"She isn't Jewish."

Esther was thunderstruck. "You damned little hypocrite!" she cried. "For years you made my life a misery with your observance, and now you've got yourself a Goyah!" She leant back in her chair and crossed her arms triumphantly. "Well, well, well! My holy brother wants to marry out. Wait until Mama and Papa get wind of this."

"They gave their blessing to Alistair and Yehudit's union only too happily."

"Ah, yes, but they're good little Christians. You're different."

"It happened against my will, believe you me."

"Ha! '. . . And subdue our evil inclination . . .' Have you tried that? You never believed it when I said it didn't work for me."

"If you ask me, she has more respect for our teachings than Taliah Demsky! What good is it being Jewish if you've no heart for God?"

"God has made an eternal covenant with us. We're a special people."

Caleb pounced on her; he wanted to get his own back. "You're contradicting yourself! One moment you say God is of no importance to you, the next you claim you've a special relationship with Him because of His covenant."

"I didn't say I didn't believe in God. I just can't see the point of endless, meaningless discussions about the small print of religious observance. Look what it has done between us. And just walk through Me'a She'arim, the Ultra-Orthodox quarter here. Is that what faith is all about? I believe in God, but not the god that was hammered into us in the synagogue." Esther was angry now. She piled the plates together noisily.

"I agree. That's why I wouldn't return to Orthodoxy. But wait till the *Bar-Torah* comes."

"And I suppose you think Messiah will tell you it's lawful to marry a Goyah? Anyway, wait till the girl sees you with a kippah on your head. That'll make her think again."

"Rut wasn't Jewish."

"Ah, yes, but she converted before she married Boaz."

"How could she? There was no Beit Din then as we know it today. Anyway, Celia might convert."

"Celia. So that's her name, is it? As you know jolly well, to convert just to get married is forbidden. She has to do it of her own free will and without any ulterior motives. And do you now expect her to convert to the Orthodoxy that you've rejected for yourself? What hypocrisy! Don't you think it's *your* reasoning that's a bit erratic now?"

With a tired gesture, Caleb dropped his head into his hands and rubbed his eyes. As much as he enjoyed a good Jewish family argument, today was not a good time. And certainly not for debating the love of his life.

~ 15 ~

Cecil Court, 10th October 1936

The first days of autumn were glorious. Celia enjoyed every moment, racing Foxtrot back to hunting condition after their extended summer break. She bridled him after a long canter as they approached a beech wood. Gratefully, she wondered at the wood's striking array of greens, golds and browns, perfectly set off against the deep blue sky. Instead of just gazing at the beautiful scene, she found herself thanking her Creator as Caleb had taught her: "Blessed are you, O Lord our God, who has arrayed the plants in splendour and beautiful colours."

Foxtrot snorted and Celia hugged his sweaty neck joyfully. "Come on, my darling. It's time we went home for lunch."

Back at Cecil Court, Celia untacked her mount and gave him a carrot before she went over to the house and inspected the letter tray. It contained a copy of *Horse and Hound*, *National Geographic* magazine, the *Jewish Chronicle*, a letter from Dorothy, and another letter in an unfamiliar hand, addressed to her. Curious, she opened it first. As she did so, the butler cleared his throat discreetly to announce his presence.

"Lord Holsworth-Leigh is waiting in the library, m'lady."

Celia murmured a "thank you" and returned to the mysterious letter. It turned out to be from Judy Levine. She was inviting her to dinner and to watch a film that Caleb and Esther had made in the Holy Land. Celia felt somewhat hurt and angered. The invitation came just from his sister and included no personal note from Caleb. Despite a wounded heart, she turned towards the library with her head held proud and high.

She was greeted by a familiar voice. "Good morning, Celia."

Sebastian was as cheerful as ever and genuinely pleased to see Celia. She looked fresh, energetic and healthy, her hair dishevelled by the wind and her cheeks glowing. "Oh, hello. Nice to see you, Buzzy."

Sebastian was calling so frequently these days that she had nothing new to tell him – well, nothing that would interest him. Unnoticed, Lady Norah slipped in and eyed her daughter critically. A bottle-green jumper covered in horsehair and unpolished, muddy boots. Her hair was unkempt and she had a bundle of magazines under her arm. Hardly a sight to make an admirer's heart beat faster. She closed her eyes and wished for a fairy godmother to transform, with a mere wave of her wand, her dull Cinderella of a daughter into a princess.

"What brings you here?" Celia asked. Her mother shuddered involuntarily.

"I was wondering if you'd come to the hunt ball with me? It would be really jolly if you could."

Lady Norah's faith in fairy godmothers rose. Her scruffy daughter was being asked to the ball by a wealthy and handsome Prince Charming. But Celia was not flattered by his gallant offer. Sebastian was well known for his way with the ladies; he had broken many a young girl's heart. Celia had no intention of being included in his list of romantic conquests.

"Oh, I'm most flattered but I already have an engagement for that evening."

Lady Norah was thunderstruck. Her daughter never ceased to amaze her. Never before had she missed the grand ball that marked the opening of the hunt season. It was one of the few certainties in Celia's otherwise irregular life. "Celia, dear, no! You've never, ever, missed the hunt ball before. Can't you cancel your other engagement – whatever it is?" Lady Norah waded in, trying to help the young Lord land his catch.

"I'm afraid not. There has to be a first time for everything. I'm terribly sorry, Mummy."

"What a pity. Oh, well, I suppose it can't be helped." Sebastian looked at his watch to conceal his vexation at being snubbed. "Must go; I'm late as it is."

Celia was rather relishing the moment.

"Won't you stay to lunch?" pleaded Lady Norah, watching her prince slip away.

"No, thank you, Lady Norah. I wish I could but it will have to wait for another time." Sebastian ended his visit, a well-practised smile covering his disappointment.

As soon as she heard the door close, Celia doubted the wisdom of turning him down. Her relationship with Caleb had cooled, while Sebastian was making flattering advances. It would make much more sense to turn down Judy's invitation. Was this really the best moment to start offending and rejecting Sebastian?

"How on earth could you be so stupid as to turn down Sebastian's offer?" Lady Norah was very cross. "Are you that blind that you can't recognise a suitor when you see one? He came all this way to see you, you silly little goose."

"Do you think so?" remarked Celia coolly, not allowing her own doubts to show.

"I know it! Trust me. You'll be a bigger fool than even I think you are if you turn him down."

"Mummy, he hasn't proposed. And this is 1936, not 1910. The Great War has changed everything. Nowadays it hardly means a thing if a gentleman visits a lady more than once."

"Then you'd better start working jolly hard to make it meaningful, you stupid child."

Lady Agatha's arms were wide open. "Ah, welcome, my dear. You should come and visit your old grandmother more often."

Celia gave her elderly relative a lingering kiss on the cheek. "I know, Grandma." She felt genuine remorse. "I'll really try to do better in future. This year has been so busy, and you know there's no love lost between London and me. If it weren't for you, I wouldn't come to this beastly city ... ever."

Celia handed her coat to the butler, the under-butler took her bags, and the maid brought some tea. A welcoming coal fire was smiling brightly at her in the drawing room. Celia knelt before it and rubbed her hands.

"Now, tell me, dear. What's this visit all about?" Lady Agatha settled herself comfortably on the large leather settee. "You mentioned being invited for dinner by a young lady – Alistair's fiancée. I read about their engagement in *The Times*. She's the daughter of a good friend of mine. Alistair's a lucky young man. They're a delightful family."

Celia almost spilled her tea. "You know them then?"

"Of course. Everyone involved in charity work in town knows the good professor and his dear wife. I've met them several times at various dos. Lovely couple." Lady Agatha nodded her head in approval.

"Do you know the whole family?" enquired Celia cautiously.

"They have three children, a son and two daughters. I've met the youngest daughter, Judy. Sweet little thing. The elder daughter is a doctor in Palestine and the son is a solicitor. But I haven't met them yet." Lady Agatha chuckled. "A typical Jewish family. Very musical."

"Do you like Jews?" asked Celia, trying to sound casual while her heart missed a beat.

"Do I like them? Well, I don't know enough to be able to judge them as a whole. But I like and respect most of those I've met. You know me, dear. My views are most unorthodox. 'Live and let live' is my maxim. I was given a lot of freedom when I was growing up and I'm very grateful to my parents for that. Yes, they were two very unusual people. Just as you are." The old lady smiled at her granddaughter, her face creasing into happy wrinkles.

"Why did your way of bringing up children never work for Mummy?" Celia sighed.

"I think your mother always felt a bit embarrassed and ashamed of her parents, me especially. Your grandfather didn't mind my drawing room being frequented by non-conformists, free thinkers, evolutionists, artists and intellectuals. Indians, Africans and Jews – even Communists. They were all welcome here. Our house had a dangerously Bohemian reputation. Many of London's most beautiful and finest disapproved of me, and their children tended to look down on poor Norah as a result. So she made a choice: she decided to live by the standards of our class rather than follow in her parents' dubious footsteps. It is always easier to follow the crowd than the dictates of our conscience."

"But not always nobler."

"Well spoken! Not many are called to walk this rocky road. Being different for the sake of being different is just silly, though. You must always know why you have decided to be different. That's what makes it worthwhile." Lady Agatha levered her old frame into a more comfortable position and folded her hands regally. "Now, why are you suddenly so interested in Jews and Judaism? Your mother mentioned it to me. She doesn't approve. The Levines are Christians anyway, and not Jews; all except their son . . . Celia!" Celia blushed. What her own mother had failed to discern, her grandmother had detected over a cup of tea. "My poor, dear child. You've never made life easy for yourself, have you?"

"What should I do, Grandma?"

Lady Agatha sighed again. "When first love hits us, we have few defences. We just have to let the waves wash over us. If we don't drown, and few people do, we learn to swim. I was once in love with someone who was – well – a bit unusual."

"You?" Grandmother, young and in love? It seemed unimaginable.

"Bopinder. A young Indian. He was a teacher and a gentleman from a good home. He was impeccably mannered and well spoken and had a sweet and gentle, artistic spirit. Oh, and the love letters he wrote were . . . so beautiful . . ." Lady Agatha paused and reminisced for a moment. "Of course, it would never have worked out. Different race, religion and class; the obstacles were insurmountable at that time. Then he was killed in an accident. I was utterly heartbroken." Lady Agatha fingered a lace handkerchief, which had appeared from the sleeve of her navy dress. "I burned all his letters when your grandfather and I got engaged. I couldn't keep them. Your grandfather never knew. It was better that way. It would have hurt his feelings too much had he known there was someone before him. Your grandfather believed he was my first and only love, and it made him feel special. You must take good care of your heart."

"Haven't you got any bitter memories? Don't you have lots of unanswered 'what-ifs'?"

"No. Our memories are the only paradise we can't lose. So just treasure them in your heart. Bopinder gave me something I'd never known before, something your grandfather was never able to give me. You must live every minute of your young love, my dear. And who knows, you may be spared bitter disappointment. But, as you love this young man and he loves you, remember that he has already given you something precious and everlasting. No one can ever take it away from you. Whatever may happen in the future, you will always know the sweetness of love. Perhaps you can now judge less harshly those who get foolishly carried away by love. Don't worry and don't be afraid. We all have our skeletons in the cupboard. I take it, from your cautiousness, that your mother doesn't yet know how you feel about him?"

"Not at all. Mummy has a fixation with Buzzy and can't see beyond that." Celia shook her head and rolled her eyes.

Her grandmother chuckled. "And he would be a most excellent catch."

"Yes. And just as slippery and wriggly."

There were three guests already at the front door when Celia and Alistair arrived at the Levines' house. A chilly November wind swept through the street, but the rooms facing the quiet road were warmly lit, creating a homely and welcoming atmosphere. The door opened at last and a young maid apologised for not answering the door more promptly. With five guests arriving at the same time, the hall was crowded. The maid was juggling unsuccessfully with their coats.

"Oh dear. You must have conspired." A lady in her early fifties came to the poor maid's rescue. Taking the coats and hats, she passed them to her in a more organised manner.

Celia stood close to Alistair; she disliked going anywhere new and was always nervous with strangers. He took the first opportunity to introduce her. "Mama – Mrs Levine – this is Lady Celia Lancaster."

"Lady Celia, I'm so pleased to meet you. Judy has told us how much she enjoyed her stay at Bleckham Manor – thanks to the trouble you took to entertain her."

Celia felt guilty, knowing the resentful and jealous feelings she had first had towards Judy. But the dear child had obviously not noticed them. Suddenly she wondered if Caleb had forgotten – or been too embarrassed – to mention her to his parents. Hiding her hurt and doubts, Celia smiled politely and replied with a few friendly words.

While she was speaking to Caleb's mother, she was struck by her vintage beauty. She carried herself with much natural grace, and had an air of liveliness and gentle kindness about her. Lacking haughtiness, and the false humility so quickly detectable in arrogant people, she exuded a straightforward, heartfelt openness. She had classical good looks, a beauty unfaded but enriched by womanly maturity. She might not be sharp and intoxicating but, like old wine, she was mellow, heady and still captivating. Her blond hair paraded a few strands of grey, enhancing her mature femininity. Celia took an instant liking to her and noted that she had some of Caleb's attributes: the same fearless glance, the fine mouth, the way she turned her head, and a most pleasing voice. Her English was almost without accent.

"Are you holding a conference in the hall then?" An amused voice pressed into the crowd and Celia was introduced to Professor Isaac Levine. The contrast could not have been more striking: Professor Levine was small, not even as tall as his wife. He had a slender frame and his face bore eastern European characteristics. When he stretched out his hand, she noticed it was small and delicate. He smiled kindly through his greying, well-groomed beard. Was Celia mistaken, or was there a shadow of sadness in those dark eyes, a melancholy relieved only by his smile?

At last Judy came over to welcome her new friend, hugging her like an old one.

"Oh-oh! Here comes trouble." Alistair looked up and their eyes followed his. Celia watched two young people come down the stairs while the hall gradually emptied into the drawing room. "Just remember what I told you. Keep calm and you might keep your head on your shoulders," he whispered loudly into Celia's ear.

"Alistair Hornby! What lies are you now spreading about me?" demanded one of the new arrivals.

"I'm giving Celia a few tips on how to survive life with Esther Levine," Alistair admitted teasingly.

"Don't believe a thing he tells you," retorted Esther with playful earnestness.

Her eyes, naturally bold and enquiring, rested on Celia, who squirmed inwardly under her penetrating gaze. She had to remind herself that she was a Lancaster of ancient, noble family. No one had the right to browbeat her. But a little voice whispered, "Your family tree may date back to the Norman Conquest, but hers reaches back 4,000 years to Abraham." Involuntarily, Celia looked away to avoid Esther's searching look.

"May I introduce you to Mr Leon Brann?" said Esther, continuing rather formally, "He's been sent to London from Palestine by the Jewish Agency to warn us of the urgency of the Zionist cause and of the pressing needs of the pioneers. He'll be speaking to Jewish societies and clubs while he's here."

Celia shook hands with the suntanned man who, she noticed, spoke with a rather heavy German accent. He looked less overwhelming than she had imagined from Caleb's letters from Palestine. He politely offered her his arm and they went through to the drawing room together.

Celia watched Esther out of the corner of her eye while she chatted to another guest. Esther was tall for a woman and very slim. She was wearing a rust-brown winter dress, which did nothing for her complexion. Her hair, wavy and almost black, was one of her most striking features. It was held fast at her temples by two large combs and was woven into an amazingly thick plait that reached down to her waist. Her face was long, its length accentuated by a long, curved nose – probably an inheritance from her father. She had prominent eyebrows, almost joining above the nose, over large, dark eyes. They gave her a slightly wild expression. From a wide, generously lipped mouth, she spoke in a voice that was both husky and charismatic. She had natural authority, and her whole body spoke in a decisive, bold and resolute language. She was no beauty, but she radiated a powerful presence. She had sat down next to Leon, seemingly calm and in control, but her fingers moved, never still.

"She reminds me of a black cat on a wall watching a bird," Celia thought.

Leon, on the other hand, was quiet and polite, a perfect and well-behaved guest. He was talking to Mrs Levine in German, who was clearly delighted to be able to use her mother tongue. Celia noted a definite physical likeness between Esther and him. They had the same long face and swarthy appearance. And he had Caleb's high cheekbones, but much more striking and deeply set eyes, which gave him an air of oriental mystery. He had an unusual but far from handsome face, she concluded.

"I've barely spoken to you." Judy's pretty voice was full of self-reproach as she came over to Celia. "I'm a most terrible hostess. Please forgive me! My only excuse is that I haven't seen Alistair all week . . ."

"It's as good an excuse as any. Have you set a date yet?" Celia swallowed back the heartache this question had provoked. And where was Caleb? Why was he not here to welcome her?

She chatted for a moment with Judy. Then Mrs Levine bade her guests come into the dining room. The professor led Celia to a seat near the top of the table between Leon Brann and Mrs Levine. She was opposite Judy, who had an empty chair to her left. The professor sat on Mrs Levine's right, at the head of the table. Celia overheard Mrs Levine say, "Well, if he doesn't come within the next few minutes, we'll start without him. Otherwise the dinner will be spoiled. Everybody else has managed to arrive on time."

Alistair had heard the remark too, and added, "I'll eat my hat the day Cal misses the onset of Shabbat."

"Shabbat?" asked Celia, surprised.

"Why? Didn't Judy tell you?" said Mrs Levine. "We have arranged a kind of Jewish evening to help our friends understand the Jewish roots of our Christian faith a little better. And Friday evening, when the Jewish Sabbath begins, is always a good opportunity. We do this from time to time, and today we have something extra special to share with you after dinner. We shall be watching the film Caleb and Esther made in the Holy Land."

"I'm sorry, Mama. I forgot to mention it to Celia," apologised Judy.

"I'll be only too happy to join in, Mrs Levine, but I know absolutely nothing about Jewish rites and rituals. I do hope I won't do anything wrong and spoil your evening."

"Don't worry at all, my dear. You just enjoy yourself. It's not a religious service. If you want to ask anything, please do so," assured Mrs Levine. She was warm and kindly.

The meal began as Mr Levine rose, welcomed the guests to this Erev Shabbat meal, and said a few introductory words of prayer. Mrs Levine placed a triangular white lace scarf on her head. Then the doorbell rang.

Alistair checked his watch. "I told you so."

Moments later Caleb slipped into the dining room and sat down next to Judy. He glanced at Celia, smiled quickly and apologised for his lateness. He sat quietly, looking at his plate. He was tired and absent-minded. Celia could not understand his behaviour. What was the matter with him? He showed no pleasure at seeing her, no intimate smile – nothing. Had she hurt or offended him in some way, Celia wondered? He could be so sensitive. Please, Caleb, talk to me. Don't just withdraw.

Caleb, however, knew that tonight he would have to show her who he really was. He would have to tell her what really happened in Palestine. Tonight she would see him as Caleb Levine the Jew, the real Caleb, not the half-assimilated crossbreed from Lenkham Hall. How would she react? Probably like all Gentiles. Caleb braced himself. He was dreading this evening.

The maid switched off some lights. Mrs Levine stood up and lit the two white candles in silver candlesticks in front of her. She said a blessing in Hebrew, which Celia was pleased to realise she half understood. She watched her profile as Mrs Levine continued praying, with great care and earnestness, a gentle smile on her beautiful, candlelit face. There was something about the mother and the moment which Celia could only describe as ethereal . . . or was it holy? She felt a great peace come over her; maybe even a kind of Presence. Was this perhaps the Presence that Caleb had spoken about? The room was dimly lit, illuminated only by the two flames that shone out like little beacons. Mrs Levine raised her voice in a Sabbath prayer-song, at the end of which those around the table said a quiet "Amen". The professor, as head of the household, ended the song with a mighty, oriental-sounding crescendo. Then he poured a little red wine into his glass. He stood to pronounce a blessing in his peculiar religious language.

It was at that moment that Celia noticed Caleb's kippah on his head. A sudden, unanticipated flood of conflicting thoughts and emotions charged through her: feelings of fear, distance, separation and isolation. What a huge difference that inoffensive little piece of cloth made. As with Dr Jekyll, the Caleb whom she knew and loved had suddenly turned himself into Levine the Jew, a stranger, her Mr Hyde. Celia pictured him wearing his kippah amongst her aristocratic friends. Thoroughly confused and bewildered, she looked at the professor, then at Judy. She thought of Esther and Leon sitting beside her. What on earth was she doing in a Jewish home? It was all so foreign, so alien . . . so un-British. She suddenly realised she was not amongst her own.

But was the Caleb Levine she had loved during the summer in reality any different from the Caleb Levine sitting here, unobtrusively wearing one of the identifying symbols of his religion? He must have felt her look on him, for their eyes met. He had discerned her instinctive negative reaction. But how could a non-Jew eradicate, by an act of will, 2,000 years of ingrained, latent anti-Semitism? It lurked in the heart of even the kindest of Gentiles, hidden, living, only just below the surface. His eyes filled with the tender sadness in his heart. Celia watched Caleb with horror, realising that he knew exactly what she had been thinking. She turned her face away dumbly, confused, and watched the professor distribute small pieces of white bread torn from a brown and shiny plaited loaf, dipped in salt. She was reminded of communion and wanted to decline but obediently took the piece he offered her. The melancholy she had noticed in the professor's eyes reflected the sadness she had witnessed in Caleb's. Could she have provoked feelings of exclusion and segregation in Caleb? Red shame poured over her face and neck as she stared at her napkin. Her eyes began to sting and she wished herself far away from this place.

Caleb noticed and tried, clumsily, to divert her from her distress. "Those dumplings are called *kneidlach* and are cooked in chicken soup. My mother makes the best."

Celia stared at the plate of soup in front of her. She did not remember anyone putting it there.

"Are you all right, dear?" enquired Mrs Levine.

Celia's burning blush had been replaced with a marked paleness. "Yes, thank you."

"Let's open a window. It is rather hot in here."

The dinner continued. Celia engaged in conversation with the Levines and even with Leon Brann. The atmosphere between her and Caleb remained tense, their eyes ill at ease with each another.

Much to her own and everyone else's surprise, Celia distinguished herself. She was remarkably well informed about the situation in Palestine and was able to express her views clearly and seriously. Despite her family's ridicule, her investment in reading the British and Jewish newspapers was now paying off. She won Leon's heart. "You seem to know more about our situation than I'd ever have dared to expect from a young English lady," he commended.

"Oh no, not at all. But I admit we English are usually lamentably uninformed about other peoples and countries. The Bible is full of Jewish history, promises and prophesies, but one rarely studies the Old Testament. I think the Jews are a very remarkable people, who believe in a very special God."

"So, you sound as if you might even support the Zionist cause?"

"I think so. I believe increasingly that Jews have a number of justifiable claims. The Balfour Declaration and the League of Nations have given Britain some undeniable and binding obligations towards the Jewish people."

Leon smiled at her. The professor picked up a dropped thread of conversation and wove it back in: "Do you study the Old Testament to understand Jewish people and Jewish history, or to learn about God?"

"I don't know. But I believe the fact that the Jews still exist as a people after so many centuries in the Diaspora is a clear proof of His existence and covenant. The ancient Egyptians, Babylonians, ancient Greeks and Romans have all disappeared, even within their own national frontiers. But the Jews and Judaism have endured, battered and scattered, but still intact and very much alive. I recently attended a synagogue service in Norwich, hoping to understand Judaism better."

"And do you?"

"No. I didn't understand a word of the service and found the congregants rather unfriendly and not very helpful," admitted Celia. She realised she might have caused offence and blushed again. She added quickly, "A bit like in our parish church, really."

"I'm truly sorry to hear it." The professor seemed genuinely concerned for her. "It's not a good witness but, with a history of pogroms and persecution, our people have become rather suspicious of strangers. It has become a tradition not to be too welcoming, in order to test the attitude of the visitor. If a visitor is still not put off after three visits, the Rabbi can safely assume that he is a serious enquirer. He will then open up and be more friendly."

Mrs Levine joined the discussion.

"But, of course, modern Judaism is not a proselytising religion. It teaches that only the Jews are the special People of God. All that non-Jews have to do to earn salvation is keep the seven Noachide Laws. That's one reason Jews keep themselves to themselves and don't concern themselves with Gentiles. Jesus, however, teaches that every man and woman – Jew and Gentile – has to repent of their sin and accept the salvation which comes only through Him."

"Well, yes, but Jesus was a Christian after all," Celia pointed out naively.

"Oh dear, no! He was a Jew. He was born in the land of Israel, His mother was a devout Jewess and He was brought up as a full and active member of His local Jewish community," Mrs Levine exclaimed, nodding affirmatively.

Celia was surprised. Jesus a Jew? How strange that sounded. But it did seem most probable.

"But not many people seem to know this. That's why we hold these little gatherings for friends; to teach them about Jesus and His Jewish roots."

Celia thought for a moment. "Do you think Jesus would have kept the Jewish Sabbath too?"

"Oh yes, and pretty much in the very same way you are keeping it tonight."

"But why, in that case, don't Christians keep the Jewish Sabbath?"

"Well, Jesus came to fulfil the Law. He died on the cross,

so we would no longer be under the curse of the Law . . ."
Mrs Levine poured some gravy over her chicken.

"*Great peace have those who love Your Law*," Caleb muttered under his breath, looking darkly at his mother, his brows lowered.

"I'm sorry, Caleb, I didn't hear you." Mrs Levine looked up.

Caleb repeated the scripture he had quoted with pointed intonation. A sudden chill swept across the top end of the table. Judy reached quickly for a serving dish. "Would you care for some more sprouts?" she chirped with a tense smile.

After dinner, Caleb, Esther and Leon set up the film projector while the guests were served tea or coffee. The film was well received. It started with well-known places of interest in and around Jerusalem. Celia recognised many of them from Caleb's descriptions in his letters. They were followed by scenes of a barren, semi-arid countryside. Sand, rocks and stones were everywhere. "Rather boring and just like Egypt," Celia thought.

Celia had very few pleasant memories of Egypt. The family trip to see the land of the pharaohs had been a disaster. Her father had spent most of the time in bars and had caused much shame and embarrassment by his drunkenness. Her parents had rowed furiously in private. In the end, she and her mother had returned to England alone. Celia glanced sideways and saw the professor in the flickering light of the projector. He had taken off his glasses and was wiping his cheeks with a handkerchief. Surely he wasn't crying?

"And now comes the best bit. Pictures of a Zionist raw recruit." Esther laughed.

There was Caleb, dressed only in boots and shorts, first sitting at the top of a drilling tower, then nailing and screwing planks of wood together, and finally smiling and waving to the people down below. These scenes were followed by Caleb in a sponge fight outside the communal washrooms, and then brazing a lead drainage pipe.

"The water pipe in my room had started to leak, and I was told to repair it myself or use the washrooms. To be honest, the washrooms were much more fun. After a while you do feel guilty about having your own sink."

Professor Levine was impressed. What a clever son he had; one who could braze. He said as much.

"To be honest, Papa, I loved doing all these different things. Even laying concrete . . ."

"We call it Living Zionism." Leon threw in an explanatory comment.

"Do you indeed." In the semi-darkness, everyone could hear the professor's amusement at their youthful enthusiasm.

Leon was undeterred. "I keep telling you, Cal, you're wasted in Britain. You should join us in Palestine."

No one saw Celia's face contort with anxiety at his light-hearted suggestion.

The next few minutes showed Caleb teaching some youngsters the steps of a folk dance; the youngsters tying their legs into knots; Caleb in a field binding sheaves, with dark sweat patches all over his shirt; Caleb bundling the sheaves; Caleb's sheaves falling apart; Caleb asleep under a tree; Caleb no longer asleep, with Esther carefully dribbling water on his face; Caleb chasing Esther; Esther having her arm twisted on her back; Caleb and Esther collapsing in a heap, laughing; and Caleb in the canteen dishing out stew with a gigantic ladle. "Isn't that women's work?" enquired Mrs Levine cautiously; "It's living Zionism," said Leon; Caleb working on electric wiring under the supervision of a kibbutznik; and, finally, Caleb joining a Hora dance circle.

"At Bleckham Manor I couldn't even get him to dance with me," Celia thought. But what struck her more than anything else was how entirely different Caleb was when he was with fellow Jews. He could laugh till tears rolled down his cheeks. He was full of fun, ready for anything. She thought of the social wallflower who had accompanied her to the garden party.

Caleb's whole family showed a lively, genuine interest in the film. Throughout the showing, the professor had asked countless questions about life in Palestine, and Mrs Levine had been terribly proud of her son. Judy said she envied her brother for all the fun he had had.

Caleb stopped the film.

"Oh, is that it? I thought you were going to show us some scenes in Jerusalem taken during the High Holy Days," said the professor, clearly disappointed.

"I wanted the evening to finish on a happy note. The dancing you just saw was on my last night at K'far Altermann. That very night we were attacked and a young Jewish mother was killed. After that I somewhat lost interest in filming," Caleb said.

He switched on the main lights; the show was over.

The Levines urged their friends to have another drink for friendship's sake. Celia found herself in the company of a kind but elderly spinster. She was very sweet but very boring. Celia tried hard to look interested.

Alistair and Judy gazed into each other's eyes, until Judy dragged him off to the piano in the next room. Soon she was seated at the piano, accompanying herself singing a gentle song in her precise but uninspiring voice.

"She's killing it!" Esther growled and marched into the music room. Caleb and Leon exchanged looks and followed her, determined to save Judy from being mauled.

"You're playing it as if nothing could be more sweetly hopeless and pointless than looking to Zion," complained Esther. Her feet were well apart and her hands were clenched threateningly on her hips. In self-defence, Judy hurriedly vacated her seat. Esther adjusted the piano stool and then scaled the keyboard a couple of times, while Caleb picked up a violin. Leon stood by with a clarinet. Then Esther's fingers began to glide over the keys, not entirely accurately, but somehow it didn't matter. The life, joy and determination she squeezed out of the black dots on the music sheets was awesome – until Caleb stopped abruptly in mid-flow.

"What's the matter?" Esther snapped, irritated.

"It's B minor, Es. You keep playing E minor." Caleb pointed at the sheet music with his bow.

"But I always play E minor. Leon?" She looked to the clarinettist for support.

"B minor."

"Papa?"

The professor was unable to resist an impromptu concert and had unpacked and shouldered his accordion. "I'm afraid it's B minor, Esti."

"Very well, B minor it is then." She submitted with ill grace.

The small ensemble played beautifully, but it was Esther's voice that stole the show. It was not professionally trained, but it was powerful, dark and throaty, and very well controlled. She ranged from passages that would have shamed a drill sergeant, to those of a mother gently crooning her baby to sleep. Celia excused herself and listened to their song. Although she did not understand a word, the music spoke for itself. Whenever she thought she had worked out the rhythm and theme of a song, everything would be turbulently transformed, without losing any of its charm and fascination. The music seemed to reflect Jewish history: each time they settled somewhere some new evil would befall them. Then, terrified and homeless, in fear for their lives, they would move on, their tenacity and perseverance undiminished, their ability to express joy and sorrow unrepressed. Celia could not help but admire these strange and fascinating people.

"Do you like this kind of music?" Judy asked.

"Oh, it's fascinating. I first heard Caleb playing it when he came to Bleckham Manor."

"It is called Klezmer, and comes from Poland and Russia. Papa's family originates from Poland. So it's in our blood. We used to play together as a family, until Papa converted. Then Mama said it was time to sing a new song, and encouraged us towards classical music and more contemporary songs. But Esther and Caleb have kept up the family tradition."

The musicians drew their session to a close. They were rewarded with enthusiastic applause from the listeners in the drawing room, who had really enjoyed the performance. To the players it was far more than a performance; it represented the overflow of their hearts. Only the professor bowed his head to acknowledge their praise. As they put away their instruments, Celia walked shyly over to the piano.

"That was beautiful. Wonderful. I particularly liked the first song. What's it called?"

"HaTikvah," replied Esther. "It's about the confident hope our people have of returning to Palestine – despite every adversity and opposition. But it must be difficult for a Gentile to understand our vision." Celia felt repulsed by her biting sarcasm.

Caleb was angry. "We'll speak about that later, Esther," he hissed. Esther, quite unruffled, continued tidying her sheet music.

Turning to Celia he asked, "Would you like to help me to pack up the cine-projector?"

It was the only excuse he could come up with on the spur of the moment to speak to her in private. Celia understood. The whole evening had been a confusing disappointment for both of them. Maybe Caleb would now shed a little light on why his behaviour had been so boorish over the past few weeks.

He just continued to wind up the extension lead slowly and said nothing. Celia spoke first. To save her wounded feelings more pain, she had decided to deal with the matter as she would with a terribly injured horse: just fetch a gun and put an end to its suffering.

"Look here, Caleb. I can see you are struggling, so I'll try to make it easy for us both. I don't know what happened in Palestine . . . but maybe you've changed your mind about me and just want to end our friendship . . . You did warn me, so I won't be angry or hurt . . ."

"That's the last thing I want."

"Then . . . I don't understand."

"Things around me have spiralled out of control, and I'm being swept along by them. Celia, so many things have happened to me over these last five months that . . ." He looked at her with such a pathetic plea for understanding. "I've been to Palestine and have seen with my own eyes my people toiling and fighting for the right to live as human beings. I've left my own sweat and blood in a land that they call their own, our Land; my Land. I just can't walk away and pretend it means nothing to me. I am a Jew and I will always be a Jew. Now I feel it more strongly than ever." He paused. Then, with a great effort, he made a second confession. "And I nearly killed a man . . ."

"You did what? How? Why?"

"When the kibbutz was attacked. During the raid. I shot at an Arab. Deliberately."

"But it was self-defence, surely." Celia tried to behave normally despite the shock of his admission. "Anyone would do the same. And it doesn't change my feelings for you . . ."

Caleb hugged her tightly. She was his special someone, someone to hold on to, to lean on . . . He breathed in her scent from the soft skin just below her ear.

"I've got something for you from Jerusalem," he said, forcing himself to let go, and pulled a small leather box from his trouser pocket. "It's not much, really," he said apologetically as he handed it to her, "but I had you very much in mind when I bought it. From a Jewish jeweller in the Old City. I thought it would go well with the colour of your hair."

It was a beautifully crafted silver bracelet inlaid with emeralds. Celia was taken aback and dumbstruck.

"It's so beautiful," she said at last. "Would you put it on for me?"

Moments later Mrs Levine appeared in the doorway. "Here you are! Our guests are leaving, and Alistair's offering Celia a lift home," she said. She was bewildered to find her son alone with Judy's friend, a bracelet in one hand and her hand in the other.

~ *16* ~

Norfolk, 8th December 1936

The riders were outside the spinney, fogbound in the steam rising from their mounts. They were waiting for the foxhounds to make a call. They had lost the fox once again. Celia was bored stiff and cold. She shivered in the December breeze, drenched by a gentle but persistent rain. What an abysmal hunt it was, and all for one mangy old fox. Over sixty riders, dozens of hounds, damaged land, fences and hedges . . . There had to be a more efficient way of ridding the countryside of vermin. And she was angry with herself because – like an itch in the small of her back – she was unable to shake off an irritating niggle in her conscience. In a recent letter, Judy had happened to mention – in no uncertain terms – her distaste for fox-hunting, Celia's favourite winter pastime. When Celia had asked Caleb what he thought, he had just said: "It is written, 'A righteous man regards the life of his animal'."

Regards the life . . . of animals. And "animals" had to include foxes. The logical consequence of this would be to give up hunting. But that was clearly impossible. She simply did not want to change her ways and give up something she'd always enjoyed passionately. And what would people say? No. It was unthinkable. Yet Celia already realised, uncomfortably, that she was no longer getting as much pleasure from hunting as she had. An inner change was taking place. But, like all human beings, she was afraid of change; afraid that it might leave her insecure and her life impoverished. Anyway, why did she have to do what Judy and Caleb said? Judaism was not her religion or her background, and she was not bound by it. Nor was Christianity. But why was she so upset by what the Levines might think of her? What did it matter what the Rabbis taught about hunting for fun? Yet here was the crux: if she wanted the God of Israel, could she reject His teachings? Ignoring Jews was one thing; ignoring God was quite another. She could not brush God aside.

"You look jolly bored, Celia. Rotten hunt, isn't it?" Her introspection was disrupted, first by the friend waiting beside her, and then by the drawn-out death cry of the fox. "They've got him at last. I'm absolutely frozen. Let's go back and get warm."

The young ladies returned to the manor and sat in front of the fire, a warming glass of sherry in their hands. Other hunters joined them and the hall was filled with the noisy recollections of the day's non-events: the hunt and kill had been unexciting, there had been no serious falls to dissect, and there were no newcomers to comment on and judge.

"It's a cruel death for the fox," Celia heard herself say. Suddenly all eyes were on her. She blushed. "I mean, none of us would want to die like that, would we?"

There was a stunned silence. Then Sir Rupert laughed. "Celia, for goodness sake, what's got into you, girl? Our keenest huntswoman going soft on foxes? Ridiculous!"

A week later Celia found herself out with the hunt again. Although it was a clear and frosty morning, and the winter sunshine made her cheeks thrill, she did not really want to ride to hounds today. The hunt was gathered at a neighbouring pub, sipping sherry and sloe gin, and waiting for the last huntsmen to arrive. Celia watched the scene she had been part of a hundred times before. A proud little boy of ten rode into the courtyard. Celia knew him well. Today was his great day: it was his turn to be blooded. It was a simple enough – if gruesome – ritual to initiate him into fox-hunting: his eager young face would be smeared with the blood flowing from the severed tail of the fox. In all probability it was a relic of pre-Roman pagan hunting rites. It was not dissimilar to other vestigial initiation rites still practised in some English public schools and universities. Celia thought back to her own blooding: she had felt excited, hot-blooded, her heart pounding proudly, her spirit bold and fierce. She had felt a sense of belonging, superiority over those who were not "one of us". But what had once been the most important aspect of her life, what had excited her more than anything else, to her surprise now left her cold and unmoved. Passion was waning; the fire was going out.

The Master led the hounds out of the yard, his little copper horn tooting the traditional hunting call, and the huntsmen followed. Celia dropped to the back, then quietly turned Foxtrot round and rode home. She hoped no one had noticed her slipping away.

Caleb had let his parents know that he harboured certain tender feelings for Judy's friend, feelings that were not unrequited. Mrs Levine was delighted; the professor hesitant. "But where is it leading, Cal? I know you're a sensible young man, so you will already have asked yourself the difficult questions. Whoever marries a Jewish girl, her children will be Jewish. But for a Jewish man . . . What about your future children?"

"Did you take that into account when you converted to Christianity?" Caleb retorted. His father did not pick up the gauntlet, not today. He waited for another response from his son. "Celia has asked me what it means to keep kosher," Caleb said proudly. "That's more than Alistair would ever consider."

Gertrud Levine intervened; she drew the line at that. "Good gracious, you aren't telling me you want the poor girl to come under legalism and bondage, are you?"

Isaac intervened immediately. "We all know that Caleb and you will never see eye to eye on that issue. Could we keep focused on the real one, please?"

"Papa, I've explained to Celia – and she understands it – that our backgrounds are very different and that this will inevitably create difficulties in our relationship. We have made no promises, yet, but I do want you to understand that I'm sure she is the right person for me."

How these words rang in Isaac's ears. He had told his own father exactly the same thing 33 years ago. A sad smile touched his face; he knew every twist and turn of this long and painful path. He did not envy the young couple their walk.

"You're of age, Cal. I hope, and pray, you are going to do the right thing."

Later that night, Isaac was getting changed for bed and Gertrud was brushing her hair. She sensed her husband's troubled spirit. "You're not happy about Caleb's news, are you, darling?" She smiled encouragingly in the mirror; she understood his concerns only too well.

"I have to admit it. I'm not. Oh, Trudy, why does history always repeat itself?" The professor shook his head and sat down on the edge of his bed to take off his socks. "I often wonder whether I've done right towards the children. I've made so many decisions that have returned to haunt me." He paused, resting one bony elbow on his knee while he reached for his sock with the other hand. "Worst of all, perhaps I've caused one of them to turn away from God." His narrow shoulders bowed under the burden of his doubts. The responsibility he felt for his children was too great for him to bear.

Gertrud turned to face him. She wanted to share the anxiety of her companion of so many years. Her hands were in her lap, calm and still, holding her brush. "Izzy, my dearest love. How many years have you tortured yourself with this? You know you're not to blame. How could we possibly deny the light and the truth of our Messiah? God did not spare His only Son, so how could we spare our own? He has to walk his own path, make his own decisions. God is the only One who can cause repentance and give His Holy Spirit; you can't save him despite himself. Caleb is proud and stubborn, and wants to do everything his own way. The Lord will have to break him before he'll be of any use to Him. He is expecting the Messiah, but he's looking for the Messiah of Judaism. Caleb will discover that for himself one day. We both know there's no salvation in Judaism."

"How can you possibly say that, Gertrud! If the Tanach isn't a 4,000-year history of redemption, what is it? To say there is no salvation in the Old Testament is tantamount to saying that Abraham and Moses are burning in hell. And that's nonsense."

"Of course I know that. Izzy, all these years we've rehearsed the same arguments over and over. You won't change my views. You know what Reverend Thomas teaches. And he's right. The Old Testament saints were waiting for the Messiah to be revealed. Once He was revealed – in Jesus – where else could redemption come from but from Him? It's to Him we all have to look for salvation – Jews and Gentiles – not to Judaism."

"I know, I know, Trudy. You are right. But the Christianity we know doesn't have all the answers either. When I think clearly about Christian doctrine and practice, quite a lot of the pieces just don't seem to fit together properly. It's as if there are some missing pieces, and others have been forced into places where they don't belong. The Torah always pointed to the Messiah and continues to do so; you can't just throw it away as if it were now irrelevant."

"Of course not. The Old Testament prophesied about the coming of Jesus, and Torah kept the Jews a distinct people until His coming. But once Christ was revealed, the Torah had fulfilled its purpose. It has become obsolete."

"You might as well say that we Jews have become obsolete." There was a rare sharpness in the way he spoke to his wife. "Or that the church has replaced Israel."

"Well, in a sense it has. If the Jews are meant to be a light to the world, then I haven't seen much of it. Jesus teaches us to love our enemies, do good to those who hate us, overcome evil with good, to imitate our Father in Heaven and be transformed into the likeness of His Son. I have seen none of that in Judaism. None. All I've seen is arrogance, corruption, lovelessness, rigidity and legalism. And I'll have no more to do with it. I only pity the poor girl. She's no idea what she's letting herself in for if Caleb leads her down that road."

The professor knew his wife well enough to realise there was no point continuing this conversation. "Maybe Lady Celia is looking to Judaism because our son is actually doing what Israel should have been doing since Mount Sinai," he murmured to himself.

Lady Agatha gave Caleb a grilling that made the Spanish Inquisition – or that was how Celia later described it – look like a picnic at Balmoral Castle. She was very protective of Celia and did not want her to be hurt. Then she gave the young couple her blessing and they decided to celebrate a little. After consulting Lady Agatha, they decided to go out *en couple*, dispensing with the chaperone that correct society still insisted on.

So, for the first time ever, Caleb rather self-consciously booked a table for himself and a young lady who was not his sister. But, when they arrived, they were told the restaurant had been overbooked. Sir and Madame would of course understand that a mistake had been made, a very regrettable and unpardonable mistake, but a mistake nonetheless. Caleb was very angry and disappointed. He felt he had been made to look a fool in front of Celia. "So what do we do now?" he said, as they stood outside the restaurant in their formal evening dress. "Try to find another place?"

"Caleb, please don't laugh at me, but I'd love to have some fish and chips." Celia's eyes sparkled. She was in love and nothing could spoil her evening. "I've never tried them before."

"I wanted to take you out, to spoil you rotten. But oh no! Instead of the caviar, salmon soufflé and champagne that I offer her, all my beloved wants is soggy potato chips and cod wrapped in newspaper. With a generous dose of salt and vinegar, of course." But she had saved his face and he was grateful to her. "Very well, fish and chips it is – for two." He laughed and looked down at their evening dress. "I think we're a fraction overdressed for dinner at the chippy. Would you like to eat at my flat?"

After hesitating momentarily, Celia agreed to this bold adventure. "But don't ever breathe a word of it to Grandmother. Even she would never permit that."

They got into a taxi, bought the food on the way and stopped outside a modern block of flats. The lift took them to the third floor. The view of London would have been impressive, had it not been night and raining.

Celia found the small bachelor flat enchanting and cosy, with its little hall, tiny spartan kitchen and a sitting room less than half the size of her father's study. She clapped her hands in delight: it was like a doll's house. They put their bundles wrapped in old newspapers on the kitchen table and Caleb fetched two plates. Celia looked around.

"The kitchen looks very clean and empty," she remarked.

"I hardly ever use it. Would you like German or French white wine? Or beer?" Caleb opened the refrigerator.

Celia was enchanted. "You've even got a refrigerator! How frightfully modern you are. At Cecil Court we're still using the icehouse. Drinks – oh, whatever the wine waiter recommends."

Caleb glanced at her and was convinced there was no more wonderful a person in the world than Celia. Standing here in his kitchen, in her silk evening gown, she was bright-eyed and radiant. Her happy, funny little face was framed by curly strands of red hair; her sweet, pure voice transformed into heart-melting laughter . . . who could not love her?

Caleb smiled, shook his head and showed her into the sitting room. A polished mahogany table for six filled the space by the large front window. He put the plates down and returned to the kitchen to fetch the drinks. Celia spotted a pair of candles and, as the table appeared rather bare, she took it upon herself to set them in place and light the candles. When Caleb returned, he stopped at the sight of the two little lights.

"I've done something wrong, haven't I?" she said, seeing the expression on his face.

Caleb went to the table and arranged the drinks without looking at her. "No, they look lovely . . . only . . . they are my Shabbat candles."

He struggled inwardly: his precious candles being treated as table decorations. But how could Celia have known? She wasn't Jewish.

"I'm so terribly sorry." Celia said, genuinely concerned. "Of course. I shouldn't have taken such a liberty in your home."

"I think the candles will survive their profanation. You meant it well and they do look pretty." He conquered his upset and graciously pulled out her chair for her. She sat down.

He had placed them at opposite ends of the table and they suddenly became aware of the compromising situation they had manoeuvred themselves into. They felt as if they were playing at husband and wife. Rather embarrassed and self-conscious, they ate their congealing fish and chips without speaking. The small clock on the mantelpiece seemed ear-piercingly loud, the light too bright, every crackle of the fire a gun shot, and every click of the cutlery a hammer blow. Caleb glanced at Celia, whose eyes were fastened on her chips. He broke the tension. "I've nothing sweet to offer you, except a box of chocolates."

The word "chocolate" breathed life into Celia. She tore her eyes away from the plate. "Oh, how super," she enthused.

"Well, you sit by the fire while I clear the table," he said, taking the plates to the kitchen. When he returned, the girl had taken off her shoes and was nestling into the settee. Caleb squeezed himself in between the armrest and Celia. She leant against him and he began to stroke her hair. Celia watched the dancing flames. She drew his arm around her.

"A penny for your thoughts," Caleb said.

"I'd like to die now."

"Good gracious! What a morbid thought. I hope I don't have that effect on everyone."

"Most people die when they're unhappy. I want to die when I am happy – leave the party at its height."

"And you're happy right now?"

"Yes." She snuggled more tightly into his arm. "Very."

Caleb tried to keep his thoughts kosher. "You're happy and content with no more than an improvised dinner, a bottle of beer and a warm fire. I know no other lady who'd be so easily satisfied."

"Perhaps I'm not really a lady then."

"Why do you always say these things? Can't you say anything nice about yourself?"

Celia did not reply. Caleb had a way of drawing all these things out of her – like a priest in a confession box. But she felt safe when he was around. She could unburden herself. It was so good to have him as a friend. And any pretence or hypocrisy would be an insult to his intelligence.

"*Bei mir biste sheyn*," he said softly in Yiddish. "You are beautiful, Celia. Has no one ever told you that?"

Celia knew very well that his compliment was sincere. A whole new, beautiful and dangerous vastness of unconditional love lay open before her. But her timid spirit was too abused to explore it. She knew happy moments never lasted long; she knew that as a fact. "Beauty is in the eye of the beholder. And you're not an impartial judge, I'm afraid," she said. She knew she needed to protect her heart and keep love's assault at arms' length.

"Stop it! I'm serious. It's true."

"I've nothing to offer you. Nothing. I'm neither pretty nor intelligent and I'm less than mediocre in all I do. You don't even know half of what goes on in my heart; my conceit, pride and hypocrisy. Do you know why I hide away in the country? The farmers have to respect and honour me. With them, I feel superior. I'm above them socially and allow myself to be a little patronising. If I keep others small I can feel grand about myself. Did you know that even servants have their pecking order? I'm a nobody among my own class, so I make do with the recognition of my social inferiors. Oh yes, I know it's not because of any personal merit; it's just because of my birth. For once I can take advantage of the silver spoon I was born with." She got up to put a lump of coal on the fire. "You see, I'm not so lovely after all."

Caleb chose not to contradict her. If she really believed this about herself, then a facile reassurance from him would not be helpful. Only when she truly recognised her need to change would real change happen. But, without realising it, she had also held up a mirror for him to see himself in. "Keep the Gentiles far from a Jewish hearth," was the attitude, "so that the Jew can revel in his own piety and purity." And did not the Jewish people have their own jealously guarded hierarchies? Apart from the despised and untouchable Christian converts – who weren't Jews *any more* – the Dutch Jews stood lowest in the ranking. The Spanish Sephardic Jews were a class apart, standing on the top rank of the social ladder, proudly looking down on him, a mere Polish Ashkenazi. But at least he could boast descent from the Chortkower dynasty of Chassidism. He realised that he too was not above the pettiness of the Jewish class system. Did he not look down on others, just a tiny little bit, when he had the opportunity? At heart, all mankind was the same.

And here he was, in love with a red-haired Goyah; what merit was there for a Jew in that?

It was time to take Celia back to her grandmother.

~ *17* ~

London, 20th December 1936

Celia's quiet world was being seriously shaken. Past certainties were beginning to topple. She was now re-examining her life from every angle. At times she found it difficult to keep her balance – in a manner of speaking – and became emotionally unsteady and restless.

On the flimsy pretext of needing to buy more Christmas presents and call on Grandmother again, Celia took the train to London in search of . . . what? She did not really know. And so she found herself standing outside the Levines' house one Saturday morning. She knocked, not really knowing why. The maid opened the door and let her in. She remembered her.

"Lady Celia. I'm not sure you're expected. I'm so sorry."

"No, no. I was just passing."

Music drifted into the hall and Celia cocked her head to listen. "It's the professor," said the maid with a proud smile. "Sometimes I just can't help myself. I just stand here and listen." A hint of cockney spiced her carefully practised parlour English. "May I show you into the drawing room?"

The maid wanted to tell the professor that Lady Celia had called, but Celia restrained her. She did not want to interrupt the professor. How delicately his clarinet sang. To what could she compare its sound? To a gentle summer breeze swaying the heads of wheat? Or an elusive dragonfly darting between waterlilies? Or the Spirit of God hovering over the waters? The door to the music room was ajar. Celia could not see the professor. She sat down on a chair, absorbing the peace and spirituality of the moment. When the music finished, she walked over and knocked gently on the door; she did not want to startle him while he was putting away his instrument.

"Lady Celia, what a lovely surprise." Professor Levine left his clarinet to greet her with unfeigned pleasure. "How very kind of you to call. Please, do sit down. I'll ring for some tea. Unfortunately my wife's not back yet. I'm a very poor host, but she should be here any minute."

"I must confess I've been sitting here for a little while already, just listening to you play."

"Not many people like Jewish music. It's very intense in places and you have to understand it in order to appreciate it. We Jews are a highly-strung people and so is our music. Laughing one minute, crying the next, and in between we just argue to stay sane." He smiled at her.

The last comment made Celia laugh. "But at least it comes from the heart – and reaches the heart – doesn't it?" she added more seriously.

"Yes, it does. If you let it. I see you're starting to understand us already."

"I enjoyed my evening here very much."

The professor knew. Celia had written to thank them for a delightful evening. She had learned so much. "You made some very valid points about Judaism and Christianity," he said. He was deliberately encouraging her to continue. He knew it would be hard for someone like Celia to move on from polite small talk to the more serious subject he sensed had brought her here.

"Thank you for your encouragement. But I've ended up with more questions than I started with. May I pick your brains?" She did not wait for him to reply. "For example, if Jesus was a Jew, and the Torah is very holy to a Jew, why would Jesus abolish it? And what about the Sabbath? Caleb says its observance is vital for a number of reasons. Isn't Sabbath observance a command for the Jewish people for every generation? And isn't it a sign of the Mosaic covenant?" Celia surprised the professor when she pulled a small Bible from her handbag and turned its pages. She found the passage she was looking for and read: "Blessed is the man that does this, and the son of man that lays hold on it; that keeps the Sabbath without polluting it, and keeps his hand from doing any evil." She turned to another passage and continued, "If you turn away your foot from the Sabbath, from doing your pleasure on my holy day; and call the Sabbath a delight, the holy of the LORD, honourable; and shalt honour him, not doing thine own ways, nor finding thine own pleasure, nor speaking thine own words: Then shalt thou delight thyself in the LORD." Celia looked at her host expectantly, and waited for his pearls of wisdom.

"If I'm not mistaken you were quoting from Isaiah 56 and 58? Now, how can I explain this to you? The seventh-day Sabbath was meant to point towards a deeper spiritual rest still to come. Psalm 95 and Hebrews 4: 1–11 will explain this in more detail. This rest has now come in Christ Jesus who said, 'Come unto Me . . . And I will give you rest.' In Him, we are also to rest from the works of the Law. Christ established a new and better covenant, a covenant sealed with His blood."

Celia thought for a moment. "I think Caleb has told me that Sabbath observance is an eternal commandment. Is it?"

"It is, but only because we have an eternal rest in the Messiah. And the literal application of this commandment – to keep the Sabbath, and keep it on a Saturday – applies only to the Jews, not to non-Jews or Christians."

"Oh, I see . . . But if you are Jewish, doesn't this mean the Sabbath is still for you, even if you are also a Christian? And there is another thing I cannot understand. It says here in Isaiah 56: 'Also the sons of the stranger, that join themselves to the LORD to serve him, and to love the name of the LORD, to be his servants, every one that keeps the Sabbath without polluting it, and takes hold of my covenant; even them will I bring to my holy mountain, and make them joyful in my house of prayer.' I think this passage includes me as well, even though it was the Jews God made a covenant with, not us pagans. So that means . . ."

Here the professor felt compelled to interrupt her flow. "Dear young lady, please allow me to assure you of one thing: first, never feel inferior to a Jew. All men – and women – are created in God's image. God gave the Jewish people the high calling to be a light to the nations. But they failed to live up to it. Instead, they profaned the name of the Holy One of Israel. God made a covenant with us but we broke it many times. So He exiled us from our Land and dispersed us in the nations. Had it not been for a Christian who first preached the Good News of Jesus to my wife, we, too, would still be dead in our sins and transgressions. I am so very indebted to my fellow Christians. Second, through the new covenant the old wall that separated Jews and Gentiles has been torn down. In Jesus we are all united, Jews and Gentiles, men and women." The professor was at his most serious.

"But why does the Bible speak of the foreigner being joined to Israel and keeping the Jewish Shabbat?"

"It's referring to the old Mosaic covenant under which proselytes – that is converts to Judaism – were required to keep all the Torah."

"And aren't they obliged to do so now?"

"No, not in Christianity. Only in Judaism."

"But Christianity says we should keep the Ten Commandments, including the Sunday Sabbath. Yet it rejects the Torah. So Christianity is fundamentally different from Judaism, which has the Torah at its heart. It's all so confusing. But it seems to me that if Jesus was the founder of Christianity, then He must have rejected Judaism and the Torah. And if He rejected Judaism and the Torah, surely He can't have been a true Jew."

This was the only logical conclusion that Celia seemed able to draw. The professor scratched his head and sighed. He too was becoming perplexed. Was a Jew who did not keep Torah still a Jew? He thought of Caleb. Did he keep Torah? Yes, he did, even if only the minimum "essential" Jewish observances. He certainly did not keep the thousands of traditions and rituals of Orthodox legal Halachah. But Caleb would die rather than deny the validity of Torah. And what about Esther? Who could say what she did? But she was obviously still a Jewess, although she rejected Judaism. And Judy? She was a Christian and certainly did not keep Torah. But she had a broken and contrite heart; she walked humbly with her God; she persevered in prayer and faith, and was loved by all those who knew her – both for her sweet nature and for the many good deeds she did so unobtrusively. Wasn't this pleasing to God and an essential requirement of a good Jewess? How far could a Jew depart from Torah before he ceased to be a Jew? And how far from Orthodox Judaism? The Muslims practised certain aspects of Judaism, but claimed Islam to be a higher and better revelation than Judaism or Christianity. But that didn't make Mohammed a better Jew. He drew his wandering thoughts together. Where did he stand? It was simple: Jesus was the Messiah of Israel and he, Isaac Levine, had sacrificed everything for Him. He had adopted a Christian lifestyle and religious beliefs in order to serve his God in the way he believed he should. He had never questioned whether this break with Judaism was necessary in order to have a living and vibrant relationship with Jesus Christ. He had simply taken it for granted.

"It's been a while since I last discussed these things so thoroughly. I really must congratulate you on your insights, Lady Celia. One of the snags you'll discover with theology is that it's not as simple as pure logic or mathematics. Faith is the engine that powers our walk with God, and without faith there can be no true revelation of God. It is our faith in Christ Jesus that reconciles us to God. And, once reconciled to Him, God reveals His truth and shows us what He requires of us. Without faith – and humility – we are quite incapable of understanding God, however hard we try. We need His Holy Spirit to give us revelation and spiritual insight."

Now it was Celia's turn to be confused. She pressed fingers to her temples, desperately trying to understand what Professor Levine was saying. To have a revelation of the truth required faith, and faith involved believing in God, but she did not yet know which was the true God, so how could she believe? She felt caught up in a vicious circle that led nowhere. She tried to explain her dilemma.

"Before I can have faith in God, I must know which God is the true God. There are so many gods. You say Jesus is God, and the Holy Spirit is God, and the Father is God, and yet they are all one God. Caleb says your gods are not *the* God, and believing in them is simply idolatry. He's taught me the Sh'mah from Torah: 'Sh'mah Yisrael, Adonai eloheinu, Adonai echad – Hear, Oh Israel, the LORD is God, the LORD is One'. I really do want to believe in this one true God, but I don't know who He is yet."

"Lady Celia, I do understand how you feel. I know it's not easy for you right now. But, if you will seek God with all your heart, He will be found. It's so tragic that man can no longer recognise his Creator because of his sin . . ."

But he was cut off in mid-sentence; Mrs Levine had returned. "Lady Celia! How delightful to see you. And I'm so glad you felt at home enough to make a surprise visit.

Have you been here long?" She swept in like a spring breeze, full of fresh air, life and joy, and blew away the cobwebs of theological debate.

"We've already put the world to rights," the professor told her. "And it appears we've added another bright new lawyer-theologian to our list of friends."

"What a pity, dear; you've come all the way from Norfolk and Caleb isn't even in town. He's in Paris, as you know. It's become a bit of a Christmas tradition with him." Mrs Levine sighed apologetically.

"Yes, he told me," Celia said.

She had been genuinely upset when he told her that he would be away over the festive days. When she had enquired whether he would appreciate a present from her – wrapped with all her love and just for him – he had asked her not to include him on her Christmas list. He then carefully explained why he was so unyielding about it. In the end, to Celia's own surprise, she found herself agreeing with his stance, even supporting it.

Caleb's statement had been categoric: "Jews don't celebrate Christmas."

Mrs Levine felt for her. While other Christians celebrated in the bosom of their families, she knew she would not receive even one single little gift from her son. And neither would poor Lady Celia. "Well, that's just the way he is. He does feel so very strongly about certain things," Mrs Levine said, and sighed again.

Celia knew. Since Caleb had moved out of the parental home he had steadfastly refused to cross their threshold as long as the abominable Christmas tree was in the house. He had quoted from Jeremiah 10: "Hear the word which the LORD speaks to you, O house of Yisra'el. Thus says the LORD: Learn not the way of the nations, and be not dismayed at the signs of heaven, for the nations are dismayed at them. For the customs of the people are vanity; a tree out of the forest is cut down, the work of the hands of the workman, with the axe. They deck it with silver and with gold; they fasten it with nails and with hammers, that it move not."

~ *18* ~

Paris, France, 21st December 1936

With a fair bit of Gallic hand-wringing, the Lerocs had set their hopes on Caleb Levine. After all, he would surely be able to talk some sense into their poor son, Albert. They had always found Caleb a sensible young man, responsible and steady, if a little full of British phlegm. Albert, their youngest son – one of four – had been excitable, impressionable and not yet settled in his beliefs; in short, a normal and healthy young man. So why should he have turned out the way he had? Arm-waving was perfectly justified in the circumstances.

The Lerocs were good, well-to-do, middle-of-the-road, bourgeois Parisian Jews. Like most of their neighbours, whether Jewish or French, they enjoyed life and its good things without being unduly bothered by religious observance. Now Albert had turned Orthodox. *Quelle catastrophe!* They hardly saw their baby grandson these days. Rows and arguments about the level of observance had divided the family, separating father from son and mother from daughter-in-law. This must be stopped. But how? Thankfully, it was now Christmas again and Caleb would be paying his annual visit to them. He would be able to talk some sense into their wayward son. Of course it was all right for Jews to flirt with Christmas traditions and laugh at the Yuletide excesses of their Christian neighbours, but to convert, as Caleb's parents had done, was rather extreme – *quand même*. Still, the professor was a gifted and useful medical colleague, so it was wisest not to say everything one might think.

Caleb liked Paris; he had first stretched his wings there. His parents had sent him to the Lerocs for six months as a lad to perfect his French. He had loved being with Jewish boys of his own age again, doing the things boys liked doing. When not in Paris, they had climbed the Pyrenees, cycled the Roussillon – where the Lerocs had a house and vineyards – and swum in the Mediterranean. Since then he had returned to Paris each year, always to find the Lerocs as solidly settled and orderly as ever. And, only last year, his friend Albert had become engaged and married to a charming, very Parisian, young Jewish princess of good family. Caleb had taken time out of university to attend his joyful and noisy wedding.

When he arrived in Paris, Mme Leroc recounted her tale of woe. She poured out her heart. "He kept telling us he wanted to be a proper Jew. He felt his upbringing had deprived him of his true identity. At first we thought he just wanted to be a little more *frumm*. And what's wrong with that, if that's what you like? Personally, we really don't think one has to take being Jewish too seriously. Anyway, we thought it would make him happy if we went along with it. *Mais c'est terrible!* It got worse and worse. Then he met this son of an Orthodox Rabbi. But, *alors!* He left university and told us he wanted to become a Yeshiva student. Suddenly my food was not good enough for him any more. Can you imagine that? My food! And when we bought him a winter coat he went straight round to a Jewish tailor and had all cotton threads replaced with woollen ones. But that's excessive, *non*? Before he visits us on Shabbat we have to tear the toilet paper in advance because that's 'work' for him. *Tu peux imaginer*? He insists that at least one member of the family should uphold the purity of Israel. As if we were dirty ghetto Jews! *Ça va pas, non*?"

Mme Leroc was visibly shaken – and insisted that every self-respecting mother in her situation would feel as she did. She snuffled noisily into a little lace handkerchief and the clean, pleasant fragrance of Eau de Toilette filled their elegant Louis Quinze living room. "You're our last hope. You had an Orthodox upbringing but you've managed to lead a good Jewish life without becoming a fanatic. Yes, a fanatic, no less. Maybe you can talk some sense into him. Oh, my precious child!"

More lace appeared and the maternal nose was delicately but thoroughly wiped. More scent wafted towards Caleb. So overwhelmed was Mme Leroc at the horrific state of her youngest son – her darling little Albert – that her dark ringlets began to tremble in sympathy with her sobs.

"*Ma pauvre chérie*. You can see how upset she's become," apologised her husband, supporting his wife's solid shoulders in his equally solid arms. Dr Leroc carried himself with much dignity and respect, as befitted a great doctor.

Caleb kept his promise and visited Albert Leroc's home in Le Marais, the Jewish quarter of Paris. It was a much less affluent area than the stuffily bourgeois 16th Arrondissement, where his parents lived.

He asked for directions several times before he found the house. He climbed the steep, winding stairs and noticed the damp walls, crumbling plaster and pungent odour of cabbage and onion. What on earth had got into Albert?

"Praise God! Caleb. Caleb Levine. *Baruch HaShem*!" Albert, now bearded, recognised the visitor in the dim light of the staircase. He was obviously pleased to see his friend. "Come in, come in," he urged. "I was just on my way out, but it's not pressing. Can I offer you something?" He was eager to be a good host.

Caleb looked about discreetly. The place was scrupulously clean, the carefully mended blanket over the settee was spotless, and the cracked windowpanes were grime-free and polished. "No, thank you, I'm fine." To take anything from this man would be robbery.

"No, please, you must. I want to bless an old friend in my own home," insisted Albert.

"Very well then. A lemonade, please."

Albert jumped up and Caleb heard a woman moving in the kitchen. Albert returned and handed Caleb a glass. He accepted it with a smile. "Thank you. And congratulations again on your marriage. I heard you've a little baby already?"

"Ach! It's so good to see you. He's a little boy, *baruch HaShem*! I've often thought of you and wanted to write, but being a Yeshiva student is very demanding. Please, forgive me. I've so little time to spare."

Caleb put his glass to his lips before he caught Albert's shocked look. "We always say a *Brachah* before we eat or drink."

Caleb said the traditional blessing and Albert was satisfied. "Missing an opportunity to bless Adonai wounds Him more than us."

Caleb watched him closely. He noticed he still had his old habit of biting his fingernails, but there was a new excitement and fervour in his eyes.

"So, tell me. How are you? I wouldn't mind meeting your charming wife again, and seeing your little boy of course."

Albert's look became serious and, he dropped his voice. "You can't see her; it's that time of the month. She's in her time of *niddah*. She can't come in here."

Caleb swallowed hard. He had expected Albert to be different, but was unprepared for so drastic a change. "I do apologise; I didn't know, of course."

Albert's smile reappeared as suddenly as it had vanished. "Of course. And I'd fetch little Moishe for you, but he's having his morning sleep. He's such a marvellous baby, and I will do everything to give him a proper Jewish upbringing." Albert was a proud and committed father.

"What do you mean by 'proper Jewish upbringing'?" Caleb was easing his way round to the real point of his visit.

"I just want to be like you, Caleb. Ever since we first

met, and you told me about your life and upbringing, I've realised that my parents deprived me of my true Jewishness – the traditions, the lifestyle – you know what I mean. I've never had that. But now that I've found it, I'll certainly hold fast to it. It's so wonderful."

Caleb took a deep breath. "Is this . . ." his eyes swept the impoverished little flat and ended up on his friend's Chassidic frock coat, "Is this your definition of 'true Jewishness'?"

Albert shrugged. "I know it's not much . . . yet. But at least it's a start."

"So, what is it you are really looking for, Albert?" Caleb asked, challenging and entreating. "At the bottom of your heart, what are you really searching for? Is it God? And if it's not God, what is it? Is it an Orthodox lifestyle? If it's just a Jewish identity, aren't you making an idol of Orthodoxy? I believe that might just be a minor breach of the second commandment." He tried to be light-hearted, not wanting an argument.

But Albert gasped and jumped up. Had he not always looked up to Caleb? Wouldn't he, of all people, understand? "How can you say such a thing, Caleb? That's ludicrous; you're just twisting my words. Worse, what you say is blasphemy. Of course Adonai is the centre of all my devotions. Have I not proven it by turning my back on my profane past? It's for Adonai that I've given up my material security and sacrificed my relationship with my parents. Don't you see? My only desire is to lead a holy life as Adonai commanded us."

"Your sincerity is commendable, Albert, but is sincerity enough? Can't one be sincere, and at the same time sincerely wrong? What do you hope to achieve by all this?"

"To be holy, pure and acceptable to Adonai. What else?"

Caleb slid to the edge of the settee and looked his friend in the eye. "You don't honestly believe you can earn yourself

206

a place in God's favour, do you? Better men than us have tried. I tried from the day I was born – but to no avail. What's more, a few months ago I was forced to look into the dark abyss of my own soul. None of my careful religious observance had cleansed my heart in the way the prophet Yekhezqel – Ezekiel – talks about. At least not in the way I'd expect it. No, it is only by Adonai's grace and mercy that we can stand before Him."

"Now I understand why you feel that way." Albert looked straight at Caleb. His body language revealed that he took himself very seriously. "You have known from childhood what it means to be a Jew. But – shame on you – you've turned your back on Adonai and have forsaken His mitzvot. That's why you feel so miserable. It's your own fault, don't you see? And now you are trying to drag me away from godliness. Pshah! A fine Jew you are." Albert sneered at Caleb. He then remembered that he was supposed to deal kindly and mercifully with a sinning brother, and his attitude softened. He continued, almost pleadingly: "Look at me! Do you remember how I was? I was always trailing behind my cleverer friends, never succeeding in anything I did. Now I've found acceptance from my brothers and the true meaning of life. I'm happier than ever before. I have a wife and a child. I'm respected. Have you anything to show for following what you are now trying to tell me is the right path?"

"I didn't say it was a perfect path, only that there must be a better one. I believe that something has to happen in here . . ." He patted his chest over his heart. "It's our hearts that need to be circumcised, not just our flesh. *Moshe Rabbenu* says so. And our hearts can never be circumcised by religious observance, only by the hand of God." His voice had dropped as if he were communicating a deep mystery. For a moment he had gripped Albert's attention. He was getting through to his friend at last. Then the door to his mind closed.

With a superior smile, Albert shook his head. "You know what? If I didn't know you better, I'd be tempted to think you'd become a Christian. Are your parents' lies and stories getting to you?"

"Nonsense!" Caleb's assertion was less confident than it sounded.

Albert went on, countering and challenging his friend. "It's Torah that commands us to circumcise our hearts. But the only way to do that is to keep the mitzvot."

They were now sparring with each other as two fencers might: cut, thrust, parry, twist. "Do you have a Talmudic reference for that interpretation? And do you think God smiles on you because you shut your wife in the kitchen eight days each month?"

"Why do you keep referring to my wife?" Albert's voice was raised and heated.

Caleb struggled to keep calm. "Look, Albert, we're brothers. I'm concerned for you. You think you'll find peace and God in Orthodox religious observance. I tried to, but just ended up angry and bitter towards my parents for what I felt they had done. And you're making exactly the same mistake. Only now have I started to understand that life is much more complex. We pride ourselves on our Orthodox Halachah, yet it is these same rules and traditions that cripple us. That's why we feel guilty and condemned all the time. Have I failed to keep the mitzvot just so? Then HaShem won't accept me. *Oy vey*! It's nonsense, Albert, just nonsense. That kind of religious bondage is as bad as slavery in Egypt. It breeds pride and arrogance . . . and guilt and hypocrisy. Torah was given to release life in us, not condemnation. Torah gives us freedom, not slavery to observance. You say you felt unworthy because you lacked what you now call 'authentic Judaism'. Guess what? I'm despised by my Jewish family because of your precious 'authentic Judaism'. Does Adonai want His people to hate one another?" Caleb was in full flood and his friend could not get a word in edgeways. "You try – and very badly – to quote the Talmud at me. But do you realise that you are living an eighteenth-century, eastern-European form of Judaism, that has almost nothing in common with the Judaism taught by *Moshe Rabbenu*? So be humble and merciful, and you will receive mercy. If you live by Rabbinic Judaism, it is by the standards of Rabbinic Judaism that God will judge you. Why? Because you have despised His mercy." Caleb was talking himself into a fury.

"But we are supposed to carry the yoke of Torah," Albert managed to interject.

"Yes, but it was never given to crush us. It's meant to be our light and joy." *For my yoke is easy, and my burden is light.* Where did that thought come from?

"You're just looking for excuses for your wanton lifestyle."

"My lifestyle is not wanton, Albert. You're blindly slipping into religious fanaticism. It's a road that leads ever downward; by following it we make fools of ourselves and a mockery of Judaism. When was the last time you had contact with a Gentile or a non-Orthodox Jew?"

"The Gentiles are unclean. And non-observant Jews aren't much better. Why should I deliberately make myself unclean? We're called to holiness."

Caleb rubbed his eyes and held out his hands imploringly. "Uncleanness is not a sin. We can't avoid becoming unclean; we live in a fallen, unclean world. And did our own people not defile themselves by committing all sorts of abominable sins?"

"We become unclean if we don't keep the mitzvot, that is true. Obedience is better than sacrifice," Albert replied, categorically.

"But what good is outward cleanliness, if the inside is dirty?" *For from within, out of the heart of men, proceed evil thoughts. All these evil things come from within and defile a man.*

Caleb closed his eyes momentarily, angrily. If only the words of the Man from Nazareth would go away.

"I have wronged no one," Albert insisted. "Test me, if you think I have sinned. I used to once, but now I'm a repentant Jew; I've undergone ritual immersion. Now my Rabbis teach me. They praise my observance and they are kind and encouraging to me. It's wonderful."

"But if you're relying on your religious observance to attain forgiveness, what place does that leave for God's mercy? If you believe you can attain God's favour through your own good deeds, you no longer need His mercy. And if you don't need His mercy, you have robbed Him of one of His greatest attributes. Do you realise: by your scrupulous observance you are robbing God; making Him smaller? That surely is blasphemy. And if you are no longer justified by God's grace and mercy, you're looking for righteousness by your own good works. So you no longer need God!"

"I've just realised what you are saying, Caleb: to be a good Jew I must stop keeping Torah and become like my parents again? Tchah!" There was a note of triumph in Albert's voice. He believed he had finally beaten the man he considered such a clever lawyer.

Caleb breathed deeply, partly in exasperation and partly to control his temper. "No, it's not that at all, Albert. All I want is that you consider seriously what I've said. What is your real motive for becoming Orthodox? Is it a true search for God – or are you just looking for your Jewish identity?"

"I appreciate your concern, but it's quite unfounded. Really." Albert felt that Caleb had loosened the tight didactic grip he had around him. He smiled with a mixture of relief and friendship, the argument behind him, his Orthodoxy undented. "You will stay for dinner, won't you? We haven't got much, but at least it's kosher."

Caleb felt frustrated. He was utterly unable to reach Albert's heart or mind. He dutifully informed M. and Mme

Leroc of the failure of his mission to rescue Albert from Orthodoxy. They were devastated.

And Caleb was disturbed. He knew his friend was right in one way. A Jew must keep Torah; and he, Caleb Levine, was not keeping it. It was a sobering thought in a drunken world. There were Jews like his father who, despite an Orthodox Jewish upbringing, had abandoned Torah because of its harshness. And there were Jews like Albert who, for want of a Jewish upbringing, became zealously Torah observant. Where did he fit in to all of this? In neither category. He had discussed these issues with liberal-minded Jews, but God and Torah were of little or no consequence to them. But he longed for a kind of Judaism that was filled with the life of God. It would surely be something like the religion his parents had, only more Jewish. Caleb's battered heart yearned for a place he could call his spiritual home. But did such a perfect home exist? And if it did, would he ever find it?

As his train rattled through the cold, dull plains of northern France – towards Calais, England and Celia – the rhythm of the clattering wheels hammered out a repetitive message: "All your fault, all your fault, all your fault." Albert's words had left a barbed thorn of guilt and confusion embedded deeply in his flesh.

~ *19* ~

London, 14th January 1937

Caleb's fragile peace of mind, now somewhat stronger since returning from Palestine, was crumbling fast. His unforeseen discussion with Albert had opened old wounds. Soon he could bear it no longer. He telephoned to request an appointment with Rabbi Levine.

His secretary was very sorry but the Rabbi was not available at present.

"But I must speak with him. It's important," persisted Caleb.

"I'm sorry, but Rabbi Levine is ill," said the calm voice. It had a strong Yiddish accent.

"I know he is ill. Tell me . . . how ill is he?"

"I'm sorry. This is all I can tell you."

Caleb was desperate. "I'm Caleb Levine. I am his grandson."

Twenty-four hours later, Caleb was standing on the steps he had run up every day as a child. How low they seemed now. They had appeared steep and impressive to the small boy; going up to the Rabbi's house had felt like climbing the steps to the Temple in Jerusalem. How he had longed for today, and yet how he was dreading it. What was he expecting from his grandfather? A miracle? Words of wisdom? Could he free him from the deep anxieties that resulted from his being banished from the Jewish community?

He walked up the steps, his heart full of foreboding. The glass in the front door reflected a clean-shaven man in a black hat and coat ringing the doorbell. Despite the murmur of voices behind the door, it was a while before anyone opened it. Caleb wanted to turn and run, but then Rivka was suddenly standing before him.

"I knew you'd come," she said in Yiddish. As she let him in, her eyes were bolted to the floor: as befitted a strictly Orthodox Jewish woman, she was not permitted to look at other men. A strong female voice was calling in the same familiar language: "Who is it, Rivka?"

Rivka did not reply. An old woman came down the hallway and looked intently at the caller. She would have dropped the tray she was carrying, had Rivka not seized it.

"I'll take it," Rivka said, disappearing into a back room.

"Caleb, my son!" The old lady gave a dry, choking sob. "Blessed be He who is taking my husband, but restores my son."

Being the offspring of her favourite son and his trouble-some wife, she had taken particular care to teach Caleb the highest Orthodox standards. Chaya Levine had fought with all her strength and cunning against the influence of his profane mother; she had battled for the soul of this boy, in prayer and deed – and here he was at last. Adonai had answered her prayers as He had those of Sarah, Rebekah, Leah and Rachel. She could not hold back her tears of gratitude and joy. Smiling and laughing, she looked at the young man again and again. How like his father he was. She wiped her eyes with her apron.

"Shalom," Caleb said. Despite his outward composure, the emotions flooding the young man were strong. There stood his *Bubba*, his grandmother, who had fed him biscuits and listened with delight while he recited the weekly Torah reading. He remembered the narrow hallway with its unique aroma of books and chicken soup. Bearded young men in dark coats and black hats stood on the stairs, staring at the clean-shaven stranger.

"I came to speak with the Rabbi . . ."

"Of course," Chaya replied.

Caleb Levine had returned. A miracle! But then, what was more natural than for a lapsed Jew to repent? Her own flesh and blood was returning to the House of Israel. She led him upstairs, past the uncomprehending stares of the Rabbi's disciples. Chaya Levine could raise her head again. He could still become a Rabbi – one of the best. She would be vindicated in her old age. She knew she had given her gentle but headstrong seventh son too much freedom. She had been shamed, but now God was restoring her good name.

The Rabbi lay in his bed, thin and frail. His breathing was heavy but his eyes were clear. Bony hands rested on the bedspread, trembling with age but at peace. His long white beard was carefully groomed. The bedroom was as neat and clean as a hospital ward.

Chaya asked her grandson Avraham – one of many – to leave, with his wife and five children. Avraham gave the stranger a suspicious sideways glance. Where had he suddenly appeared from? Chaya wasted no time introducing the estranged relatives. Later there would be time enough to catch up with the past. Avraham, puzzled, hesitated while she nudged the family out of the room. She carefully closed the door behind them.

Chaya approached her husband's bedside. "Mendel, someone has come to see you."

"Who is it?"

"A lost sheep of the House of Israel."

Encouraged by his grandmother, Caleb stepped, hesitantly, towards the bed. "It is I, Rabbi. Caleb Ben-Yitzchak, your grandson."

The old man's outer shell might be withering, but inside it a passionate zealot roared. He gasped for breath. "I have no son called Yitzchak." His voice, still strong, shook with anger.

Chaya left the room, leaving Caleb alone with his grandfather. With quivering lips the Rabbi turned his face away. He was fighting, fighting with himself, even on his deathbed. He loved this young man; he had taught him Torah and Talmud; he had let him ride on his knee while teaching him Hebrew. And his words had been like God's to Caleb. The old man had interpreted Torah all his life. He knew what was right and Godly. He had observed the Orthodox traditions meticulously; had upheld and guided the community. He was revered and looked up to. He still had to do right in all things. But God alone knew fully the many struggles, regrets, errors and mistakes the Rabbi harboured in his soul. Every Yom Kippur he lived with the hope – but not the certainty – that his name was written in the Book of Life.

How often had his heart ached for his lost son? Were Yitzchak ever to recant, he would take him back that very instant. Now his grandson was seeking reconciliation. How he longed to clutch him to his chest as Isaac had embraced Joseph. His emotions fought with his reason and religion: be reconciled with a non-person, a non-Orthodox, a non-Jew? How could such a thing be? And yet . . . The battle raged in his heart.

After a while the Rabbi turned his head; tears were streaming down the deep lines of his old face. "Caleb!" he cried in a pitifully thin voice.

"Grandfather!" Caleb fell on his knees and rested his forehead on the Rabbi's hand. "Bless me like a true son of Israel. Do not die and leave me an outcast. Have mercy on me. I have not bowed my knee to the cross. My parents have submitted to idolatry but I have not. Must I forever be made to pay for the sin of my parents?"

"I loved your father as I love all my children. I did not cast him out – he cast himself out; he ran after other gods. He

215

broke our hearts. But I had to look after the House of Israel. I had to keep it pure and undefiled. The cancer had to be cut out. I had no choice. I had no choice . . ."

The old man's body shook under a renewed onslaught of emotion. A pathetic whining sound bubbled from his mouth. And together they cried, the old man and the young; a broken and persecuted people, given no rest, tossed by commands and demands, torn by their enemies, their pride, and their sufferings.

Chaya tapped on the door and came in.

The Rabbi wiped his tears. "Chaya, call Moishe. Now. There is something I must settle before I pass on." His voice had the urgent vigour of a dying man.

Chaya hurried off. Caleb kissed the old man's hand for the last time. "Will you bless me, Grandfather?"

The Rabbi blessed his grandson, his dying voice transformed and invigorated by the beautiful and long-remembered words of the traditional Hebrew blessing from the Torah:

The Lord bless you and keep you;
The Lord make His face shine upon you, and be gracious to you;
The Lord lift His countenance upon you, and give you peace.

Two days later, his obituary appeared in the Jewish newspapers. For 24 hours, Professor Isaac Levine declined all food.

Uncle Moishe kept the promise he had given to his father. When the formal period of mourning was over and normal life could resume, he invited Caleb for an Erev Shabbat meal with his family.

The past was wiped away. He was warmly welcomed and they laughed, praised God and bade him sit down. There was such a to-do as everyone tried to find a place, the

216

women sitting on one side of the room and the men on the other. Caleb relived the hubbub and memory to the full; this was how he remembered Shabbat. Many of his relatives he did not recognise; many wives and children had been added to the family in the years he had been an outcast.

Peace descended as Aunt Malkah lit the Shabbat candles and recited the ancient prayers. The traditional Ashkenazi cold fried fish was wonderful. The meal was punctuated with songs from the Psalms and a Midrash on the name of Abraham the Patriarch. Happiness and laughter abounded. Everyone enquired after his well-being.

"How old are you now? Twenty-two? And not married yet? *Oy gevalt*," commented Uncle Shloyme, half jokingly and half seriously. He patted Caleb on the shoulder. "Don't worry. Leave it with me. I'll talk to Mrs Mandel first thing tomorrow morning. She'll find you a nice Jewish girl." Uncle Shloyme was thrilled at the prospect of yet another wedding in the family.

Caleb wasn't. The woman he had already chosen was a Gentile. She was totally alien to his family, and his family was totally alien to her. They would never understand each other. Tragic family history was beginning to repeat itself before his very eyes.

The evening was suddenly and irretrievably spoilt for him.

* * *

Berlin, Germany, 15th January 1937

It was late and dark when Celia's train pulled into Lehrter Bahnhof. A gentleman offered to help her with her many suitcases, which were crammed with woolly jumpers, long underwear and thick socks. Lady Norah could not understand why her daughter was determined to travel in the middle of winter. Neither did Celia, but it took her mind off Caleb's unsettling behaviour. He was once more acting strangely, and was irritable and distant towards her. Something was obviously troubling him again. Celia had expected that the reconciliation with his late grandfather would have healed the deep, old wounds. She was obviously mistaken. She had so wanted to draw close to him and get to the root of it all, but Caleb would not let her. Well, she reasoned to herself, Alistair had spoken to her of these periods Caleb went through from time to time.

For the moment, she was not willing to tolerate his mood swings. She needed a break. If he could go to Paris without her, then she would jolly well go to Berlin without him.

Caleb's encouragement and love over the past six months had given her the confidence to start growing towards maturity again. It was a terrible shame that they were unable to see each other more often, Celia sighed to herself. Caleb was busy in his budding career as a young solicitor. He was under constant pressure to meet court deadlines, advise clients and attend legal hearings. Celia could understand that. Caleb was not a Sebastian. Sebastian lived off his family's fortune. Caleb had to work for a living. Then there was his involvement with Zionist groups in London. They laboured 24 hours a day to alleviate the growing desperation of German Jewry. She could understand that too, and loved him all the same. But Celia was wrestling with her preordained role as a woman, a role demanding that she wait for her man to turn up when it suited him. Men could pursue a calling, a career, a mission, a vision. Women, especially of her upbringing, had to put up with their spouses' ambitions and private pastimes. They had to wait patiently at home, raise children and comfort their husbands after their demanding day at work.

Well, Celia was not yet anyone's wife. She would go to Berlin and stay with her brother, Francis. He had his own flat, fended for himself and, judging by his letters and occasional telephone calls, enjoyed a degree of Bohemian freedom. It was exciting; she too was free and could do just what she wanted.

So here she was, standing on the platform, all alone in a foreign city. It was bitterly cold and her feet were like ice. After the busy crowds had dispersed, annoyance and anxiety crept over her. With the people gone, she noticed the billboards. Most of them were dedicated to Adolf Hitler, bearing swastikas and party-political slogans. Personally, Celia found Hitler's propaganda idiotic; it was aimed more at the emotions than the intellect. She wondered why such an intelligent people as the Germans put up with such nonsense.

A smartly dressed and very handsome man in his late twenties was approaching her across the station concourse. "Hello, Francis!"

Celia's brother gave her a courteous peck on the cheek. He looked rushed and preoccupied. "I'm sorry for being so late, Celia. I was held up at a meeting. The time you chose to come was not the most convenient."

"I know, but I promise I won't be a nuisance."

"I'll see if I can find a porter," he said, and disappeared.

Celia sighed. More waiting. By now her feet were numb. She stamped to get some feeling back. Francis returned with a porter in tow. "So, why were you so keen to come here? There are much nicer places to go than Berlin at the end of January. Why not Switzerland or Monte Carlo?"

"I wanted to do something outrageous, something out of character. I've at last decided to throw myself – hook, line and sinker – into the world."

Francis looked at his sister with bewilderment. Was this the little girl he remembered? Was she finally growing up? There were seven years between them. She had been born as he was packed off to boarding school. He hardly knew her and they had virtually nothing in common. He found her trotting alongside him a nuisance. Under no circumstances was he going to nanny her. If she were unable to look after herself he would pack her off home again on the very next train.

They got into a taxi, which stopped outside a block of flats in a street lined with chestnut trees. The house had a heavy wrought-iron and glass door. Celia was rather impressed by the marbled entrance hall, with its Baroque mirrors and carpeted stairs. She was disappointed when they passed through another door leading to an inner courtyard at the back. Across it was a modest, dull house with a linoleum-covered staircase and painted walls. The smell of cooking hung in the air.

"The posh people live in the front house, the workers' class live here," Francis explained as the cab driver dragged her suitcases up the stairs behind them.

He fumbled in his pocket for the key to his second-floor flat. With an oath, the exhausted cabby put down the luggage. The door opposite opened and a woman peered out. Taking her time, she eyed Celia with a critical air. Sniffing pointedly, she made a sarcastic comment in German and closed the door again. "Take no notice of her," Francis mumbled under his breath. "She's just a nosy old woman."

As soon as they had closed the door, Celia demanded an explanation. "Excuse me, Francis, but my German is good enough to know that the woman opposite was wondering if I was another sister. I am your *only* sister!"

Francis did not rise to her bait. He felt under no obligation to justify his private life to his little sister. "This isn't a monastery, and I'm not a monk." He opened a door and pointed to a double bed in a good-sized bedroom. "This is where you'll be sleeping. I'll get your things."

The room was comfortable enough. Yes, she could manage with this. Francis returned with her cases. "Is this your guest bedroom?"

"This is *the* bedroom, my bedroom. I don't have a guest room. I'm a poor bachelor, remember?"

"Oh, Francis!" She was genuinely concerned. It upset Celia to deprive her brother of his comfortable bed. "Where are you going to sleep, then? You should have said you couldn't put me up. I would have gone to a hotel nearby."

"Nonsense. I'll sleep on the settee in the living room. It's quite comfortable really. I sometimes stay with friends so I'm used to making the most of sofas."

"Friends? Or sisters?"

Francis gave her a withering look. "I'll warm up some soup for you."

After freshening up, she went into the kitchen. It was very basic compared to Caleb's. The icy windows overlooked an unexciting back yard.

Francis served her a very nourishing barley broth with large pieces of beef in it. Their conversation about home, friends and family progressed haltingly but it eventually took off over a cup of coffee.

"Do you want to know the real reason why I wanted to come to Berlin?" Celia offered. She wanted to tell him. "I've met a Jewish family and think they're lovely people. Well, most of them." Celia was thinking of Esther. "Professor Levine's family. In London. Friends of Grandma's. Mrs Levine comes from Berlin. They invited me to dinner and to see a film about Palestine. They also showed me and explained some of their Jewish traditions. I found it fascinating. And their music . . ." Words failed her and her hands continued the conversation. ". . . it's so beautiful." She thought of its soul-embracing, life-encompassing rhythms and tunes. It brought a shine to her eyes.

Francis was astonished. "And that made you come here?"

"No. Not just that. I've also been reading a Jewish newspaper and swotting up on Jewish history. Did you know that the Jews have been treated terribly by Christians in the name of Jesus? Most people have no idea," she said emphatically.

She was warming to her subject. Francis was unimpressed. Her sudden interest in Jews was no doubt the passing fad of a bored and silly girl. "But why take up the banner for the Jews? Why not the Negroes? Or our own working class. They're going through a pretty rough patch at the moment."

"You are absolutely right, but you see ..." Could Celia tell her brother about her discovery of Torah and God and religion? He would just ridicule her. She decided to feel her way forward carefully. "I'm also intrigued by the Jewish teachings of the Old Testament. They seem to make so much sense. Mankind would be much better off if people would keep their laws."

But Francis had smelled a rat. He put down his slice of bread. "You haven't caught religion, have you? Not Judaism? That of all things."

"What do you mean: 'That of all things'? You're not anti-Semitic, are you?"

"No. And I'm not a Nazi sympathiser either, if that's what you're hinting at. But I certainly don't feel excited about the Jews."

She felt it would be wise to let the subject drop. They finished their meal and moved into the warm living room. Francis fell into an armchair and lit a fat cigar. He needed to warn his little sister about the realities of life in Berlin.

"About your sudden interest in Jews and Judaism. Not a good time, actually. Rather unpopular with the Germans, you see. And with a growing number of our own fellow countrymen, I hear. Judaism has never been much *en vogue* at the best of times. But you've probably discovered that already."

Francis looked at his sister provocatively. He wondered how long it would be before she ran out of arguments to justify her new fad – her silly flirtation with the unusual and exotic. She rose to the bait. "I suppose you think I'm desperate to give my life meaning, don't you? Or that I'm throwing myself into the arms of the first new religion I discover? You must have a pretty poor opinion of me." Celia steadied herself, seeing from his grin how pleased Francis was that she'd responded to his tease. "It's much more than that. Don't you ever think about anything more serious than girls and money and having a good time? Don't you ever ask yourself what the point of life is? Don't you sometimes think there must be an Absolute Truth, something or someone who is absolutely reliable, absolutely good and absolutely pure? I think God must be like that. Holy, true, righteous – all the things we're not. I want to be a better person. Don't you? What I've discovered is that the Old Testament – the Torah to be more precise – teaches me how I should behave. It's challenged me in so many ways – views, perceptions, traditions, actions – the things we just take for granted. Without realising how damaging they are. It covers so many areas of our lives."

"Celia, this is all utterly ridiculous, and – I want to be frank with you – jolly worrying. You're just being a silly idealist, a dreamer. And for goodness' sake, don't broadcast your ideas around Berlin. You won't be popular if you do, and it'll be your own fault if you get into trouble." He stopped to blow smoke rings into the air. "Just as silly as I remember her," he thought. Then, to her: "Anyway, your life is your own to mess up, so the best of luck. And do let me know when you've become a 'better person'."

"If you just want to criticise and humiliate me, we might as well stop now."

He spun round on her, thoroughly irritated by her piqued and self-righteous expression. "But why Judaism, Celia? Christianity is far more convenient; not only that, it's the obvious religion for people like us. No one will hassle you for going to church. Not unless you're a bigoted, born-again fundamentalist and wanted everyone to believe what you do, of course."

"Do you really want to know why? All the Christians I know are hypocrites. Just think of the churchgoers we know in Marsham."

"You used to be one of them. Does that make you a hypocrite too?"

"Only because Mummy made me go. People would have talked if we hadn't gone."

"I suppose you think Jews and Judaism are better – less hypocritical?"

"I think there are probably good and bad people in all religions. But my interest in Judaism is more a question of Truth. If there is only one true God, why would He teach one thing to one people, and another to someone else? It doesn't make sense. Also, if you are really convinced it *is* the Truth, you have to live by that Truth."

"Ah, Truth – with a capital 'T'. That's the muddle-headed claim of every religion. And anyway, how can you possibly be sure that what you believe is . . ." Francis paused dramatically and waved his arms in a grand theatrical gesture, ". . . the Truth? Many people have claimed to know the Truth. Jesus even claimed to be the Truth incarnate. What utter poppycock!"

Celia was not upset by his scepticism. Despite the tension in the air, she felt a real peace. She was on home ground now; she and Caleb had discussed this many times. "Truth is absolute, it's the plumb line of all existence. It can stand up to examination, scrutiny and challenge, and exposes and breaks those who set themselves against it. But in the end Truth depends on the existence of God. He, and He alone, is the definition of Truth; He sets the absolute standard of the Truth."

"If you believe in God, that is." Francis thought he had found a weakness in her argument.

"No, that's not what I'm saying. The question is this: If God exists, what am I personally – each one of us – going to do about it?"

Francis was surprised to see how well his sister argued. Of course, he disagreed with her on the subject of religion; that was normal and sensible. But, from a philosophical standpoint, he knew she was right. If Truth were absolute, then this Truth should be applicable to all mankind and should be lived out. But where was one to find Truth? It did not grow on trees, and it certainly did not originate in the mind of man. He sighed. It was late. Man would never get it right. There was as much point in embarking on a search for Truth as there was in hunting for the Holy Grail. He ended the discussion with a rather lame: "It all depends on how you define God. Anyway, who taught you to think about this sort of thing?" he asked.

"I told you, I've met some Jews," she said with a pleased, half triumphant smile.

It was freezing cold and already light when Celia woke up. The winter sun, weighing in at minus fourteen degrees Celsius, tried hard to fight its way through the thin curtains. Although she prided herself on being hardy, she had to admit she was missing having a maid to light the fire before she got out of bed. Celia put on her clammy clothes in a hurry, smoothed over her bed and went out into the hall.

"Francis?" she called.

No reply. She eventually found a scribbled note on the kitchen table. "The concierge will come later and light the stove. There is bread in the bread bin and cheese and jam in the larder. Alternatively, have breakfast in the café at the corner of the street. It's warm there. Don't wait up. F." A set of keys was lying beside the note.

The bitter cold hit her with a vengeance as she left the cheery café after a filling German breakfast. Once outside, she stopped to slip on her gloves and spotted a note in the window: *Juden sind hier nicht erwünscht* – "Jews not wanted here". Celia had heard about such warnings, but was shocked to see one for herself. The waitress had been so friendly and welcoming. How could she possibly live with such a hurtful prohibition?

She took the underground to Unter den Linden, the beautiful avenue where the French emperor, Napoleon I, had celebrated his triumphant entry into the city. Celia walked up it towards the Brandenburger Tor, the famous gate at the far end of the avenue.

She became aware of the faint strains of a brass band. Berliners, wrapped up warmly against the cold as they hurried through their beautiful wintry capital, paused and looked for the source of the music. Then, from around a corner, the military band came blaring out some bright, hearty march. It was followed by three ranks of helmeted, goose-stepping soldiers. Those nearest to them raised their arms in the notorious Nazi Hitlergruß salute.

Celia rather liked the spectacle and music – there was one particularly catchy tune which had her tapping her foot to the beat – and tried to ignore the aggressive strutting and waving. Then she felt a sharp pain in her back and whirled around to give the culprit a piece of her mind. But instead of the overexcited ragamuffin she had expected to find, she was confronted by a pair of hard, steely eyes and a repellent grin masquerading as a smile. "Aren't you going to salute when our Führer's heroic soldiers march past?"

Celia identified the man as a member of the *Schutzabteilung*, the SA, Hitler's brown-shirted bullyboys. She had seen photos of the uniform in English newspapers. Also in the *Jewish Chronicle*, which was following German political developments with rapidly growing unease, if not panic.

She had no intention of complying, but he exuded an aura of naked intimidation that frightened her badly. His rhetorical question was an order that was not to be resisted by an unescorted woman. Celia glanced around; all her neighbours in the crowd had their arms raised. The stout, middle-aged woman next to her gave her a condemning look and said, in a deliberately raised voice, "Disloyal wretch. After all the Führer has done for us! What are you? A Communist? Or even a Jew?"

Celia thought about what the bullyboy might do to her if she resisted him. Her initial defiance crumbled and, like a hypnotised rabbit, she turned towards the parade and raised her arm woodenly. The last thing she recalled was his triumphant smirk as the SA guard bent and hissed into her ear, "If I catch you again, you little piece of filth, I won't let you off so lightly."

At last the band passed and the crowd dispersed. Celia checked to see if the fat woman was still there before lowering her arm. She had never felt such an overpowering sense of threat, intimidation and fear in all her life. The Germans called it "Angst"; there was no equivalent word in English. Perhaps the Germans knew more about fear than other people. How could she, a British subject and an aristocrat, have been coerced into submission like a meek little lamb? What could that brute really have done to her? Very little. So how could one man, Hitler, twist a nation's soul so hard that it had become like this? It was hard to imagine.

She continued her way towards the Tiergarten, crunching snow underfoot. The bare trees in the most famous of Berlin's parks were shivering; the cold winter sun filtering down through a thin layer of white mist. She had wanted to visit this place ever since Mrs Levine had told her how, as a child, she had come here most days with her nanny. Children ran past, their leather school satchels bouncing on their backs with muffled thuds, books and pencil cases rattling inside. How perfectly normal the day was. An elderly couple walked past, arm in arm. Surely things were not as bad as her instinct suggested? Her imagination must have exaggerated the incident with the SA at the Brandenburg Gate. Celia's mood brightened again.

It was already dark when she returned to the flat. The lights were on and it was wonderfully warm inside. A clattering was coming from the kitchen; Francis was obviously getting dinner ready. Celia was eager to tell him about her day, and began to chat while still in the hall taking off her heavy winter coat and scarf.

Her mouth dropped open in astonishment when, cigarette in hand, a strange woman with an amused smile appeared in the kitchen doorway. "You must be Celia. Your brother's not back yet. I'm Barbara Reinhardt, by the way." She spoke with an American accent. "I'm a secretary at the US embassy here in Berlin. My mother is American and my father is German. And that's that." They shook hands formally. Barbara continued walking around as if she lived there. "I take it Francis forgot to tell you that I'd be dropping in today? I've cooked us some dinner – pork chops, potatoes and cabbage. I hope that'll be all right."

It was not a question. She flicked her ash onto a saucer on the kitchen table and turned the chops without putting down the cigarette.

"Are you my 'sister'?" Celia asked.

Barbara laughed. Celia wasn't sure she liked the laugh of the attractive brunette, whose airs were more cultured than her behaviour. "Has the busybody opposite already been on at you? She should mind her own business."

She pricked the boiling potatoes to see if they were ready. The thick, damp smells of boiled cabbage, cigarette smoke and fried pork chops streamed down the kitchen windows and hung in the air. Celia suddenly longed to be home again.

"So, how do you like our Berlin?" asked Barbara.

Celia told how she had bought herself some new boots

and had found her way round the city. But the conversation did not flow easily. In the end she excused herself and withdrew to her room. She came out of hiding when she heard Francis' key in the lock. Looking into the kitchen, she saw him, his arm around Barbara's waist, kissing her neck while she giggled and squirmed, the fork still in her hand. She was not embarrassed to see Celia watching them from the door. "I think your little sister wants you," she said with a worldly-wise smile.

Deeply embarrassed for having inadvertently spied on them, Celia tried to regain her composure. She flushed, and felt an easy target for ridicule. One thing was sure: she was in a totally different world now and knew she was ill prepared for it.

Francis had not noticed her embarrassment. "Come on in, Celia. Let's sit down and eat. I've brought a bottle of wine to celebrate the occasion."

They sat down at the kitchen table, Francis making do with a stool, which he pulled from under the table. To Celia's relief, Barbara made the effort to find some topics of conversation they could all contribute to. But her relaxation was short lived and her reservations soon returned. Francis and Barbara were so very different from her. They spoke in innuendoes she could not follow and always treated her like a child. And that was precisely how Celia felt.

~ 20 ~

Berlin, 17th January 1937

She woke up just as cold as on the previous day. She heard the latch on the front door click and assumed that Francis had gone to work. Wrapped tightly in her woollen dressing gown, she shuffled across the hall to the bathroom. To her surprise, she found Francis in the kitchen.

"Coffee?" he asked.

"Oh, please!" Anything hot to clasp in her hands sounded good. "I thought you had just left." She did not look at her brother and wondered if he had heard her hint of accusation.

"No, not yet. That was Barbara. And, before you feel the need to ask any discreet questions, yes, she did stay the night. And we did sleep on the settee. Both of us."

Poor Celia. Her trip to Berlin was turning into quite a process of learning and re-education. The world she knew was falling apart as she watched it. She was growing up; nothing seemed to surprise her any more.

"I didn't say a thing," she said lamely, defiantly.

"Good." There was a pause before Francis enquired about her plans for the day.

"I thought I might visit some art galleries and museums. It might be warm in there."

"Sorry about the heating. I'll ask Frau Meyer to come earlier. I don't want you to think I'm trying to freeze you out."

The day passed almost pleasantly. Celia had breakfast in the same café, but felt too timid to challenge the waitress about the note in the window.

She visited an art gallery in the morning and had lunch at a restaurant at Alexanderplatz. As she ate, she thought about the paintings she had seen. There had been many old masters – Breughels, Dürers and Rembrandts – which she had enjoyed.

But there were also canvasses that reflected the vision of the New Germany, on which the paint was barely dry. Male and female nudes were depicted with beautiful but carica-tured Aryan bodies. The men were tall, blond and muscular, with hard-set and determined faces; the women were lighter, but with full child-bearing hips, and firmly soft and feminine. There were family groups, with old and young living in harmony before striking backdrops of grand German country scenes; their arms were around one another; they were holding the nation together. Other groups, dancing in traditional folk costume, were joyfully shaping the empire to last a thousand years – the Third Reich. She mused that brown shirts, jackboots and swastikas were prominent by their very absence from the paintings. How like Stalinist Russia, where art was less an outpouring of the human spirit than a statement of political ideology. Painting on demand, not by inspiration. On the other hand, she thought, all art conveys some form of personal, social or political message. As Jewish music did. So why shouldn't the Nazis do the same?

In the afternoon, she wandered through the side streets of central Berlin. In Taubenstraße a building – almost a palace – caught her eye. On the façade, in bold, gold-plated letters, was written "Gebrüder Ebenstein". Just above it was the name of a coat-exporting company, Binyamin & Caspary. All around were manufacturers and businesses with Jewish names; names such as Leopold Levy, Rosenthal & Jacobson,

Lesser & Joseph, Heinrich Pagelsohn, Appelbaum – and even Immanuel Brann. The road was more or less owned by Jews in the clothing trade, advertising their bourgeois furs and ready-made clothes. Celia was especially delighted to have stumbled across Leon Brann's family business.

So, pleased with her new discoveries, she crossed the road. She spotted a confectioner's by the name of Gersohn. On the shop window someone had painted, in large, crude letters: *Deutsche. Wehrt euch. Kauft nicht bei Juden* – "Germans. Defend yourselves. Don't buy from Jews." But Celia was undeterred; this time she would not give in. Boldly, she stepped into the little shop and was instantly immersed in the marvellous scent of chocolates, hazelnut pralines and coffee. A brass bell tinkled and an elderly lady peeped cautiously through a flowered curtain. She looked relieved and approached Celia, asking her what she would like.

Celia wanted to say something kind. "Oh, your pralines all look so lovely, I don't know which to choose from. I rather like truffles, the dark ones." Celia felt proud of her German. Sir Arthur was a keen linguist, and had always encouraged her to learn foreign languages.

"The Germans who killed and were killed in the Great War were just poor sods like the rest of us. We were all deceived by our respective governments. Once you begin to understand what your enemy is saying, you may discover, to your great surprise, that he's a human being just like you."

Sir Arthur's views had always been somewhat unBritish.

The lady recommended a particular type and Celia asked for a generous two hundred grams. Francis was bound to pinch some, she thought.

The lady tried to make polite conversation as she weighed out Celia's chocolates. "You're not from here?"

"No, from England. By the way, I happen to know a Leon Brann from Palestine. His parents own the business next door, don't they?"

The chubby old lady's face suddenly lit up and she started gesticulating. "You know Leon?" She called excitedly into the back of the shop. "Oh, Samuel, Samuel, come quickly. Here's someone who knows our Leon." Then to Celia again: "Why did he ever have to leave his parents and go so far away, especially now?"

An elderly man came through the curtain at the back of the shop. He had the same initial look of suspicion in his eyes.

"Samuel, this young lady knows our Leon. Isn't that a wonderful surprise? His Mama comes regularly to buy coffee and chocolates from us. Oh, what a fine lady she is."

"They closed the firm yesterday," said Mr Gersohn.

Celia, who was having her change counted out, looked up. "Closed? Who closed it? The Branns?"

"No. The police. They came, searched the building and left a notice on the door saying 'This firm is closed until further notice'."

Mrs Gersohn looked very worried but tried to master her anxiety. "Who knows what this is all about. Perhaps they'll be back tomorrow to remove the notice. There must have been a misunderstanding."

"And that?" said her husband pointing to the window, "Is that a misunderstanding, too?"

Celia realised he was referring to the anti-Semitic smear on the shop window. The old lady shrugged her shoulders in resignation. "If we scrape it off it will just be painted back on. Or worse."

At that moment, the Gersohns' faces froze into masks of fear. Two SA men entered the shop. They slammed the door, clicked their shiny jackboot heels and saluted their Führer by shouting "Heil Hitler!". Mr Gersohn's response to this greeting was so unconvincingly lame, that it reflected an insult.

"*Guten Tag,*" whispered Frau Gersohn, greeting her new customers politely. Celia pretended she wasn't there.

"Very well, if that's the way you want to play it." One of the SA men – a solidly built, middle-aged man with fat, wet lips – walked up to Celia provocatively. "You, Fräulein. I'm talking to you. Are you deaf? Can't you read either?" He planted himself a few inches from her face and sprayed her with Aryan superiority. "Germans don't buy in Jewish shops. Unless, of course, you're a Jewess," he sneered.

She cowered involuntarily, hating herself for being weak. She wanted to wipe her face.

His comrade, a young lad of about seventeen, laughed. Celia did not think it funny, and scraped together all the dignity and pride she could muster. The subliminal moral support of the Gersohns gave her the courage to hide her fear. She spoke up, head raised, looking the bully in the eye.

"I am a British citizen and I shop where and when I choose."

"We'll see about that. Papers!" He snapped his fingers inches from her nose. "Or, if you prefer, you can come with us for a little private chat at the police station."

Celia swallowed. Francis had told her to carry her passport at all times. Just in case. Whipping up her outrage, Celia opened her handbag and slapped her passport into his hand. It was a precious little dark-blue booklet with the insignia of the British Empire embossed on its cover – her passport to safety in any storm. The big man took his time, scrutinising every page. She realised his behaviour was just psychological warfare, but it was still unnerving.

While this was going on, the younger SA man had helped himself to a tin of coffee from the shelf and examined the label. Then he slowly scattered its contents over the floor, begging the elderly couple's forgiveness for being so clumsy as he did so. Celia's tormentor pointed to the mess.

"You see, Heinrich, I told you Jewish shops are dirty. Insanitary. They should all be shut down." He handed Celia her passport, eyeing her up and down. A wet sneering sound like "English. Pffff!" slithered past his fat lips and landed on Celia.

He turned to leave. The younger man grabbed a handful of chocolates from behind the counter. "Thanks," he said with a false smile, and followed his leader out of the door.

Celia felt suddenly very sick. Mr Gersohn went to fetch a broom.

"Dear young lady, you look quite ashen! Come, do sit down. Can I get you a glass of water? Or coffee? Or maybe, being English, you'd prefer tea?"

The good woman was doing all she could to help Celia through the trauma of the past few minutes; the unfortunate incident had dishonoured the good name of her establishment.

"Woe when the peasant becomes king!" murmured her husband. He bent down with difficulty to sweep up the coffee. Celia felt his humiliation almost physically; his stoical submission to his fate, his silent rage, his powerlessness.

"Please. Do let me do it," she said, bending down to help him.

All the stories Caleb had told her came to mind, and Celia now felt nothing but compassion and sadness for these people. For the first time, she began to understand the millennia of degradation and persecution they had suffered – and the fear and antagonism that had risen in their Jewish hearts against all Gentiles. She could now relate to Mrs Levine's desire to deny her Jewishness, to escape her past. Forget, deny, close your eyes, pretend it's not there. And Caleb, Leon and Esther's tenacious fight to create a Jewish homeland, a place of refuge from the torment of their Diaspora. It was all starting to come together in her mind, demanding her involvement.

Celia finished sweeping up the last coffee beans and straightened up.

"Leon is very happy in Palestine. He says it's very hard and hot, and there is no end of work to be done. But he believes firmly in what he's doing. Why don't you go to Palestine too?"

"Dear young lady, do you know how old my wife and I are? *Einen alten Baum verpflanzt man nicht.* – 'You can't replant an old tree'. We were born here and have lived here all our lives. And what would become of my 89-year-old father? If Herr Hitler is getting rid of lunatics and cripples quite shamelessly, what do you think he'll do to an old Jew?"

"Fräulein, the tea is ready. Would you like to come through?"

It was suddenly as if nothing unpleasant had happened; Mrs Gersohn was simply behaving as if an old friend had dropped by. Celia was amazed. It must be that Jewish survival instinct, that ability to carry on as normal in all situations. Like Jewish music, she wondered?

"This will not be the last time," Mr Gersohn prophesied with gloomy resignation. "They'll be back."

Celia made her way straight home, passing her café. The note was still visible in the window. What would happen if she challenged the café owner? Would he call the block warden, or the SA? What if they already knew where she lived? Would they make problems for Francis?

"My God!" thought Celia, "I'm already trapped in their web of fear, suspicion and unwilling collaboration with the Nazis. Evil thrives where good people do nothing. Is not fighting evil as bad as *being* evil?" she wondered. Her head began to ache.

"No, I really want to go." Celia insisted.

"You're mad. You're just asking for trouble. What do you want to prove anyway?"

"Nothing. But I want to go. I need to go. I will go. You don't understand!"

"No! I certainly do not. And this I really won't allow."

Francis shook his head in utter disapproval as she turned to put on her coat. They were arguing over Celia's intention to attend the Saturday morning service at the synagogue in Joachimstaler Straße. The service started at ten, she had to hurry.

"It's not the Jews who keep the Shabbat, but the Shabbat that keeps the Jews," Caleb had said. She knew she had to go.

By the time she arrived, the surroundings appeared calm – there was not a Brownshirt in sight. Busy Saturday traffic hurried past, and people pushed along the pavements to do their shopping before the Christian Sabbath. Jews were streaming into their synagogue; they were still obeying the commandment – which God had given them almost 3,500 years ago – to remember the Shabbat and keep it holy through all their generations.

She felt privileged to have come and went to the women's gallery. There she watched as the men prepared themselves, pronouncing a blessing before wrapping themselves into their tallitot – their prayer shawls – and reciting the day's prayers. Celia wondered what it was like to be under a tallit. She remembered how, as a child, she used to hide behind a curtain when upset. She had thought, "If I can't see them, they can't see me." Did these men also feel that they were hidden from the world? They looked strangely beautiful in their tallitot, a swaying group, a covenant people standing on His ancient promises of deliverance. Once, years before, God had led His people out of bondage. It was now the 20th century; would He save them again?

As a quorum of ten men – a minyan – was now present, the official part of the service could begin even though people continued to arrive until well into the service. The cantor sang magnificently, his baritone voice scaling the most demanding parts of the chants like an opera singer's.

Celia tried to follow the service over the highly distracting background chat of the women, who were very kind in their attempt to draw her into their conversation.

The peace that the congregation had found in the synagogue was only a transient interlude. With the service over, the people had to re-enter the world. Who knew what the rest of the day would hold? Who knew who might not be there for the next Shabbat?

The congregants had been right to feel anxious. On leaving the building they were confronted by a gang of at least two dozen SA men. They were hissing, sneering and shouting abuse. Celia was unaware of this commotion until news of it filtered back into the building. Anxiety and fear accompanied the message and seized the hearts of the gathering. All the words of praise to their God and of mutual encouragement seemed to melt away. Celia was too preoccupied with her own fears to understand that she was reliving a scene from the Torah: one moment she was witnessing and proclaiming God's mighty deeds of power and deliverance; the next she was terrified of the pursuing Egyptians. But this was not Egypt, nor was she leaving it. This was a European capital in a civilised 20th-century country; there would be no mighty miracles and she was not one of the tribes of Israel.

Her instinct for self-preservation urged her to push through the crowd and, if stopped by a Brownshirt, claim immunity from their hatred as a British citizen. She decided to squeeze past the fearful congregation and take stock of the situation outside. The outlook was not good. SA men were now attacking the worshippers physically, grabbing hats, slapping faces, laughing and jeering, pushing, punching. An unfortunate man stumbled over an outstretched leg, and two or three bullyboys began kicking him gleefully. Jewish women and children cried and screamed. A lady was pulled to the ground by her hair. The contents of an old lady's handbag were emptied onto the pavement while mocking eyes peered at her private treasures. Passive German onlookers watched with eyes that did not see and ears that did not hear. Passers-by turned their faces away so as not to have to testify to the brutality being perpetrated in their midst. Celia witnessed this with horror, the events rolling before her eyes in slow motion, a film in which she was a helpless, paralysed extra. And there was no one to stop the film. Celia took her chance and slipped away – slunk away – horrified, petrified and ashamed.

To live with her dishonourable, cowardly act was worse than suffering abuse herself. She returned to the flat, barely able to hold back her tears. In the privacy of her bedroom, the anger and despair over her moral shipwreck found release in a flood of tears. All her high-sounding, valiant and imaginary principles had been crushed by the hand of hard reality. She should have opened her mouth to help and save the people she loved and respected. But instead she had, dumbly and faint-heartedly, retreated and capitulated in the face of personal danger. She felt insignificant, insipid, unfaithful, trite, arrogant and two-faced. She just wanted the ground to open up and swallow her. One moment she had been boldly proclaiming God's greatness, the next, all her paper crowns were lying in the dust. Was her bravery just a figment of her own imagination?

Shivering, she went into the kitchen to make a cup of tea. The British always made tea in times of crisis, she thought numbly. Clasping the hot cup in cold, trembling hands, she returned to her bedroom and wrapped herself in a blanket. Resting against the headboard, her eyes searching the plaster design on the ceiling for inspiration, she tried to take stock of her position.

She felt honestly sorry for the German Jews, and something had to be done for them. No one had a right to treat other human beings like dirt, to humiliate and ridicule them, or traumatise old people, women and children. But what was her role in all this? She was not Jewish; not a single drop of Semitic blood flowed through her veins. She could prove it; her family tree could vouch for it. So why on earth was she taking such a passionate interest in this people? And why did they refuse so obstinately to be assimilated into the world? Was it any wonder they made enemies? And they did not even want her among them. Therefore, at the synagogue, she had carefully concealed the fact that she was not Jewish. To avoid disagreeable comments being made. So why should she stick her neck out for them? Had the Jewish community in Norwich gone out of their way to make her feel welcome? Not at all. And then there was Judaism itself. Everything about it was outlandish: everything about Judaism and being Jewish was far removed from her life and culture; its philosophy and lifestyle were utterly alien to her. That she might aspire to love these strange people and their religion seemed absurd in the cold light of day.

She tried to imagine breaking the news to the family that she was considering converting to Judaism. What an outcry there would be! "One" was British; "one" was Christian; being British meant being Christian. And being British meant upholding one's traditions, standards, values and principles, and rejecting all that was foreign and inferior. Morris dancing and maypoles, Westminster and the Grand National, hunting, shooting and fishing, Christmas and Easter – these were solidly British, Christian even. What had they to do with Passover, Shabbat prayers and keeping kosher? Nothing at all. If Celia were to reject Christianity, she would be rejecting Britain; and if she rejected Britain, she would forever be considered a traitor and a foreigner. But if she believed in the God of the Christians she must reject Torah, and most likely also Israel as the people of God. Could she not believe in God without becoming a Jewess?

Must she pretend to be someone she was not? It was one thing to know God had chosen the Hebrews to be a special people, and she really did believe in God now. But she wrestled terribly with the Judaism attached to this idea. Why could she not demonstrate love and fear of God the Christian way, without having to accept Torah observance? After all, other Christians, such as Mrs Levine and Alistair, seemed to be able to do it all right. But if you loved the one true God, the God of Israel, Caleb said, you must follow His commandments the Jewish way and keep His Shabbats. If you loved Jesus, you kept Jesus' commandments. Caleb believed that. As much as he believed that Jesus was a different God.

Celia knew she lacked the personal courage and religious conviction to take this step into Judaism. She had not grown up on the sour milk of mockery and persecution; rejection and expulsion had not been her daily bread; nor had hatred of the feared Goyim been her bib and tucker. Caleb had warned her; he knew what it meant for a Gentile to join the Jewish people. The thought of Caleb made her cry again. Caleb would never let go of his Judaism, and she knew it was impossible for her to deny her Britishness. This unbreachable cultural and religious barrier must be the "Dividing Wall" Caleb had spoken of when he had first loved her. She now realised that every word he had said was true, and each one pierced her heart.

Francis and Barbara found her in this distressed state when they returned to the flat. He was annoyed, and felt not a little self-righteous about his sister's trouble at the synagogue. She could have avoided it all if only she had followed his sensible advice. And her apparently irrational emotional state was an awkward intrusion into his life and equanimity. All he could do was scold her and bluster: "I warned you, you silly girl. Didn't I tell you to drop this stupid interest in

Judaism? It's pure foolishness – just childish nonsense. And very dangerous."

Eventually, Celia could take his scolding no longer. She fought back, tearfully. "My interest goes much deeper than you think," she blurted out. "It's not just altruistic or religious. Haven't you understood? I'm in love with a Jew."

~ *21* ~

Cecil Court, 1st February 1937

Celia's experiences in Berlin had changed her thinking as radically as Caleb's visit to Palestine had affected him. Her long journey back to England gave her ample time to reflect, and she arrived at Cecil Court physically and emotionally exhausted.

"You don't look well, dear," observed Lady Norah. "Perhaps you should see the doctor. It's probably all that foreign food that's upset you. Didn't Francis look after you?"

"He did, Mummy. And, no, it wasn't the German food. It was all that went with it."

That evening she had a telephone call. A familiar voice was at the other end of the line. "Hello, traveller. How are you?" To hear Caleb's soft, cheerful voice was balm to her soul. Celia closed her eyes and cradled the receiver in her neck. "How was Berlin?"

How was Berlin? "Bad," she said.

There was a moment's pause. "What do you mean?" Then, "Celia, are you all right?"

"Yes, I'm fine. I just can't explain over the telephone."

"Would you like to come to London next weekend?"

Celia closed her eyes. How could she possibly explain to him her fears? And her growing doubts about the future of their relationship? The hurt she could cause him would be immense. She needed time, time to think. "No. I need time to recover from the journey and think."

Another pause. "What if I came to see you?"

"I'm sure Sir Arthur would love your company. Even if it's only for a couple of nights."

Caleb noticed Celia's reservation about coming to see him. "Are you sure you want me to come?"

"Yes, my love, of course I do. I just feel tired. It's been a challenging couple of weeks. I'd really appreciate some rest here in the country."

For the time being Caleb would have to be content with what he considered an evasive explanation.

Next morning, after a late breakfast, Celia put on her riding gear. The soft leather against her ankles was a sensuous and welcome return to normality. Striding into the yard revived her further – the soothing sounds of a stable routine, the grooms greeting her respectfully – and affirmed her sense of being home again. Twenty minutes later she was galloping across the wintry fields, delighting in the familiar jumps. She crossed shallow, sparkling streams and waded through snowdrop-carpeted woodlands. Soon daffodils and blue-bells would fill the air with the warm scents of spring. Celia dismounted on a knoll overlooking Sir Arthur's estate and looked around with deep satisfaction. She breathed in the landscape that spread out before her, embracing all she called Home. She felt love and tender kinship rising in her towards this tiny spot of land, irrelevant to the outside world, yet pulsing within her life's blood. Her intense attachment to this little piece of England suddenly over-whelmed her. She picked up a lump of soil, rubbed it between her fingers and smelled its rich fragrance. "Home," she sighed.

After sharing her thoughts on Germany with Sir Arthur over lunch, Celia returned to Cecil Court. She badly needed to catch up on some long-overdue correspondence. As she walked down the portrait-hemmed corridor to her bedroom, her eyes lighted on Lady Anne. Celia looked at her serene face, into the calm eyes of someone who had given her life for her beliefs. She had held to her Protestant faith, despite her husband's reversion to Catholicism, and had been burned at the stake in 1558 by Bloody Mary. Now, nearly four hundred years later, a descendent of Lady Anne was again troubled by religious deliberations. But there were important differences: Celia was still very unclear about her beliefs and was not facing a life or death choice. Lady Anne had given her life to resist submission to the Church of Rome's authority and teaching, and had died honourably, as an English Protestant martyr. No one would ever doubt her Englishness. She might be a traitor to the Crown of her day – that was open to debate – but at least she was an English traitor. Jews saw things differently: if you professed that Jesus was the Messiah you became a Christian and a citizen of your host country. You ceased to be a Jew. Celia began to understand Caleb's predicament; why his Jewishness meant everything to him. When he had hinted at the struggles that lay ahead, she now realised, he was not just pointing to the political powers of this world. There were also spiritual powers hidden within each one of us – controlling, resilient, unseen forces binding us to our native cultures. Dark Valkyrian forces battled against the righteous demands of God, opposing them as alien and dangerous abuses of trad- itional Gentile lifestyles.

Caleb was also facing new challenges. The first Shabbat with his large Orthodox family had made a deep impression on him. How he had loved his time with them, talking Jew to Jew, not having to constantly justify himself and watch his back for hidden Christian daggers. He had sat amongst his family, his *mishpochah*, laughing, arguing, without worrying about treading on sensitive English toes. He felt like a thirsty traveller who had reached an oasis at last. Aunt Blimcha's *cholent*, a uniquely Jewish stew, was still the best, and he still disliked *gefilte fish*. Uncle Shimon made sure that news of the prodigal's return spread in the community and, wherever Caleb went, he was welcomed with open arms. He had to admit he was enjoying it, his heart rejoicing to be with the people he had missed so bitterly. But he also knew he would have to make serious commitments before returning to Orthodoxy. It would mean giving up Celia. And did he really want to bind himself to a stern religious lifestyle again? He was undecided. He was the descendant of two worlds: his father's strictly observant, close-knit family and community had made him feel accepted, Jewish and safe, while his mother's religiously liberal background had opened doors to opportunity and freedom.

His heart and mind blew hot and cold as he visited his relatives. Occasionally Caleb would be found discussing spiritual matters with uncles and cousins until late into a Friday evening. But, while he enjoyed the intellectual stimulation, he often questioned the value of what he was told. Uncle Moishe addressed only the "how to do" of Judaism, but never "how to be" a Jewish person – a weakness his parents loved to point out. He sometimes wondered if his father, for all his many errors, did not have more practical, honest-to-God wisdom about the day-to-day issues of righteous living than learned Rabbinic sages. Admittedly, there were many gems of wisdom in the great books of Judaism, but Caleb had to admit there was also much that left him unsatisfied. And he was irritated by the balloons of hot air expended in sincere, but utterly futile and fruitless, argument. He understood the arguments for and against Orthodox Judaism and knew he was being given time to feel his way back into the community. But he also knew the Rabbi would soon expect him to make a firm decision. Caleb was not looking forward to this interview.

Celia met Caleb at the station and took him straight to Bleckham Manor. She still did not know how to share what was happening in her since Berlin, or how to explain her doubts that they could ever share a future together. Caleb suspected none of this and guessed her quietness was due to the late hour and her tiredness.

The next morning, on the stroke of eight, Celia walked through the doors to the very breakfast room where Caleb had first seen her. The shadow of preoccupation he had seen the night before was still hovering over her, and Caleb vowed to do his best to cheer her up. They went on a hack, but Celia did not dare touch on the matters that were burdening her. Instead, she carefully kept their conversation light and superficial, their last tender encounter now appearing illusory and far away. She was quite unable to reconcile her feelings for Caleb and the fears provoked by the brutal reality of her German experiences.

Thick and dark, winter storm clouds began to push in fast, taking them by surprise. "That don't look good, that do," Celia said in a poor imitation of the local dialect. "I know a nearby barn where we can shelter."

The first large raindrops thundered down and she spurred Foxtrot into a fast canter. As soon as they reached the barn, they flung open the doors and pulled the horses in. Having secured the reins, they sat down on a thin layer of hay and watched the floodgates of heaven open before them. For a while they listened to the sound of the gushing rain.

Caleb, who lay propped on his elbows beside her, was silent. Celia felt him looking at her and turned to him with the mischievous smile that always melted his heart. He felt it was now or never. "Celia, may I kiss you?"

"Of course you may," she teased.

"I mean, as a man kisses a woman . . ."

Though not quite sure where this might lead her, she surrendered her lips to his. A bit shyly at first, he began to take from the sweetness of her mouth with increasing intensity. What joy to be wanted, what joy to give, what joy to receive!

Celia's anxieties dissolved and she was again entirely filled with his beloved presence. Her whole being yearned to be one with him. And he knew she was all he needed to make him complete, as it had been ordained from the beginning of time. She sought his face, his mouth, the very essence of his soul. In her awakening passion she would willingly have given herself completely to Caleb had he asked her. Instead – to her utter confusion and shock – he suddenly jumped up and rushed outside. He left behind in the hay a thoroughly bewildered and hurt Celia, at a loss to explain his abrupt and inconsiderate action.

Through the half-open barn doors, she watched him standing in the rain, head hanging, fists clenched, drenched and cold. It suddenly occurred to her that she must have appeared a very easy and cheap woman. Tears of guilt and shame filled her eyes, and she hid her face with her hands. Caleb returned to her and took her in his arms, asking gently and without the slightest reproach, "Celia, do you know how it is between a man and a woman?"

Celia understood what he was asking and her ignorance and naïveté brought a deep blush to her cheeks. No, she did not know, not really, about the way it was between a man and a woman. Nothing, that is, that went beyond the common farmyard knowledge she had about horses, chicken, frogs and cats. Sir Arthur had looked after her well and ensured that she knew no more about "the birds and the bees" than befitted a young lady of her upbringing. She shook her head, not daring to look at the young man. Caleb wondered for a moment whether it might be appropriate for him to explain it to her . . . In the end, he suggested she talk to a trusted girl friend.

Once in her room, Celia tried to come to terms with what had happened in the barn. Deeply unsettled, she dressed carelessly for lunch. Catching sight of herself in the mirror, she stopped and stared at her reflection. Something major had happened today: she was no longer a little girl. She was moving irretrievably towards womanhood, and was afraid. In many ways she liked being a little girl: she had no real burdens, responsibilities or accountability. But she also lacked power, power to control her own life and choose her own path. She was sure Caleb would propose before long, and knew she could make him a very happy man – or deny him that joy. But to become a wife? Nothing could have been further from her thoughts until he had stolen her heart. Now she must talk to him. Soon. She thought of her serene and martyred ancestor; yes, Lady Anne would help her say what she had to say.

Celia's parents had gone out for the day, so she telephoned to ask Caleb over to Cecil Court after lunch. When he arrived, she suggested a visit to the portrait gallery. "I'd like to introduce you to someone."

Having kindled his curiosity, she led him through the long corridor lined with darkening portraits. "Where are you leading me? To the White Woman, your residential ghost?" Caleb grinned.

His guide stopped in front of one of the many paintings. "This is Lady Anne. She's my favourite ancestor."

"She looks very serene. Why's she your favourite?"

"Surprising, isn't it? This portrait was painted shortly before she was delivered into the hands of her enemies by her husband. Then she was burnt at the stake for heresy."

"Ah! So you've got heroes of religion in your family as well. We've got quite a galaxy of those: crucified by the Romans, slaughtered by the Crusaders, tortured by the Inquisition, burnt by the Catholics and mutilated by the Cossacks." Caleb counted the events on his fingers. "And goodness knows what else we have yet to experience."

Celia looked offended by Caleb's cynical comment, so he added, apologetically, "I'm sorry. You're just not used to being persecuted."

This was the opening she had been waiting for. "Yes, Caleb, you're right: I'm not used to it. That's precisely my point. Lady Anne died for her convictions. Her faith was strong. Mine isn't – if I have any at all, that is. I'm a coward, Caleb. That's the truth." And now Celia poured out all that had been weighing down her spirit since her return from Germany.

Caleb listened in silence. When she had finished he asked, sombrely, "So, what are you really saying?"

"I don't know what I'm saying. I love you and I don't want to lose you. But I can't pretend to be someone I'm not, or claim to believe in something I don't. Not even for you. I just can't go through the anguish of leaving everything behind and becoming Jewish, let alone be persecuted and slaughtered for it," she confessed, overwrought.

"I know, I know. I know every ache you are feeling, and have known every shade of it since I first loved you. I knew that I'd bring you only pain. Please forgive me for my self-ishness." He took hold of her as if he could shelter her from his own onslaught of doubt. Should he release her and end their relationship? Should he make it easier for her by playing the cad and walking out on her now? He took one look at her and knew he could not do it – they were in this together; they would have to play out their duet to the end.

That evening, Celia decided to present her parents with a *fait accompli*. She told the butler that there would be two guests for dinner – Sir Arthur and Mr Levine – but neglected to mention this fact to her mother or father. They would either swallow hard and make the most of Caleb's unwelcome presence, or insist he leave and suffer the indignity of making a scene in front of Sir Arthur. Her plot was only discovered five minutes before her guests arrived. When Lady Norah asked why there were covers for five instead of three on the table, Celia told her the truth. "Caleb Levine is visiting Bleckham Manor, and I thought it would be nice to invite Sir Arthur and him for dinner."

"'Nice'? It most certainly won't be 'nice'. How many times have I told you, that person is not to cross our threshold? How dare you conspire with the servants behind my back. Henry, for goodness' sake, say something."

The Earl of Besthorpe hesitated. The whole world was treacherous and wicked, so what difference could one more Jew make? He just wanted to be left in peace. And, he thought, Purley was a snob and an idiot who had often enough deliberately tried to make him look a fool at the club. So why not welcome someone who had put Purley's nose out of joint? Even better, it would rile Norah.

In the end they had a polite, non-confrontational evening, much to Celia's surprise, except that Lady Norah sulked and hardly said a word. That she was dining with the man who would shortly be asking for her daughter's hand in marriage did not even cross her mind. The Jew was so far removed from her world that the idea was utterly preposterous.

~ 22 ~

London, April 1937

Although Celia was very open and honest about her fears, Caleb continued to trust in their future together. He hoped she would come to terms with her worries about living as a Jew. He knew she was a brave girl. She had to be. She had greater reserves of strength and faith than she knew. Yes, it was true; there was a frightening chasm between her perception of her courage and the dangers she saw. But he was trusting in God and the overcoming power of love to bridge that gap.

There was also the problem of his steadily growing involvement in Zionism and all that that implied for them. Celia's report from Berlin stressed the urgency of the situation. And there was also Uncle Moishe, who was still waiting for his decision. How would he react to the idea of him marrying a Goyah? Caleb didn't want to think about it.

Everything was coming to a head at the same time. He called at his parents' and found his mother deeply upset. An old school friend had just written asking her not to write in future. She explained that her son had been promoted to the rank of Colonel in the Wehrmacht. He had been posted to army headquarters in Berlin as a staff officer. It was obvious that this now made it impossible for her to maintain any connection with Jewish individuals. Gertrud was so sensitive; she would understand. "Even as I write," she wrote, "I cannot be sure that this letter will not cause me or my family any problems. I am truly sorry. Yours lovingly, E. von J."

"I just can't understand it, Cal," his mother cried. "She was my best friend; we were like sisters. We went to school together and I visited their home many times. How can she call off a friendship that's lasted a lifetime?"

"Mama, I'm sure it was very difficult for her to write that letter. Maybe even dangerous. But she wanted to take that risk so that you would understand the position she's in. You can see clearly, if you read between the lines, that she doesn't want to end your friendship permanently. We can't imagine what it's like for her in Germany at the moment. And I'm sure you'll be able to pick up where you left off as soon as the Nazis fall from power." Caleb was being positive for his mother's sake. But he felt sure he was lying.

"Well, what do you make of this then, Cal? It came in the same post." The professor handed his son a second letter. It bore the same distasteful profile of Adolf Hitler on the stamp. With a grim expression, Caleb scanned its contents. Dr Zink, a doctor in Berlin and a good friend, was asking his parents if they would let his three grandchildren come and live with them in London. He was quite blunt about it. He was becoming very concerned for their safety. "Every day they are having more and more problems at school. We could send them to one of the new Jewish schools that are springing up everywhere, but . . ." he wrote, "Personally, I don't think we Jews have any future here under the Nazis."

Caleb shrugged. "So his grandchildren have been bullied and beaten up, and the teachers did nothing about it. What's new about that?"

Gertrud saw it very differently, and said so. "This is not the wild East End. Or a sadistic English public school, for that matter. His grandchildren go to one of the most prestigious state grammar schools, in one of the most refined and civilised suburbs of Berlin. That does worry me." She spoke with emphasis.

Caleb smiled. "Have you decided what answer you'll give Dr Zink?" It was obvious to him that his mother had already made up her mind.

"We'll have them, of course. Judy will be getting married soon and leaving us. We could do with a bit more young blood around us. It won't be for long, after all."

"In the end, we never really manage to wash off our Jewishness," Caleb thought. Not even in a Christian baptismal font.

These developments helped show him the way ahead. He asked for an appointment with Uncle Moishe, which was granted at short notice and with great joy. He found himself, once again, standing in his grandfather's office. Caleb looked round the familiar room with fondness. Its curtain-subdued light protected the precious volumes arranged carefully on the shelves lining the walls from floor to ceiling. Rabbi Uncle Moishe Levine was sitting behind a massive desk. Two dark-clad and respected elders of the community were standing sentinel behind him.

The Rabbi opened the interview. "I'm glad you have come to see me. We've much to talk about. I thought it right to leave you to make the first move." His dark eyes looked at the young man, firmly but kindly, from his large, black-bearded face.

Caleb sat down. He took a deep breath. "Uncle Moishe, I'm afraid there are two remaining issues I'd like to discuss with you. I understand that they may well prevent my return to Orthodoxy. But I hope we can resolve them."

The Rabbi did not flinch at the disappointing news. "What are they?"

"Well, first – no, there is no first, really. They are both equally important."

"Are they more important than the study of Torah?"

Caleb continued, ignoring his uncle's comment. "First,

there is a young non-Jewish woman in my life. I intend to marry her."

His words crashed like thunderbolts through the room. The elders both inhaled sharply but the Rabbi's raised hand held their tongues in check. He had enough self-discipline to hide any reaction to Caleb's shocking words. He felt sure this desire to marry out was no more than the foolishness of a young and deceived man. He had spent too many years with the Goyim; this had obviously corrupted his understanding and observance. But this could be corrected in time. There was no fault that intensive Torah and Talmud study could not wash away.

"And, secondly, I believe fervently in the establishment of a Jewish national home in Palestine."

"You already know this will not happen until the Messiah comes. Zionism is nothing more than a misguided work of man, wilful and unholy. Men cannot force the hand of God." Uncle Moishe spoke with calm authority. Then followed a moment's pause while he considered how best to respond to Caleb's first point. "This woman you mentioned: don't you think that any daughter of Israel is better than the best of the Gentiles?" He was pleading, softly, teasingly. Emotions were involved; they could cause problems if confronted too abruptly.

Caleb sighed, despite himself. He was relieved he had not been excommunicated on the spot. But he knew that, whether now or later, this would be the inevitable consequence of his decision.

"I believe that she is my soul mate, Uncle Moishe, strange as that may sound to you. We know that there are many challenges and trials ahead of us, and much love and patience will be required to overcome them. But it says in the Talmud – in the Midrash from Genesis Rabba 39:21 – that 'anyone who draws a Gentile close to Judaism and converts him is equivalent to having created him.'"

The Rabbi was unmoved. "It speaks about *converting* them. Not marrying them."

"But there are many examples in the Torah of Gentile women who converted and married Jews: Ruth, Rahab, Zipporah . . ."

"Yes, but let her convert first. Then you can think about marrying her. You know as well as I do that she will never be one of us really. And . . ."

"And why not? Did not the great Rambam chide a teacher of Israel for treating a Gentile proselyte as inferior to a Jew?"

"Their uncleanness will never wash off, not in all the ritual immersion baths of Israel. A Goy is a Goy. You know that, Calvele." The Rabbi was pleading, his arms out-stretched. "You're of my own family. Why defile yourself? Look, now: we'll find a beautiful and pure Jewish girl for you, one who will make you very happy and give you many good sons and daughters." Uncle Moishe was arguing out of sincere affection. He was not going to give up on Caleb: a Jew's life was at stake – a Jewish relative's life, moreover.

"But I love Celia." Caleb leant forward in his chair and looked intently at the Rabbi. "Uncle, don't you know what love is?"

The Rabbi's tender, pleading tone changed. "Love is keeping Torah. Don't get confused. All the rest is emotion. Emotions are a bad counsellor, Caleb."

"But if you've never experienced love, how can you care for those God loves? If we Jews don't demonstrate the love of God for men, who else will? There are millions of desperate Gentiles out there in the dark. Aren't we meant to be God's light to them? Isn't that Israel's calling and our task?"

"You're talking like a *meshumad*, an apostate. And you're deliberately trying to change the subject."

"No, I'm not. I love her and I want to see her in the fold of Israel," Caleb maintained stubbornly.

"Then bring her here and let her convert first. When she's well and truly in the fold, then you can marry her."

"I don't want to wait for years. And I don't want her to convert because she feels she must in order to marry me. That's against Rabbinic teaching anyway."

"That's very true," conceded the Rabbi. "But if you choose to obey one command, you must obey all the others as well. And they all make it overwhelmingly clear that a Jew cannot marry a Gentile."

"Not completely. Torah says a Jew may marry a female captive. It does not say she must convert first."

"Don't be ridiculous. We're not at war."

"No, but I have conquered her heart."

The Rabbi relented a little. Despite his evident foolishness and immaturity, he liked the way his nephew was trying to argue his case. Like a true Jew. "I see you have considered the issue a little. But not enough. A little knowledge is dangerous. You're not authorised to make Halachah. You have to submit to the decisions of the religious courts. King Solomon was led astray by foreign wives."

"He was led astray by his own lust and disobedience."

"Are you better than Solomon?"

Caleb did not answer. It was pointless. Even if Celia converted 50 times, she would always be considered an outsider by Orthodox Jews. The wall of partition between Jew and Gentile was still firmly in place in the 20th century; the present was still in the past. Once his father had stood here and pleaded with his grandfather to accept and bless the bride of his own choice. She may have been ill prepared for the ways of the family she was joining, but at least she was Jewish. Celia was not even that. Now it was Caleb's turn. And the wall was as high and strong as ever.

The Rabbi used another powerful argument, his trump card. "And, of course, you know your children will never be

Jewish." He was convinced it was the winning argument, that Caleb would now capitulate.

But he had misjudged him. Caleb was furious and slammed the flat of his hand down on the desk. "Torah never says that! God's concern is that a Jew must be circumcised and observe Torah. If the son of a Jewish father and a Gentile mother is circumcised and observant, who can deny him the right to call himself a Jew? Answer me that, Rabbi! Or do you have a monopoly on deciding who is a Jew? I know I'm a Jew, whatever my parents are, whatever you say. Yet I'm still expected to become a *t'shuv*."

The Rabbi was also losing his composure. "If we all thought like you we'd end up in spiritual anarchy. And who are you – in your ignorance and arrogance – to judge the wisdom and rulings of the Sages, let alone Torah?"

Caleb knew he was getting nowhere but refused to give up the fight. "Why do you have to make conversion so damned difficult? Why do you make commands and excuses to prevent Gentiles from joining Israel? What would you lose by just making a sincere Gentile feel welcomed, accepted and an integral part of the Jewish community? You make him a proselyte and tell him he must keep the same endless minute observances you keep. Yet you still refuse to accept him as a true brother."

"Why do we make it so hard for Gentiles to convert? Because of the dangers of assimilation and the resultant annihilation of our people – through the neglect of Torah, Talmud and the Traditions. They don't seem to mean anything to you any longer."

"Which leads me to my second point," Caleb continued. "In the Diaspora we will always struggle to survive in the face of persecution and assimilation. We're treated as unwanted vermin and will always be at the mercy of our host nations. The only place where a Jew is guaranteed a haven is in an internationally recognised national home in Palestine. That's why we must all pursue the Zionist ideal: the rebirth of our homeland, maybe even independence and self-government, to be a free people in our own Land – Eretz Yisrael. We all need a place where we can keep the commandments of Adonai under a Jewish Government . . ."

Uncle Moishe cut across Caleb's political outpourings. "I know you're a Zionist, but your arguments are based on a false interpretation of the Prophets. Zionism may be very popular at the moment, but it's also very wrong. So even on this point we hold diametrically opposed views."

"So you're against the Zionist cause. I knew as much." Very many Orthodox Jews sincerely shared Uncle Moishe's convictions. But failing to support Zionism's aims was, as far as Caleb was concerned, both incomprehensible and reprehensible. He felt sure he had now come to the end of his interview. He took a deep breath. This was the end. "I knew we'd fail to agree on the two most important areas of my life. Our views are too divergent. You must now understand that it is impossible for me to commit myself to Orthodox Judaism. I'm so very sorry, Uncle Moishe." Caleb did not say these words lightly; he knew the writing was now on the wall for him.

"I'd forgive you for your Zionist sympathies, but I cannot forgive you for being so determined to marry out." The Rabbi was entering the last act of the drama.

"I know that."

"Are you really prepared to turn your back on your people? Think about the consequences. One day you will bitterly regret what you are about to do." The Rabbi's voice was steely cold.

"I'm not renouncing my roots by supporting Zionism. On the contrary, I'm planting them. And I know the consequences of my choice of wife. Have you forgotten that I've already lived half my life outside the Jewish community? I know what I'm doing."

The Rabbi's face turned to stone. "Then we can have no more dealings with each other. This is my final word."

Caleb rose and said "Shalom" to the three men. They made no reply. He walked to the door slowly, his head lowered. With the doorknob in his hand, he hesitated. Then he turned to them and said quietly, "I am Caleb Ben-Yitzchak. I shall be mourned by that name."

His grandmother was waiting expectantly for him in the hall "Well?" she asked, bright-eyed with hope. Her smile died as she looked into his tense face.

"I shall not be coming again, *Bubba*. Forgive me for having aroused false hopes in you all. My path is not leading me here. But I still love you all." Caleb bent down, embraced his Bubba and gave her a kiss. Chaya Levine was stunned; big tears filled her eyes and ran down her cheeks. The old lady had known so little happiness in her life and all he had done was to rekindle old sorrows. Would he ever forgive himself for this? He let go of the heartbroken old woman and hurried away. Once outside, he pulled his hat down over his face to hide his tears. "But," he thought, "this excommunication is different from the last. This time I have made my choice; I'm not just an innocent victim."

Rabbi Moishe Levine and the elders rent their clothes. And Chaya Levine bewailed the loss of a grandson.

It took Caleb until late June to recover fully from this painful experience. But the smarting sore of so many years had at last been cleaned and was now healing. He had mentioned only briefly to Celia what had been said at the Rabbi's office. Sensing the hurt and upset it had caused him, she did not press him for details.

Throughout his time of searching, Celia had been afraid that Caleb might want to return to his Jewish family after all. However, she had vowed not to influence him, and any decision on this matter had to come from him, and him alone.

Now another hurdle had been taken successfully. Celia could not deny that there were times when she felt stretched to snapping point by the strain this complicated relationship put on her. Religion, politics and lifestyle were such an intrinsic part of Caleb's life and nature that she found it hard to keep up with him.

After his short stay at the welcoming inn of his Orthodox family, the wandering Jew was on the road again, his eyes on the far horizon. He now knew where he was heading, and marched resolutely towards his goal. He would dedicate his life to the Zionist vision: to freeing his people, once and for always, from bondage, persecution and fear. Despite the sadness he had felt, the break with his Orthodox roots was liberating. And mounting anti-Semitism in Europe fired his Zionist zeal. In the light of the international situation, Caleb knew that practical help was more pressing than hair-splitting Talmudic niceties.

Caleb found himself being drawn into a growing friendship with Daniel and Sarah'le Glicksman. He had met the couple at a Jewish Agency meeting and there was an instant rapport between them. Dani had been an active Zionist for over 30 years. He had lived in Palestine twice; once as a young man, then later after he had got married. He had tried to make a living there but malaria had nearly killed him. In the end, he had been forced to leave his heart in Palestine and return to England. Although he suffered from the disease to this day, his vision was as sharp and clear as ever. Caleb quickly grew to love him. He admired his alert mind, common sense, wit and gracious heart. Dani was as enthusiastic about Zionism as Leon but, unlike Leon who had rejected God, Dani read the Tanach every day. He had found that he needed the Bible to keep up his strength and hope in the face of pressing world events.

"Do you think we should encourage Gentiles to join Judaism?" Caleb asked him one evening.

"Judaism is not a missionary religion, but . . . why not? We worship the One and Only God, so He must be the God of the Gentiles too. The Almighty made us all, after all. But they'd have to follow Him in the same way He has commanded us. Kind of 'Torah for the Gentiles'. Can you imagine it: the whole world practising Judaism? Now that's an idea to fight anti-Semitism with." Dani chuckled at the thought. "But for it to work, we first have to overcome our own religious arrogance. Our attitude towards the Gentiles must be one of humanity, of moral courage, and mutual tolerance and mercy – not rejection. They aren't perfect, but are we? Indeed, their hostility towards us is all the more reason for showing mercy and humanity towards them. I'm quoting AD Gordon here: to Him I hold; everything else is interpretation." He chuckled at his own deliberate twisting of the Rabbinic maxim.

"What would you say if Ben or Joshua wished to marry out?"

Dani looked hard at Caleb. "I'd discourage it, of course."

"But you just said . . ."

"Well, that's the difference between theory and practice. I said I'd discourage it, not forbid it. Love and life always find a way. Love always elevates; it never tears down. If a Jew loves a Goy, they'll become equals. And, seeing that Judaism is the only true religion, I think it would be more correct to say that the Goy is 'marrying in', rather than the Jew is 'marrying out'. While I'm opposed to the idea of mixed marriages, I'm not fanatical enough to break with my children over it. But it would take a pretty remarkable kind of person to put up with us lot. The chance of finding anyone like that in England is pretty remote, don't you think?" Dani laughed.

Caleb didn't. "I want to marry a Goyah, Dani."

The news hit Dani like a bombshell. For a long moment the veteran paced his small back room considering what counsel to give. Calvele was a man after his own heart. He was like himself at the same age. Cal would go far. But to take a Goyah as your wife? What a waste. He eyed Caleb up and down, then looked him straight in the eye.

"Are you sure she's meant for you, Cal? I mean, how could she possibly be?" Dani turned up his palms and shrugged. "If she's not Jewish, she doesn't know our ways, our traditions. She's got no idea what it means to be set apart as God's people. I've got nothing against Gentiles – some of my best friends are Gentiles. But Calvele, think: how will it be for her? Jewry . . . Judaism . . . Zionism . . . life in Palestine . . . all that. How will she be able to adapt and fit in?"

"I've made my decision. After much thought, and in the face of opposition and sacrifice, I intend to propose to her as soon as I can." Caleb was unwavering and entirely sincere in his intention.

It was not Caleb's fault that he got seriously embroiled in a clash with the black-shirted Mosleyites the next day. When a gang of them started to push around an old Jewish couple, he felt compelled to support his street-fighting brothers. They had to show these young fascist thugs that British Jewry was a force to be reckoned with. Here, in England, Jews were not going to submit meekly to bullying; here, the Blackshirts would meet an iron resistance. Caleb took their blows without flinching, and returned them with interest. Until the mounted police arrived. Now Caleb wore his campaign medals with pride: a black eye, stitches above the brow, a cut lip, and two cracked ribs. Too battered to attend court along-side his friends and enemies, he was granted bail. With this unexpected free time on his hands he decided to pay his parents a surprise visit. Celia chose to call on them unan-nounced at the same time. It was to be a fateful encounter.

She had just taken off her coat and gone through to the drawing room when the doorbell rang again. It was Caleb. When he came through and saw her, he beamed through his painful disfigurement. Celia was shocked and horrified.

"Caleb! What on earth has happened to you? When did you get hurt?"

Caleb felt proud, a bit like a little boy caught fighting off bullies. He ignored her question at first. "You didn't tell me you'd be in London. What a wonderful surprise. You've certainly brightened my miserable day." He shuffled and felt his tender face. "I'm sorry. I had a bit of a brush with the Mosleyites. They were trying to frighten some elderly Jews again."

"You see what I have to put up with, Celia?" teased Mrs Levine, to mask her own worries.

Transfixed, Celia stared at Caleb. The beaten and humiliated Jews of Berlin flashed before her. This is what it really means to be a Jew, she thought. Anti-Semitism was an omnipresent and uncontrollable living reality, lurking just beneath the surface of every supposedly civilised society. Yes, I do see what you have to put up with, Mrs Levine. But do I want to live a life of fear and intimidation, beatings and humiliation? However hard I try, I cannot come to terms with it. Celia plunged from the breathless cliff top of love and dashed out her heart on the rocks of fear and evil far below. She shook her head, fiercely: no!

"I apologise, but I have to go."

"But you've only just arrived, my dear . . ."

Understanding exactly what was happening, Mrs Levine tried to save the situation. Celia grabbed her gloves and handbag and rushed from the room. Caleb followed and caught up with her in the hall. Panic-stricken, she was struggling to put on her coat.

"Celia, listen . . ."

"No! It's of no use! I tried to tell you when you came to

Cecil Court, but you – love – wouldn't let me speak my mind. Then I began to hope again. I wanted everything to work out all right. But looking at you now . . . like this . . . No, Caleb, I can't live like this all my life. I refuse to live like this, fearing for you every single day, not knowing if you will come home well or half dead – or even come home at all. I'm not a Jew. Don't you understand? I'm English. I'm a Lancaster. As hard as we might try, the cracks would soon show. I'd just make you unhappy and keep you from what you treasure most. I came here today desperately needing a sign, something to tell me what I should do. That sign has now been given. I can't pretend it hasn't."

It was not Celia who was speaking any more; it was some other, stronger, person inside her. It was a different Celia who was resolutely refusing to let the inner Celia, whose heart was being torn apart at this moment, speak her mind.

"So it's all over. Is that what you are saying?" Caleb's words sounded muffled in his ears. A decision he had hoped he would never have to make had been thrust upon him. Here. Now. He believed in fighting for what he wanted, taking on a visible enemy and beating him into submission. But now he suddenly found his own Jewishness had turned on him and was fighting against the Celia he loved. She was a Goyah: there was nothing he could do about it. Helplessly he found himself standing back and watching the Jew in him accept the destruction of the love between them. He just waited, passive and broken. He knew he was waiting for the whiplash to fall across his resigned and bent Jewish back.

"Yes. That's what I'm saying."

Caleb did not protest against her decision; he did not say a word. Instead he kept his promise of long ago. He opened the door and let her walk free.

He stood on the top step outside and watched her walk down the street until she turned the corner. She did not even look back once. His eyes stayed riveted, locked to the spot where he had last glimpsed her. He was frozen in pain and disbelief, lost.

Only then did his mother come looking for her child. She found him still clutching the doorframe, his knuckles white with tension. "Are you all right, Cal?" she enquired anxiously.

"I will be," he said. He let his hand drop. Then he closed the door.

Later, in his flat, his eyes rested on the two Shabbat candles and the pot of soil from Palestine. He thought bitterly that the Almighty must be smirking triumphantly, reminding him that the covenant was eternal and that He was not letting him go. Caleb was still a slave, a slave to the God of Israel. In a burst of impotent rage, he swept the mantelpiece clear. Then he dropped to his knees and wept till he had no more tears to cry.

And someone else was weeping, at the same moment, in the seclusion of her room. Her strength gone, Celia had slid to the floor, her back against the locked door. She wished herself dead. It was over. The Jew and the Gentile could never live together, but the Gentile did not know how she could ever live without the Jew. Why had she ever allowed herself to love and to hope? Had she still not learned that loving and hoping always led to bitter regrets? She was obviously not meant to love and be loved.

She spent the whole afternoon shut in her room upstairs. At dinner, Lady Agatha enquired after her health. She thought Celia did not look well. Celia picked at her food until she found the strength to answer. "I'm fine, thank you."

"Have you had a disagreement with Caleb?"

Celia put down her knife and fork and arranged them neatly on her plate. She spoke very formally and slowly and in a very little voice. "I gave my heart to a very noble and worthy man. But I now see that I made a mistake: the present situation makes any continuation of our relationship utterly impossible. I have decided that it is better for us not to see each other any more. This has been a very painful decision for me. I would prefer not to talk about it, if you don't mind."

The following morning, Celia left for Marsham. From there she planned to visit an old school friend in Devon and stay with her for the summer.

~ 23 ~

Campania, Italy, late September 1937

The sand was soft, the sky deep blue, and the waves lapped idly in the late-afternoon breeze. Celia stretched out on a bath towel and her toes flicked sand over her back. Her thoughts meandered through the universe, stopping at no fixed place, drifting. But they always returned to the same fixed point: Caleb. Sebastian appeared and reminded her she needed to change for dinner. She sighed and reined in her thoughts.

Her summer holiday in Exeter had not brought the distraction she had hoped for, or the peace and clarity of mind. Celia had returned to Norfolk, unsatisfied and empty, to find Sebastian waiting for her at Cecil Court. He was delighted to see her, and the sight of him did her good. She was grateful for his attention.

"Sir Arthur has been complaining that Bleckham Manor is falling apart without you. And that Foxtrot is pining for his mistress. And, as for me, well I've been suffering along with him . . ."

Celia laughed. "You? Without a lady friend? Is that possible?"

"I'm serious, Ciel," Sebastian had replied.

And things had developed from there. Sebastian became a frequent visitor at Cecil Court again – much to Lady Norah's delight – and life became easy and pleasant for Celia. "For the first time ever," she thought.

Sebastian was nice and uncomplicated and never caused any hurt or embarrassment. She was flattered by his attentions and started to enjoy being seen with him. This added greatly to the credit balance of her social account. Of course. People who had ignored her previously, now underwent an amazing change of heart. Naturally. And Celia allowed herself, gradually and passively, to be sucked into social circles she had avoided before. Why not? Her mother became kind to her and almost likable, and would advise her with enthusiasm on what dresses and jewellery to wear. Celia acquiesced and complied; it bought peace and quiet at home. Even the Duchess of Garnbrook discovered she had hidden talents. Who dared question the choice of someone as distinguished and accomplished as the young Viscount Holsworth-Leigh? Celia adapted to her new lifestyle, caught in the web of Sebastian's attentions and inoffensive amiability. And, smiling quietly, she died a little each day. His charm and gentlemanly flatteries appealed to, and affirmed, her femininity. He made her feel valued and important as she nursed her still-bruised spirit back to health. He knew how to nurture her womanly needs and she became increasingly dependent on him. Everyone was delighted with the change in her and she grew brighter and busier; her days of rustic quiet a thing of the past. Only Sir Arthur sighed for his lost Celia and imagined he could hear Foxtrot crying, abandoned in his paddock.

And now they were in Italy, accompanied and chaperoned by two elderly aunts from Sebastian's large family. Florence, Pisa, and Rome were already behind them, and lazy days on the hot beaches of Campania stretched to the horizon. Sebastian dined in the best restaurants that catered to English palates, and she sparkled at his side like champagne. Sebastian was much sought after by the expatriate English community, and she rested lightly and beautifully on his arm at soirées. Sebastian, who spoke no Italian, enjoyed the prearranged Cook's Tours excursions, and she and a crowd accompanied him. Sebastian loved archaeological sites, museums and churches, and she showed a dutiful interest in the things that appealed to him. But she knew that Caleb had been to Italy and, in her heart, she wished he was with her instead of Sebastian. Caleb would have brought life and colour to the cities and countryside. Caleb could get by on broken Italian and they would have wandered freely. Caleb knew how to make the most of the simple little bistros where the locals ate and drank and sang and loved. Wherever Celia went, Caleb's face and voice went with her.

Gradually his haunting presence became more real to her than the flesh-and-blood Sebastian by her side. But, despite the scream of warning bells in her heart, when Sebastian proposed to her in Venice in mid-March 1938, Celia accepted him, passively. She telegraphed the news home and Lady Norah replied, ecstatically. Celia knew her mother's heart: the long battle was won, the Lancaster estate was now financially secure. Now she could, at long last, focus all her energy on climbing the giddy social ladder again.

Caleb learned of the engagement through the announcement in *The Times*. Then he met Celia briefly in London at some tiresome official function. She had changed so much that he had to look twice before he recognised her. He spotted her wearing what he considered a skimpy, high-fashion dress, her head crowned with a hideous hat. He thought her make-up glaringly offensive and her laugh artificial. The descriptions "classy", "brittle" and "charming" came to mind and stuck in his gullet. Would she eat fish and chips in Sebastian's palace, he asked himself? Would they ponder the wonders of creation and the mysteries of God in the moonlight? And, more importantly, would Lord Sebastian Noble-Charming truly take care of her, love her, and bring out the best in her? Would he encourage her good qualities and budding intellect? Could he soothe the wounds life had dealt her in her youth? He doubted it. However he looked at it, Celia's marriage to Sebastian would turn her life – and Caleb's – into a prison sentence.

Celia had seen him, too, and her heart had missed a beat. He looked well, successful, and in charge of his life. She felt a little hurt; he had obviously come to terms with their parting. Was there maybe already someone else? Should she approach him? What could she say? She pulled herself together and walked across the crowded room. She must grasp this opportunity to take her destiny back into her own hands. She was now strong enough to deal with such situations. There would be many occasions in the future when she would have to walk boldly and smile sweetly, despite a troubled heart.

"Hello, Caleb. How are you?"

Caleb bowed slightly at her self-assured and classy charm. "How do you do? I saw you earlier across the room. I didn't have a chance to say hello. Too many people I had to talk to."

"Yes, I noticed. You're in great demand."

There was an open chasm between them. Whatever they might still feel for each other had, of necessity, been carefully locked away. If they could keep assuring themselves that this was the way it was going to be, they might, perhaps, believe it.

"You look very different," observed Caleb. He did not mean it as a compliment.

"Well, I've grown up. The country mouse has moved to town."

"Yes, I remember the tale. Then the country mouse became very unhappy and returned to her home in the country."

Celia was taken aback by his comment but was rescued by Sebastian, who came to join them.

"My congratulations on your engagement." Caleb's voice was barristerial, courtly, cutting. "When is the happy day?"

"In four weeks."

"As soon as that?" Caleb raised his eyebrows.

"We didn't want to wait any longer." Sebastian replied, "I still can't believe it took me so many years to recognise this jewel on my doorstep." He put his hand on Celia's back, gallantly. Caleb wanted to put his into Sebastian's face, forcefully. "We would have got married earlier, but there are all those endless boring preparations to see to. It'll be a grand ceremony, of course. And then I'll mount my white charger and carry off my new princess to my fairy castle."

"And ravish her," thought Caleb.

Celia was pensive and looked away. She was remembering Caleb's touch and gentle ways, the air of love and security that surrounded him, his strong sense of belonging. Sebastian possessed none of these qualities.

They politely wished one another goodbye. Half an hour later, Celia begged to be excused on the pretext of a sudden headache. "Yes, the hall is frightfully crowded, and it's jolly stuffy," admitted Sebastian.

They retired gracefully and he dropped his betrothed off outside her grandmother's house. He gave her a peck on the cheek and reminded her of the dinner party they were to attend the following evening. "Something I'm so looking forward to," thought Celia with bitter sarcasm.

What was there to look forward to? Another party with more people who meant nothing to her. In clear-headed moments like these, the old Celia rattled her chains: she screamed at her guards from the top of her gilded tower and swore revenge for her seduction and kidnapping. "To thine own self be true," Shakespeare had commanded through the mouth of Polonius. At what precise moment had she finally strung herself up like a puppet? And why exactly had she allowed herself to do it? "God, help me, if I'm not about to make the biggest mistake of my life," she cried silently.

She changed her clothes and took a cab to one of London's East End Jewish quarters. Wandering aimlessly in the busy streets, she watched the throng, observed the bustle and soaked up every impression like a dry sponge. So this was where Caleb had grown up. Bearded men with wide-brimmed black hats passed her by, debating and gesticulating. She stopped outside a Jewish bookshop and went in out of curiosity. A well-nourished, middle-aged man with a bushy black beard, his head crowned with a black velvet kippah, sat at a desk piled with books. He peered suspiciously at the intruder over his bunker wall; she was obviously not a Jewess. Celia wondered if this fact were stamped across her forehead.

"I just want to browse around a little," she declared, over-awed by the alien other-worldliness of this place and its strange inhabitant.

The man barely nodded to acknowledge her presence before returning his attention to the books. Celia was the only customer in the shop. She perused the rows of precious books – in Hebrew, Yiddish, German and even English – and picked one out and flicked through its pages. She felt the shopkeeper's eyes on her back. He was probably nervous about a Gentile touching his precious hoard. At the far end of the shop were shelves with miscellaneous Judaica: candlesticks, mezusot, wall plaques, kippot, and beautifully calligraphed Torah quotations. Among these was a good selection of tallitot, which attracted her attention; she had always felt drawn to the prayer shawls. Now she could see them close up. She stroked the garments which, for hundreds of years, had been a symbol of Jewish identity and religious observance. Could women wear them as well, she wondered? She unfolded one and held it up; the white woollen *tzitziot* dangled from its four corners. A Hebrew blessing, to be said before wrapping oneself in the fringed garment, was embroidered on the top edge. Celia could not read it and sought the assistance of the bearded Jew. His response was an incomprehensible machine-gun burst of rapid Hebrew. She did not dare to repeat her question; she would just have to work it out herself.

"I'd like to buy this one," she said.

"You're not Jewish," the unfriendly voice stated. It was strongly guttural.

"No," admitted Celia with an accommodating smile.

The Jew nodded and took the tallit to the back of the shop. When he returned, the *tzitziot* had gone. "Why did you take off the fringes?" asked Celia, upset.

"We don't sell *tollises* with *tzitzis* to non-Jews," he mumbled. Celia could not understand why he was being offensive, and protested. "Do you still want it, or not?" he asked unmoved.

Celia took a deep breath. She would have to find someone to help her to attach some new ones.

She was delighted with her purchase – despite this new and unpleasant experience of Jewish religiosity – and left the shop happier than she had entered it. Once home, Celia hurried to unpack her prized acquisition. She unfolded the prayer shawl with reverence, realising that there was more to this piece of cloth than met the eyes. It was like touching history, the history of an ancient, stubborn people. It was like a link to God. Love and comfort emanated from it. Mental associations with childhood security and clutched blankets returned to her: "How precious is your loving kindness, O God. And the children of men take refuge under the shadow of Your wings." Celia held the tallit over her head, then let it come down slowly, and pulled it over her face as she had seen the Jews in Berlin do it. Suddenly, she knew that God was. It was awesome and her eyes filled with tears.

"Sh'mah Yisrael, Adonai Eloheinu, Adonai Echad. Hear, O Israel, the Lord our God, the Lord is One."

As she spoke these solemn words in the seclusion of her bedroom, a Bible verse from long ago came to mind: it was something about proclaiming liberty to the captives and opening prison doors to those who were in bondage. The shackles that had held her bound these last long months fell off, and a spirit of strength and resolution filled her heart. Celia sat for some time wrapped in the prayer shawl and wondered about her next steps.

"What on earth was the matter with you tonight? You were horribly argumentative with the Brandons' guests." Sebastian felt the need to admonish her severely after her shocking behaviour at the dinner party. "Just as well they are Germans, and a bit stolid and not too easily offended. I felt I had to apologise for your rudeness. For goodness' sake, never do that to me again, will you?"

Celia thought she had misheard him. "You felt obliged to apologise for me? Am I nothing more than a naughty child to you? And didn't you hear what that Herr Dieber said about Jews?"

"As I said before, you're in a beastly mood, and I won't discuss it with you. With a bit of luck, you'll be back to your old self before I see you again. It was jolly embarrassing for me, you know. And I'd really appreciate it if you'd stop flying a banner for the Jews. And do keep your opinions on British politics in Palestine to yourself. The subject is a matter of utter indifference to a viscountess and your attitude has caused no end of raised eyebrows already. Everyone but you thought the Diebers a charming couple. And, I must admit, what they had to say about eugenics and euthanasia makes a lot of sense."

Enraged and humiliated, Celia bit her tongue and said nothing. But, in the stillness of the night at home, she asked herself in bewilderment, "Am I really going to marry this man?"

~ 24 ~

London, 5th May 1938

By seven o'clock the small hall was filling rapidly. The Zionist meeting was scheduled to start at seven-thirty. Celia was glad she had come early. Now she sat, expectantly, on a hard, uncomfortable chair in a dingy, run down community hall in London's East End. Weak light bulbs glowered from the ceiling under cheap paper lampshades. The paintwork and whitewashed walls, like old masters, were discoloured from decades of cigarette smoke. Most of the people, from thirteen year-old boys to men in their late seventies, were poorly dressed. Despite wearing her plainest coat, Celia stood out from the crowd because of its quality. Now and again she was given an odd look. Was she here merely out of rebellion against Sebastian's insufferable behaviour? What did she expect from her adventure? She was not Jewish, did not know any Jews – except Caleb and the ones she had met at the Levines' – knew little about Judaism and entertained only hazy, if romantic, ideas about Zionism. So why was she here?

Now there was standing room only, but men and women were still pushing in, among them Caleb, Dani, Ben and Joshua. "We've been warned to expect the Blackshirts again tonight. They've promised to disrupt the meeting if we go ahead," Ben said.

Caleb shrugged, "I don't think we've got anything to lose."

His eyes scanned the hall. A lady in a front row caught his attention; she was much better dressed than her neighbours. She turned her head and looked around.

"Do you recognise her?" asked Dani, following Caleb's stare.

"It's Celia," he exclaimed. "The lady in the cream-coloured coat."

"Where? I thought you'd parted company. What's she doing here?"

"I've no idea. I must speak to her. If the Blackshirts are out to make trouble tonight, this isn't the place for her." Caleb wanted to push past Dani, but he held him back.

"No, leave her. Let's see what she does." Dani clasped his hands behind his back and rocked on his feet. "It's not often I've the chance to see how a Goy takes the kind of abuse we have to put up with. Don't worry; she'll be fine. Our fascist friends will spot her for what she is and pack her off safely."

Caleb's only concern now was for Celia's safety. He fidgeted. On the dot of 7.40 pm – punctually, ten minutes late, as is the Jewish custom – the speaker stepped up to the podium and greeted the crowd by introducing himself as Morris Sherman. He was about to come to the purpose of the meeting when loud voices were heard in the entrance to the hall. Seconds later, three dozen Blackshirts pushed in and took up strategic positions around the room. The people looked tense but the bespectacled speaker said nothing. He remained calm, waited until the initial shuffling had died down, and then continued his speech. It was not long before the Blackshirts began to heckle. At last the speaker paused and asked for silence. This provoked roars of laughter from the intruders. The gang leader jumped onto the stage and formally called for silence.

"Quiet, gentlemen. I'd like to hear what the Jew-Boy has to say. Maybe we'll learn something from him. How parasites get into their hosts, for example," he mocked.

Celia was appalled. How could he call himself British? He caught her eye and glared.

"Here, Miss. You don't look very Jewish. What are you doing here?"

Celia, embarrassed that she had attracted his attention, wished she could make herself invisible. But she was determined not to back down in the face of intimidation this time. "I wasn't told that the meeting was closed to non-Jews," she retorted, hiding the tremor in her voice.

"Of course the meeting is not for the British. You'd best leave right now. That's if you're worried about the health of our nation – and your own, of course." He spread his legs, crossed his arms, and adopted a commanding fascist pose.

Celia was indignant. "You can advise me to leave, but I may choose not to heed your advice. I've come here to listen to what the gentleman speaker has to say. Maybe you would care to refrain from any further disruption – or leave?"

Celia turned her face away from him and smiled nervously at the speaker. No, this time she would not run away – not in her own country. After all, this was England; she knew who she was, and she knew her rights. She could feel her heart pounding with tension and looked straight ahead. It felt hot in the hall. One could have heard a pin drop. The Blackshirt responded to her challenge.

"All right!" he said, as calmly as a rambler might explain the route to fellow walkers. "This is your last chance: anyone who wants to go can go now. If you stay, I daren't promise that nothing will happen to you. You see, my friends and me are very upset that you lot are spreading your dirty Jewish lies around. And don't come snivelling to me afterwards and say we didn't warn you."

A handful of people got up and left as the fascists jeered. The rest stayed. At the back of the hall, Dani removed his glasses and put them carefully away in a small leather case. "Are you sure this is your young lady?"

"It's Celia all right."

"What a *chutzpah*. Shame she's going to marry a Goy."

Caleb's proud smile died. "Let's see if we can get her out of here before she gets hurt," he said, annoyed by Dani's jibe.

The last person to leave closed the door, and the Blackshirt leader gave the signal. His men pounced on the assembly, hitting men, women and children indiscriminately. But the Jewish street fighters had come prepared. Chaos exploded, chairs crashed, glass smashed, women cried, scratched, bit and spat, and men cursed, punched and grappled. The Blackshirt leader made straight for Celia, grabbed her arm and tried to drag her out.

"I could hit you for being one of those rotten gutter rats," Celia shouted in his face, her fighting spirit breaking out. Then she bit his hand as hard as she could. He let go of her, swearing and cursing. For good measure, Celia spat at him.

That was too much for him and he grabbed her wrist with an iron grip, twisted it hard, and hissed, "You know who the worst enemies are: it's traitors like you. They're just filthy little Jews, but you're the real scum, because you're an Englishwoman and you're siding with them bastards."

He hit Celia in the face with the back of his hand as hard as he could. She stumbled backwards. He let go of her wrist and she crashed to the floor, chairs scattering. She scrambled to her feet and felt her cheek burning. But that was all; she felt no fear, only a surge of blazing anger. She looked around for her assailant but he had walked off. Then she heard someone call her name and felt a light touch on her shoulder. Celia flung around and found herself looking straight into a pair of beautiful hazel eyes with long, silky eyelashes. "I think it's time to leave, Lady Celia. You've had enough fun for one evening."

The short, balding man in a cheap suit smiled at her and she followed him obediently. They reached the door without too much trouble. It was drizzling outside. She could still hear the noise of fighting. Curious onlookers watched the door from a safe distance, breathless for action. Bobbies were blowing their whistles furiously as they rushed towards the hall. "Ah! Here comes the cavalry." The Jew squinted into the darkness. He reached into his breast pocket for his glasses and put them on his nose ceremoniously. "Shall I call you a cab, m'lady?"

"Thank you. May . . . may I offer you a lift?"

"That's most kind of you, but I have to stay around and clear up tonight's carnage. You're very brave, if I may say so. Do you do this sort of thing often?" The Jew's eyes were serious, but they had a spark of laughter in them.

Celia began to shiver. "There have been two, no, three occasions when I've looked the other way and been ashamed. We all make mistakes, but I was determined not to let it happen again. I hope I haven't made the situation worse for you." She was suddenly concerned about the riot. Had she inadvertently sparked it off with her defiance?

"Not at all! On the contrary. Tonight you blessed many people. Thank you." Her rescuer was reassuring.

Celia stretched out her gloved hand. "Goodbye, Mr . . ."

He took her hand. "My friends call me Dani."

"Goodbye, Dani. I hope we meet again some time."

"I'm certain we will."

It was not until Celia was sitting in the cab that it occurred to her that Dani had called her by her first name.

Despite the judicious application of ice packs, Celia's face swelled up beautifully. She squinted at her black eye in the mirror. It had been a stunning physical blow, but inside she felt jubilant, triumphant. She might have lost the battle but she knew she had won the war. Three times she had cowered away, afraid. On the fourth occasion she had faced up to her adversary and had conquered her fear. Fear? She had felt no fear, just a fierce anger at the evil she had been a witness to. But how could she make Sebastian understand? The more she supported the Jews, the more antagonistic he became towards them. He ridiculed them as a people; he sneered at their religious practices, and he mocked her search for truth and meaning. So she had given up talking about it altogether. Now there were only two weeks left until the wedding, two weeks to go before she was locked into marriage with a man she had little in common with. She did not even respect him; he had never done anything to earn her respect. Celia looked at herself in the mirror. Was she really looking at the future mistress of Lenkham? It was only in the past few days that Sebastian had kissed her on the lips for the first time. She had thought of Caleb's kisses in the cold barn.

She was not a complete fool, after all. She knew only too well that her fiancé had other sources of pleasure. A wife for the drawing room, and a mistress for the bedroom, like his father, and his grandfather before him. Theirs was an open family secret. She knew that Sebastian did not love her; she was just a sandpit playmate for him. He had enjoyed the chase and the triumph of taming the notoriously difficult Lady Celia. She knew in her heart that he intended to break her spirit and carry on with his old life as if no marriage had ever taken place. Soon she would not dare to raise so much as an eyebrow at his infidelities. After all, was she not just poor and stupid little Celia? Should she not be eternally grateful for having landed Lord Sebastian Holsworth-Leigh?

The only person who had ever really considered her to be an interesting and attractive human being was Caleb. Caleb had wanted her for herself. In every way. Sebastian had not made even one serious attempt at seducing her. When travelling in Italy, he had taken her up to her hotel room every evening, given her a chaste peck on the cheek, and wished her good night. Then he had slipped out into the warm night. Sebastian was a trout: bright, beautiful, elegant, slippery and cold-blooded.

Some time previously, Francis had come for a week's visit. Barbara Reinhardt had come with him. She looked very different from how she had been in Berlin. Now she was smart, attractive, charming and difficult to impress. Mummy did not like her but Daddy thought her a good sport. And Celia? What did she think? To her surprise, she had actually grown to like her. Barbara was worldly-wise and independent, but she possessed a unique brand of natural kindness and carefully disguised compassion.

Sebastian had called one evening. When Barbara walked into the drawing room, unannounced, his face froze. "Sebastian Holsworth-Leigh. What a small world it is." Barbara, completely unruffled, had stretched out a hand.

Sebastian struggled to conceal his shock. "Hello, Barbara."

"You know each other?" Celia was surprised.

"Yes, we do. Don't we, Sebastian?"

"Yes, of course. My, who'd have thought . . ." said Sebastian. The evening had carried on from there. Celia felt herself tense up, watching them.

The following day, seeing Barbara's bedroom door ajar, Celia tapped on it. "Come in." Barbara was sorting out her laundered silk lingerie on the bed. "Oh, it's you, Celia." She turned back to her underwear. Celia leant against the dresser and watched her for a moment. Barbara smiled at her as if she were her baby sister. It was a kind, understanding smile. Celia folded her arms, rather pointedly. "Barbara, I was born in this house. I know the noise each door makes and the creak of every floorboard."

"Of course you do."

"Last night I heard my brother's door, and then yours."

"Indeed?" Barbara's glance spelled a challenge.

"I know that you and my brother are still lovers. Why don't you simply marry him?"

"Because he hasn't asked me," Barbara replied, with a disarming, sad smile. It knocked Celia off her high and mighty horse called Self-righteous. "Francis is not the marrying type, I'm afraid. Just my bad luck."

"But why do you allow him into your bed . . . room, then, when you don't have to?"

Barbara smiled that older-sister smile again. "What is it you want to know? Really? What men and women do in bed? Are you worried about your wedding?" Barbara knew about life. She also knew about the fears and worries of young, inexperienced upper-class girls. She was trying to be helpful and encouraging, inviting Celia to open up to her.

Celia blushed and retorted, "I know more about these things than you grant me. I'm not that naïve."

Barbara let the bluff pass unchallenged. "Of course you aren't. But if that's not the reason why you knocked on my door, then what is?"

"You know Sebastian too. How well do you know him?"

"Not as well as Eve knew Adam." Barbara seemed not in the slightest bit offended by the implication of the question. "We met at a number of parties in Berlin."

"Parties in Berlin? What kind of parties?"

"Parties for high-ranking Nazis. Seb was always given preferential treatment. In everything. You understand me. He's one of their greatest admirers. It must have been in – let me think – '36. Yes, that's right. During the Olympic Games. Big official parties. I'd been sent there by my paper. That's when Francis and I met."

"Oh . . . And I thought . . . I'm terribly sorry . . ."

"Well, I haven't exactly given you any reason to think differently, have I?" Barbara sat down on the bed and fingered a pair of stockings. She did not look at Celia. "Look, Celia, it's none of my business. I'm no one special and I don't pretend to be. My parents divorced when I was ten. After that I had to survive on my own wits – more or less. I know men like Sebastian; I know their tastes and I know the circles they move in. Celia, you're a sweet, clean girl. I mean it. Stay that way. Don't get corrupted and dirtied by a man like Sebastian." Celia did not defend her fiancé. She didn't feel any need to. "You don't love Sebastian, do you?"

Celia stuck out her chin aggressively. "Of course I do. What kind of woman do you take me for?"

"Don't misunderstand me. I know the look of a woman in love. You simply haven't got it." Barbara was being cruel to be kind. "You're still in love with that Jewish gentleman, aren't you? The one you mentioned in . . ."

Barbara could not finish her sentence. Celia had stormed out of the room.

How long would she be able to play the part she had been bred for? She had acted it out so well that Sebastian had proposed. Three years? Maybe five? No more.

~ 25 ~

London, 6th May 1938

Her heavy make-up, broad-brimmed hat and dark veil hid the worst of her bruising from the Zionist meeting in the East End. When he had seen her the next day at his London town house, Sebastian had been shocked and concerned for her. But, as soon as she had told him where and how she had earned her beating, his tone had changed. He had become angry and abusive and accused her of being foolhardy and stupid. Had she been? Perhaps. But whatever he might think, she had had as much as she could take of his critical attitude towards her and the people and things she valued most. He had created an opening for her to say something that had been on her mind for several months. And she was angry enough to say it.

So she told him about her conversation with Barbara. She asked him if what had been said was true. Sebastian reacted very angrily and, for the first time, he revealed his true nature. He said many ugly things: in summary, that Celia was a nothing and a nobody, both *to* him and without him; that her father's social graces and reputation were a notorious scandal, and that her mother's intelligence and sordid social aspirations were a public joke. He said other things relating to Judaism and Zionism that Celia would not have wanted to repeat in polite society.

"Blow you, Sebastian," Celia thought. "You and all your damn wealth and titles. You twisted trout."

His deeply hurtful outburst had not really reached her

heart; he had never touched it in the first place. But it made taking off the engagement ring as easy as blowing out a candle. With her head held high, she had dropped the costly thing onto a silver tray. He was enraged that a feeble, silly girl should dare to turn him down – him, Lord Sebastian Holsworth-Leigh – and he said so. Celia was unmoved. She wished him all the best for the future and walked out of the house a free woman.

The easiest bit was over, unpleasant as it had been. Now she must tell her parents that she had thrown away the chance of a lifetime. The big society wedding they had been bracing themselves for would never happen and her future lay in tatters. And what reasons could she give? She hardly knew herself. That Sebastian was a philanderer, a Nazi sympathiser, and anti-Semite? How many English aristocrats were the same? These were hardly convincing reasons for jilting Sebastian. Everyone she knew would say she was out of her mind, childish and utterly irresponsible. Those would be the kinder names they would call her. So where could she go from here? Right now it looked like nowhere. She had made an incredible mess of her life. All she could think of, at that moment, was that she needed to be alone, to lick her wounds, to gather up her last reserves of strength and courage.

As soon as she arrived back at her grandmother's home, the butler appeared.

"Ah, Lady Celia. Lady Agatha requests that you join her at your earliest convenience. She's in the drawing room. She has a visitor."

"Thank you, Taylor, but I'm really not feeling very well. Please could you convey my apologies to my grandmother?"

"But Lady Agatha gave me very clear instructions, m'lady. She was most specific that you should join her as soon as possible."

Celia could see his agitation at being put in such an awkward situation. It had been instilled into her that it was simply not done to embarrass the servants. So she said, kindly and with a sigh, "Thank you, Taylor. In that case I'd better go right away."

"There you are, my dear," exclaimed her grandmother when Celia entered the room. Then, turning to her guest, she said, "You see, Caleb. I think your patience may have been justified after all."

Caleb looked at Celia. She was wearing a simple mouse-grey town suit and her stockings were still damp from splattered rainwater. He beheld a very insignificant and crumpled Zionist heroine looking more like a little girl than a grand lady. But she was his girl, whether she admitted it or not. He rose politely, not knowing quite what to say or how to say it. Celia just wanted to disappear.

Lady Agatha got up too. "Oh! I've just remembered. I have a letter I must finish before luncheon. If you'll excuse me . . ." She smiled at them and left before they could reply, closing the door behind her.

"How do you do, Caleb?" Celia did not look at him. She went to the tea tray and busied herself with a cup and saucer. Her hands were shaking so badly that the fine china rattled. She closed her eyes and took a deep breath to regain her composure. Events were catching up with her; she knew she could not take much more before she burst into tears.

"Please. Let me do that." Caleb took charge of the teapot.

"I'm sorry for being so clumsy. I don't feel very well." She sat down. "Why are you calling on Lady Agatha?" She felt embarrassed at asking so blunt a question, but she had to know his answer.

"To hear how you are. Our last encounter was . . . well, not a very happy one. I didn't want that to be my last memory of you."

The conversation died. Celia sat on the sofa, demure, and

stared at her tea. "Don't worry. There isn't going to be a wedding."

Caleb thought he had misheard. "You've postponed the wedding? Why?"

"No, not postponed. I've broken off the engagement. The wedding is cancelled."

His brow creased into a frown of disbelief. "The wedding cancelled? Since when?"

Celia looked at her watch. "Since an hour ago. At ten o'clock, to be precise."

Caleb paced the room, his mind in turmoil. Celia was free again; the unbelievable had happened. He had always known that she was meant for him. The engagement had perplexed and upset him and, in the end, he had been forced to abandon his hopes and dreams. And now, figuratively speaking at two minutes to twelve, all his love and longings came flooding back with such speed and power that he was left breathless. Unaware of his excitement, Celia too was dreaming, caught up in a living nightmare. She had insulted, rejected and abandoned the only man she had ever truly loved. How could she turn the clock back? It was utterly impossible.

"Dear God," she cried silently. "If it's possible, please give me another chance."

Caleb was the first to break the silence. He spoke with barely contained excitement. "There's a big bruise under your eye. How did you get that?" He needed to hear it from her own lips.

"I ran into a door."

"Weren't you looking where you were going?"

"It was dark."

"That's not what I heard."

"Oh?"

"You were at a Zionist meeting last night and got embroiled in a fight because you sided with us Jews."

"Who told you that?"

Celia was taken aback. She was struggling to work out just what to say or how to behave. To try to appear a heroine in Caleb's eyes would be cheap melodramatics. That was not her style. She could not encourage him to think her better than she was. She had treated him appallingly and had deliberately kicked away his happiness. And now she was being given a second chance. But she did not want him to think she was running back to him. He might think her someone who, when thwarted of her high social aspirations, was simply grabbing at the first, less attractive, offer to come her way. Such an attitude would demean both of them, and that she could not countenance.

"No one told me. I was at the meeting myself."

His heart was beating violently. In his mind he was carefully phrasing his crucial next question. Her answer would either bring him back to life . . . or bury him forever. He was dreading Celia's reply; he would more happily face a dozen angry Arabs than this moment. His question lingered nervously, trying to form itself into the right words. Before he was ready for it, he asked, "Celia, if you could turn back the clock, would you still walk away from me?"

"I didn't know then what I know now."

Caleb was encouraged by the vagueness of her whispered reply. At least she had not said "No." He determined to try again. "All right, let me rephrase my question. If you were again to face the reality of all it means to be Jewish, would you now be able to accept it?"

He looked at her intently. Celia found his probing an agonising ordeal. What did he want to hear from her? A confession of guilt? A plea to be received back, now that she had jilted Holsworth-Leigh? Was he trying to rob her of all dignity, to humiliate her utterly?

"No. Yes. I don't know," she said weakly and a little crossly.

"For goodness' sake!" Caleb could barely contain himself.

"Do I have to spell out the question? Celia, can I cherish any hope of our future together? If you still care for me, just a little bit, then tell me, I beg you. If not, tell me that too. I have to know. I promise I'll never trouble you again if that's what you truly want."

Her reply was a tearless sob. Caleb rushed to her, enfolding her in his arms and covering her with kisses.

"Caleb, please forgive me for deserting you," she cried. "I've missed you so much. Every day, every hour. These last few months have been the most wretched I've ever lived."

Caleb rocked her soothingly. "There's nothing to be ashamed of. You know that. You didn't understand because you didn't know. But now you've confronted your fears and have won. You've believed strongly enough in what is right to overcome your cowardice. People who are not afraid because they have nothing to lose are the most terrifying enemy. But you had everything to lose and still you stood up for us – and truth and decency. And now you're covered with battle scars, my poor darling. I promise I'll never scold you when you come home looking a mess like that." He lifted Celia's face to his and gently, soothingly, kissed the bruise and wiped away her tears with his lips.

"Celia, will you marry me?" He said it very softly, very sincerely. It was the most wonderful, incredible question Celia had ever heard. Had she heard him right? She chuckled.

Caleb suddenly became aware of the inappropriateness of his timing. Quickly he added, "I mean, when you've had time to think it over. I hope you'll then consider my proposal."

"Yes, my dearest Jewish love. I will consider your question very seriously." She giggled. "Maybe I could keep the wedding cake. I could cross out 'Sebastian Montgomery Charles' and replace it with 'Caleb'."

Suddenly Caleb jumped up, romance swept aside. "Good gracious! I have to be at a court hearing at twelve. I'm late already."

Celia saw him out. Waving goodbye from the top of the outside steps she called, "Caleb. I've had enough time to consider. The answer is: I will!"

"Oh, has he left?" Lady Agatha emerged from her writing room. "What a shame. I wanted to say goodbye."

"He has to be at a court hearing at twelve. Grandmother, could I have a little talk with you?"

Celia took the afternoon train to Cecil Court. This was the moment she was dreading, when she had to start justifying her outrageous decisions. She told her mother first that she had ended her engagement. The storm crashed around her; Lady Norah was beside herself with fury. "And she's still blissfully unaware of my engagement to Caleb," Celia thought ruefully.

"For goodness' sake, Norah. Can't all this wait till the morning?" The Earl had missed the cause of the row and was irritated that his peaceful evening had been interrupted.

"No, Daddy. I'd much rather we discuss this thing now. Otherwise we'll all have a sleepless night. I've just told Mummy that I've called off my engagement to Sebastian. I know he's a gentleman of good character and standing – and very wealthy – but I'm convinced we're quite unsuited for each other and would be very unhappy as man and wife."

"And why do you think that?" asked the Earl.

"I think I've outgrown the social cradle I was born into. There's more to life than producing babies to continue the Holsworth-Leighs' noble family line. I don't want to spend the rest of my life wondering what on earth I'm doing, and why. I'm not really cut out to walk the same road that generations of ancestors have trodden before me. I want to leave footprints behind me along the paths *I* decide to walk down. I admit that what I've chosen looks more like a jungle track than a gravel path through stately gardens. And I know I can't see beyond the next tree. But I also know that God will look after me."

"For God's sake, leave God and religion out of it," mocked the Earl. "And what makes you suddenly think that He will look after you?"

"Next she'll be telling us that she wants to devote her life to 'serving God'," Lady Norah scoffed.

Celia took the opportunity offered by this impromptu remark to approach the lion in its den. "As a matter of fact, Mummy, Caleb Levine proposed to me this morning. And I've accepted him."

"Good God, girl! Are you out of your mind?" The Besthorpes were aghast.

Celia braced herself. Normally the Earl was quiet, introverted and peace-loving. But he was prone to violent, unpredictable outbursts, like a sleeping volcano. Lady Norah knew them well and Celia had feared them since childhood.

"You're mad!" he bawled, with such unrestrained anger that he made his daughter jump. "A filthy little Jew-Boy? A hook-nosed Judas? Marrying into my family? Never! Do you hear: n-e-v-e-r!" And then, as if addressing his enemy: "Oh, you are a clever one, Mr Levine. You think you can wheedle and trick your way into my home. Not on your cunning little Semite life!"

"But he loves me, Daddy. He's good and honest. He's better than some of our own countrymen."

"He loves me, he's good and honest," the Earl parroted. "That you'd turn down Holsworth-Leigh at the last minute I can just about understand. And I admire your courage for doing it. But don't come telling me you've been hoodwinked into getting engaged to a Jew. No! No! No! I will never give my consent to that. Never! A Jew will not worm his way into my family. Never! The Lancasters will not sink that low."

"Daddy, you don't know Caleb. How can you say such horrid things?"

"Don't know Caleb, eh? I don't have to. Everybody knows that Jews are a brood of vipers. Even the Bible says so. And my demented daughter can't do any better than throw herself at one."

"I warned you, didn't I?" Lady Norah chipped in, triumphantly. "Once they get a foot in the door you can't get rid of them."

"Oh, be quiet, Norah!" her husband snapped.

Celia felt humiliated, angry and afraid. But she had her father's Lancaster fighting spirit. "How dare you compare me with an empty-headed social tramp who's prepared to throw herself at the first bidder! If I were like that I'd go for Sebastian, not Caleb, wouldn't I? And how dare you treat me with such contempt? How can you – yes, *you*, Daddy – maliciously slander someone you hardly know? I've learned more about goodness, love and gentleness from a Jew in two years than from you in twenty. Caleb's ten times more of a real gentleman than either you or Sebastian are. And you want me to keep God and religion out of my life, do you? Well, you make claims for 'Christianity', as you call it, but do you actually keep any of Christ's teachings? Oh, no! You just make up your own rules as you go along, rules to suit your own purposes. Or you twist Jesus' words to make them say what you want to hear. You don't know God. When was the last time you prayed? How often have I heard Mummy say that one only needs God at Christmas, Easter, weddings and funerals? Have you ever considered the demands God is making on you? I bet you haven't. You use God when it suits you. For any other purpose you keep Him locked away. Well, He is the Mighty One of Israel. And I will marry Caleb Levine. Whether you damn well like it or not!"

Celia's parents were stunned by their daughter's outburst. Their discussion stopped abruptly when Lady Norah slapped her daughter. The Earl of Besthorpe stamped out of the room without another word, steaming with fury.

Celia quietly and nervously joined her father at the breakfast table. He was engrossed in his paper and ignored her completely. He did not speak until she was onto her second piece of toast.

"And when is this wedding to take place?" He was still hiding behind the *Daily Telegraph*.

"We haven't decided yet. Everything has happened so fast. Caleb wanted to propose six months ago, but I wouldn't let him. I made a terrible mistake, which delayed him." Celia was keeping as calm as possible.

The paper crackled and came down. It revealed two whisky-shot eyes beneath bushy eyebrows. "And are you still dead-set on marrying him?"

"Yes. Absolutely."

The Earl looked at his daughter closely. He noticed her bruised face for the first time. "Did your mother do that last night?"

"No, it's the result of an encounter with Mosley's fascist thugs."

"Good gracious! How did you get mixed up with that lot?"

"I was at a Zionist meeting. They decided to break it up."

Lady Norah appeared and, very pointedly, ignored her daughter.

"Celia is still insisting on marrying that chap, Levine."

"I'm not interested in whom she wants to marry. She can marry a jungle-bunny for all I care."

"Hold your horses, will you? We need to sort this thing out. The Jews are a shifty lot, but maybe there's one good egg among them. Maybe my daughter has picked such a rarity.

The world won't come to an end because of it. Besides, it's not up to Celia to continue the family line. That's your son Francis' job. And he's done a pretty poor job so far. So far he's fathered nothing legitimate."

Lady Norah was not amused. "If Cecilia marries the Jew, I for one will not be attending the wedding. And who knows who else won't come. Look at the shameful spectacle she's made of herself and her family. It's a scandal. And where's your sense of duty, girl, to kith, kin, Crown and country?"

Celia was not going to let her mother's bitterness deflect her. "It will be a test for our friends and family, not for us. Our true friends will come. The rest can stay away, and good riddance. The same applies to family."

"You came prepared for all this. Is that what your Jewish friend has told you to say?" The Earl gave his daughter a sideways glance.

"Not at all. I've had lots of time to think things over. I've become very calculating these days. I've had to be. And his name is 'Caleb', not 'my Jewish friend', if you don't mind."

"You see, Henry! Judaism's already rubbing off on her. I told you," Lady Norah sniped.

"Anyway, Grandmother has given us her blessing and she'll definitely be at our wedding. Mummy, don't you think people would think it a bit feeble of you not to come too?"

"Cecilia, there are some things one just does not do. And one of them is jilting a Holsworth-Leigh after breakfast and getting engaged to a foreigner of disreputable descent before lunch. You've brought it all on yourself."

"The Levines are not disreputable. Caleb's father is a highly respected medical scientist and a British citizen. In fact, Grandmother knows the Levines well. They've even dined at her home and she at theirs. Would she do that if they were 'foreigners of disreputable descent'?"

"My own mother. Letting down the family again." Lady Norah closed her eyes. She was genuinely horrified.

The tapping of the Earl's knife on the table was the only sign that showed that he was deep in thought. A Jew in the Lancaster family? Good God, the Lancaster line included traitors, heretics, murderers, thieves, kidnappers, torturers, and goodness knows how many adulterers and bastard children. He had enough skeletons in his cupboard to fill a graveyard, but there was probably room enough to squeeze in a Jew – or two. Although he didn't say anything at the time, Celia knew intuitively that the battle had been won.

Pleased with the outcome of the family confrontation, Celia returned to London as the bearer of good news. After a lengthy and less explosive discussion, her father had eventually agreed not to oppose the union. But he had insisted that the Levine family – herself and Caleb included – should restrict their visits to Cecil Court to an absolute minimum. Celia felt hurt at being banished from her childhood home, but knew it was a small price to pay for Caleb, and little compared to what he had paid for her already.

The Levines were genuinely happy at their news, especially Gertrud. Now that her son was to marry a Gentile, he might at last drop his bitter and critical attitude towards them and their Christianity. At a dinner in celebration of the engagement, the delicate subject of the wedding ceremony was broached. The professor made the wry comment that this year was going to be rather costly, with two of his children standing under the *chuppah* canopy.

"How exactly were you thinking of celebrating your wedding?" Mrs Levine asked, feeling her way forward.

"For a start, there'll be no church wedding and no *chuppah*," Caleb said adamantly.

Celia had been devastated when he had first told her. It had been a severe blow and had shattered her girlish dreams of a white wedding. The young bride had had to swallow hard.

"What do you have in mind then?"

"The Registry Office," Caleb said.

"The Registry Office?" Gertrud was genuinely shocked at this bombshell. "But that's for divorcées, adulterers and atheists. Are you sure we couldn't arrange something nicer?" Gertrud put her hand on Celia's to comfort and encourage her.

"Trust me, Mama. It's the law of the land. We must abide by it. Given our present situation, no Rabbi or Christian minister would bless, let alone marry us. Officially, we're of different religions."

Celia put on a brave face. "We'll have to improvise and be imaginative," she said. "Just because the legal and religious ceremony won't be as grand as we'd envisaged doesn't mean the reception can't be. Let's make the most of that, shall we?"

~ 26 ~

London, June 1938

The wedding day was set for the first Friday in July 1938.
Celia had compiled a new wedding list and sent out the invi-
tations. In passive protest over this obvious misalliance and
the scandal Celia had caused, she received many apologies.
And, after all, how could a Registry Office wedding be considered a respectable society wedding? Even Georgina felt
she could not come. The broken engagement to her brother
was forgivable . . . these things did happen . . . but to get
engaged to someone else so soon . . . and to someone of such
low birth . . . Georgina might come herself . . . but there was
her husband and his position to think of. No, she really could
not afford to make such a faux-pas. It was the first really
hurtful blow Celia was to receive.

Despite the pressure of their wedding preparations,
Caleb accepted Dani's invitation to celebrate an Erev
Shabbat dinner with his family. The invitation obviously
included Celia, the Gentile fiancée of a good Jewish boy. He
guessed what lay behind the invitation: Dani and his wife
wanted to have a good look at Celia and were curious to discover why on earth she wanted to marry a Yidl. Caleb knew
his friend had deep-seated reservations about this union, but
was confident that Celia would win them all over. And it
would enable her to experience a real Erev Shabbat. Caleb
wanted her to observe the Glicksmans' kind of Shabbat in
their own home: it was sincere, happy and relaxed . . . and
not too serious. But what if Cielie didn't like it? What if she

preferred the showpiece Shabbat that she had experienced at his parents' home? Or what if she were to reject altogether his desire to keep certain basic Jewish traditions and observances in their home? What if she just wanted a purely English home . . .? No, he would not allow that dreadful thought to enter his head.

It had been hard enough for Celia to forego the traditional "white" church wedding she had dreamed about since she was little. He was Jewish; her background was Anglican. No Rabbi would marry them unless she converted to Judaism first; and he, Caleb, would not submit himself to a Christian church wedding. End of story. He felt a bit like a big bad wolf who had robbed a beautiful Little Red Riding Hood of her innocent dreams. But, in the end, Cielie had understood. With sad eyes and a lump in her throat, she had agreed to lay her grand wedding plans on the Altar of the Impossible. And, after he had caused her this little heartbreak, he was loath to broach the other important subject that was on his mind.

This Erev Shabbat invitation was to prove a new and challenging experience for Celia in more than one way. The Glicksmans lived in a London borough crammed with working-class families and dingy little two-up two-down terraced houses. Caleb knew the area well; Celia did not. The Glicksmans' street looked depressingly like a thousand other identical streets. Small side streets branched off the main road with endless rows of soot-blackened red-brick houses. Apart from weeds in the pavement there was no greenery at all, and a narrow pavement was all that separated the peeling front doors from the road. Runny-nosed, shabbily dressed children played in the noisy streets. The cries of the smaller children mingled with the shouts of the older ones as they chased and fought. Others were playing hopscotch, while the better-off kicked a football against a wall. Could this really be where his respected friend lived? Celia was feeling very uncomfortable and held on tightly to Caleb's arm. Her nervousness amused him. "You've never been to a place like this before, have you?"

Eventually they came upon a door that was indistinguishable from the others in the street. A man opened it. Celia recognised him at once. He smiled broadly at her as he let them in. "Didn't I say that we would meet again?" Dani took Celia's coat. A short, dark-haired woman with a paradoxical air of strength and femininity approached. "This is my dear wife, Sarah'le!" Dani put his arm tenderly around his wife's shoulders.

She greeted her guests, a reserved but welcoming smile on her expressive face. She was aware that the modesty, if not frugality, of her home was in stark contrast to the opulence her lady guest was accustomed to. Sarah'le stretched out her work-worn hand and Celia shook it politely.

"Please, come through. We are just about ready," said Dani, leading the way to their little back room.

Four people were waiting to greet them: two handsome, adolescent boys and an elderly couple, who were introduced as Mr and Mrs Sabotnik, Sarah'le's parents. The boys were Ben and Joshua, their hosts' sons. Dani pulled out a chair for Celia. She was to sit next to Mrs Sabotnik, who did not look too pleased. Celia noted that few of the pieces of cutlery, glass or crockery, so neatly laid out on the threadbare white tablecloth, matched. She sat down and stifled a shriek, as her chair wobbled precariously under her.

"I'm terribly sorry. Ben, I asked you to swap the chairs around," admonished Dani. There was a lot of commotion in the overcrowded room as the chairs were switched.

"Well, we aren't rich and she'll just have to make do," Mrs Sabotnik muttered to herself.

Sarah'le appeared from the kitchen. "I'm ready when you are."

Dani smiled at her. Then, with beautiful solemnity, the Glicksmans, the Sabotniks, a Levine and a Lancaster welcomed Shabbat. The atmosphere in this house was quite different from that which Celia had experienced at the Levines' Erev Shabbat meal. Sarah'le's candle-lighting prayer was light yet solemn; and there were no curious onlookers, interruptions or explanations. It was not a performance. This was real. It was an act of worship; a family and their friends meeting with the God of gods in the intimacy of their poor home. Dani blessed Adonai for the bread and the wine. Then the dinner was served. Caleb unobtrusively placed another bottle that he had brought on the table. The boys tucked themselves away in a corner – there was not enough room for all of them at the table. Nobody seemed to mind. Dani helped his wife hand the plates round. His cheerful nature and light-hearted conversation made them all laugh.

The Glicksmans treated Celia as a member of the family. She soon discovered that the Sabotniks were *real* socialists. Mrs Sabotnik challenged Celia, provocatively: "I suppose you don't have much to do with the working classes? Apart from your servants."

Celia did not know what to say. She felt lost here, out of her depth. At home, the common people had been taken for granted, accepted as the underclass, treated graciously and patronisingly, but never fraternised with. Here, she was among the common people; they were her host and she their guest. They had their own peculiar culture and ways of behaving, and it was Celia who now felt intimidated and, somehow, looked down upon. The little people were proud too, and proud of being proud.

"I do help with the harvest in the summer," she said at last.

"Harvest? What, picking berries and so on?" Mrs Sabotnik asked.

"No. It's mostly wheat and hay."

Ben raised up his head. Balancing his plate precariously on his knees, he said, "Do you know how to bind sheaves then?"

Celia gave him an amused smile, "Yes, of course."

"Do you remember, Dad? We were taught to bind sheaves last year. It took me so long to learn. Which reminds me, the *HaBonim* have organised a little dance tonight. May I go?"

Joshua giggled. "Ben only wants to go because the Stinski's Rosie will be there." His older brother elbowed him in the ribs.

"*HaBonim*? I've heard about them. Don't they run agricultural schools for Jewish youth?" Celia asked.

"Oh, yes. They're worth going to . . . especially the social gatherings. A lot goes on at them . . . well, I mean . . ." Ben affirmed eagerly.

"Growing olives and citrus fruit isn't the only thing that's important for Eretz," Caleb added, winking.

Dani understood what he was getting at: Rosie was a nice girl from down the street and an ardent Zionist. And she and Ben liked each other. "What do you think, Mother?" He looked at his wife. Sarah'le's smile and eyes were full of affirmation. "Well, you'd better go then," said Dani. Ben finished his dinner in record time.

Dani picked up their conversation where they had left off. "So, you know a little about agriculture, do you, Lady Celia?"

Celia felt on safe ground now. "I know a lot about sugar beet, but that's more by accident than design. I'm more interested in cereals, but my real love is livestock."

"Cattle? Poultry?"

"Yes, but mostly horses."

"Pshah! Horses. They're just something for the rich." Mrs Sabotnik objected strongly to having to share a table with a *shicksah*; worse still, she was a property-owning *shicksah* from the ruling class. "Do you know how many workers

303

queue up at the London docks each morning for hire as day labourers?" she asked. "Thirty thousand. And only six thousand get jobs. And you breed ponies. Pshah!"

Celia felt quite indignant at this unprovoked attack. "Mrs Sabotnik, I breed horses, not ponies. Mainly working horses: Clydesdales, Shire horses and Suffolk Punches. Horses help the workers." Celia very pointedly stressed the words "working" and "workers".

"Can you plough?" asked Dani, amused to see Celia standing up to his formidable old mother-in-law.

"Yes. And I can harrow and drill."

"Not bad."

"Do you know anything about preserving – jams, pickles, that sort of thing?" This was Sarah'le's speciality. She was clearing the table to make room for the pudding.

"A little."

"And can you cook too?"

Celia wished she hadn't asked that question, and paused before answering. Caleb came to her rescue. "*Chaverim*, it's Shobbes! Can't we postpone this inquisition to another time?" He laughed and offered everyone more wine.

Over the sweet, the subject turned to Zionism. Celia was astonished at Sarah'le's knowledge. While she sliced up the steamed pudding, she joined in the discussion on political philosophy. Caleb and Dani listened seriously to what she had to say. While she ladled out the custard, she quoted Herzl, Buber, Ha'Am and Pinsker. Suddenly, Celia felt very small and ignorant. This humble and apparently simple Jewish mother and housewife knew more about social science, economics and politics than anyone she'd ever met. Sarah'le Glicksman was an exceptional woman. She might be miserably poor, but she had a dignity that towered above her frail tablecloth. Her wisdom and education lifted her spirit high above her poverty. She was an individual who stood head and shoulders above the masses because she believed in a cause to the point of sacrifice. The world-changing power of God lived in the anonymity of a poor Jewish home.

"Shall we go through to the front room?" suggested Dani. They left the table while Sarah'le tidied up. Dani lit a pipe and puffed away, filling the room with sweet-scented smoke.

"I do admire Sarah'le," said Celia quietly to Caleb. "She's so clever."

Mrs Sabotnik overheard her. "If you so admire her, why don't you give her a hand with the washing up? We don't have any servants here, you know."

"Mother!" Dani reacted with a stream of agitated Yiddish. Even Mr Sabotnik joined in on Dani's side. Eventually, after a strong rearguard action, his wife withdrew to the corner by the fireplace and pulled a face. Celia too felt embarrassed. For the Glicksmans and Sabotniks, this ramshackle place was home, and hard work was their daily bread. Money was short and their few possessions had to be made to last as long as possible. Maybe Mrs Sabotnik was right. Maybe she really was spoilt. It was true: household chores were for the servants, not for her. What right had she to brag about breeding horses, while Sarah'le soldiered on uncomplainingly in her poky little house? Celia slipped out of the front room and joined Sarah'le in the kitchen. She was already filling the sink from a heavy kettle. Celia rolled up her sleeves, determined to help, but did not know what to do. She felt utterly lost. Sarah'le realised that the poor girl, for all her fine clothes and fancy manners, had no idea how to manage in a kitchen. But she did not want to discourage her; it was not every Shabbat she had a willing helper.

"The tea towel is over there," she pointed, smiling. Celia started to dry up. She worked slowly; she had never been taught how to work fast and efficiently in a kitchen. She took an age to polish one cheap glass and wipe a chipped plate.

The concentration on her face made Sarah'le laugh. "You'd never make a living in service." Sarah'le took the towel from her and showed her how to dry the cutlery and plates. Celia was amazed at her speed. "And don't worry. It's not Royal Doulton china. See, do it like this. It's much quicker and gets them just as dry." She handed the towel back to Celia with an encouraging smile.

"I am sorry. I know I'm useless. But I've never done this before"

"Don't worry. I'd be useless doing what you do."

Celia felt a stab of anxiety: what did she actually do that was of any real worth?

Meanwhile the rest of the family was relaxing, digesting the nourishing Shabbat meal.

"I bet right now my Sarah'le and Celia are complaining about us men. Women are the same everywhere. That's why they're so protective of their kitchens, and we're not allowed in." Dani puffed contentedly at his pipe. Caleb felt he had been promoted from a bachelor to a husband, a man of stature and worth. It made him feel proud. Mr Sabotnik closed his eyes. Dani reached for a small accordion and played a gentle melody. "The *chalutzim* taught me this one. Why not join me, Cal?"

Caleb could not resist the invitation and took down the violin from its place on the wall. Dani played a tune, and then built an arrangement around it. Caleb picked up the harmony and added new variations. Before long the Sabotniks had joined in, first humming, then singing a round while they drummed out the rhythm on the armrest. After the song ended, they paused a moment, wondering what to sing next.

Sarah'le joined them from the kitchen. "There. With Celia's help, I got through the work in half the time."

Caleb smiled, satisfied. His fiancée had done the right thing in a challenging situation. "Where is she?" he asked.

"She's gone to powder her nose," Sarah'le said. For the Glicksmans, "powdering one's nose" meant a trip down the path to the wooden shed at the bottom of their narrow garden.

It suddenly occurred to Caleb that he had not kissed his fiancée for at least two hours. But that could easily be put right. Maybe he could snatch a discreet kiss when Cielie returned. He had noticed a small bench in the garden behind the house; they would not be disturbed there. He left the room, pretending he needed a book from Dani's bookshelf in the back room. He waited, impatiently. Celia returned, washed her hands at the kitchen sink and freshened up her scent. As she left the kitchen, he put a hand lightly on her shoulder. Seeing his finger held to his lips, she smiled conspiratorially and kept quiet. He indicated the little bench through the window. They tip-toed out.

It was dark and the air was mild. They relaxed in each other's company. After they had done what one does when one is young and in love and sitting on a bench, Caleb withdrew his arms. The delicate matter that had occupied his mind for the last few weeks needed to be brought into the light. He shuffled a little, dropped his head and played with his fingers, nervously.

"Are you all right, my love?" Celia asked, at once concerned. She stroked his back to reassure him.

"There's something I've kept putting off talking to you about . . . because you were so disappointed over the wedding arrangements. But we must talk about it. It's very important to me . . . well, for both of us . . . for our future together." He looked at the London sky. The stars were barely visible. He took a deep breath. He was collecting his thoughts, marshalling his words and arguments. "Celia, my love, you know I'm a Jew. That means I'm not a Christian: I don't believe in Jesus; I've never been baptised or confirmed; I've never taken communion, and I've never even read the

New Testament. I don't, I haven't and I never intend to. For me, Christianity is a false religion – polytheistic, pagan, worshipping three false gods, and all that. What's more, over the last 2,000 years, my people have suffered more at the hands of the Christian church, and in the name of Jesus, than from any other source. I know that Alistair says, 'But they weren't real Christians,' and tries to convince me I should become a 'real Christian'. To be frank, I don't care who's a 'real' Christian and who isn't. To me, a Christian is someone who practises Christianity or simply says, 'I've been baptised.' He celebrates Christmas and Easter, weddings and funerals, and doesn't care about what he eats. Alistair hasn't the haziest notion what he's really asking me to do. For me, to convert to Christianity means I must deny my roots, my people, my Land, my God and my religion. And even you have no idea how deep the wounds are that I still carry from the time I was thrown out of the family when my parents became Christians. Whether I like it or not, I'm a circumcised Jew, a son of the covenant, a descendant of Avraham, Yitzchak and Ya'akov. To become a Christian – 'real' or otherwise – makes me an outcast, an apostate and a Goy. It's like my asking you to become a . . ." he searched for a suitable analogy, ". . . a Shintoist Geisha girl at a time when Japan and England are at war. In fact, the whole idea is so repellent to me that I don't ever want to see a New Testament in our home, or hear the name of Jesus mentioned. Are you able to promise me that? Please . . .? If not . . . I don't know what . . . where we can go from here."

He paused, visibly upset. He shrugged in a gesture of helplessness. Celia knew that he was shocked at his own willingness to sacrifice their marriage over this issue. And she was shocked too, and hurt, but not daunted. By now she had begun to understand – to glimpse – his desperate struggle to free himself from the trauma he had suffered as a child. She didn't want to be the cause of more pain. She knew he was waiting for her answer and she already knew what she must say. She had been expecting this moment for some months and was glad that, at last, her beloved felt secure enough to confront this demon.

She thought of Rut the Moabitess who, 3,000 years ago, had been willing to abandon her own home, family and culture to become an Israelite. She surrounded his hands with hers. Using Rut's own words from the Bible, which she had carefully memorised, she solemnly promised Caleb that she was willing to do the same: "Entreat me not to leave you, or to turn back from following after you; for wherever you go, I will go; and wherever you lodge, I will lodge; your people shall be my people, and your God, my God. Where you die, I will die, and there will I be buried. The Lord do so to me, and more also, if anything but death parts you and me." She laid the fingertips of one hand gently to his lips to hush any sudden, ill-considered reply. She cupped his cheek in the other, caressing it softly. For a moment they both dwelt in, and on, the deep confession of love, surrender, obedience and fidelity she had just made to him.

Then Caleb took her hands in his, squeezing and caressing them gently. Eventually he broke their intimate silence: "I love our traditions and the Torah; I love the sense of belonging and joy and good cheer of our Shabbats and High Holy Days; I love the argument and debate as Jewish men tease out the fine points of the Law and seek to apply it to their lives; I love being a living, vibrant member of the oldest surviving nation on earth. But I don't want to follow all the far-fetched halachic interpretations of the Orthodox. The Rabbis mean well, but such interpretations are derived from a misuse of Torah. And I really don't know who benefits from hair-splitting observances . . . I want our home to be identifiably Jewish, which means we'll still keep many of the wonderful traditions of our ancient culture. But I promise you one thing: I will never lead you – or myself – into steely, unyielding religious observance. I will teach you our culture and traditions. We'll grow together as we share and participate in this ancient life. We'll try to live Judaism together as I understand it should be lived. And you'll come to love it as I love it. Our love for one another will grow in the process. It'll be a most wonderful time, as we learn to live one life together. We will become truly one – Echad – as God is One and indivisible. This too was inherent in Rut's 'betrothal vow' with the Land and people of Eretz Yisrael. Are you willing to walk this walk with me? Hand in hand, together?"

Celia looked straight at him and nodded solemnly. She did not need to speak. Caleb hugged her to him and kissed her. It was the happiest day of his life. For once, things seemed to be working out right.

The back door was opened and closed noisily. A man coughed discreetly. Caleb quickly withdrew his arms, but kept his fiancée's hand in his. Dani appeared. "Ah, I wondered where you'd gone."

"We're *benching*," Caleb said with a grin.

"I say. That's what you call it. I always thought it meant Jewish prayer. No wonder it never worked for me. I must have been doing it wrong all along." He winked at Celia. She blushed, but no one could see it in the dark.

～ 27 ～

London, first Friday in July, 1938

Caleb Levine and Lady Cecilia Eleanor Matilda Lancaster were married in a London Registry Office. It was a private ceremony and only friends and a few relatives attended. The bride and groom were delighted that both Esther and Francis had been able to come from Palestine and Germany. Barbara was also invited, and came with Francis.

So there they stood, in front of the registrar. Celia wore a beautiful, cream silk outfit, embroidered with tiny, multi-coloured flowers. In her hand she carried a small bouquet and her matching hat and veil added to her height and grace. Caleb was in a tailored morning suit and wore a grey top hat. Those who truly understood the young couple admired their commitment.

The Registry Office ceremony was brief, almost to the point of being humiliating. The elderly registrar did his best to make it special and meaningful as they went through the few steps the law required. But both bride and groom felt a little disappointed. There was no *chuppah*, no peal of church bells, and no grand reception. The moment Celia had dreamed of since she was a little girl was not to be: no gliding down the stairs of her home, to the whoosh of yards of silk and lace, her hand on her father's arm to be given away . . . Well, never mind. At least she was being married to the man she loved.

Caleb knew how she felt and was doing his best to make up for it. When the moment came to kiss the bride, he made sure that everybody present understood how he felt about her. Celia wished this moment might last forever. Alistair and Francis signed the register as witnesses and the wedding reception, with kosher catering, was held in a nearby hotel. When Caleb put his on, many more white kippot suddenly appeared. Celia felt proud. She played the role, sincerely, of the joyful bride but could not help glancing over her shoulder at the wedding plans she and Sebastian had made. There would have been over four hundred guests, a seven-course buffet lunch at Cecil Court and . . .

Caleb did not mind the relative simplicity of the wedding. He had got his princess, his *sarai*, and that was all that mattered to him. All the rest was icing on the cake.

Isaac was a little sad, though, that his son was taking a Gentile wife. How Isaac would have loved to hear his son speak the same ancient, tender, binding words that he had pronounced over his Gertrud: *Behold, you are consecrated unto me by this ring according to the Law of Moses and Israel.* He sighed. Celia had so naïvely and trustingly taken her place alongside Caleb in the history of God and man; joining the divine link running between heaven and earth through Judaism and its Messiah. How blissfully unaware she was of the consequences of her action on this happy day. What would the future hold for them? Isaac sensed that something impenetrably dark and evil loomed over the horizon. Ach, but the young couple were so happy . . .

The good father suddenly felt very emotional. Great anxieties for the future and overflowing joy for the moment were filling his heart. He had to do something. He decided to give his son and new daughter something that no man could touch or steal. So he stood up in front of everyone and said, rather formally, "According to Jewish tradition, I am permitted to pronounce the Seven Blessings for Bride and Groom over you both. And so that's what I propose to do."

The professor put his hands on their heads and chanted the ancient benediction which had been carefully handed down over the millennia. Although she could not understand much of what was said, Celia could tell that he was putting his heart and soul into his prayer. Then he blessed them again with a smile of deep satisfaction. The grateful bride and groom gave him a warm hug while the guests clapped. It was the highlight of the wedding.

The reception and luncheon went well. Caleb and Barbara took an instant liking to each other and Barbara congratulated Celia on her choice. "This one will make you much happier," she assured her and gave her an affectionate hug.

Celia was happy to see how sincerely Barbara was sharing in their happiness. She had lost a lot of her former "friends" through the scandal of her broken engagement and her too-hasty and unsuitable betrothal to Caleb. It was high time she made some new friends.

All the Lerocs, except Albert, had come to the wedding, amply accompanied by wives and children. This Franco-Jewish invasion livened up the event considerably. If there was one thing the French had really mastered, it was a well-planned, spontaneous family celebration. And, as Jews outnumbered Gentiles, the occasion ended with traditional lilting wedding songs and dances. Celia's face shone as she and her new husband whirled around the dance floor, accompanied by singing, cheering and clapping. Suddenly an accordion squealed. Dani had not been able to leave it at home; it had never yet missed a Jewish wedding. Lady Agatha got carried away by the celebration and clapped her hands with great gusto, very much to Lady Norah's consternation.

The latter had yielded, with the strongest possible protest, to her husband's command not to "be so bloody toffee-nosed and jolly well attend her daughter's wedding".

Throughout the celebration, Lady Norah sat at the top table with a sour expression pinching her face. Jewish guests who came to congratulate her were treated haughtily. Celia felt ashamed and secretly wished her mother had stayed at home.

Lord Besthorpe did not quite know what to make of this truly unorthodox wedding. He delivered a clumsy speech but, for Celia's sake, made a genuine effort to be sociable. Had he ever seen her happier? He couldn't remember. So he gave a piece of advice to the bridegroom as he shook his hand. "Now, my Jewish relative, you've got what you wanted. A little warning from me: if you don't make that girl happy, I'll break every damned bone in your body."

Caleb assured the Earl that he would do his best.

As a special wedding contribution, François, one of the Lerocs' sons, had made his summer home available to the young couple. So they spent a hot and blissful honeymoon in a small market town in the Roussillon.

* * *

On July 14th, 1938, Britain placed a restriction on the admission of qualified Jewish doctors and dentists from Germany. Only 185 had so far been permitted to practise in Britain. On the 25th of that month, the German government forbade Jewish doctors to treat all non-Jewish patients. Marianne Zink and her brothers would have to stay with the Levines for a little bit longer. Under such circumstances a return to Berlin was clearly out of the question. The professor tried to find a post for their father in England, but the British Medical Association insisted that their quota was full. When, in September 1938, the German government forbade all Jewish lawyers to practise, Caleb took it as a very personal insult.

Since January 1933, 40,000 refugees from Germany had come to England and the public were starting to mutter about a refugee crisis. At school, the Zink children were starting to feel that they were no longer welcome. To make matters worse, the United States was still sticking rigidly to its planned immigrant quota: 27,370 Jews a year. At that rate, it would take till 1958 for all of Germany's Jewry to find asylum in the USA, not counting the equally desperate Austrian Jews. Only the Netherlands, Denmark and the Dominican Republic kept their gates open to German Jews.

Leon and Esther had joined the Haganah, "gone to Aunt", as it was referred to in Palestine. "Let's face the realities," Esther had written, "The world hates us, and no one will come to our rescue. We are on our own."

While changing trains in Paris on the way home from their honeymoon, Caleb and Celia had witnessed heartbreaking scenes. The station was swarming with German and Austrian Jewish refugees clustered like bees without a hive. They were huddled together in little family groups, their few personal belongings squeezed into bundles, suitcases and trunks. Standing on the platform waiting for their connection, they watched, spread out before them, a tableau of multi-faceted human misery, painted in infinitely varied shades of suffering, fear and deprivation. Caleb's heart had bled for them, and he cursed his inability to do anything about it. Nothing had changed in 2,000 years. His people were on the run again, and again they had nowhere to go. And no one cared about them. God had promised Avraham offspring as numerous as the stars. Yet at this moment, God's stars had lost their sparkle and were being swept from the sky.

"Oh God, Cielie. What shall we do? Where can my people go?"

To Celia it seemed unbelievable that anyone could strip a people of their rights and dignity. From one day to the next, they had been reduced to a silently suffering, heaving mass of homeless, defeated, spiritless "inferior beings". She was shocked and frightened. A very pregnant woman was sitting uncomfortably on her suitcase in the midday heat. Arching her back and shifting constantly, she caught Celia's attention. She made her think of Mary riding on her donkey to Bethlehem. Shame overcame her. Here she was, nicely dressed, travelling freely and safely from a lovely honeymoon in France to a beautiful home in England. And something else struck her: she wasn't Jewish. *She* was a Gentile; *they* were Jews. That made all the difference. What if she had been born into a Jewish family? Might she, too, be sitting here, having lost her home, her possessions, her certainties and the security of her domestic routine? Might she, too, be uprooted, separated from friends and family, not knowing what tomorrow might bring? What an immature child she had been to cry on leaving Marsham for her beautiful new home in Epsom, a most generous wedding gift from Sir Arthur. She had freely chosen to leave and embark on the adventure of setting up home with the man she loved.

Caleb wanted to join the Haganah, too, but felt he could not. This just increased his restlessness and frustration. "We Jews are being expelled from Germany and Austria, while I'm supposed to be happily engrossed in silly little legal squabbles. And in my free time I dabble in a bit of boy-scout Zionism."

Celia had other concerns; she was still trying to work out how to be the wife she wanted to be. "If we lived in London, would it make things easier for you?" She was preparing herself for another radical step. She loathed even the thought of living in "the Smoke".

Caleb felt guilty at times because he took Celia's loyalty and support so much for granted. "The Torah gives us one year all to ourselves after marriage. So I can't join the Haganah till then." While his heart and mind were elsewhere, the young husband still wanted to fulfil his God-ordained duties to be a blessing to his wife.

"Do you think German Jewry can afford to wait a year?" Celia had asked.

Prime Minister Chamberlain continued to appease Nazi Germany. In March 1938, Hitler's troops had marched into Austria. In April, the Aryan Austrians expressed their delight to be annexed in a national referendum. The Czech people were less delighted to be swallowed up by the Thousand-Year Reich. Chamberlain hurried to Munich. On the 29th September, Hitler fobbed him off with a Non-Aggression Pact. "Peace in our time," Chamberlain triumphed, waving a worthless piece of paper. The Czech people were betrayed and abandoned.

As early as 1934, Britain had very reluctantly committed itself to rearmament, beginning with the Royal Air Force. In 1935, voices called for a national defence strategy. Now it was autumn 1938. Sandbags appeared in the streets of London and elsewhere. Air-raid shelters were excavated and trenches dug. Pill boxes were dotted along the south coast, and the beaches were garlanded with barbed wire. The public was advised to carry gas masks at all times and taught how to black out their windows.

That gloomy Shabbat afternoon the weather had changed. It was cool and was raining steadily. Celia sat sketching, humming a tune. Caleb tried to concentrate on a book. Now and then he looked up and stared hard at nothing in particular. Celia glanced over the top of her pad and noticed his behaviour. She knew what he was thinking. He had talked about little else for weeks. Eventually he put down his book and fetched the jar with soil from Palestine. Opening it, he poured some into his hand and broke up the lumps between his fingers. Then he poured the fine sandy soil from one hand to the other.

Celia watched him for a while. "You're miles away in

Palestine, aren't you? That's where you want to be, now more than ever. You'll be called up at any moment, but I know you don't want to join the British forces." Celia put down her pad and straightened her back. "There'll be war very soon, and then we'll all have to do our bit for king and country. But you've got another country to fight for, haven't you? And that's where you'd rather be."

Caleb sighed. "It's not as straightforward as that. Hitler wants to dominate Europe and in the process is destroying the Jewish people. And there's a refuge and home in Palestine for the persecuted Jews of Europe – which is totally closed to them now. I have two choices. Should I fight with the British against a murderous megalomaniac to save my people in Europe? Or should I fight anti-Zionism in the Middle East? That means fighting against the British – whose passport I carry – who are at this moment misguidedly, insanely, tightening restrictions on Jewish immigration into Palestine. In doing so they bar one of the precious few escape routes our people have. German Jewry are like sheep penned in with the wolves. And it seems that the British government wants to make sure the sheep stay in the pen. It's a hard decision. But what about you? What do you think I should do? I'd understand perfectly if you want me to stay here to defend your country."

In reply Celia once more recited the passage she loved from the Book of Ruth: "'Your people shall be my people, and your God shall be my God. The LORD do so to me, and more also, if anything but death parts you and me.'" Caleb was deeply touched. He had married a true Rut – a Gentile whose heart was one with Israel. "So when will we be leaving?" Now she was graciously creating an opportunity for him to discuss the subject closest to his heart.

"We? Who said 'we' should go? I will go. You will stay here."

"But isn't it also written, 'entreat me not to leave you, or to turn back from following after you; for wherever you go, I will go, and wherever you lodge, I will lodge . . .'"

"'. . . And where you die, I will die, and there I will be buried,'" Caleb ended her passage from memory. "I'm sorry, but you aren't coming with me. I don't want you dead and buried in Palestine. Not that I've any intention of getting myself killed, mind. No, you're definitely staying here. Besides, Rut never went to war alongside her husband."

"Don't you think I'd be of some use to you in Palestine?"

Caleb sat down next to her and closed his eyes. "It's not going to be an exciting grand adventure; it's going to be a war. I need to know you're safe and waiting for me when I return."

"So you don't want me with you," Celia said, somewhat archly.

"I'd love to have you with me, Cielie darling, but I can't always have what I want. Please understand." He took her face in his hands and kissed her.

Still, in early October they celebrated *Chag Succot* with as much joy as the political circumstances around them allowed. Caleb constructed a beautiful *succah* in the garden. Celia helped him to decorate it. "From now on this will replace decorating the Christmas tree," she thought, with sudden mixed feelings. But they were quickly chased away by the pride and joy she saw on her husband's face. He had built a *succah* for them as a couple. Soon, Caleb hoped, for them as a family.

The first few days of the Feast of Tabernacles were cold and wet. Nevertheless, they committed themselves to eating their dinner under the green leaves of the *succah*. Only when a heavy shower started to water down their *kneidlach* soup did they agree to go inside. Then the weather turned and the young Levines proudly invited the family to join them for this great occasion. So they feasted – along with the whole

Jewish community around the world – in the late Indian summer sunshine. They were observing the commandment to feast and rejoice before Adonai for eight days, something they had learned to do with much gusto over the past 3,500 years. For a short while they forgot what was happening on the Continent. Papa Levine was at his liveliest, made music with his son, told traditional stories, and shared the latest anti-Nazi jokes which Jewish refugees had brought to Britain. On more than one occasion, he slipped into Yiddish.

On their first visit to the newly-weds some weeks earlier, Papa Levine had given Caleb two mezusot containing a few words from the Torah; one for the front door and the other for the back. He had slipped them into his son's hand discreetly, knowing that Gertrud would not approve. Since then, a quiet understanding had grown up between father and son, an understanding that said, "We are Jews after all." The mezusot were now fixed to the doorposts of the house. Without thinking, Isaac returned quickly to the habit of touching them whenever he went in or out. Yes, his son was a Jew and his house was Jewish. And how he loved being with his son and daughter-in-law, in their own home.

~ 28 ~

London, late October 1938

As the year progressed, Isaac Levine's concern for the Zink family grew daily: Nazi chicanery seemed to know no limits. They found new ways of humiliating their Jewish community that bordered on the demonic. Jewish people were forced to add either the name *Sarah* or *Israel* to their names, depending on whether they were male or female. On October 5th, 1938, the authorities confiscated their German passports and issued them with new ones stamped with a large *J*. Two weeks later, 17,000 Polish Jews living in Germany were expelled.

But, however hard Isaac tried to persuade Friedrich Zink to come to Britain with all his family, he refused to abandon his Jewish patients. Although his family begged him not to, Isaac decided to go to Berlin in person. He had to convince his old friend before it was too late. "They can't touch me; I'm a British citizen," he assured his family.

Before he left, he gave Celia a small, well-worn book. "I want you to look after this until I return," he said. It was a leather-bound New Testament.

Celia took it hesitantly. "Caleb doesn't want to see any of these in our home . . ."

"I know. But I just want you to look after it for me. Please."

Celia struggled with her conscience. She did not want to upset her husband, or be rude to Papa. She had promised her husband not to bring Jesus into their home. Dare she break her promise? But then this little, innocent-looking book was not 'Jesus', was it? If she kept it tucked away in her drawer until Papa's return it could surely do no harm, or could it? What was more, how on earth could she turn down the only personal request Isaac had ever made of her? She made up her mind. "Very well," she said, still hesitantly, not yet understanding what might lie behind Isaac's request.

Isaac patted her hand and gave her one of his special smiles. "Thank you, Celia. You won't regret doing this for me."

The younger Levines' day always started the same way. The housekeeper arrived at 6.15 am. She would light the fire in the dining room and then prepare breakfast. Celia came down, a warm dressing gown wrapped tightly around her, to face the first cold spell of the season. From spring to autumn, she was bright and fresh in the mornings. But it took all her self-discipline to get up to a cold and dark house as winter approached. When Caleb had the audacity to comment on her bouts of morning grumpiness, all he got was a brusque, "Well, I'm sorry, but your bright and cheerful little lark has migrated to warmer climes."

She was pouring hot water into the teapot, only half awake and still bleary-eyed. The telephone rang. Celia was immediately alarmed: who would be calling at this hour?

It turned out to be Gertrud Levine. "Celia, have you heard the terrible news? Last night the Nazis burnt down all the synagogues in Germany. And Isaac is still in Berlin."

It proved to be the onset of a time of devastation and horror for the Levines, as it was for all of European Jewry. It heralded the first peak of Nazi terror, a peak that would be horribly surpassed in the next seven years. All through the day, news of what was happening in Germany unfolded. The *Kristallnacht* reign of terror, later to be known as the Night of

Broken Glass, or the November 1938 Pogrom, was the Nazis' revenge for the murder of a German diplomat in Paris by a Jewish youth. Through the night of 9th to 10th November 1938, synagogues were burned to the ground, cemeteries were systematically desecrated, and Jewish buildings, shops and homes were looted and smashed. 26,000 male Jews were arrested and imprisoned.

All that morning Gertrud tried to reach the Zinks, but no one answered the telephone. Celia tried to contact Francis, without success, and then hurried to London to be with Gertrud. Caleb and Judy joined them at lunchtime. At 2.30 pm the telephone rang. Gertrud was relieved to hear Emilie Zink's voice.

Moments later her world fell apart. "Isaac is dead?" It was said more as a question than a fact. Her gaze was empty as she looked at her family, one by one.

"You must have misheard, Mama. Surely!" Judy cried.

Gertrud shook her head. "No." She was numb, speaking in a trance.

"Mama, what exactly did she say?" Caleb was barely able to control his rising panic.

Gertrud staggered to the nearest chair and collapsed into it. She spoke woodenly. "SA men banged on the front door of their flat at around midnight. Friedrich was afraid they'd break it down if he didn't open. They'd already been watching what was going on in the street from the balcony. The SA then vandalised the flat. Isaac protested, but he was pushed to the floor and . . ." Gertrud stopped to suppress a sob. "Isaac apparently had a massive heart attack at that moment. Emilie says there was nothing Friedrich could do. A neighbour took him to hospital. He was dead on arrival. They have arrested Friedrich . . ." She dropped her face into her hands and sobbed.

Judy rushed to comfort her. She could not believe it: her Papa, dead? The others were stunned and silent. The heart and soul of the Levine family was dead? Isaac, the gentle, quiet man who was filled with compassion for every living being, irrespective of class, colour or religion, was no more? He had always been so understanding. He was never condemning or judgmental towards anyone. Was he really gone?

Caleb was paralysed. My Papa dead? It had taken ten years to restore their fragile relationship. Now, with old wounds healed and a true understanding beginning to grow, God, in His unfathomable wisdom, had decided to take him. Why? Why, God? Caleb was convinced that his father wanted to renounce Christ and return to the Jewish fold. But now it was too late. Caleb only hoped that God had granted his father sufficient time to recite the *Sh'mah*.

When he came home from school, Hansi Zink ran straight to Caleb. Delighted by this wonderful surprise visit, he grabbed his hand. "Will you play with me, Uncle Caleb?"

"No. I'm sorry, Hansi. Not today. Just tell your brother and sister to get changed and come down for supper."

"Is something wrong? Have I been naughty?" The little boy felt convicted by the total absence of happiness in his favourite uncle's manner.

Caleb was moved by Hansi's readiness to admit any fault if only he would play with him. He stroked the boy's blond hair. "No, Hansi, you haven't done anything wrong. You're fine; you're a splendid little chap."

"Is it about Mutti and Vati?" Big blue eyes searched in his face.

"Don't worry. For now, just do as you're told." Hansi scuttled off.

Except for a blessing for the food, their supper was eaten in total silence. The children looked at each other uneasily. Finally, Erich asked, "Something bad has happened, hasn't it?"

"Just eat your food," his big sister, Marianne, ordered him.

He did not feel at all hungry. Adults were terribly secretive at times. They always tried to hide bad news from children. But they usually did it so badly that the children became more alarmed than if they had been told the truth straight away.

After supper, Caleb broke the news. "Uncle Isaac will not be coming back from Berlin. He had a heart attack. I'm afraid he is dead."

The children looked up, wide-eyed. They had never faced the death of someone close before. The thought that they would never see Uncle Isaac again made their stomachs knot with anxiety. Hansi asked if Uncle Isaac was an angel now. Caleb was angry at this silliness and stared at him hard through narrowed eyes.

But Gertrud spoke softly: "No, Hansi. But Uncle Isaac is with God now. Because he believes in Jesus. He's very happy now, singing and laughing and worshipping the Lord. We're very sad because we miss him terribly and won't see him for a long time. But he's not sad at all. He's in heaven where there's no pain, crying or suffering." Gertrud was emotionally exhausted and was hardly able to speak or think clearly. She was surprised to discover she had been comforted by her own words. Despite her grief, she smiled a little smile.

With a loud clatter, Caleb dropped his knife and fork onto his plate, crashed back the chair and stormed out of the room. "Uncle Caleb is very upset," Gertrud continued. She still did not have the strength to tell the children about their own father. That must wait till later.

With his hands thrust deep into his trouser pockets, Caleb stared sightlessly out of the window. As every person does at such times, he was wrestling with the vexing question of life after death. How could his mother be so very sure that his father was forgiven? Had his father worshipped only the

One True God, the God of Israel, Caleb might have found solace in the thought. But, as it was, he had chosen to worship three false gods. The thought that his own father was now condemned to live eternally in Gehennah – the place of eternal fires – filled him with fear and fury.

Gertrud followed him into the music room and went up to her son. "Caleb, dear. Please," she said quietly. She touched his arm gently but he shrugged off her hand. "I know how you feel about what I said to the children. But it's the truth. You wouldn't want me to tell them a lie deliberately, would you? There's great peace and comfort in that truth. I know that I'll be reunited with your father when I die. There is a way out of . . ."

Caleb's rage and impotence boiled over. "I can't believe you can tell Jewish children such an unbelievable . . ." He was lost for words that would not be too insulting. "My father is a Jew. He would have recanted – rejected Christianity and returned to Judaism – if it wasn't for you. You're responsible for his apostasy. You are guilty of leading him astray. And I – and God – hold you accountable for his soul," Caleb was shouting at his newly widowed mother. All feeling for her grief was banished by his own. And by his anger.

Gertrud had braced herself for a vicious response, but was taken aback, nevertheless. His verbal slap in the face had been much harder than she had expected. So, nothing had changed in all these years. Caleb had not moved an inch in his views. Her heart was crushed by her own son at a time when they most needed each other. Yet, above all, she felt pity for him. At last, after years of pain, their broken relationship had seemed to be mending. Now this ill-timed tragedy was splitting the family again. Their painstaking reconciliation would be blown apart for ever if she said anything wrong. "O Isaac, why did you have to leave us now?" she cried in her heart. But how could she possibly deny the only truth she knew? Could she refuse the children this ray of hope and comfort? Just because of Caleb's religious hard-heartedness and blindness? Why had God still not removed the veil from his heart? What should she say? Nothing, despite the unjust insults her child had heaped on her. "Please, Lord Jesus, deal mercifully with him and save him," Gertrud prayed silently. A fresh wave of grief and tears swept over her.

～ 29 ～

London, 10th November 1938

It was Caleb who told Esther the news. He telephoned her at the Hadassah Hospital, hoping she would be on duty. It took a while for them to be connected. The line was terrible.

"Hello," said Esther curtly, not sure who was at the other end.

Hearing his sister's voice brought him some comfort. She would understand his Jewish soul. "Shalom, Esther. It's Cal."

"Shalom, Cal. Goodness . . . Are you calling from England? Is everything all right?

"Esther, our father is dead . . . He had a heart attack in Berlin . . . during *Kristallnacht* . . . It's all a mess here and . . ." he faltered. There was a long pause at the other end. Caleb wondered if they had been cut off.

Then Esther spoke again: "Is Mama all right? And Judy?" She had to shout down the line.

The crackling was so bad that Caleb could barely hear her. "We still can't take it in. It's too unreal . . . Can you come back to London?" Silence.

Then, "I can't talk freely. Aunt needs me . . ."

"It is a mitzvah to honour the dead, especially one's father and mother . . ."

"You don't have to tell me that, Caleb. He's my father too. But we must put the living before the dead. That's what Papa always says. I'll do my best to come. But I must go now . . ." Esther was not showing her emotions; she was not someone who cried easily.

"Shalom . . . And God be with you . . ." Caleb prayed that another Levine would not be getting killed in the near future.

"Shalom."

Alistair, Judy and Gertrud found solace in the certain hope of the resurrection in Messiah. They thanked God that Isaac had run a good race and had now received his crown of life. Having reflected on these things, they now felt they could think more clearly.

"Where's Caleb?" asked Judy.

"He and Celia have gone to the undertaker's to arrange for Papa's arrival in London. Celia's brother is being terribly good. He's making sure that everything – the embalming and coffin and everything – goes smoothly on the German side." Gertrud sighed, grateful that this burden had been lifted from her.

"How is he?" enquired Alistair.

"Caleb? In a very bad way, I'm afraid. We had an appalling confrontation yesterday. It's not the dead I worry about, it's the living."

"I know, Mama. But he doesn't understand yet," said Judy. "One day he will."

"I wish I had your faith. Oh, Judy. Papa has died and it's starting all over again . . . Celia did him so much good . . . But now, again . . ."

"But think how isolated he must feel," said Judy. "He has no assurance, no answers, only a very vague hope. He's releasing his fear as anger. It's not really you he's cross with; it's his own stubbornness and refusal to yield to God. He's like a ram butting its head against a wall. Imagine the pain he's going through; he's got no true comfort or hope. He's so much worse off than we are."

There was a sad smile on Gertrud's face. "You talk like your father."

Obituaries appeared in the papers. They all extolled Professor Levine's medical achievements and his dedication to charitable causes. Gertrud and Judy read them over and over again.

"He did what any good Jew should do; he was a light to the Gentiles," asserted Caleb. His family did not challenge his view.

"We all know that Papa carried God in his heart wherever he went." Judy was sticking to the common ground of their faith, to truths they all shared.

Caleb's frame of mind had not improved and he was now asserting his Jewishness – and their heretical Christianity – more aggressively than ever. Even Celia found it trying but excused him because of the great emotional pressure she knew he was under.

Caleb was struggling most painfully. He just could not understand why this wonderful man, his father, who had taught him so much about life and living, had been taken from him – and to a place where he could not reach him. He would and could not accept the finality of death and divine judgement. His conscience was becoming a burden to him: he felt guilty about every small opportunity he had missed to express his love for his father, and for denying him access to his heart. Such thoughts tormented him, night and day.

Gertrud and Judy watched what was happening with concern, and hoped and prayed it would pass. This was the main reason why they did not object when Caleb insisted that he perform the last Jewish rites for his father before the coffin was finally closed. He in turn came to accept that Isaac would be buried in a Christian graveyard, not a Jewish one. In both Jewish and Christian eyes, Isaac had converted to Christianity. He was no longer Jewish. But for Caleb he had always been, still was, and would for ever remain, a Jew.

The quiet, intensely private ceremony took place in the undertaker's back room. Caleb covered his father with his tallit according to the Jewish custom. Celia, who had accompanied her husband, could not bear the grisly sight and turned away. Next, he cut off the *tzitsit*. It was the heaviest and most heartbreaking duty he would ever perform. How could his father's body look so small and frail, the face so tiny, and the mouth, which had spoken such wisdom, be so closed? For ever. Why would the slim, delicate hands never again play a musical instrument, bring comfort through their touch, or healing through their skill? Why could these melancholy eyes, whose look could penetrate the soul, not suddenly open again? Why, Papa? Why not, God? Papa's eyes used to evoke remorse and repentance faster in his children than all of Mama's chidings and smacks. His gentle, penetrating gaze could melt a child's heart into a confession of guilt and grief over some little naughtiness. Papa never once had to spank his son or daughters. To upset their father was considered a heinous sin by the Levine children. By the time he came to the last *tzitsit*, Caleb's eyes were blinded with tears.

Finally, he placed his father's long unused tephillin in the coffin and sprinkled a jar of sand from Palestine over his body, soil from the Jewish homeland he had never seen. Caleb remembered the exact place where he had scooped it up. He could not have anticipated how soon he would need this precious soil for his beloved father.

"Now, Papa, now you are free from the Torah," he said quietly.

A few days after the funeral, at the request of his mother, Caleb went through his father's tidily kept desk drawers. At the back of the bottom drawer he came across a bundle of unopened letters. They were all neatly tied together with string. Caleb looked at them, curious. All the letters were addressed to his grandfather Levine. He asked his mother if she knew about them. Gertrud took the letters and held them for a moment, thinking, her fingers tracing her husband's handwriting.

"Your father wrote to him every six months, at Passover and Rosh Hashanah. The letters were always returned, unopened. I didn't know he'd kept them." Gertrud handed them back to Caleb. "You can read them. I know what they say." Or so she thought.

Over the next few days, Caleb read and re-read his father's letters. The first was dated more than a decade earlier. Isaac had tried to explain why Jesus was the Messiah, and why he had to obey His call. It was about six pages long and used arguments and biblical passages that Caleb knew well. He did not spend much time on them. Over the following years, Isaac had written about his family more. He had recounted how Esther was doing so well at Cambridge, and what a kind, happy and loving girl Judy was; she was growing into the apple of her parents' eye. He had also spoken about Caleb: that he was becoming a strong and confident young man, the son that every father could be proud to have.

Caleb paused in his reading. His father was writing in his own unique and gentle style, with sensitivity, warmth and earnestness. But underlying everything was the longing of a banished child to be understood, and the urgent plea for reconciliation with his father. After his fateful and devastating decision, he was subconsciously begging to be acknowledged by his own father. But his appeals struck no chord of mercy in the old man. Caleb began to feel a deep sorrow for his father rising within him. How did his father feel each time a letter was returned? Did he feel a bitter stabbing pain whenever his offer of love and peace was rejected? What desperate heartache must he have felt? And all this time he, Caleb, had only added to his anguish by his scornful and derisive behaviour. Yet Papa had described him as a son every father could be proud of. Caleb's conscience winced at the wholly undeserved and gracious way in which he had been loved and cherished by Isaac. It was strikingly evident that Professor Levine had loved him unconditionally, despite all the hurts and rejections he had received. "Oh, Papa, if only I had told you how much I loved you, how much you meant to me. If only I had once explained how much I yearned for your fellowship and spiritual company. If only we had prayed together as Jews, just once as father and son. If only . . ." The sheet of brittle paper crumpled as his throat tightened and his fist clenched.

The letters got shorter and shorter as time went by; maybe Isaac's hopes of a reconciliation were fading. But this began to change as soon as Celia entered their lives. Yitzchak started to share his growing doubts about some aspects of Christian doctrine. He was being challenged to think things through for himself. This young lady, who had no theological training, had seen weighty biblical issues with innocent clarity and astounding perception. Through her influence, Yitzchak had started to re-evaluate some of the teaching he had hitherto accepted unquestioningly.

"At heart she is a Jewess," he had written. "One day she asked me why we do not keep 'shabbos' if we so fervently believe in obeying the Ten Commandments. I explained why, but realised the contradictions in my own argument as I was speaking. I was merely repeating what I had been told, not what the Scriptures actually said. Jesus pointed out to His listeners, 'You heard it said, but I say to you.' I began to wonder whether I had more faith in what I had 'heard said' in the church than in what our Saviour and the Scriptures were actually 'saying to me'."

Caleb found this comment, and others in a similar vein,

most perplexing. Surely, his father was starting to understand at last that Jesus of Nazareth could not be the Messiah. The true Messiah of Israel would never abolish Shabbat, the day that the Jews say has kept them as a people. So, what on earth or in heaven was now keeping Isaac from renouncing Christianity? But here the letters ended. He would never know the answer to that last question.

Gertrud had hoped and prayed that, out of respect for his dead father, Caleb would at last take Isaac's faith to heart. Instead, Isaac's words were leading Caleb in the opposite direction. His father's tacit doubts about some aspects of Christianity only reinforced Caleb's belief that, given time, his father would have recanted.

Celia too was unsettled and troubled. Dani and Sarah'le had urged the young Levines to join in the celebrations of the Purim Ball in February 1939. They hoped it would lift Caleb out of his depressed and morose mood. Caleb reluctantly agreed and, to Celia's delight and surprise, was quickly caught up by the joyful, back-slapping festivities. He flung himself into the arguments his friends were having with enthusiasm, waving arms, shrugging shoulders and raised voice. She watched as he earnestly furrowed his brows at some shocking notion, only to smooth them out with a laugh a moment later. Yes, Caleb was back in his element again. Snippets of German, Yiddish and Hebrew floated past her. Watching him, Celia saw an entirely different man emerge. She would barely have recognised the Caleb she was now watching had she not already seen him in the film from Palestine. She was grateful, and happy for him. She remembered when they had first met at Bleckham. Their roles were now reversed. "Now it's he who's a part of the wallpaper," she thought. "And it's I who am the stranger in their midst."

Most of the Jewish ladies at the Ball seemed to know each other well. Caleb had quickly mingled with the men folk and had assumed his wife would do the same with the ladies. But Celia had found herself politely excluded from their conversation once it became clear she was not Jewish. Celia understood how and why Caleb had felt so uncomfortable in her own social circle. Jews *were* different. She felt poles apart from the people her husband was so at ease with. She understood how Esther could have viewed her as an alien, as someone who did not belong among their people. The Jews had survived for so long only by stubbornly sticking to one another and to their traditions and culture; fighting off every alien invasion. Esther had simply assumed that Celia was, and would always be, incapable of meeting the emotional and spiritual needs of her beloved brother.

Celia's thoughts kept wandering. She loved to watch him when he opened his letters at the breakfast table. With a frown of concentration on his forehead, his eyes would glide over the sheet of paper. She would look at his hand, the fine shape of his ear, the bold line of his nose, and his dark curls. They gave him an air of dignity and independence. At times like this her love for her husband would overflow within her and Caleb became the object of her heartfelt devotion.

But there were other moments, darker moments. Such as now. Then she even caught herself thinking that it might have been better if he had married a Jewish girl. She would be able to understand his complicated nature and upbringing so much better. They would have been able to share their common historical past and predestined future; she would have better understood the everlasting covenant they would both have been part of. Celia felt their hearts were inseparably intertwined, and yet . . . There were moments when she felt fearfully distant from him, as if she did not belong to him at all. She suddenly felt very rejected and tearful.

"May I ask for the next dance?" Dani had noticed her sadness and loneliness. With a heavy heart Celia accepted

335

and allowed him to lead her around the dance floor. "Has something upset you?" he asked. She shook her head; she did not want to talk about it. Dani made an enlightened guess. "Many of us feel like this at English social gatherings, you know. Our Purim Ball must be very unsettling for you. You are suddenly surrounded by all our lovely and extraordinary *mishpochah*. You've so many new friends and family you never knew you had. And you are now seeing the man you love and thought you knew in a new light. You're seeing him as he really is." He looked carefully at her as they danced. "Give yourself time. Culturally, you've already come a very long way. But there's also still a long way to go. No wonder you're feeling a little disheartened. I understand that. What with the upheaval in Germany, getting married, your father-in-law dying . . . You've had a bit too much to cope with. But you're a strong person; you'll make it through the desert."

"Oh, Dani. You're so kind to me. I don't know how I'd manage without you and Sarah'le," Celia replied gratefully. She was comforted and strengthened by the faith he seemed to have in her.

In all the turmoil, Celia had forgotten that she still had Papa Levine's New Testament. It was carefully hidden in the drawer of her bedside table. Should she give it back to Gertrud or Judy? As Celia went to fetch it from its hiding place, she remembered the moment Isaac had given it to her. Holding the leather-bound book in her hand, she now wondered what Isaac's thought had been. Why had he wanted to give it to her? Puzzled and curious, Celia sat down on her bed, crossed her legs, and flicked through the pages. She stopped at passages Isaac had highlighted, or where he had added a comment in his tiny, neat handwriting. He had underlined one passage in the Gospel of Matthew, which read: "Do not think I came to destroy the Law or the

Prophets. I did not come to destroy but to fulfil." The professor, applying the normal Jewish meaning to the words "Law" and "fulfil", had crossed them out and replaced them with the words "Torah" and "interpret it correctly". The Bible passage continued: "For assuredly, I say to you, till Heaven and Earth pass away, one jot or one tittle will by no means pass from the Law till all is fulfilled." Again, the word "Law" had been replaced with "Torah", and "fulfilled" with "correctly interpreted". So the full text now read: "Do not think I came to destroy the Torah and the Prophets. I did not come to destroy but to interpret it correctly. For assuredly, I say to you, till Heaven and Earth pass away, one jot or one tittle will by no means pass from the Torah till all is correctly interpreted."

Celia was staggered. By changing two little words, the New Testament suddenly sounded so Jewish. Had Jesus really claimed He had come to interpret the Torah correctly? Caleb had already told her that this was exactly what the Rabbis taught that the *Bar-Torah* was going to do when He came. Isaac had changed other passages in a similar way. She read: "Whatever you want men to do to you, do also to them, for this is the Torah and the Prophets." And: "And then I will declare to them, I never knew you; depart from me, you who do not practise Torah." In Isaac's New Testament, the Gospel of Matthew was thickly underlined and annotated. Another passage read: "But if you want to enter into life, keep the mitzvot, the commandments of God." Was Jesus really telling people to keep the mitzvot? This had been the great point of dispute between Caleb and his father all along.

The Jews had long argued that, when He came, the Messiah would uphold and interpret the Torah correctly. Christians agreed that He had come to fulfil the Law, but they interpreted "fulfil" to mean that He had made the Torah obsolete, abolished it, made it null and void. Yet had she not just read that Jesus had said: "Do not think I came to destroy the Torah"? Celia continued to read Isaac's astonishing Bible notes. They continued thick and fast in the Book of Acts. She read: "They preached the word of God in the synagogues of the Jews. But when they departed from Perga, they came to Antioch in Pisidia, and went into the synagogue on the Shabbat. So when the Jews went out of the synagogue, the Gentiles begged that these words might be preached on the next Shabbat." The Book of Acts showed clearly that Jesus' disciples had kept the Jewish Sabbath. So why did the church deny it so insistently?

As she read on, Celia could hardly believe her eyes. She discovered that the book was full of practising Jews who believed in Jesus. What was more, even the Gentile believers went to the synagogue on Shabbat. Why had she never been told this before? She read on: "But some of the sect of the Pharisees who believed . . ." The Pharisees had also believed in Jesus? This too was new to her. And: "You see, brothers, how many myriads of Jews there are who have believed, and they are all zealous for the Torah." This was incredible: so it really was possible to believe in the Messiah and remain a Jew and zealously keep the biblical commandments of the Torah? Finally, in the last chapter of Acts, she read that the Apostle Paul said, "I have done nothing against our people or the customs of our fathers . . ."

The implications were enormous. First, what if Jesus of Nazareth really was the Messiah whom Caleb was so earnestly waiting and longing for? And second, what if the New Testament really did show that Jews who believed in Him were allowed, even expected, to keep the Torah? How would that affect Christians such as Judy and Gertrud who were Jewish by birth? Celia sighed deeply. Could the whole of Christendom be wrong on these issues? She shook her head; that was absurd. Two thousand years of Christianity and millions of Christians could not all be wrong on these points. Or could they? What a preposterous thought. She heard the front door open and close, and Caleb call out a greeting to his wife. Celia jumped off the bed and hid the forbidden book again.

~ 30 ~

Epsom, early March 1939

"How wonderful that we could meet again so soon," said Celia. She gave her sister-in-law an affectionate peck on the cheek. "You're just in time for morning coffee. It would be lovely if you'd stay for luncheon as well. You can, can't you?"

The new wife was always grateful when Judy called. Life here in Epsom was so very different from Marsham. Here she had to assume her new role as the Honourable Mrs Levine. It did not come easily to her. Socialising was still not her strong point, nor Caleb's, for that matter. Foxtrot had been put into livery at a nearby riding stable but, as Celia did not hunt, she was a little frowned upon by the local gentry. She shuddered at what they might think about her Jewish husband . . . She itched to help at the stables, but had to watch her position in society. Epsom was not Bleckham. And she had to consider Caleb's professional reputation. On the other hand, Celia shrank back from the thought of being sucked again into those familiar upper class circles or, worse, being wooed by the *nouveau riche*. It was simply not her world. So she was almost childishly grateful for Judy's company. Without her gift for making friends and introducing Celia to them, Celia might well have ended up as just another social wallflower, well heeled into a soft bed of splendid isolation.

Over coffee they chatted about the inconsequential trivia of family news. But before long the conversation turned to more serious matters. "And how is Caleb?" Judy asked. She stirred her coffee and glanced at her sister-in-law.

"Fine," said Celia. She did not want to be indiscreet, or complaining or disloyal.

"I mean, how is he *really*? In himself." Judy's probing continued and Celia felt a little cornered. But she knew Judy wasn't prying; her questions arose from a heartfelt concern for a brother she was honestly worried about.

Celia was hesitant with her reply. "He doesn't laugh as much as he used to, and the music he plays these days is so melancholy."

She thought back to an incident that had occurred last week. She had found him standing in the hall holding the telephone receiver. "No one there?" she had asked.

"No," he had replied. "I wanted to call Papa and then remembered . . ."

This had really worried Celia. "Why don't you start going to the synagogue again, Caleb? I'll come with you, if you like."

"No. I don't seem to get anything out of the services any more."

"But you went for Yom Kippur."

"That's what you do on Yom Kippur." Caleb had then cut the conversation dead and gone into his study, his head hanging, his shoulders hunched. He had closed the door on her, shutting her out of his life and his pain.

"He's still grieving terribly for Papa," she eventually said in answer to Judy's question. "But I'm hoping the worst is over now. There are a few encouraging signs, and Sarah'le and Dani are being wonderfully supportive." Celia paused and lowered her eyes. "But sometimes a dreadful frown crumples his brow. He doesn't even seem to realise it. If I ask him what he's thinking, he won't tell me. Only last night he mentioned that we can never really be sure whether God ever forgives us. I think he's tormented by the thought that he might never see his father again. And guilt over something that's happened in the past, I suspect."

"He needs to know he's forgiven in Christ Jesus. It's his only hope. He needs salvation." Judy spoke gently, but with real conviction.

"I knew you'd say that."

"I mean it. No one can earn forgiveness from God. It's His free gift to all who believe in His Son, Jesus."

"But surely you don't need to believe in Jesus to be forgiven? Doesn't it say somewhere in the Bible that God forgives all who repent and keep Torah? How else could Moses and David be forgiven for their sins?" Celia did not want to appear provocative.

"No, the Bible doesn't say that. Repentance and religious observance alone don't bring salvation. And yes, Moses and David were forgiven, but they believed in the Messiah to come, the ultimate Redeemer of Israel. So does Caleb. Sadly, somewhere down the line he's missed the point that the Messiah is Jesus and that He has already come. He's waiting for another messiah, a false messiah who isn't Jesus."

"But why can't we just believe in God and repent when we sin? Why is believing in Jesus so important?"

Judy was pleased that the conversation had reached this point. She knew she was on firm ground. "Let's look at the Letter to the Hebrews in the New Testament," she said. She fished a small New Testament out of her handbag and flicked through the pages till she found the passage she wanted. "It says here that, according to the Law, almost everything must be purified with blood. Also that, without the shedding of blood, there's no remission of sins."

"Yes, I think I understand. But that won't help Caleb, will it? Where can he go to make a sacrifice for his sins? The Temple in Jerusalem doesn't exist any more. The Rabbis are much more helpful. They say that God forgives Jews their sins if they confess them and make *tzedakah*, works of charity.

And through sincerely seeking reconciliation with God and our fellow man on Yom Kippur, of course."

"I know they say that; they even say you are 'saved' on the sole grounds that you are Jewish. But this isn't actually founded in Scripture. Why do you think God allowed the Temple to be destroyed in 70 AD? He needed to make it impossible for His people to keep the sacrificial system He had initiated in the Torah. He wanted to make the point that Jesus had come and paid the price for our sins with His own life. He shed His blood as a sacrifice for the forgiveness of our sins, once and for all. The blood-sacrifice system of the Torah has continued to this day, but in a modified form, with Jesus' death being the eternally effective sin-offering the Law requires. It goes a bit further than that, but that's the bare bones of it."

"But why? Why did God require Jesus to die as a sacrifice? Wasn't the animal sacrifice that the Torah commanded sufficient to earn forgiveness for sins?"

Judy was thrilled by Celia's genuine interest. She loved nothing more than sharing what she called "The Very Good News", and explaining the Scriptures. "Once every year, on Yom Kippur, a special atoning sacrifice was offered for the sins of all the people. That's what the Law demanded and what God expected of Israel. If this animal sacrifice had been able take away all sin, why was it repeated year after year?" And here Judy quoted the Bible by heart: "'For it is not possible that the blood of bulls and goats could take away sin'."

"Why not?" Celia asked innocently, and listened carefully for Judy's answer. For the first time in her life she really wanted to know what Christians like Judy honestly believed. Her knowledge of the Christian faith was so fragmentary and confused that it had never made any sense to her. Now she was prepared to look anywhere for help for her troubled and suffering husband.

"Because . . ." Then she looked up and read a passage to Celia. "'For, as by one man's disobedience', He means Adam's disobedience," Judy explained before continuing, "'many were made sinners, so also by one Man's obedience' . . . He's referring to Jesus' sacrificial death . . . 'many will be made righteous.' You see, Celia, sin came into the world through a man, Adam, so it can't leave through an animal. It has to leave through a man, Jesus. We have to leave the room through the same door we came in by. That's how God, in His righteous justice, has decreed it should be."

"Wait!" Celia jumped up and hurried upstairs to fetch Isaac's New Testament. "Where's that passage?" Suddenly she was aware that she had something that had been very precious to Judy's father. "I'm sorry. I should have given this to you sooner. It was Papa's. He gave it to me to look after before he went to Berlin. Strange, isn't it?" Celia handed the book to Judy.

Judy held it for a moment, looking at it searchingly. Then she made up her mind. "I'm sure Papa had a reason for giving it to you. I want you to keep it." She placed the book gently into Celia's hands.

Together they looked at several passages. Understanding was starting to take root in Celia's mind. She said, "I've been reading it secretly. I find the Apostle John's letters especially beautiful and comforting; every line just overflows with love. I think I'm beginning to understand why you became a Christian. But one question bothers me: is Jesus really the Messiah of Israel? You know Caleb's arguments, and I think his objections are valid. But I think I'm starting to understand why the Messiah had to come, suffer, die and be resurrected. But there's something else. The Torah and the Prophets were given to Israel by God, weren't they? And the Jews are called to lead the nations to God and salvation." Judy nodded, wondering what she

344

was driving at. Celia continued, "Then it follows, doesn't it, that the Messiah has to live within the framework of Judaism?"

"That's absolutely true, Celia. He did."

"But why then did his disciples reject the Torah and abolish the Sabbath? Why did they begin to keep new festivals incorporating pagan timing and symbolism? It seems so wrong and confusing."

"Jesus fulfilled the Law. He set us free from bondage to the Law and legalism."

"If the Torah is bondage and legalism, why did God give it to Israel in the first place? Does God want His people to live in bondage or under legalism? I don't think so. Moreover, why does He say, 'You shall therefore keep My statutes and My judgments, which if a man does,' – and by 'a man' I think He obviously means 'all mankind', not just Jews – 'he shall live by them: I am the LORD'? And there's another thing, Judy. You said that Jesus has set Christians free from the Law of Moses. Does that mean you can steal? Can a Christian say, 'Jesus kept the command "You shall not steal" for me, so it's fine for me to steal'? I don't think that would make sense, would it? But I want to show you something else. Look." Celia pointed to some of the passages Isaac had underlined and corrected.

Judy was perplexed. "I've no idea why he did it, or where he got those ideas from. It's so unlike Papa to tamper with the Word of God."

"Do you think it's possible the church could have made a mistake in translation? Do you think it's just remotely possible that Christians should keep the Torah today?"

"Now really, Celia! Certainly not. That's going much too far." Judy was quite categorical. "You do have some funny ideas. A little knowledge is a dangerous thing, you know. But do read the New Testament. God's Holy Spirit will guide you. He'll show you the truth."

And Celia did. After reading the four Gospels she was certain Jesus was a Jew, even if she was still not totally convinced that He was the Messiah. But when she got to the Apostle Paul's letters they confused her again. Suddenly, eating the food God had declared unclean in the Torah was allowed. And again, the observance of certain festivals – Celia assumed them to be Jewish – and holy days, months, seasons and years was strongly discouraged. His letters to the Galatians and Colossians seemed to deny any possibility of Christians keeping Torah.

She started to meet Judy regularly. Celia was hoping that she could shed some light on the apparent contradictions she had discovered. But some of Judy's explanations seemed only to make matters worse. Whenever Judy produced an argument against keeping the Law, Celia could find one for it. At times they got frustrated with each other and even a little heated.

Celia had begged Judy not to tell Caleb about their meetings but Judy was unhappy about this. "You shouldn't have secrets from your husband," she warned. But Celia insisted, and she gave in to her. "Perhaps the end justifies the means," Judy reasoned. "If Celia comes to believe in Jesus as a result, perhaps it may help Caleb find his way to Christ too."

That Celia was now suddenly showing a renewed interest in the Bible and Talmudic teachings pleased and amused Caleb. He was teasing her good-humouredly one evening. "Either you're planning to surprise me on my birthday with a Certificate of Conversion, or you're already well on the way to becoming a Rabbi." But instead of asking him about the teaching of Rabbi Maimonides, Celia asked what Jews believed about the resurrection of the dead, sin, and the relationship between man and God. He grinned. "Has Judy been having a go at you? Look, *sarai*, I'm not a Rabbi."

"But you ought to know these things," Celia teased him back.

Now Caleb had to laugh out loud. "*Oy gevalt*, I've married a *frummer* Goy." In his heart he was a proud and happy man that his beloved wife was showing such an interest in Judaism. But it was too soon to tell her.

Celia was so absorbed in reading her New Testament that she did not hear the key in the front door. Only when Caleb called a loud "Surprise!" did Celia start. Panicking, she hid her Bible behind the sofa cushions.

Caleb walked into the drawing room with a broad smile and a beautiful bunch of flowers in his hand. "You didn't expect me this early, *sarai*, did you? You're blushing. So I still make you blush? Wonderful." Caleb took his wife in his arms. Celia's blush deepened. Yes, her husband still had that effect on her. But her present embarrassment was caused by guilt over the hidden New Testament.

"I also have two theatre tickets. And I've booked a table at Boswell's. So . . . I suggest we send the housekeeper home early and have some time to ourselves before we go out for a romantic evening together." He grinned.

"I'll make us a cup of tea, shall I?" he called up the stairs to Celia, who was changing into her evening dress.

"That would be lovely. I'll be down in a minute."

Caleb chuckled and sighed. In God's eyes a day might be like a thousand years, but why must a woman's 'one minute' always be like half an hour? He brought the tea tray through to the drawing room and poured himself a cup. Putting it on a coffee table he dropped down contentedly onto the sofa. Something hard dug into his back. Looking for the cause of his discomfort, he found the New Testament and a notebook. Celia had just started a new one. At the top of the first page she had written, "Why Jesus is the Messiah". It was followed by a list of arguments in favour of this proposition.

Transfixed, Caleb stared dumbly at the New Testament in one hand and the notebook in the other. So that's why his sister and his wife had been meeting so regularly; that's why Celia had shown such a keen interest in the Jewish texts. It wasn't because she was interested in Judaism. It was because his very own baby sister was working behind his back to convert his wife to Christianity. Caleb was heartbroken and afraid. Would it never stop? Would Jesus always be able to reach out to sever bonds of love and friendship between people – even from beyond His grave? Was He not dead and buried, crucified outside Jerusalem 1,900 years ago? Yet His teachings survived. Somehow, the words of "a Jew", Jesus – worshipped as a good, loving and Holy God – had managed to spread hatred for "the Jew" who had become, in Gentile minds, a symbol of all that is evil. And, ever since, "the Jew" had paid dearly because of what "a Jew" had said and done. How ironic. Ideas seemed to be immortal and uncontrollable. They were born and bred in one mind and passed on, unquenchable and unstoppable, from mind to mind and generation to generation. How can one fight such an invisible and terrifying enemy as a false idea? How could "the Jew" ever defend himself from Christian anti-Semitism?

As a Gentile, Celia was a much easier target for conversion than he was. This he had always known. She was his vulnerable and soft underbelly. That's why he had made her promise never to abandon his faith. But did Christian trickery know no bounds? Was there no honour among the thieves who were now trying to steal the heart of his beloved? How could his own flesh and blood – Judy – do this to him? "Adonai, what can I do? How can I halt the damage and division Jesus keeps wreaking in my family? Will it never stop? And now this Jesus-plague has broken out inside my own four walls – within my own bed. Please, God, don't let this tragedy happen again in my family," he cried out in his heart. "Don't let me have to live in a constant struggle against the demon Christianity in my own home for the rest of my life."

"I'm ready. If you'd just button me up . . ." Celia walked into the room, fastening her watch strap. When there was no reply, she looked up. She saw a deathly pale Caleb standing in front of her. "Caleb, my love. What on earth has happened?" She rushed to him. He held out the books to her. Celia understood. She tried to stay in control of herself and the situation. Caleb would be reasonable. Surely. "I meant to tell you, darling. You see . . ."

"You've deceived me. You've betrayed every ounce of trust I ever had in you." Caleb's voice was hoarse and broken. "You knew I never wanted to see this thing in my home. Never. You promised me."

"Caleb, it's only a book . . ." Celia tried appealing to his reason. Unsuccessfully.

"A book! Don't you know the pen is mightier than the sword? That's not a book. It is a weapon of mass destruction for my people. Most of the slaughter, torture, expulsions, poverty and deception perpetrated against us Jews has been justified from the pages of that book. To us the cross is a symbol which means the annihilation of Israel and her God. And you know that." He was working himself into a rage. Suddenly his voice fell to a whisper. "I'd never have thought you, of all people, could have brought this sacrilege into my house. I truly believed you loved my people and me. I've trusted you as I've never trusted anyone before. That's why I married you. I went against every teaching and warning I'd received. Even my common sense. Now you've betrayed me as my uncle said you would. And we've barely been married nine months. I'd forgive you if I'd found you in bed with another man. But this secrecy, this treachery . . . Celia, you just don't understand what you've done to us . . . to me . . . Why did you do it, Celia, why . . .?"

349

"Please Caleb . . . I didn't mean any harm. I was just afraid you'd stop me if . . ."

"If you didn't mean any harm you won't mind my getting rid of this . . . thing." He threw his father's New Testament into the fire. Without thinking, Celia rushed to rescue it from the flames. It was singed but otherwise undamaged. "That's how much you value it, is it? I see it's so precious you'd happily burn your fingers for it." Caleb felt wretched, an emotional wreck.

Celia was kneeling down brushing off the smouldering ashes with the back of her hand. She didn't look up at him. "No, it's not like that at all. This Bible belonged to Papa. He gave it to me for safekeeping the last time we saw him. Before he went to Berlin. But I wish to God I hadn't kept it."

Her words were like a dagger thrust into Caleb's heart. "My own father?" In an eternal moment the bottom dropped out of his world. His very own beloved father had been working towards her conversion as well? Caleb had been grief-stricken when he had died. He had naïvely believed that Papa was returning to the true faith. But all along, behind his back, he had been trying to convert his wife. With one hand he had given him his mezusot and with the other he had given his wife the teachings of Christ. Caleb felt trapped by his own family, a sheep encircled by wolves, a fish caught in the dragnet of their Christianity. Would they stop at nothing to get him, even striking at him through his own beloved wife? But he was not beaten yet; he had a fighting spirit. He would not take their treachery lying down. He would avenge himself . . .

Caleb stormed out of the room. Celia hurried after him and caught him with the doorknob already in his hand. "Caleb, please . . ." She grabbed him by his coat sleeve.

With his back to her, his head hanging, Caleb raised both arms in a gesture of rejection. "Just don't touch me. Not now

. . ." He opened the door and walked out. Moments later, Celia saw him drive off.

"I could forgive you if I'd found . . ." How could he say such a terrible thing to her? Oh, why had she not been honest and open with him, as Judy had urged her to be? The full consequence of her secretiveness began to dawn on her. Caleb's strained emotions had made him tense and jumpy enough. This latest, tragic discovery must seem to him an incomprehensible breach of trust.

"Oh God, forgive my terrible foolishness," Celia prayed from the depth of her fear-ridden heart.

Caleb, furious, drove at breakneck speed to the Hornbys. He had to have it out with Judy and Alistair. Now. Once and for all. The tyres churned the gravelled drive leading to Grange Hall, which Alistair and Judy shared with his parents. Caleb opened the front door without ringing the bell. Shocked, the butler hastened to greet him.

"Ah, Mr Levine. Er . . . Good evening . . ."

"I must speak to Mr Hornby. Alistair. Where can I find him?"

"In the upstairs drawing room, I believe, but . . ."

With the tails of his coat flapping, and taking two steps at a time, an enraged Caleb – a proud and wounded son of the covenant – leapt up the stairs. Breathing heavily, he barged into the drawing room. He found Alistair and Judy, relaxed, quietly reading.

"Cal! Goodness! What on earth's the matter?" At the sight of his troubled friend, Alistair jumped up and hurried to him. As soon as he got close enough, Caleb grabbed him by the lapels and pinned him to the wall. Judy shrieked.

"We've always been straight with each other, Al," Caleb hissed through clenched teeth. Alistair could feel his breath on his face. Their noses almost touched. "And I'm not going to change now. I'll come straight to the point. When your" –

351

Caleb spat out a blasphemy against Jesus – "and Christianity begin to affect my wife and ruin my marriage, I'm not going to sit back and do nothing."

"What do you mean?" Alistair croaked, shocked by his friend's sudden and unprovoked attack.

"We both know our wives have been talking about Judaism and all your Christian stuff. Now listen very carefully: my marriage is sacred and I won't allow you or Judy to undermine it. I know perfectly well that you're doing it intentionally, that your sole goal is to convert Celia and me. Don't think you're deceiving me. But I won't allow it. Do you hear me? And if it doesn't stop, perhaps the time has come for us to go our different ways. You're Christians; we follow the Jewish faith. They're different religions. And they're going to stay that way."

Running out of steam at last, Caleb let go of Alistair, who breathed a sigh of relief. He straightened his jacket and tie and retorted, sharply and angrily, "For goodness' sake, man! Pull yourself together. And what do you mean by all this anyway, Cal?" He was thoroughly upset by his friend's rude, aggressive and appallingly ungentlemanly behaviour.

"I found my father's New Testament in our house. And now I discover that your wife . . ." Caleb stabbed his finger past Alistair's shoulder in Judy's direction, ". . . is trying to convert Celia."

"You honestly expect me to discourage Judy from trying to save a soul from eternal damnation?" Alistair would never forget the expression he now saw on his friend's face – the cold stare full of calculated hostility. Alistair remembered the line Caleb had once drawn between them and knew that Judy had overstepped it. So Jesus had finally got between them. But he was too angry to back down. "I'm sorry, Cal. Maybe the time has come for us to redraw the boundaries."

"Yes, maybe it has."

Alistair was taken aback. He had hoped for a constructive

dialogue, not a separation. Then Judy intervened. She was distressed by her brother's treatment of Alistair and felt she had to do something to calm Caleb down. He was quite unable to hear the truth in his present state.

"What kind of home have you got, Caleb? And what kind of man are you? Is your poor wife not allowed to decide for herself whether Jesus is the Messiah? Do you want to hear what Celia and I have been doing? Will that restore your peace of mind? Is the truth too shocking for you? All Celia did was ask me to explain why the Messiah had to come. And why He had to suffer, die and be resurrected. And she understood – sort of. But she wouldn't accept the fact that Jesus was the Messiah. Do you want to know why? Because He didn't insist His disciples should keep the Torah. Talking to her was almost as bad as talking to you. This is the truth, Cal. You have to believe me. Celia said she understood why I believed in Jesus, but said she would not, and never could, believe in a Messiah who wasn't a Torah-observant Jew. Because, in her own words, 'it would be too illogical'." Judy had succeeded in getting her brother's attention and now continued in a much softer tone. She went to him and put her hand on his arm. "Cal. Celia loves you more than you know. She knows how much you've been suffering since Papa died. She was willing to do anything to ease your pain. She even went as far as looking for the Messiah in case He might be able to help you. As it was, she came to the conclusion that the Jesus of the Christians isn't 'The One' she's looking for. And that was all."

Caleb relaxed a little but remained very angry. "I'm warning you both," he growled. He raised his finger, pointing at Judy and then at Alistair. "Stay away from my wife." Then, slapping the astonished couple across the face with one last look, he turned and left.

It was very late when he got home. On the way, he had pulled off the road and turned off the engine. He had sat for a long time, thinking. He was utterly weary, exhausted in body, soul and spirit. His hurt and anger had been such that he had not really taken in what Judy had said. "She was probably lying anyway," he thought. With a family like his, he and Celia would always be vulnerable to grimy and underhanded conversion attempts. Had not Alistair made this abundantly clear tonight? The only choices that the Jews in the Diaspora had were persecution, conversion, assimilation or death – or emigration to Palestine. Caleb turned the key and the engine coughed and caught. He knew what he had to do. And the sooner the better.

He opened the front door quietly. The hall was dark. He noticed a light under the drawing room door. Was Celia still up? It was well past midnight. Quietly, he opened the door. Celia was fast asleep on the sofa. She lay on her side, hands tucked under her face, her legs pulled up. She was obviously cold. Caleb took off his jacket and covered her. Then he sat down on the floor in front of her and watched her sleeping. A strand of hair had fallen over her nose. Before long it would tickle her and disturb her. Caleb pushed it away.

"Oh Celia, my love," he whispered. "I won't let them do to us what they did to my parents."

While reading his father's letters, he had realised that his parents' outwardly happy marriage was not all it had seemed to be. In his letters, Papa had poured out his heart to his own father, sharing things he had been unable to discuss with his wife. Why? Because she was so faithfully wedded to the doctrines of the church. But why had he given his New Testament to Celia before he left? It just did not add up. He looked over his shoulder. Celia had put the singed, leather-bound book on the mantlepiece. He got up, took it and put it on the desk in his study. Then he returned to the drawing room, picked up Celia carefully, and carried his sleeping bride upstairs. "Come on, *sarai*. Time for bed. We've had a miserable evening."

~ *31* ~

Epsom, mid-April 1939

Judy knocked on the front door the next morning in time for morning coffee. "I was just passing and thought I'd drop in." She took off her gloves and coat.

Reluctantly, Celia showed her sister-in-law into the drawing room. "That navy suit looks nice on you," she said politely, and wished Judy was a thousand miles away.

They chatted inconsequentially about this and that until Judy came to the point of her visit. "Caleb came to Grange Hall last night. He was in a terrible state and made a dreadful scene. He'd found Papa's New Testament and was accusing Al and me of trying to convert you. I just wanted to make sure you were all right. Is he still very angry?"

When Celia had woken that morning, she had found herself in bed, half dressed, with Caleb already gone. She had telephoned him at the office. The secretary was very apologetic: Mr Levine was with a client and could not be disturbed. Was he making excuses to avoid speaking to her?

"Do I ask *you* personal questions about your marriage?" Celia asked, her voice shaking.

"No." Judy did not feel the need to add an apology. Celia's cold response had confirmed her worst fears. She knew her brother. He was gentle, kind and compassionate . . . until someone touched the raw nerve of his Jewishness. Then he would attack like a lion, or cower, snarling and defiant, like an injured beast. At those times, pain and misery made him aggressive towards everyone around him.

This must have been the state Caleb was in last night, and poor Celia must have been the only victim on hand for him to maul. "If I can help in any way . . . or if you'd like Alistair to talk to him . . ."

"Help? You mean 'interfere'." Celia's only thought was to push away her uninvited guest, her Job's comforter. "I wish I'd never asked those stupid religious questions in the first place. Everything Cal warned me about has come true."

The bitterness and desperation in Celia's voice took Judy aback. She felt partly to blame for the situation. If she had followed her instincts and obeyed the Spirit of God, this might never have happened. Lies and duplicity never paid off. "What can I do to make amends?" Knowing the dark side of Caleb's character, Judy wanted to do all she could to alleviate Celia's anxiety. "I'm so sorry," she said, still unaware of the Pandora's Box she was opening.

"'Sorry' is an inappropriate word, Judy; 'ashamed' would be better. You were only too keen to convert me in the hope of getting to Caleb, weren't you? You were born a Jewess but turned your back on your heritage. You, more than anyone else, could have anticipated his reaction at finding a New Testament in his home. And what it would do to me and our marriage. But – oh no! You're more interested in making Caleb a Jewish convert for Christianity. And you all want him to abandon his identity as a Jew, don't you? You want him to become like all the pagans and Christians around him. I weep for Caleb, I'm afraid for myself . . . but I'm sorry and ashamed for you. We've all been betrayed – you and Alistair included. I think Papa was beginning to realise that. But how could he swim, all alone, against the current of 2,000 years of Christian teaching and tradition?"

Judy was speechless at Celia's outburst and her unfair accusations. "Maybe I'd better leave," she said. She too was upset and shaking now; she could take only so much. She had come in love and friendship, but she was not going to become the scapegoat for everything that had gone wrong between Celia and Caleb, or for the division between Judaism and Christendom. She said a quiet, polite goodbye and left.

Celia turned her back on her sister-in-law to hide her tears.

Caleb had taken the afternoon off work to visit Dani. He was glancing over his laden bookshelves while his friend clattered in the kitchen with tea caddies and spoons.

"You wanted to discuss something with me?" Dani asked. He returned with two mugs of strong tea without milk. "Oh, you take milk, don't you?" He shuffled back to the kitchen. Reappearing a moment later, he sat down at the dining table.

He looked like a defeated and tired soldier. "I went to see Mrs Rosenthal today. She's two young children. Her husband killed himself last week. Jumped out of their second floor flat window. She found him impaled on the railings outside. He'd just been released from a concentration camp in Germany where he'd been held since *Kristallnacht*. He was arrested for trying to protect his synagogue's Torah scroll from being burned. And now this little family is destitute. And you know what's worse? I've absolutely nothing to give them. Here, look at my hands; they're empty." Angrily, Dani showed Caleb his open palms. "No help, no hope, no chance, nothing. We're as powerless and wretched today as we've always been. We're sitting ducks waiting to be shot." Dani wheezed asthmatically. He stared at the table-cloth and coughed.

Caleb disagreed, passionately. "No, Dani, this time it's different. This time we've a place to go to; we've got Palestine."

"Oh yes?" replied Dani cynically. "We may have a place, even a home, but the Brits have slammed the door shut in

357

our faces. And they'll keep the key until they give it to the Arabs."

Caleb was appalled. It was the first time he had ever seen Dani so defeated. "*Nu*? So we just climb in through the windows, overpower the colonial British squatters, and open the doors. I have been approached by representatives of the Haganah . . ."

"And then what? Once we've kicked out the Brits, do you honestly believe the Arabs will make any room for us? They hate and despise us more than the British do. They'll never let us live in peace."

"Everyone hates us. They always have. There's nothing new about that."

"And have you ever wondered why?"

"Because we're the chosen people of God."

Instead of replying, Dani asked Caleb to pass him the Tanach – the Jewish Bible – from a desk piled high with books and papers. He flicked through the pages. "The Romans could never have carried us off to every corner of their empire if God hadn't allowed it. For goodness' sake, Caleb, think. When we first entered Eretz – the Promised Land – after leaving Egypt, we faced far more powerful enemies than a handful of Brits and tribal Arabs. We defeated them all . . . easily. Why? Because God was with us. And now? We have to struggle for every inch of land." He thumbed his Bible. "Here it is: 'Outside the sword bereaves, at home it is like death'. Isn't this precisely the situation we're in now? And the prophet tells us why: 'For I rebelled against His commandment'."

Caleb threw his hands in the air. "*Chaver*, old friend. I understand why you're so depressed. Poor Rosenthal's death is horribly tragic, and what led to it, utterly unforgivable. But you can't blame that on our sins. If God is so displeased with us, why has He so miraculously opened a way for us to reclaim our homeland?"

"Why? That too was prophesied." Dani turned to the Prophet Yekhezqel – Ezekiel – and read: "'For I will take you from among the nations, and gather you out of all countries, and I will bring you into your own land. Then I will sprinkle clean water upon you, and you shall be clean; from all your uncleanness and from all your idols, I will cleanse you. A new heart also will I give you, and a new spirit will I put within you, and I will take away the stony heart out of your flesh, and I will give you a heart of flesh. And I will put My Spirit within you, and cause you to follow My statutes, and you shall keep My judgments, and do them. And you shall dwell in the land that I gave to your fathers; you shall be My people, and I will be your God.' And . . ." Dani's finger slipped further down the page: "'Not for your sakes shall I do this, says the LORD God; let that be known to you. Be ashamed and confounded for your ways, O house of Israel.' Does that answer your question?"

"Not really. I think you're saying that God wants me to sit here and do nothing and watch our people being systematically persecuted and slaughtered in Germany."

"Of course not. What are you implying? But we all need to know what lies ahead for us. This is not a fairytale war where the good people always win. If God is with us, we can leap over a wall, but if not . . . 'How could one chase a thousand, and two put ten thousand to flight, unless their Rock had sold them, and the LORD had surrendered them?' No, before Israel is able to live in peace, something drastic has to happen. It will be terrifying and marvellous, and it won't come about because of our own strength. God will make sure of that. If it did, we'd just become more arrogant than we already are." He stood up and looked out of the window, his back to Caleb.

Then he went on, "I know many fine men and women in Palestine. They're all zealous for the Land and love it with all their hearts. They're ready to give their lives so that our

359

children have somewhere to live in freedom and peace. But there are many amongst them who reject even the idea that only God can do it. I love our people with all my heart. I've a burning desire to see them living in security and peace as they did in the times of King Solomon. But, in our pride, we fail to see that it was God, and Him alone, who made us a people and gave us the Land. We've been through more suffering than any other peoples. Yet I sense we've all missed something that's hidden in the Scriptures. It's as if a veil is over our eyes. I'm not an *overly* religious man, as you know, but I want to understand why the same things keep happening to us over and over again. What is it we've done wrong to deserve this? And how can we put it right? Think of Mr Rosenthal: it's Germany, the most civilised and progressive country in the world, that caused his death. How could that happen? Why does God not protect us? Has He forgotten us?"

"Maybe these events are leading up to the coming of the Messiah?" Caleb replied. But he did not sound very convincing, even to himself. He sensed there was something in what Dani had said, a message that made him sit up and listen; it struck chords that had played in his mind before. It made him uneasy that a man as strong and bold as Dani could sit here, all small and burdened with doubts. Where had his great vision, experience and optimism gone? After a long pause, Dani gave a deep sigh that came from the bottom of his heart. He shook his head, as if to clear it. "What does Celia think about you joining the Haganah?"

"We haven't discussed it yet." Caleb fidgeted. "We had a terrible row last night."

"Oh?"

"I found out that Celia had been studying Papa's New Testament behind my back. And that my own family is working secretly to destroy my – our faith. They'll stop at nothing."

Before Caleb's shocked eyes, Dani reached to the shelf behind him and took out a New Testament. "Do you mean one of these?"

"Don't tell me you're a secret Christian too! You must be in a much more desperate state than I realised."

"Calm down. Why on earth have you made such a mountain out of the molehill of this little book?" Dani took the book and flicked through the pages with his thumb.

"Molehill? This is the monstrous mountain that split my family. How can you say it's just 'a little book'?"

"Have you read it?"

"Of course not. Never. I've hardly even touched one," Caleb proclaimed proudly.

"Then you're a fool and a bigot, Levine. That disappoints me. It has caused us Jews so much trouble; the least we can do is know the book our persecutors get their tactics from."

"Next, you'll be telling me you've read the Koran as well."

"As a matter of fact, I have." Caleb was stunned. Dani continued, "Now Caleb. Let me see if I've got it right: you discovered Celia – in *delecto flagrans*, so to speak – the New Testament in her hand, proclaiming her conversion to Christianity. And then she left you."

Caleb fidgeted. "No, it wasn't quite like that. I was upset when I saw she had a New Testament. I said and did things I shouldn't have and stormed out of the house."

"What happened? Tell me the whole story, Cal."

"Apparently, Celia was worried for me after Papa's death. And she got it into her head that Jesus might be able to help me. With my sister's help she was looking into the biblical teachings on the Messiah. She came to the conclusion that Jesus couldn't be the Messiah if he hadn't kept the Torah. I didn't discover all this till afterwards, mind you. I know now she didn't mean any harm by it. Anyway, I was so angry about all this that, after losing my temper with

Celia, I drove round to see Judy and Alistair. I nearly punched Al in his stupid, smug Christian face. And that's the end of our longstanding friendship."

"*Oy veh*! So . . . you're really up to your neck in it?"

"Yes."

"And now you want to join the Jewish underground in Palestine. I'm not stupid, Cal."

"A Jewish homeland is the only solution to 'the Jewish problem'. There's no other way to protect ourselves against the persecution and murder – whether physically or spiritually. I wanted to join before, but you wouldn't let me. Remember?"

"I didn't forbid you. What's the point? I know it's useless to deny Mr Caleb Levine anything he's set his mind on. I simply suggested you should concentrate on making a success of your marriage, not rush off to war. Anyway, let me sum up your situation as I see it: your marriage has received its first little knock, so now you want to go and give your life to 'reclaim Palestine for the Jews'. Men like you are dangerous, Cal. God won't build Eretz Yisrael on a foundation of unhappy lives thrown to the dogs of war. We may be a stubborn and awkward people and we've many faults. We may be the Almighty's biggest headache, but one thing we are not: we've never been a people who run after death. If your own life doesn't seem worth saving, make sure you're not recklessly risking the lives of others. Our homeland must be founded on a hunger for life and living, not a death wish. Be a man: beat your pride into submission, not your wife. Go on; make it up with Celia. She's a good woman. And – I'll remind you of your own words – she meant you no harm. Then – and only when you have her blessing – go and join the Haganah. If you still feel it's right to go. If you then get killed, there may just be some meaning to your death. And your wife will be able to forgive you and come to terms with her loss."

Dani was speaking with gentle warmth and Caleb felt ashamed of his recklessness. Papa and Dani were alike in so many ways. Now Papa was dead. But God had not left him without a friend and counsellor.

"You're a good man, Calvele. Just a little hot-blooded and impulsive at times." Dani patted his young friend on the shoulder. "Don't be disheartened: God, in His wisdom, will work out His plan for your life."

After a long and thoughtful pause, Dani reached for the New Testament again. "Have you ever asked yourself this question: what if Messiah has come and gone, and we missed Him?" Caleb almost erupted, but Dani gestured him to listen. "Let me put it like this: if He came today, would we recognise Him? I mean, you and I are eagerly awaiting His coming. But how can we be sure He's really Mashiach? And what if He's already amongst us, right now?"

"For a start, He'd be kicking the Arabs and British out of Palestine."

"Really? Have you ever heard about Ben-Yossef?"

"Whom?"

"Ben-Yossef; son of Joseph. According to Rabbinic teaching there are two Messiahs: Mashiach Ben-David, the son of David, our King Messiah, and Mashiach Ben-Yossef, who will come as a Suffering Servant. Yeshua Ben-Yossef . . ." Dani pondered aloud. "The Rabbis also say, if Israel is worthy to receive Him, King Messiah will come riding on the clouds of heaven. But if Israel is unworthy, He'll come riding on a donkey."

The gilt letters on the cover of the leather-bound New Testament suddenly seemed to blaze with light in the dingy back room. Caleb looked away. "As a friend I must tell you, Dani, you really must not read the teachings of that evil apostate."

"I've read worse. When I was young I read everything I could get my hands on. My father beat me for it, but my hunger for knowledge was so great that a few bruises couldn't stop me disobeying him."

"Why was your father so angry at your studying?"

"My father was a well respected and very observant man. He couldn't afford to be seen with a rebellious son, even less a boy who asked questions he couldn't answer. And do you know why he was so ignorant? Because he'd never dared face any challenging questions himself."

"You never told me you'd had a religious upbringing."

Dani shrugged his shoulders. "It's not something I boast about. When I was fifteen, I ran away to Palestine. I wanted to see the Land I'd heard so much about. I met many liberal-minded Jews who expanded my horizons wonderfully. They introduced me to the ideas of Marx, Lenin, Buber, Herzl, Pinsker and goodness knows who else. Also the Greek philosophers . . . and Jewish thinkers like Kant and Lessing . . . what a world! Yes, and Nietzsche . . . Oy, my father would have stoned me. Did it harm my faith? On the contrary. If our faith is truly rooted in God, then we can read and discuss anything without feeling threatened. It's the weak ones, or those who want to lord it over us, who have to treat us like imbeciles to be controlled with threats and prohibitions. Everything is permissible, but not everything is profitable. Oh! And did you know that Paul of Tarsus was a very learned man?"

"The Greeks and their gods and priests were *meshuggeners* anyway, crazy." Caleb tapped his forefinger to his temple. "Paul renounced the faith and became one of them. There's no threat in that because everyone can see what he says is nonsense. But deception is very different: it's subtle, a drop of poison in a glass of Shabbat wine, a lie disguised as truth. Every lie is dangerous, especially the lie that pretends someone is the Messiah of Israel who isn't, and especially if the lie claims he's God incarnate. Many sincere Jews have been deceived."

"How can you be so sure that Jesus isn't the Messiah of Israel?"

"Every good Jew knows he isn't."

"Levine, you're talking poppycock. You'd be hounded out of court if you used that kind of argument in a legal prosecution! Hardly any Jews have the slightest idea what to expect of the Messiah, or whom to look out for. Why? Because it's not a subject the Rabbis teach on. They censor a lot, believe you me! Their maxim is: if we don't like the truth, it isn't the truth. Well, I for one am not impressed or intimidated by Rabbinic fundamentalism. I'm a man who thinks for himself. If I want to read the New Testament and make up my own mind about it, I jolly well will. And so should you. If you weren't so scared about what you might discover in it. I'll tell you straight: I've found nothing in the teachings of Jesus that contradicts Torah. He certainly put some head-in-the-clouds and nose-in-the-mud Scribes in their place. He was a *mensh*; he was all right. If I had a Rabbi like this Jesus, I'd go back to the synagogue again. And, by the way, do you know what 'Jesus' means in Hebrew?"

Tired, Caleb shook his head. Dani was really getting to him. "I don't care. But you're going tell me anyway, aren't you?"

"It means 'Yeshua': salvation. Isn't that a wonderful name?"

"And Yeshua is just one variant on the 'salvation' theme, like Yehoshua, Hoshea, Yoshia and so on. What's so special about that?" Caleb felt too drained to face the issue seriously. At least not now. He got up. "But thanks for your time, Dani. And your advice."

"I'm sorry if I've knocked the wind out of you a bit. Of course, you must join the Haganah if that's what you honestly believe you should do. And thanks for listening to my spiritual meanderings." They embraced warmly. They had spoken the same language, and had dared to voice the same questions and doubts. They had shared their hearts, and battled through their differences. Like true sons of the same Father. Like Jewish men. "And, Calvele, why not talk to Celia? She's your wife after all. And she loves you; trust me. You're a man: if you've made a mess, recognise the fact. Just clean it up before someone else steps in it."

At the top of the street, Caleb turned and looked back at Dani and Sarah'le's little house with the number twenty-six. Would he at least be able to recognise a prophet if he ever met one, let alone the Messiah?

As he walked through the front door Celia was standing in the hallway, waiting for him. She looked like a little puppy who had done wrong and didn't know whether she would be punished or not. Caleb put down his briefcase and hung his hat on the stand. He leant against the dresser and pushed his hands into his trouser pockets. "I've had a terrible day. How about you?" He peered at her questioningly from under his brows.

Celia took his words as a sign that reconciliation was imminent. She flung herself at her husband. "I am so, so sorry. Please, please forgive me. I know I hurt you terribly. It was silly and it was unforgivable of me to keep a secret from you. I promise I'll never do it again."

Caleb squeezed her lovingly. "I said and did a lot of things I shouldn't have, too. And I lost my temper. That was unpardonable. And I didn't mean what I said."

"I know you didn't."

After they had made up, as newly-weds usually make up, Caleb fetched his father's New Testament from the study. He offered it to Celia. She turned it down. Dani was right: he had made a mountain out of a molehill. What had he been so frightened of? Had not Rabbi Maimonides said definitively that Jesus was not the Messiah over 900 years before? Therefore He couldn't be. That was the end of the story. Had his reaction to Celia last night been calm and considered, they could have discussed the issue intelligently and put the whole affair behind them. Perhaps, if he had simply suggested that Celia continue her study of the New Testament and had listened to what she discovered, he could have exposed Jesus for what he knew Him to be: a Jewish apostate and a charlatan.

Dani was right again: running away from problems did not solve them – quite the reverse. Had not the Caleb of the Bible been a determined giant killer – like King David? From now on he would imitate his namesake. Who was the greater: Jesus or the God of Israel? In Caleb's mind there was now no doubt. Why had he not had this revelation earlier?

Later, Caleb put the dreaded little book with his father's letters in the furthest corner of the bottom drawer of his desk. If he was to suffer that thing in his house, at least he didn't want to be reminded of it.

~ 32 ~

London, beginning of June, 1939

Caleb Levine stood on a platform at Victoria Station en route to Palestine. He had made his decision at last and joined the Haganah as a volunteer. The general policy of the Jewish Agency was for British Jews to enrol with the British Forces. This had a double merit. First, it demonstrated Jewish loyalty to King and Empire; second, it ensured the cost-free military training of men for later use by the Haganah against the British and Arabs. But Caleb was deaf to their arguments. "You honestly expect me to wear the uniform of the country that's now pressuring the Balkan states to arrest Jews fleeing from Germany to Palestine? What's more, they've again suspended all immigration for a further six months." His friends saw his point and knew he'd never see theirs. So they agreed. That was life. And death. Now they were sending him to the Middle East for training.

"So, that's it, then," Caleb said. The train was straining to leave and it was time for him say goodbye. He shook hands with everyone and received their heartfelt *mazaltovs*. Celia was being the perfect little brave soldier's wife. "We've had so little time together . . . And it's gone so quickly . . ." she faltered, trying not to cry.

"It'll be fine, Ciel. It's best like this. And it's better than living with uncertainty, isn't it?" Caleb felt he must be cheerful and pragmatic. "I promise I'll write as soon and as often as I can." He rested his chin against the soft skin of her neck and wondered when he would do it again. "Take care of yourself. *Yivarech'ch Adonai.* God bless you," he whispered.

The train's guard blew his whistle and the engine hissed steamily in reply. Caleb got on board quickly and it wheezed and grunted out of the station. He waved. Celia did not dare take her eyes off him for a second, trying to memorise his face, his smile, his eyes, the unruly curls, his gentle hands ... Then he was out of sight. Suddenly her tears burst forth. She clutched a handkerchief to her mouth and tried not to sob out loud.

She felt an arm around her shoulders. "I know how you feel." Sarah'le squeezed her affectionately. "You know we're here for you whenever you need us." She thought back to the day when Dani had left her and their two small boys – something his mother-in-law had never forgiven him for. He had gone to try and make a home for them all in Palestine. But he had returned, physically wrecked and sick, just two years later.

On the 1st of September 1939, Germany invaded Poland; on the 3rd, Britain and France declared war. Celia rented out the cottage and joined the Land Army. She organised things so that she was posted to Bleckham Manor at the head of a platoon of young women. Their mission: to replace the farm labourers who had enlisted, and "grow for victory". They were cheerful townies, ill-disciplined and supercharged with hormones, who knew nothing about farming. And, while a constant hassle for Celia, they proved a gorgeous godsend for the few remaining lads in the village. And a headache for a lot of wives.

* * *

Palestine, September 1939

It was unbearably hot and it was windy. Whatever, wherever, whenever he ate, the sand always got there first. "We crawl in the dust all day, so we might just as well eat it too," he wrote home from Palestine. "It's not only that I am in the Land, the Land is also in me. Literally. Every drop of water is precious, so washing and shaving is difficult. You wouldn't recognise me. We get one hour free each day, and only six hours' sleep at night – five actually: we're on guard duty for one of them. We live on a mush of chickpeas – except on Shabbat when we get biscuits as a treat. Some begrudge us even that; they call it 'pampering the pioneer spirit', being 'counter-revolutionary' and I don't know what. Most important of all, Ehud, who is in charge of our unit, has married us to our rifles. We eat with them, wash with them and sleep with them. And at night he tries to steal them from us. If he succeeds, we have extra duties. They have made me 2nd Lieutenant along with a chap called Arik Halberstajn. I have never met anyone so professional and single-minded. I think we will work well together. "

Caleb was the new boy in the unit and felt very green. Most of his comrades were much younger and more experienced than he was. They taught him how to plot and plan, about "contacts", how to organise and smuggle – and how to kill. His decision to come to Palestine really hit home when they were taken to the Haganah's secret shooting range far out in the desert, away from British military ears. They lay on their stomachs and obediently fired at human effigies stuck up on poles like scarecrows. Caleb took careful aim at the heart of one dummy and tightened his finger around the trigger. After what seemed an eternity of squeezing, the rifle spewed out its deadly load. Caleb had snatched his shot – instinctively – and the bullet threw up a plume of dust a yard away from the target.

"*Oy*, Ben-Levi," Ehud yelled at him from the other side of the range. "What on earth are you doing, man?" Caleb wanted to bury his head in the sand; if Ehud had been closer he would probably have done it for him. "Don't you know the risks our comrades take to smuggle every single damn round to us? And all you can do is blast at thistles."

"I'm sorry. Shooting at a human shape . . ."

"What are you? Religious, or what? Then go back to wherever you crawled out from. This is the Haganah. Not a Yeshiva. We're here to defend our people and our settlements. Now do as ordered. Shoot the hell out of that bloody dummy . . ."

Caleb saw the black outline in the shimmering, sand-yellow distance. He had been brought up to treasure life – to keep this most sacred of Jewish principles. Now he was being trained to wipe out what God had created in His own image. But then he thought of Mrs Rosenthal and her husband's body draped over the railings, and . . . He aimed and fired. The dummy's heart imploded. Ehud nodded, satisfied.

Caleb had reverted to his Hebrew surname – Ben-Levi – and was intensely aware of the historical significance of all he was doing. He quickly became fluent in modern Hebrew, settled in quickly and served in his unit wholeheartedly. He grew to love his comrades and became devoted to them. Gradually, his carefully preserved Jewish roots took hold in the Land, and started to go down deep. With every breath he took, every grain of sand he swallowed, his love for the Land grew deeper. He still marvelled that, wherever he went, he was never ridiculed for being a Jew. The miracle was happening: a whole pogrom-free country filled with Jews. Here the people told jokes, argued and studied Torah and Talmud – freely and in Hebrew. Here they cursed other reckless drivers, bartered for lemons, and built homes – freely and in Hebrew. For the first time in his life, and despite the ever-present British troops, Caleb felt truly free. He would never again give up that freedom. A Jew had come home. To stay.

When he wrote home, Caleb opened his heart to his wife. Every word of his letters was underlined with deep devotion for his Land and his people. "You talk about Palestine as if it were a woman you're in love with," Celia wrote. Eight weeks later she got the reply: "Yes, I am madly in love with her."

Celia now had it in black on white. She had a serious rival. Caleb was having his first "love affair" and it was different from anything she might have imagined. She realised for the first time that Caleb might never want to return to England. This provoked a great deal of heart-searching. Looking out over the autumnal, drizzle-misted English meadows, she wondered what new challenges and sacrifices might be demanded of her.

The Phoney War ended in 1940. Hitler's incredibly innovative Blitzkrieg military machine smashed through the Benelux countries as it had torn through Poland. Then it roared into France, spitting fear and death. Within days it had rolled the British army back into the Channel and the French to the suburbs of Paris. When the Germans bombed Norwich, even this sleepy backwater of Norfolk finally caught up with the rest of Europe. On that very night, the future heir to Bleckham Manor, Richard Hornby, was born to Judy and Alistair.

Sir Arthur died in the early summer of 1941, six months after liver cancer had been diagnosed. Celia was devastated but hardly had time to grieve before Alistair was shot down over France. Reported missing in action, *La Résistance* eventually got the message out that he was alive and well. He was smuggled across the Channel in the spring of 1942, and Judy's joy at having her husband home and alive was barely dampened by the empty sleeve pinned to his left shoulder.

Celia was happy for them; they were a united family again. But it was almost three years since she had last seen Caleb. She began to envy the Land Army girls, who worked in small groups and formed life-long friendships. And, after a long, hard day of planting potatoes, harvesting sprouts or spreading muck, they could go and amuse themselves at the Village Hall dances in the evenings. As a married woman of social standing, this diversion would have been most inappropriate for Celia.

She tried not to dwell on it, but loneliness became her ever-present companion. And serious worry: even the reluctant and indifferent British press could no longer play down the fact that terrible things were happening to the Jews on the Continent. News of atrocities against the Jewish populations in Poland, Russia and France made terrifying headlines in the *Jewish Chronicle.* Voices began to speak of a systematic mass murder.

Celia kept writing to Caleb and, miraculously, her letters seemed to get through. He confirmed her fears regarding European Jewry. He had also been given a mission, he wrote. But she was not to worry. He would be all right. Celia was worried nonetheless, especially as there were no more letters from Palestine after that. Not one.

Repulsed by the imaginary threat of "Dad's Army" and the hard reality of the RAF's Fighter Command, the German invasion of Britain was averted. The Eighth Army locked horns with the *Afrika Korps* in Egypt, and nine Italian PoWs came to work on the Bleckham estate. They were welcomed with open arms by Celia's Land Army girls who did much to comfort their desperate homesickness.

As the war progressed, some pressures eased but most increased.

On Sir Arthur's death, Alistair inherited Bleckham Manor. Naturally, he took control of the management of his inheritance. It was not long before he and Celia clashed over how to run the estate. Until Alistair's premature demobilisation, Celia had managed it. Now she had to hand over her beloved Bleckham Manor to Alistair and Judy. It was a hard blow for her, but times had changed.

With Sir Arthur's passing, the old heart of Bleckham Manor had ceased to beat. Sadly, there was no improvement in Celia's relationship with her parents to counterbalance the sad loss. On her return to Bleckham, Celia called on them once a week. She regarded it as her filial duty. Lady Norah did not conceal her contempt that her daughter had married well below her station. Not once did she enquire after Caleb's well-being. Celia had even begun to entertain the idea that her mother might prefer him dead. She cut down her visits to once a fortnight, then to once a month. Eventually she stopped them altogether. They made no difference to her life or, it seemed, to her parents. Celia began to feel more and more like an ageing and unwanted spinster aunt. Judy comforted her and encouraged her to persevere. But Judy's reminders to "honour your parents" only discouraged Celia further. It seemed clear to her that her parents had given up on her.

Long months passed slowly and emptily. Then, late one morning in November 1943, and without any warning, she spotted a figure walking up the drive. He wore a British Army uniform. The Haganah's power of persuasion had finally breached Caleb's resistance.

"Caleb!"

Celia flung open the front door so that it rebounded on its hinges. Stumbling across the gravel, she threw herself into her husband's arms. They clutched, cried, laughed, and kissed. For a long time.

"I thought you might be pleased to see me," chuckled Caleb.

Entrusted with urgent documents, Caleb had crossed the Channel and delivered them to Whitehall. He now stood in one of the soulless offices while Sir Alec questioned their authenticity. Caleb looked out of the paper-masked windows. Heavy war traffic thundered past on the road below. Norfolk was within easy reach and yet so far away . . .

Sir Alec had nodded, satisfied. "Thank you. These papers are fine. You can go," he said. He called for his secretary.

Caleb did not move. "Sir?"

Sir Alec, his mind already on the next task, looked up. His eyebrows twitched a little in irritation. "Was there something else?"

"Yes, sir."

"Well, speak up, man. I haven't got all day."

"I haven't seen my wife for four years, sir. She's in Norfolk with the Land Army."

Sir Alec flicked through more papers. "I see. And what has this got to do with me? Haven't you got any orders?"

"My orders are to return to France immediately, sir."

Sir Alec looked up. He looked intently at the man in front of him. Caleb's face was creased with desperation. His sorrowful eyes were tense with homesickness. And shame. Caleb had never asked a Gentile for anything, let alone begged. His silent suffering did more for him than his words.

"Four years, what? A long time." Sir Alec's grumpiness softened. He muttered something and dialled. "Harold? Alec here. I say, about the maps you wanted to go to France. I've got a chap here who'll take them in for you . . . No, no . . . His orders are to return immediately . . . When?" Sir Alec covered the mouthpiece with his hand and looked at Caleb. "Will five days do?" Caleb nodded. His heart raced with sudden anticipation. Sir Alec spoke again into the receiver. "Splendid. Have them ready by Tuesday . . . No, Tuesday, I said." Sir Alec hung up and scribbled a note. "Report back here in five days. Understood? I need you more urgently than they do in France." He signed and stamped the piece of paper and handed it to Caleb.

375

"Thank you, sir," croaked out from Caleb's dry mouth.

"What for? You've got your orders. You're to return here in five days for further orders. What you do in the meantime is your own business." He dismissed Caleb with a smile.

Five glorious days with Cielie lay ahead of him. He couldn't wait to see her – to hold her in his arms – again.

The five days went far too quickly. During that desperately short and happy time, they hid their fears behind brave faces: the situation of Jews in German-occupied countries was reaching ever-deeper levels of horror, the news reported. They did not even dare talk about it. In later years they often wondered how they had managed to cram so many intense feelings into their hearts, all at the same time. On Tuesday morning Caleb waved goodbye to his love.

When Caleb returned to the war, they only hoped that the next time they were together it would be for good. Then wartime life returned to its uneventful and heavily rationed normality. Celia had recycled her precious tea leaves so many times that all she could now squeeze out of them was pale brown water. That morning, her breakfast tea looked particularly revolting. The sight of it made her feel violently sick.

"Blast this food rationing . . . Just look at this tea . . ." she complained.

Judy was determined to be British and stoical to the last. "The tea? There's nothing wrong with the tea except that it's a bit weaker than usual."

"Yes, of course. But just the thought of . . . and the colour . . ." Celia shuddered.

As her complaint and complaining persisted, Celia went to see the family doctor. He confirmed what had been widely diagnosed: Mrs Caleb Levine was pregnant. Celia's heart turned upside down and inside out: a baby! She was going to be a mother! She was overawed. Caleb was delighted. His letters started to be littered with funny little drawings of mummies and babies. It also affected her spiritual life. Celia turned her beloved tallit over in her hands guiltily. How long had it been since she had last prayed? She reflected that 160 generations of Jewish history were lying in her hands. Celia put her hands on her still-flat belly. Soon it would be 161 generations. She and Caleb were making history; they were perpetuating Israel's sacred mission.

Seven months later, on August 9th, 1944, Celia Levine went into labour. Their son, Ruven, was born that night. He weighed in at 7lbs 6oz and was a thoroughly healthy baby. He was circumcised a week later by a doctor.

On 8th May, 1945, Germany surrendered unconditionally. The British people were deliriously happy, as was the rest of Europe. Then began the operation of counting the dead, healing the wounded, feeding the survivors, sorting out the refugees and displaced persons, and judging the criminals. The names "Brann" and "Weiss" were found in the Auschwitz-Birkenau transport lists; Marianne, Erich and Hansi's father had died in Dachau while Emilie Zink had been worked to death in the IG Farben works. But there was also happy news: Francis renounced his vow of bachelorhood and married Barbara Reinhardt; Esther and Leon – who had got married in 1940 – were blessed with a little girl they called Shoshanah, and Gertrud Levine formally adopted the Zink siblings and gave them a permanent home.

At the end of June, Celia received a short and urgent telephone call from Paris. Caleb told her to pack whatever she could carry and join him in Paris, with Ruven. He was taking them to Palestine.

"Hold on a moment," interjected Celia with an amused little laugh. "Caleb, I can't just drop everything and move to the Middle East. We need to discuss this. Then it'll take weeks to sort through our belongings and have them crated for shipment . . ."

Caleb interrupted her, impatiently. "I've been called back to Palestine. This is our best chance for you both to come with me. You do want to come, don't you?"

Celia felt as if she had a gun to her head. "How long will we be staying there?"

"I don't know. Until Eretz has really become the Jewish homeland, I suppose."

Celia was panicking. "It's all a bit of a shock, Caleb . . ."

"I know. And I'm sorry I've landed this on you so suddenly, but I really thought you'd like to . . ." Caleb's tone softened.

"How long will you be in Paris?"

"Until you get here. But I'm under strict orders not to delay. A few days at most . . ."

Celia paused and breathed in deeply. She needed to buy time. "We'll see you in Paris, then. Give me a contact number or address and I'll let you know the earliest we can make it." I'm crazy, she thought.

"*Ani ohev otach, sarai.* I love you, princess." Caleb hung up.

Judy walked into the study to find a pale and stunned Celia standing by the desk. "Who was that? Not bad news, I hope?"

"No, that was Cal. From Paris. We're going to Palestine. Perhaps tomorrow. Within the next two days, for certain."

"To Palestine? Tomorrow? Good heavens, Celia. Are you sure about this?"

"No, but I have to go. I can't lose the chance to be with Caleb again. I'm afraid he's never coming back to England." She paused. "This time it feels quite different. When he went the first time, I knew he'd return. I was his harbour and he was anchored in me. Now he's anchored in Palestine. If I'm

not beside him . . . We've all just fought and won a horrendous war, but my war isn't finished yet, I'm afraid."

Just sixty hours later, Celia, with Ruven in her arms, was
standing by the hectic reception desk of a Paris hotel,
waiting for her husband. She would never forget the look on
his face when he spotted her, and saw his child for the first
time. He wore a most wondrous and astonished smile. He
blinked, repeatedly. He had survived this bloody war to see
his very own family. With a lump in his throat he first tightly
embraced his Celia, the most wonderful, most sorely missed
person in his life. Then he took his "Ruvele" from her arms
carefully. He kissed him, admired him, and held him close.
The crowds around him vanished and, for a moment, he and
his son were surrounded with light and peace. Then Ruvele
started to wriggle and pull towards his mother.

"Don't be upset, Cal. You're still a stranger to him. He'll
soon grow to love you."

~ 33 ~

Tel Aviv, last days of July, 1945

After only one night in Paris, Caleb urged his family on to
Marseille. He hoped to find a ship bound for Palestine, or at
least for Port Said or the Levant. They were lucky and
booked a passage on a Greek merchant vessel stopping at
Jaffa. All in all, the journey was not too bad. They had a cabin
to themselves. Somehow Celia managed to maintain a
steady supply of clean nappies for Ruven. With little else to
do, the Levines had time to start to get to know each other
again. Caleb spent every moment with little Ruvele. He
showed him round the ship, fed him biscuits, played with
him and helped him to take his first steps. Caleb was thrilled,
and his face shone with paternal pride. By the end of the
journey, one-year-old Ruven had concluded that the big
person called "Abba" was fun to be with.

Caleb had arranged accommodation for them in Tel
Aviv, but when Celia saw it her heart sank. It turned out to
be a flat above a grocery shop, which they were to share
with the lady who owned the shop and her fifteen-year-old
son, Ovid. The Levines had one large room with two single
beds, a cot and a wardrobe. The sitting room, kitchen and
bathroom they had to share. Caleb was proud and happy
to have his family with him . . . and Celia was hot, dirty and
close to tears. Had she travelled 3,000 miles for this: a
scantily furnished room, a few pieces of luggage at her feet
and a baby struggling in her arms? Oh for the green
meadows of England! How could she possibly live in a

place with no space, no garden and no greenery? She fought back tears.

Caleb saw her desperation and put his arms around her. "Don't worry, *sarai*," he said encouragingly. "It looks a bit grim now but, once we've settled in, you'll love Tel Aviv. Just as I do. It's irresistible and teeming with life. It's a wonderful example of a modern Jewish city. Come on, cheer up, old girl. You've arrived in the Promised Land." Celia made an effort to share her husband's enthusiasm. After all, they would not be staying there long.

Settling into a Middle Eastern culture proved to be a tough challenge for Celia. To make matters worse, Palestinian Jewry hated the British. Every time she opened her mouth, her tongue betrayed her origins. As a result, she was generally treated with frosty politeness; even outright hostility. She felt rejected, helpless, inept and entirely dependent on Caleb.

And then there was Miriam Mizrachi, alias Miri, their landlady. She was a big, dark, overpowering woman. She greeted them with an open and welcoming smile. As Caleb introduced his family, Miri clapped her hands in delight. She then swept Ruvele into her massive arms and kissed him passionately. She babbled at him in Hebrew and Yiddish, laughing and singing "La-i, la-i, la-i". Then it was Celia's turn to be welcomed. She smiled and put on a brave face. Miri reckoned she looked too thin and tired and needed feeding up. She would look after her. She would cook for the Levines that evening.

Caleb was touched, but Celia was furious. As soon as they were alone she burst out with, "She can't just walk in, grab my son, and tell us where, when, what and how much to eat. I won't stand for it."

Caleb reacted with more than a spark of irritation. "And why not? Were you intending to cook tonight? For goodness' sake, Celia. Don't be such a snob. We can't afford to be prissy. Tel Aviv isn't Belgravia, you know."

And that was how Celia's life in Eretz began; with hurt and disappointment. And that was how it seemed it would continue. Caleb's first job was to mediate between Mrs Mizrachi and his wife. The clash between Miri's overly generous heart and Celia's standoffish Britishness was reaching flashpoint. In the end he had to explain that English women were different, much more reserved and less outgoing. Miri nodded, vexed and uncomprehending. As she poured out to Benzion Kirschzweig, the kosher butcher next door, she would never understand why nice Mr Ben-Levi had had to marry a Goyah. Worse, an *ishah Anglia*, an Englishwoman. He was a lawyer, wasn't he? Wasn't he the sort of young man every Yiddishe Mamma longed for as a son-in-law? He could have had any Jewish girl of his choosing. She hitched up her shoulders in justified bewilderment. Mr Kirschzweig shook his head in sympathy. Miri was a good customer. And sympathy did not cost a lot, did it?

Thankfully, life gradually became a little more settled. Miri's overflowing hospitality was at last tactfully restrained, and the initial tensions eased. For her husband's sake, Celia tried hard to make the most of the situation. But English roses are bred for temperate climates and Celia soon started to wilt in the hot, humid air of Tel Aviv. The many restrictions she had to put up with gnawed at her nerves. She had to make do with a painfully restricting flat; she had nowhere to go to play with Ruven; the days were so hot that she could not take him outside, and, with no gainful employment, the days seemed endless. In the end, she enrolled for a Hebrew language course at the local school and started helping out in Miri's grocery shop.

Caleb would disappear for weeks at a time without saying what he was doing or where he was going. Celia put two and two together, but never asked any questions. She was afraid of the answers. And it was only much later that she found out about Miri's flourishing grocery business: her fruit and vegetables, so busily peddled about town by Ovid on his scruffy tricycle cart, often covered revolvers, hand grenades and rifles. And the tins of beans she sold sometimes contained material distinctly more explosive than baked beans.

It was during the first weeks of 1946 that the British Labour Government stepped up, to almost obsessive levels, its efforts to stop Jews reaching Palestine. The struggle between the British Government and Palestinian Jewry became increasingly bitter. Concentration camp survivors were again incarcerated behind barbed wire, but this time in British camps. Between January and July, eleven boats, carrying a total of 10,500 immigrants, were intercepted.

After intense diplomatic pressure from London, two ships carrying over 1,000 refugees from Central Europe were refused permission to leave the Italian port of La Spezia. The refugees refused to disembark and went on a hunger strike. Eventually, starving and desperate, they threatened to commit mass suicide by sinking the ships. In Palestine, Golda Meir and fifteen Zionist leaders joined in the hunger strike. Amidst worldwide publicity and pressure from Washington, the British Government capitulated. The refugees set out from La Spezia clutching immigration visas for the following month.

Then Celia developed asthma symptoms. It was eventually established that Mrs Ben-Levi was not suffering from asthma, but from a lack of open space, a type of claustrophobia. So, after much deliberation, Caleb decided that Celia and Ruvele must go to a kibbutz. But he was worried for their safety. With the ever-increasing tension, these isolated farming communities were far more vulnerable to Arab attacks. Eventually he found them a place at Emek Prachim – Valley of Flowers – the kibbutz Ben, the Glicksmans' son, and his young wife Rosie had helped to build in 1941.

As Celia let her eyes roam across the fields and hills of Emek Prachim, she felt as if iron shackles were falling from her heart. After the last of the winter rains, the valley and its surrounding hills were richly carpeted with wild flowers. And the farmed fields were covered with the tender green of young barley and sprouting vegetables. For the first time since their arrival in Palestine, Celia felt hope rising in her again. But their accommodation was still very restricted: one small room with two single beds, a wardrobe, a dresser, two bedside cabinets, a table and two chairs. Nothing else, not even a cot. This was what now constituted their home. Everything else was communal. All meals were in the communal dining hall and the kibbutz had its own laundry. Even the showers and toilets were shared. Little Ruvele had to sleep in the children's dormitory located at the heart of the settlement. Celia was devastated to discover this but, when she realised she had no choice, she was forced to accept the arrangement.

All in all, the kibbutz reminded Celia more of a Girl Guides' summer camp than a farming community. But it appealed strongly to her sense of adventure and she rose to the challenge. Leah Ginsberg, a stout, energetic staff nurse from Austria, welcomed her and Ruvele. She promised to help them settle in. In due course, Celia would be assigned a job on the kibbutz; what little remaining time she had would be filled with lessons in history, Hebrew, economics, agriculture, first aid, self-defence and weapons training.

Celia adapted quickly to life at Emek Prachim. She was assigned the job of running the kibbutz's small herd of cattle, and teaching animal husbandry to the youngsters. Some of these children were extermination camp survivors who had known horrendous neglect and cruelty. Watching them care for the young cattle was to become one of Celia's greatest rewards. Her life now had a purpose again. Soon, like thousands before her, she had caught the Zionist vision to rebuild the Jewish biblical homeland in Eretz Yisrael. Celia worked as hard as any of them and soon became intrigued by her fellow kibbutzniks: they were a fascinating cross-breed: peace-loving farmers-cum-fighters, resourcefully tending and defending themselves and their land with little more than their bare hands. But not everyone appreciated the *ishah Anglia* in their midst. A vociferous minority bitterly resented the presence of a Brit on their venerated Jewish soil. And they worked hard to sow seeds of mistrust in the hearts of their fellow kibbutzniks. But, somehow, even this worked for Celia's good: for the first time ever, she was now experiencing the rejection and ostracism that the Jewish people had known for 2,000 years.

She had shared the Levines' Shabbat table, admired the Jews' ancient traditions, and browsed through quaint Yiddish shops in London; in short, she had filled her heart with beautiful religio-romantic notions about the Jewish people. But to live as their apparent enemy, amongst fearsome, awe-inspiring and outspoken Jewish grannies, was altogether different. Donning a tallit in the quiet of her bedroom in an English country house was one thing; enforced identification with a defiant, no-nonsense, contrary, suspicious and not always likable people was quite another. In small doses, and sprinkled with charming Glicksmans, the Jews were lovable and amusing; here she was surrounded by a fiercely resolved people fighting, in deadly earnest, for their survival. There was no room for a romantic "Aren't-you-blessed-to-be-a-chosen-people" attitude. For the Zionist pioneers, life was sacrificial, raw, unforgiving and harsh. And often deadly.

One sunny afternoon, Celia was sitting with some of the *Gadna* boys and girls in the dappled shade of the olive trees. In this romantic biblical setting, they were cleaning a stack of revolvers and rifles. She liked this mind-numbing job: she could sit quietly, letting her brain rest and her thoughts wander.

"Here, I say, Mrs Ben-Levi. Trot along and get us all a nice jug of cold water, will you?" ordered Almah Kaminski, an elderly matriarch. She had tried to mimic Celia's typical upper-class British accent. For Celia, this was the last straw. She got up and dumped the revolver she was cleaning on the table.

"I'm tired of being treated like a servant. All I hear is: 'Do this, do that; fetch this, fetch that' from morning to night. First, there are much younger legs round this table than mine. Second, I don't respond to rudeness. I don't mind a polite request; a few 'pleases' and 'thank yous' wouldn't go amiss from time to time." Celia strutted off in a hot huff, muttering "Go and get it yourself" under her breath.

Two hours later she was summoned before members of the kibbutz's disciplinary committee. The charge cited by its chairman, Mr Kaminski, was: "You didn't carry out your orders this afternoon, *Geveret* Ben-Levi."

She was still furious. "What? I'm being disciplined for refusing to fetch a jug of water for your wife? That's nepotism. Haven't you anything better to do with your time? I know I have."

The grey-haired, bespectacled Mr Kaminski refused to be irritated by her defiance and lack of respect. He folded his arms, leant across the table and peered at her over the rim of his glasses. Very calmly and very sternly he said, "You're being disciplined for walking away from weapon-cleaning work, Mrs Ben-Levi. Our lives – yours included – depend on their readiness for use. The kibbutz has to run like clockwork. We don't have time for fancy tantrums and emotions. And, while we are on the subject, many of our pioneers dislike your general attitude."

"My attitude?" Celia thought she had heard wrong.

Mr Kaminski took off his glasses and lowered his eyebrows. "Many of these men and women, whom you look down on for their lack of good manners, have been labouring here since before you were born. They were rising before dawn to stand waist-deep in water to drain malaria-infested swamps. At noon they were fighting off Bedouin attacks, and at night they were giving birth to our sons and daughters. You aren't here to lecture us on good manners. Only two things will impress us: work, sheer, bloody, tireless hard work, and courage. We're waiting to see you so exhausted that you can't lift your spoon at your evening meal, and fall off your chair, asleep. Then you might just get our attention and respect." Mr Kaminski had not lost his calm and serious manner. "This time, we're letting you off with a warning. But make sure we don't see you here again. You may go now."

Celia felt humiliated and humbled to the core. With burning eyes she turned to go.

"Mrs Ben-Levi." Celia looked over her shoulder at Mr Kaminski. "We aren't boorish peasants here, you know. My wife has had a very hard life. And I'm very proud of her. She has my total respect and gratitude. So have all the others. Please try to understand what I've been saying."

Some days later, Celia walked past the Kaminskis' accommodation hut. The door was wide open and she could see Mrs Kaminski on her hands and knees scrubbing the floor. Red-faced, the old lady wiped her brow, panting. She looked like a good candidate for a heart attack. Celia took a deep breath. She was very tired and knew she needed her two hours' rest before joining the night watch. She knocked and went across to Mrs Kaminski. She knelt down beside her. Taking the brush and soap from her hand, she started scrubbing.

"Where have you already cleaned?" she asked.

"I've only just started."

Celia's heart sank. An hour later, she tipped out the last bucket of dirty water. Throughout this time, Mrs Kaminski had barely spoken a word. She had sat on a chair, not looking well, watching her work. Celia dried her hands on a towel. The cracks in her skin stung badly.

Mrs Kaminski took the towel back. "Wait a moment, will you?" She waddled off and returned with a big piece of cake, wrapped in a page of the *Palestine Post*. "Eat that on your night watch. It'll help you keep warm. And be careful. You've a little boy now, and Jewish boys need their mothers." It was a while before the full meaning of her last remark sank in.

The festival of Passover was approaching rapidly. With it came a frenzy of spring cleaning and heated debates over what to do with the *ishah Anglia*. Such was the interest the issue generated in this non-religious but traditional settlement that a security meeting, called to discuss the kibbutz's defences, ended by debating the question: could a Brit share in the Seder meal? This question was clearly more pressing to the Jewish minds at Emek Prachim than the threat of an Arab raid. Opinions were many and varied. Four simultaneous conversations erupted around the table.

"She's not one of us."

"Neither were the multitude who left Egypt with the children of Israel."

"She's a proselyte."

"Oh no, she isn't! She's only married one of us. She never underwent formal conversion."

"But the Egyptians sought shelter in Jewish houses. This woman labours here with us. She's under constant threat of sniper fire. Thousands of Arabs are baying for our blood. If I were her, I'd run a thousand miles from any Jewish home."

"How do you know she won't once the going gets really tough?"

"If an Englishwoman sits at our Seder table, I won't be coming."

"You must. That's the tradition. And who are you to decide who can share the Seder meal? Are you God? Or a Rabbi?"

"Let's consult the Torah."

"Don't get religious with me."

"Fetch Ben. He knows about these things."

Ben Glicksman was fetched and eventually found a Torah passage that said: "It is written: And if a stranger shall sojourn among you, and will keep the Passover to the LORD; according to the ordinances of the Passover, and according to its prescribed manner, so shall he do; you shall have one ordinance, both for the stranger, and him that was born in the Land."

There was a moment's stunned silence. This was followed by shouts of approval and disagreement. Efrem Harcarmel was chairing the meeting. He was a true *Sabra* – a Jew born and raised in Palestine – and looked it. He was dark and taciturn, and had a pronounced limp. Although middle-aged, he appeared much older. His face was weatherbeaten, and the deep lines etched into it were the result of years of struggle and personal tragedy. With a grim expression, he lit a cigarette and called for order. Lowering his eyes he decreed, "Celia Ben-Levi shall partake in the Seder if she so wishes."

"You've no right to force your decision on us. Let's vote."

Efrem glared at the speaker. "And shall we also vote to see if she's a right to a place in the bunker? Or shall we throw her to the Arabs straight away?"

"Keep religion and politics separate."

"None of us would be here if it weren't for religion and politics. When the Book says this is our Land, so be it. When the Book says that a stranger can share in the Jewish Pesach if he or she so desires, then so be it too. If you've a problem with that, get out." Efrem glowered at some murmuring pockets of rebellion. "Any more objections?" There were none.

That's how Celia came to celebrate her first Passover at Emek Prachim. She was overwhelmed and honoured that she, a non-Jew, should be allowed to share the Seder table with Jews in Eretz. And it was the God of Abraham, Isaac and Jacob who had allowed it. She felt doubly honoured. As they sat down around the table, she noticed an empty chair: the place set aside for Eliahu the Prophet. It was powerful in its symbolism. The war had only just ended and the empty seat called to mind the friends and family that each Jewish person had lost in the Shoah – the Holocaust. They were gone, never to share again in Israel's greatest festival of freedom. Around the world, there were some six million empty seats at the Seder of 1946.

~ 34 ~

Emek Prachim, 29th June 1946

Celia was up, along with many others, into the small hours of that morning. They were waiting for the arrival of yet another truckload of shattered and dehydrated "illegal" Aliyah Bet immigrants. Her joy overflowed when she spotted Caleb among their escort. He was completely exhausted, with bloodshot eyes and a dark two-day stubble. And he smelled terrible. To Celia it did not matter. She felt prouder of him than ever before. She took the rifle out of his hand and put his arm across her shoulder. She was alongside him, helping her husband – the supportive Zionist wife.

"We hit a British roadblock and couldn't get through. We had to lie low in the mountains for 24 hours. There wasn't enough water to go round . . ."

"Well, you're here now and still in one piece. That's all that matters."

She stole five minutes to take her husband to their room. He could barely stand on his feet and fell onto the bed. By the time Celia had taken off his shoes, he was already half asleep. Then he rolled onto his side and was gone, off into a deep and dreamless sleep. Celia sighed. He would not wake before the afternoon. She stroked his dark hair like a mother caressing her sleeping child, covered him with a blanket and returned to the blacked-out dining room. She had to attend to the needs of the new arrivals.

Caleb had earned a few days' leave. Celia could not believe her blessing: their first few days together for almost three months. But their joy was not to last. Just before dawn the next day, on a Shabbat, they were woken by the roar of army vehicles. Minutes later, British paratroops drove through the fence surrounding the compound and flicked on floodlights. They rounded up the stunned kibbutzniks and herded them into collapsible iron cages that had suddenly sprung up. They looked like kennels.

Celia found the soldiers' callousness and insensitivity incredible. "For pity's sake!" she thought. "Some of them have only just got out of the detention camps." When she protested out loud, a soldier grabbed her by the hair and dragged her into a cage. A few kibbutzniks who had tried to resist arrest were being punched or clubbed with rifle butts. Celia raged, stamped her foot and shook the iron bars. Lady Cecilia Lancaster had been imprisoned like an animal. This was outrageous.

"I demand to speak to the officer in command." she shouted, "At once. I'm . . ."

She shut her mouth. Something had stopped her from completing her sentence. She had wanted to yell: ". . . I'm British; I don't belong here." Did her Jewish friends "belong" in this cage then? Of course not. She let her arms fall limply. She turned and looked into the hard and closed faces of the caged people of Emek Prachim. Caleb was among them. She caught his eye. His face was motionless, his glance strange. Then she understood. Resigned, she nodded.

"Right." Caleb raised his voice. "This is what we'll do . . ." To cover any members of the Haganah, in particular the *Palmachniks*, everyone would refuse to give his name.

Twelve days earlier, on the night of 16th June, Palestinian Jewry had vented their deepest frustration over Britain's persistent unwillingness to raise the immigration quotas and end the land-purchase restrictions of the 1939 White Paper. Members of the Palmach had isolated Palestine from its neighbouring states by destroying ten road and rail bridges and damaging the Haifa railway workshops.

In retaliation, the British arrested 3,000 Jews throughout Palestine, including most of the senior members of the Zionist Executive. They also shut down the Jewish Agency building. As Clement Attlee had declared, the dissolution of the Jewish national home would be carried out by force if necessary.

Most of the arrested men and women were released later that morning. Celia was taken to the nearest British police station for questioning.

"Good morning. I'm Major Hickson. Please, Lady Cecilia, do sit down." The Major gestured to a chair and smiled at her warmly – as if this were a polite social visit. Celia was hot, tired, thirsty and scruffy. She raised both eyebrows, but chose to remain standing, her hands clasped behind her back. "I see you're surprised that I know your name," the Major observed. He scribbled on a pad for a while to give her time to take in her situation. "I hope you're not going to say that you're just 'a Jew from the Land of Israel' like the rest of them." He looked up. She did not move; she said nothing. He was starting to get annoyed by her insubordination but restrained himself. "Sit down . . . please . . . Lady Cecilia." She noted a hint of hardness in his voice and obeyed. There was no point provoking him unnecessarily.

An orderly came in with two cups of tea on a tray. He put a cup in front of Celia. The temptation to reach for the delicious, thirst-quenching brew was hard to resist. The Major lit his pipe and sucked hard a few times to make sure it had taken. Then, as if oblivious to the incongruity of it all, he continued his charade. "Please, do help yourself to milk. And do you take sugar?"

"Major Hickson. I appreciate your hospitality, but do you seriously expect me to sip tea and exchange small talk with you while my friends are being treated like animals?"

Unruffled, he took a sip of tea. Celia watched him swallow. "I never forget a face, Lady Cecilia. The last time I saw yours was in the *Tatler*, I believe. Or was it in *The Illustrated London News*? I forget now. You had just jilted Viscount Holsworth-Leigh. Good job too, by all accounts . . ." He shook his head. "Do please tell me, Lady Cecilia: how does a lady such as you manage to end up in a pickle like this?"

Celia laughed out loud. Then, a touch sarcastically, patronisingly: "And do tell me, my dear Major Hickson: how does an officer and a gentleman such as you end up doing what you are doing here? Putting Shoah survivors into cages . . ."

Hickson swivelled in his chair. He stopped and glared intently at his prisoner. "Very well, Lady Cecilia. I'll be blunt with you. I'd have thought you'd be bitterly ashamed to be mixed up with this rabble. They're murdering our chaps, undermining the Empire and jeopardising the stability and peace of the whole Middle East. Murdering bastards, all of them. And I'm sure you want to do the decent thing. We need your help: we're both British, on the same side, you know. So I'm going to have you and your husband released. In return, I'm sure you'll be only too happy to provide us with any information that might help us to bring criminals to justice." Then the officer swivelled in his chair again. He turned his back on Celia, sucked on his pipe and looked out of the window. His appeal to fair play and loyalty might work but he wasn't sure. Bloody aristocrats – usually think they can do whatever they like and get away with it.

Celia heard herself say: "Major Hickson, I'm afraid I don't know anything that could be of the slightest interest to you. I don't know any criminals."

"Your husband has been charged with being a leader in the Jewish Resistance Movement. He's in very serious trouble. I don't want you to underestimate the seriousness of the charges. He might well be facing the death penalty. Look, Lady Cecilia. I want to release you. I really do. And it's damned embarrassing to HMG to have to keep the Earl of Besthorpe's daughter in detention. So I'm offering you a deal: even if you know nothing, I'll let you go now. And we'll release your husband later once you've provided us with something useful . . ."

Celia felt weak and cornered, but knew she must refuse to co-operate. If her husband was in jail, that was where she would be too. And if she was an embarrassment to His Majesty's Government, that was a problem for His Majesty and His Government to solve, not for her. So she drank her tea and asked for another cup. An hour later she was taken to a single cell "to think things over".

To think what over? Caleb's release in exchange for treason? Had the Jews no right to Land, Liberty and Life – not even to this tiny piece of land? Where else could they live in peace and mind their own business? What demented mind still insisted on continuing this manhunt in which millions had already been slaughtered? Demented? More like demonic. Celia felt a righteous anger stir in her. And any relief she might feel over Caleb's release would be short-lived. What if he ever discovered the price she had paid for his freedom? He would never forgive her. She lay on her plank bed, her arms behind her head, and studied the cracks in the ceiling. She wanted to make the most of the respite she had been given. Hickson was right on one point though: how on earth *had* she got herself into this mess?

Next day, the Major invited her to join him again. He sent two young soldiers to her cell in case she might feel unable to accept his invitation. This time there was no tea.

"You think you're above all this, don't you? Maybe I need to point out that there's more at stake than you might think. You're caught up in events that are way beyond you. You imagine you're here on a romantic mission to plant olive trees, harvest the grapes, milk the odd cow and help a few hapless refugees. But that's a silly illusion. There are great powers at work and irresistible forces have been let loose. You can't put the genie back into the bottle. Nor can we. You need to decide whose side you are on, Lady Cecilia. You can do the decent thing and work with us to restore peace, stability and prosperity to the Middle East. Or you can take the side of a bunch of homeless, dissident and murderous Jew-Boys." The heat was oppressive. The Major wiped his brow. He was under severe pressure. His superiors expected results, but for every Jew-Boy arrested, sentenced and hanged in Acre jail, ten new ones would take his place. Control of Palestine was fast slipping out of British hands.

Celia informed the Major politely which side she was on. She was returned, rather less politely, to her cell. After days of repeated questioning, with cups of tea alternating with threats and intimidation, she was released with a stern warning.

She returned to a kibbutz recovering from the vandalism of the British search for hidden arms caches. What a sad sight Emek Prachim had become! The soldiers had driven their lorries over lovingly planted flowerbeds; they had reversed them into young trees; they had ripped walls and floors open and the kitchen had been wrecked. In the damaged outbuildings the soldiers had discovered 52 rifles and revolvers, 30 hand grenades and a few hundred rounds of ammunition. All that Emek Prachim had to defend itself against Arab attack had been confiscated. They were now sitting ducks.

Outraged, Celia laboured night and day beside "a bunch of homeless, dissident and murderous Jew-Boys" to rebuild their kibbutz. And she offered up her English looks and accent to the cause of the Haganah. Instead of doing "the decent thing" and providing useful information to the British, Lady Cecilia chose to become a Haganah gun runner.

Caleb and hundreds of others had been taken to a detention camp in the Sinai in the hope that they would "crack" and change their minds. From there he was transferred to Acre jail. He was released three months later, in October, when no firm evidence against him could be found. And his cell was needed for more important detainees. It was also in prison that Celia told him that she was pregnant again: the hope and life of Israel was very much alive and kicking in her womb.

1947 brought no change for the better. On the contrary: Arab violence increased. While Celia had been growing big with Baby Yoram, Palestine had been growing big with the threat of war. In March, Ben-Gurion summoned all Haganah officers of battalion commander rank and upwards. He instructed them to prepare for war on a scale never before envisioned. Baby Yoram joined the Levine family that same month.

In April, Caleb decided that Celia and the boys must return to England. Celia would not hear of it. "Sorry, Caleb, but we're staying here. The bunker at Emek Prachim is fine. I trust our leaders."

"I worry about you. A sniper could pick you off in the fields any day."

"You now know how *I* feel every time you leave us. Why shouldn't *you* worry about us for once? I've been worried about you every day for these last eight years." Caleb heard the resolve in his wife's voice and did not press the matter. They stayed.

In May, the kibbutz youth were mobilised. Celia saw the determination in their young faces, and was pained that their young lives were to be ravished by war. She knew each of the young men and women well and had established a good relationship with them, despite frequent arguments. It still galled her to take orders from a bossy Palmach girl when she was almost twice her age and the mother of two boys. But Celia admired – immensely – the love and dedication the older children showed towards the younger ones. In the Nazi camps they had learned to hold together and stay alive.

July 1947 witnessed the "Exodus" tragedy. Celia felt revulsion and shame for her country. The newly established United Nations talked and talked – and talked and talked – about the future of Palestine, the British Mandate and the Jews. Meanwhile, the Arab nations around Palestine prepared for war. As did the children of the covenant. Ben-Gurion called for the full deployment of Palestinian Jewry – men and women alike. Their mission was to conquer the whole country and hold it until an authoritative political settlement was reached. On November 29th, 1947 the General Assembly of the United Nations voted in favour of partition. For the first time since the enslavement and dispersal of Israel by the Roman legions in 135 AD, the Jews had the legal right to a land of their own. There was euphoric dancing and rejoicing in the streets of Jerusalem, Tel Aviv, Haifa . . . wherever Jews had gathered to listen to the outcome of the UN vote.

Celia would always remember the huddle around the radio in the kibbutz dining hall and the ensuing explosion of communal joy. Yoram was on her arm, and Ruvele tugged on her skirt. "Mamele, why are we all laughing and crying? I've never seen everyone so happy before. Will Abba come home now?"

As if in miraculous answer to this question, Caleb arrived the next day. He had presents for the children, a bottle of wine and a new dress for Celia. "I hope it fits," he said sheepishly.

It was too tight around the waist. Celia laughed. "I've had two children, you know. I'm no longer the skinny little waif you married."

"Ah, now! It just proves my love and devotion. I still see you as my beautiful, slender, 20 year-old bride."

Celia giggled and said he was impossible. Caleb swept

her off her feet. Ruven could not make head or tail of his parents' strange behaviour. "Are you going to live with us now, Abba? For ever and ever?" he chirped.

Caleb put Celia down and hugged him. "Well, nearly. The fantastic news is that I've got a whole week's leave." Caleb announced it as if he were heralding the beginning of a Golden Age. To little Ruven it was.

The day after the partition resolution, a group of Arabs opened fire on an ambulance. Others, with machine guns and hand grenades, ambushed a bus full of unarmed Jewish civilians. Four died in the attack, including a 22 year-old bride on her way to her wedding. This undeclared and clandestine war of terror and attrition lasted for five months, until April 1948. The enemy could be anyone and anywhere, bombing, killing and maiming, apparently indiscriminately. This war was a war without a front line, and without honour. During the night of February 22nd, 1948, an explosion on Ben Yehuda Street in Jerusalem killed 52 Jews, most of them asleep. But every shock and sorrow reinforced the Jews' grim restraint and fierce determination to hang on to their land.

On March 1st, 1948 the Jewish National Council voted for the establishment of a Provisional Council of State. It was to become the legislative body of the Jews of Palestine, the Knesset. For Palestinian Jewry it was the first good news in a long time. It was a very concrete step towards Jewish statehood.

~ *35* ~

Israel, May 1948

David Ben-Gurion proclaimed the rebirth of the State of Israel at 4.38 pm on the 14th of May 1948. It was a Friday afternoon, just before sunset. "Shabbat shalom, Israel." But it was a fleeting Shabbat shalom. In the morning, Egyptian planes bombed Tel Aviv. Barely twelve hours earlier, the Jewish people had been rejoicing, happy, singing, dancing in the streets. They were a nation again at last – and on the very Land that God had promised to Abraham and his descendents as their unique inheritance. God had vowed to gather the outcasts of Israel and bring them back to their eternal inheritance. And, as they celebrated the fulfilment of this ancient redemptive prophesy, five Arab States – Egypt, Transjordan, Syria, Iraq and Lebanon declared war on them.

All through the War of Independence, the people of Emek Prachim tried to carry on as usual despite the daily risk of attack and snipers. Many kibbutzim had already fallen under siege or had been evacuated.

Celia carried on caring for her herd. On this particular late afternoon, she went to fetch the cows for milking. Efrem Harcarmel, the well-respected, battle-hardened kibbutz mechanic, was watching her from the window of Leah's medical office.

"There goes our *ishah Anglia*. She reminds me of a girl I once knew."

"An old flame?" Leah looked up from her reports.

"Heavens, no. Her name was Rachel. Came from Russia. Her family had emigrated in the early twenties. Went on to America. I wonder why on earth our *Geveret* Ben-Levi stays here. I told her what Arab men do to Jewish women if they catch them. She just gave me a strange look. As if she thought I was lying." Efrem squinted through the glass, then drummed his fingers on the window frame. "Something isn't right out there. I'd better check."

He took his rifle and left the office. He followed Celia and caught up with her as she was inspecting the herd. She noticed his presence.

"Daisy should be calving down any day now," she said.

"Funny habit of yours, to give names to the cows. You spend a lot of time with these animals, don't you?" Efrem patted a cow on the back.

"I sometimes find them nicer than people."

Efrem took no offence. He knew what she meant. He turned to go. Suddenly the bushes on the hillside moved and the sun reflected on something bright. He whirled around.

"Dammit! Run!"

With surprising agility, Efrem hurled himself against Celia, throwing her to the ground. At the same instant, there was a shot. Celia cried out. Efrem fired two shots towards the bushes. There was a ditch a few yards away. "Quick. Into the ditch. Now!"

"Efrem, I can't! My leg's hit." There was another shot and dust leaped up under her nose. Celia panicked: blood was pouring from her face.

"You've got two legs but only one life, woman. Move!"

Celia pulled herself together and pretended it was just another security drill. She nearly fainted with the pain. They slid into the ditch head first.

"Where the hell did they come from?" Efrem muttered to himself. "I've got a rifle and you've got a revolver. I guess we must have 16 rounds of ammunition between us – less the two shots I've already fired. That isn't much. I'll keep back two bullets. One for you, one for me. The Arabs won't get us alive."

"Oh God . . . Efrem . . ."

"Don't worry, I'll get you out of this mess. Cal would go to pieces if anything happened to you. We can't afford that, can we? He's far too valuable. And you've got two boys who need a mother. But I'm dispensable. The kibbutz would lose nothing more important than a good mechanic and a bad accordion player." Efrem's humour was as black as the night. Celia had never heard him say so much before in one go.

Suddenly there was a fearful blast. Stones, soil, bloody chunks of cow, more blasts, more shots.

"Those bastards. They've got a mortar up there and they've already got our range. We'll have to run for it or we're finished."

"My cows! My beautiful cows!"

Tears were flooding down Celia's cheeks. She had to help her cows. Celia peered over the rim of the ditch. Efrem pulled her back. "Are you crazy?" Another blast. Celia cowered to make herself a smaller target. Eyes closed with terror, hands clutched over her head and ears, she bit her fist till it bled.

"If they haven't heard this in the village by now, they must be deaf," said Efrem.

They could hear shouted commands in Arabic. More shots. From the direction of the kibbutz this time. Rescue. Familiar faces peering down at them. Strong arms helping Celia out.

What she saw turned her stomach: the flesh, blood, bones and guts of her proud herd were strewn across the ground. Here, a cow's eye covered in dust; over there, part of a jaw.

"Daisy! Daisy . . .!" Daisy had no front legs. Celia

vomited. Tears of anger, shock and pain mingled with her blood. Leaning on her friends' shoulders and gritting her teeth, she hobbled back to the village to be patched up.

It was dark when she knocked on Efrem's door. His face was as motionless as ever. "I hear you've got something I need. Gin. Brandy. Wine. Anything."

Efrem sized her up. She needed to get drunk. "You can have a bottle of red. It's the strongest stuff I've got."

"Fine. Can you open it for me? I haven't got a corkscrew." "I've changed," thought Celia. "Where on earth did my polite 'thank yous' and 'pleases' go? I'm talking like one of them now. Worse, I don't care. I'm still alive. And so are my children. That's all that counts."

Efrem fetched the wine, pulled out the cork and passed her the bottle. Celia took it without another word. She limped into the darkness. Then she halted and looked over her shoulder. "Would you really have shot us?"

"Yes."

"Thanks for being honest. Remind me never to let myself be rescued by a homicidal maniac again. Good night."

Efrem closed the door.

Back in her room, Celia poured herself a full tumbler of wine and gulped it down. She had to hold her breath to stop from vomiting. She had always enjoyed a fine wine drunk in good company. But not tonight: tonight she was going to get drunk. Alone.

Someone knocked on her door. "Who is it?" Celia snarled, refilling her glass.

Leah came in without being asked. She closed the door. "Efrem just came by and said you'd confiscated his last bottle of wine. Mind sharing it?" Celia motioned her to sit down. Leah got another glass. "How's your leg? And your face?"

"Hurting."

"I'd give you something, but . . ."

403

"I know: 'We're low on supplies and need all reserves for emergencies.' Until I'm actually writhing in agony on the floor, I'll just have to suffer in silence, won't I?"

"Something like that. I'm sorry about your herd. Those cows meant a lot to you." Leah poured a little wine into her glass and took a sip.

"Oh, to hell with the cows. How can I mourn for them when I'm surrounded by Shoah survivors? And I don't know that my husband isn't being blown to pieces as we speak. Hey, we don't cry here. It's unpatriotic, un-Palmach-like. We're strong. We're Jewish. We're walking in the footsteps of the Maccabees." Celia lifted tear-filled eyes to the ceiling. Her mouth trembled. When she lowered her eyes again, tears were running down her cheeks. "*L'chaim.*" She raised her glass in a toast and drank to life. Whose life, she wondered?

"You're doing us an injustice," Leah said with unusual gentleness. "We all feel sorry for you and the cows. We all know what grief is. Your pain over the animals is as real to you as grief for a lost brother."

"And Efrem threatened to shoot me. Out there. The Arabs are trying to kill us and I'm lying in a ditch with a madman."

"You're still in shock. It's been a very bad day for you. I understand that. But don't ever call Efrem a madman. He knows what he's talking about. Do you know his story?"

Celia shook her head. She had heard so many stories here. Most of them were tragedies. In Celia's eyes, Efrem was a dark and sinister character and she tried to stay out of his way. Usually there were only three places where he hung out: on the *Gadna* training field, under a greasy vehicle or in Leah's office. Sometimes he would just come in, say hello to her, drink a glass of tea, smoke a cigarette and leave without saying another word.

"He's a second-generation *Sabra*," Leah said. "Had a wife, two little children, parents, and a farm. In the Hulah valley. One morning in '29, just before the outbreak of the Arab riots, he had to go to Haifa on business. When he got home in the evening his farm had been burnt down. His family had been burnt alive. You don't want to know what they did to his wife first. Then, three years ago, the British caught him. Shot him in the leg. That's why he limps. They dragged him off to prison and refused to let a doctor see him. He almost died in their 'care'. Then they released him. He spent weeks in hospital. He came to Emek Prachim four weeks before you arrived here."

"No wonder he hates me. I must be like a red rag to a bull for him."

"He doesn't hate you. Hate is simply not in his nature. If he really hated you he wouldn't have offered to shoot you. He'd simply have left you for the Arabs."

"Charming. So, I should be grateful to him, should I? Perhaps I owe him an apology."

"Never apologise to Efrem. Words offend him. Only actions count. Judaism's a religion of deeds, not words. Just buy him a packet of cigarettes. He'd probably appreciate that."

Celia changed the subject. "I'm pregnant again."

"*Mazaltov*! Cal will be delighted." Leah smiled, pleased.

"Yes, if he lives long enough to get the message. Every time he comes here I keep thinking it'll be the last time. Every time he returns to his troops, some of my strength and courage goes with him. Before long I won't have anything left to give him." Her tears were streaming now, silently but uncontrollably. Leah got up and put her arm around her. Celia buried her face in her friend's large, soft belly, her shoulders shaking. When she had quietened down, Leah helped her to get undressed and tucked her up in bed. It felt good to be looked after. For once.

The pain in her leg kept Celia awake all night. At dawn, she got up and limped to the canteen. While she was making

405

herself a cup of tea, a group of young soldiers came in. They looked tired and scruffy. Their blond-haired leader was wonderfully cheerful. His smile was designed to melt a girl's heart. He introduced himself. "Shalom. I'm Tsachi Meir. We got word there were some Arabs in the area who are out for scalps. And that you were attacked yesterday. They sent us here to get rid of them for you."

Celia nodded. "They wiped out our dairy herd." She stretched out her hand. "I'm Celia Ben-Levi."

Tsachi shook it and tilted his head. "You're not by any chance the Englishwoman who knows everything about horses?"

"Why?"

"My father breeds Arabs. The peaceful, four-legged sort. And cattle. I'm sure we can help you restock the herd . . ." The door opened and a young woman appeared. Tsachi's eyebrows shot up. She left the canteen. "Who was that amazingly beautiful creature that just looked in?"

"My right hand. Tzipporah Sachar. But be warned: she thinks young men are a waste of time. Now, about those cattle you mentioned . . ."

"You've just lost your right hand, Mrs Ben-Levi. She's the future Mrs Meir now. If you'd excuse me a moment . . ." Tsachi was off. His friends chuckled. A few minutes later he returned, rubbing his cheek. He grinned. "Negotiations on the marriage contract may take a little longer than I'd anticipated . . ."

The marriage contract was not the only thing that took longer. The next day, an Arab unit blocked the road to Emek Prachim. The siege of the kibbutz lasted fifteen days. Food was heavily rationed and many kibbutzniks went to bed hungry. While defending her home, Leah's arm was grazed by a bullet and she had to wear it in a sling. Celia was promoted to assistant nurse. Tsachi was wounded too. And only Miss Sachar's tender care would guarantee a speedy recovery, he assured everyone. Tzipporah – Tsipi – Sachar was furious: she almost tipped him off his sick bed.

By the time the siege was over, there were five new graves at Emek Prachim. Three soldiers and two kibbutzniks had been laid to rest, among them Mr Kaminski.

After four weeks of war, a truce was declared on the 11th June. Israel found herself in control of a much larger territory than she could have hoped for. But Jerusalem was reduced to a heavily besieged enclave where the Jews were hanging on by their fingertips against the British-led Transjordanian army. By the time a truce was declared, Israeli-held Jerusalem was accessible by only a slim and heavily defended corridor. The truce lasted only a few weeks. Then war broke out again.

Celia was treating the sore teat of a cow when Sheynah from the kibbutz office appeared. Her face was grave. There had been an incident, she said. Celia understood at once and her knees almost gave way. Caleb had been taken to hospital. It did not look good.

The hospital was in a state of organised chaos. Its staff were impossibly overloaded and near exhaustion. It took Celia a while to locate Caleb's bed. Eventually she was directed to an intensive care ward, where she found him in a critical condition. He was ashen and his mouth and eyes were tightly shut. He and two friends had been caught up in an Arab ambush. Caleb had been hit in the hip and shoulder and lost a lot of blood. By the time he had reached hospital, the doctors were not sure whether he would survive surgery. But, somehow, he had managed to cling on to life and this world, the *Olam Hazeh*.

"Will he live?" Celia asked the overworked nurse who had shown her to his bed.

"It's too early to say. You must talk to Dr Scheinermann."

Somewhere in the room, a woman was weeping painfully. Celia pulled a chair to Caleb's bedside and lifted his cold, grey hand to her face. She felt strangely empty and completely unemotional. The shock was too great, and her fears were too close. Sitting there, watching him, proved to be the worst moment in her life. She remembered what she had said to him, lifetimes ago, back in 1937: that she would refuse to live like this, fearing for his safety every day, never knowing if he were going to come home well – or half dead – or at all. And now she *was* sitting here. What a bitter irony.

But Caleb did survive. After lying unconscious for an eternity of four days, he opened his eyes again. He was pathetically weak but at least Celia knew she had a husband again.

"The angels said I was too much trouble . . . They sent me back to you . . . I must learn to behave myself before they'll have me . . ." he whispered with a faint smile. He could barely keep his eyes on Celia. He closed them again when he had finished speaking.

"Then I want you to be the most irascible, exasperating and impossibly badly behaved man on earth," Celia replied, choking with happiness.

After a moment's rest he asked, "Tomasz and Arik?"

Yes, Tomasz and Arik. How could she tell him without killing him? Caleb and Arik had been best friends for many years. As members of the Haganah they had co-operated with British intelligence units to help the allied cause. After Caleb had been sent to Syria and France as liaison officer between the British and *La Résistance*, he and Arik had been reunited in early 1946. Their mission – and this time not for the British – to get German-Jewish "displaced persons" through France onto Haganah ships at secret locations on the southern French coast. What could be more rewarding and exhilarating than to bring their people home to Eretz after 2,000 years in exile? Now, after many perilous operations

Caleb was a colonel and Arik a major. A dead one. Celia felt deep sorrow, as if she had always known Arik personally. Caleb had told and written so much about him.

Warm and generous, Tomasz was Czechoslovakian and not Jewish, but according to Caleb the best Gentile friend and ally a Jew could have. They had worked together in arranging for the training of pilots and paratroopers in the years before the War of Independence. Between them they had emptied a good few bottles of fabled Czech beer and the odd glass of home-made *Slivovice*, plum schnapps.

Both had now been killed; Tomasz instantly, Arik slowly with a bullet in the chest. Caleb did not speak again. He rested, holding on to Celia's hand.

Later the doctor said that only his iron will to survive had kept him alive. "No, Dr Scheinermann." Celia shook her head. "It's God's iron will to keep the Jewish people alive."

Dr Scheinermann smiled. He was very, very tired. He had just completed 28 operations on severely wounded soldiers without leaving the operating theatre once.

Within days, Caleb was sent back to the kibbutz. Under Leah's stern and unflinching gaze, Celia learned to change his bandages and massage his feeble muscles. Then she nursed him back to health.

One morning, after breakfast, Celia returned to their room to attend to her husband. She found a strange man sitting on the edge of the bed; he was old, slumped, pathetic and resigned. She stroked his hair. "Don't worry, my love. You'll soon be better."

"How's Rosie?"

Ben Glicksman had been killed in action two days earlier. "Like every mother and wife who's just lost her lover, provider and the father of her children." Celia tried to keep her voice steady.

Reaching for her hand, Caleb lifted large, sad eyes. "Can you forgive me for putting you through all this?" He searched her face for reassurance and hope, but mainly for the truth. Then he asked the unaskable, unthinkable question that was in every Jewish heart: "Do you think we'll win this war? Can we survive it?"

Celia's heart felt faint, as much at the words as at the sight of her broken and hopeless husband. Her Caleb – so fiercely independent, so immensely resourceful and so indestructible – looked crushed and helpless, like a mangy and emaciated old lion. "Please, dear God," Celia cried in her heart. "Give me some words to say to him, some encouragement, some hope, anything. Please . . ."

"Failure is the one option we don't have," Celia heard herself say with an assertiveness that was not her own. "Of course we'll succeed. We must. We've come too far to fail now. Just think: the Jewish State is back on the map; Israel's a living miracle in our days; biblical promises are being fulfilled before our very eyes. It's a struggle, yes, but we're here to stay. Caleb, you're making history, and so are thousands of others like you." Caleb put his arm around her waist and leant his head against her swelling, tightening belly.

"I don't know, Ciel. Do you remember Dani's words from '39? Something like: 'Something astounding and marvellous has to happen before Israel can really know peace.' and 'The Almighty will make sure that we don't start to become proud of our own achievements.' I can't get his words out of my head. All the surrounding countries are fiercely hostile to us. We're just a tiny handful of Jews against millions of Arabs. And just look at us: we're as arrogant and disobedient as ever. The Irgun and Stern Gang's divisiveness could still cost us the war – even our nation. And so many Shoah survivors have turned against God. Who can blame them after everything they've been through? Humanly speaking, I can't see how it'll work out. Before long we'll have the same problems as any other nation. With the addition that all our neighbours want to annihilate us. No, it's never going to end . . ." His chin dropped onto his chest.

"Caleb. We'll never give in. We can't afford to. What would we tell all those who survived the World War and whose hope and future lie here in Eretz? Tell them to go back to . . . where? To Poland? To Germany? Impossible."

"I once had a dream that, when the Land was restored to us, we'd all be able to live in peace and happiness and keep God's commandments as He always intended we should. It's not going to happen, is it? The Land has become a reality all right, but it's turned into a death trap for us. Maybe the religious anti-Zionists are right after all . . ."

"Great." Celia felt like throwing her arms into the air and pacing the room. "So where do we go from here? We must go on. There is no turning back because there's nowhere to turn back to. There might be for us, but not for the German, Polish and Russian Jews. And what about our duty to the next generation? Do you want to condemn them to another thousand years of exile?"

"You're talking like one of those damned Zionists." Caleb wanted to smile and cry – both at the same time.

"Yes. I've picked up some bad habits here, haven't I?" She laughed a little.

When she returned the ointment to the medical room, Leah scolded her for the delay. "I'm sorry, Leah. Sometimes you have to bandage more than just a broken arm." Leah peered at her student nurse over the rim of her glasses. Everyone here was pulling together, was superhumanly supportive, but . . . Deep down lurked the unuttered fear of annihilation. What if they did lose the war? It was not going well, after all. No one had any idea how on earth – or in heaven – victory might be won. The Haganah's Chief-of-Staff, Yigael Yadin, was doing everything possible to boost the country's morale – even to the point of bluffing. 5,000

Jews from abroad volunteered for the Haganah, including 1,500 from the US.

The War of Independence lasted nine months, from May 15th 1948 to February 24th 1949. It was interspersed with fragile truces. They were just long enough to allow the warring sides to lick their wounds and regroup their forces. 6,000 Jews lost their lives. The war left Jerusalem divided until 1967.

During those dark days, Celia's fellow kibbutzniks seemed to have forgotten that she was not really "one of them". Efrem even started calling her "Ruchel" and the name stuck. Caleb eventually made a full recovery.

Little Ronit first screwed up her eyes at the bright light of day on October 30th, 1948. When Leah placed the little bundle of life into his arms, Caleb cried. He had seen too much death; now he was experiencing new life in all its innocence. The perfect little woman in his arms had tiny fingernails and perfect ears and a tuft of silky hair and a little Jewish nose and . . . Caleb could not stop marvelling at the miracle of life.

After the war, many of the Jewish volunteers returned to their countries of origin. So why couldn't the Ben-Levis, Celia pleaded. "Caleb, you promised . . . You said in '45 we'd stay here until Eretz had become a Jewish homeland . . . That's been achieved now . . ."

After years of atrocities, danger, food shortages and the ever-present threat of another war, she was physically and emotionally exhausted. But Israel was now Caleb's first love, and his one and only home. Caleb had given Israel all his time, energy and heart, and, had it been required, he would have given it his very life. He expected his family to feel as he did.

He found it unbelievably exasperating that she was again saying she wanted to return to England. "We have our country back, yes, and thousands of exiles are returning. Our prime goal must be their safety and well-being. We need to train the best army in the world and uncover the enemy's plans well in advance. We must never again allow our people to be defenceless and at the mercy of their enemies. We'll show the world that Jews can and will fight back."

Celia looked at him. The look in his eyes unsettled her. He continued, "There's so much still to do. Our borders are incredibly vulnerable, and the peace with our neighbours is about as solid as hot air. Do you seriously expect me to go to our leaders and say, 'I say, chaps, frightfully sorry and all that, sir, but I just can't carry out your orders any longer. My nice little English wife needs me at home'?"

Celia winced at his mockery of upper-class English. "I've got children, work and responsibilities, but no husband with whom to share my life and family. True, you're at home more often now, but even when you're here your mind isn't. You're still totally preoccupied with work. I can see it in your face."

"It's because I happen to care for the men I have sent behind enemy lines to gather information. They help to ensure that you can milk your precious cows without being shot at."

"It seems you care more for your spies than for your children. And whenever you're here you just spend your time under Efrem's damned vans."

"At least he doesn't nag me all the time. He leaves me in peace. I can relax and recover my strength when I'm with him. That's more than I can with you."

Caleb felt thoroughly hurt and misunderstood. Angrily, he stomped out of the room and went to Efrem. After a time of working silently on a car, Caleb hurled his spanner as far as he could.

"Why won't God send sixty million Arabs . . . somewhere else? Why does the world hate the idea of Jews living in

413

peace and freedom so much? Haven't we been through enough suffering and war?" His whole body shook; his fists were clenched. Efrem retrieved the spanner from the bushes. As he walked past Caleb, he touched his shoulder. It hurt and comforted Caleb at the same time. Efrem understood how he felt. Why couldn't Celia?

He turned to Efrem. "We still haven't heard from Yoni Katz, you know . . . His father's already lost a son and a daughter. I can't bear the thought of having to tell him again that . . ." Caleb said quietly, his shoulders drooping.

Nevertheless, Celia continued to vent her frustrations. Whenever she had the chance, she repeated her message in the hope she would get through to him at some point. He might call it nagging; to her it was begging for mercy. "I've never made any demands on you. I've shared in Israel's hardships like everyone else because I believe in the Zionist cause. I let you do your duty to your country and people. But now I want us to go home, where it's safe. I don't want our children to grow up in a war zone. I don't want them to become little thick-skinned, hard-nosed, emotionally self-sufficient Efrems and Leahs. Because that's what they must become to survive in this strife-poisoned atmosphere. I want us to live, not just survive another day. Can't you understand that? Caleb, I love you. I need you in my life . . ."

"I understand you perfectly well. You'd prefer them to grow up in the warm, cosy Diaspora where we've been living and dying for the past 2,000 years. And do you really think we'll be safer outside Israel than in it? If it's so bloody safe there, why were six million of us shot and gassed like rats? Israel is the only place on earth where a Jew can live in safety. The best he can do in the Diaspora is survive." Caleb looked at his wife. "You think Israel's my hobby, don't you? 'Let little Caleb play with his toy soldiers, until Mummy says it's time to come home.' What do you think would happen if everyone here did that? 'Oh dear. I've just discovered that Israel's no heaven on earth, so we'd all better leave.' And our blood-spattered Diaspora history will go on . . . and on . . . and on. No, we must stay here. But, of course, it's impossible for you to understand that. You aren't Jewish."

Tears of hurt and anger filled Celia's eyes. "That was below the belt, Caleb Ben-Levi. And I'm not taking that from you or anyone else. I've shed my blood, sweat and tears in this God-forsaken place too, haven't I? You know exactly what I mean. I hope you told all the volunteers that they weren't really Jewish because they were going back home. You self-righteous prig. Is the blood they spilt worth nothing to you? Just because they didn't stay when you felt they should?" Celia spat out her utter frustration.

"So let them go home and bask in the warm glow of their bravery and unselfish sacrifice. Let them brag that they're heroes to their grandchildren. Let them attend fund-raising gala dinners in support of the poor idiots who are still living here. That may be fine for them, but it's not fine for me . . . for us. I want my children to walk proudly with their heads held high. I want them to be free Jews and Israeli citizens, unashamed of who and what they are. And what do you mean by 'going home', anyway? This is our home. Haven't we both carved out a life here? Don't you travel the country teaching the new immigrants about animal husbandry and farming? Haven't you played an important part in rebuilding our nation as well?"

Celia could not fault his reasoning, but inside herself she was rebelling more and more fiercely against her situation. During the war she had drawn strength from the thought that they would return to England once it was all over. Now it was abundantly clear that Caleb had no intention of going back. Ever. Sometimes she looked out over the hot, dusty land and dreamed of green meadows and the fragrance of daffodils. In England there was no threat of Arab invasion, no bombings, no snipers. In England there were lots of innocent ladybirds, dark, quiet woodlands and swallows circling high in the hot midsummer sky. Celia began to feel desperately homesick. She knew she was trapped in Israel and resented it bitterly. But how could she escape?

After years of making do in one small room, the Ben-Levi family moved house at the end of 1951. They settled into a more comfortable, two-bedroomed bungalow close by Emek Prachim, but outside the kibbutz compound. For the first time in their lives, they had the opportunity to live as a family. But it was already too late. The crack of discord between Caleb and Celia continued to widen. Their marriage was slithering silently and treacherously towards destruction. They began to lead separate lives under the same roof, each following their separate careers. Celia refused to allow herself to be upset when Caleb telephoned that he would be late or unable to come home. Blow him! So she was often asleep when he returned. She might wake as he changed for bed, but she would not snuggle up close to him as she would have done in the past. She would lie by his side for hours, wide awake – while he snored gently – nursing her bitterness and sense of rejection. Her body and soul ached for his closeness, while her pride refused to let her be ignored and taken for granted any longer. She eventually tired of fighting and simply gave up her husband to the cause he had espoused. She had been robbed of her man by a mistress she was powerless to fight against.

~ *36* ~

Emek Prachim, March 1952

"Look, a letter from Aunt Judy," Celia called. She waved an envelope as the children ran to her during the morning break.

Letters from Aunt Judy were always exciting. Without fail, she always included photos, drawings, newspaper cuttings or funny little notes for the children. Celia looked at them first, before reading her own letter. Judy was, once again, inviting them to visit Bleckham. "It's been so long since we last saw each other," Judy wrote. "Almost seven years in the hot and sticky Middle East. Don't you ever feel homesick for England?"

Celia let the letter drop to her lap. Homesick? Before her eyes rose visions of roast beef and Yorkshire pudding, proper tea with milk, served in bone china, starched, blossom-white tablecloths underneath her dinner plate, large rooms and beds; no hand-washing, no food shortages; woods and green meadows; rain . . . "Not to mention a bath tub full of scented, warm water with no one to remind me that irrigating the crops is more important than a bath. Oh the blessed cucumbers of Egypt. And Judy's children must be quite big by now. Let's see . . . it's 1952 so . . . goodness, Richard must be twelve by now and little Cynthia is just turned five . . ." she found she was dreaming out loud.

"How would you like to visit Aunt Judy?" Celia asked her children. They shouted an affirmative "hooray".

Without thinking further, Celia wrote to accept the invitation. When Caleb returned a week later from a trip abroad on confidential government business, Ruven threw himself at his father. "Abba, Abba! We're going to visit Aunt Judy and our cousins in England."

Caleb put the boy down. "You're going to England?" The opposition in his voice was unmistakable.

"Yes," Celia confirmed, exuberantly. "Judy has invited us again. I've said we'll be coming. I've already cleared it with the kibbutz."

"But we haven't discussed it. You can't just take the children and go to England without asking me first."

Realising her mistake, Celia turned defensive. "But you're never here. Besides, she's invited all of us."

"You should have waited before replying. You know full well I can't just leave at the drop of a hat."

"Twice we discussed and planned it well in advance. You still had to cancel the trips at the last minute because something urgent had cropped up. I'm not going to let that happen again. By all means join us later, if you can or want to."

A tense calm pervaded the house. Suddenly she realised how far they had drifted apart. Neither Celia nor the children had thought it unnatural to do what they had done. Caleb, not being around, was simply not consulted. He played no part in their decision-making.

Caleb sat down at the kitchen table with a troubled heart. Celia was right. He was never at home. She had to make all the family's decisions on her own. She had been forced to do this for most of their married life. "When do you intend to go?"

"In a fortnight. It'll still be cold back home, but the English spring is so beautiful. I want the children to see it."

"And for how long?"

"I don't know yet. The invitation was open-ended."

"You will come back, won't you?" The question slipped out uninvited.

"Of course we will." Celia looked up. "What a silly question." Then she tucked Ronit's blouse back into her shorts. She needed an excuse to avoid looking into Caleb's grave and questioning eyes.

Of course she would come back. But she did not underestimate the temptations of a life without unending hard work, constant security alerts, and nerves taut to screaming point. And she would appreciate little luxuries such as going to the cinema or the theatre . . . without the ever-present danger of being blown to bits by an Arab bomb. Nor was she sure she wanted to resist these delicious temptations.

On the day of their departure, Caleb took his family to Haifa. Celia gave him a farewell kiss. They both knew that it would be the last for a long time. She took the children through passport control and then up the gangplank. Her last glimpse of her husband was of a lonely man, lost in an excited crowd, waving the boat off. Their shouts were drowned by the blasts of the ship's siren.

Caleb headed for the nearest bar. He was angry: angry with himself, angry with the world and angry with God. Celia had stuck it out for as long as she could. She had no emotional reserves left. And what about him? He too was fast running out of faith and hope. What had happened to the Land and the freedom he had fought so hard to win? Were they too simply a deceptive mirage in a desert of hard reality? Were they just a trick to help him believe that his people had achieved liberty and peace at last? He had felt increasingly like a mule these last few years. He just struggled on and on. And for what? All that was left in him was a dying faith in a better future. What future? The peaceful, happy biblical Utopia he had slaved and suffered for was not materialising. Israeli society was barely interested in the Torah. At least not the way he had once imagined it. And the possibility of another war was a daily reality. The State of Israel was striving to build a humanistic society based on Jewish cultural values. God had no part in it: God, the Owner of the Land, was given no say in how His tenants lived.

He ordered a Scotch. But who could blame them, the Shoah Jews, after all they had lived through in Germany, and Poland, and Russia, and Hungary, and Italy, and Rumania and . . . Where had it not happened to them? However strong the optimism of post-war Israel, he knew his beloved country had the same troubles as every other nation . . . only more so.

What was the point of carrying on? He had believed passionately that, once his people were living in safety, everything would be wonderful. Today that hope was decaying fast. Had Dani not prophesied that this would happen? But he had not believed him. What was more, he had become deeply suspicious of God and His plans: they seemed to bring only more work, more struggle, more suffering and more confusion. Nor did he trust human wisdom and politics. It was punctuated with errors, greed, inconsistencies and human weakness. He downed his drink in one pull. "Who cares anyway?"

He ordered another Scotch. It would chase away his disillusion and self-contempt.

* * *

The train puffed and pulled its way to Marsham station. The children, heads crammed through the open window, spotted a lady on the platform waving energetically.

"That's your Aunt," Celia cried. Judy's shoulder-length brown waves had gone. They had been replaced by a short, well-styled cut. She had put on weight too, which gave her an air of dependable and motherly femininity. Her suit was tailor-made and she carried herself with the gracious poise of a self-confident Lady of the Manor. Gone was the clumsy walk of a shy young bride. "She reminds me of her mother," Celia thought.

Celia lifted the heavy suitcases down from the train before the hurrying porter reached her. Ach, hadn't she grown strong lifting milk churns and ammo boxes? Here she stood, now supposedly "back home", with her little flock of children at her feet. And Caleb was thousands of miles away. It all felt so wrong. Suddenly she felt tearful. The yearned-for relief at being back in England had slipped through her grasp. She just felt a crushing disappointment.

Judy ran to them and kissed her sister-in-law on the cheek. When was the last time she had been greeted in this way, with breeding and sensitivity, Celia asked herself. How different from a *Sabra*'s strong embrace and heartfelt thanks that she was still alive. They looked each other over, affectionately. Judy noted how Celia had changed – both inwardly and outwardly. She had certainly aged. Fine lines had appeared around her eyes and mouth. They suited her well, actually. They bore witness to the strong, unwavering maturity she exuded. But the air of plucky determination in her eyes had faded, replaced by something not unlike powerless resignation.

"Oh, Celia, it's been so long . . ."

"Yes, it has, hasn't it?" She gave Judy a little smile.

"You must be feeling tired . . ." Judy bent down towards the oldest boy. "Now, you must be Ruven. Haven't you grown?" she said in her quiet gentle English. The throaty yell of the Jewish settlers and *Sabras* seemed aeons away. "Welcome to Marsham."

Ruven responded politely to her outstretched hand and shook it seriously. "How do you do, Aunt Judy?"

Celia had rehearsed him well. Yoram was less co-operative and just stared at his aunt, wide eyed. Judy smiled with motherly understanding. Then she knelt down, close to the

421

serious-looking little girl clutching Celia's skirt. "And you must be Ronit. We haven't met before, have we?" She smiled at Ronit, whose little face suddenly burst into a big smile. "Oh Celia, what beautiful children you have."

On this spring day, for the first time in seven long years, Celia's hungry soul feasted on the scent of wild daffodils. Their fragrance wafted in through the open car window.

"I've been trying to recall these fading memories for so long. I tried hard to remember the smell of daffs . . . and couldn't. It's harder to remember a fragrance than a face or a place, isn't it?" Celia mused.

"I sensed it in your letters. You were writing about Bleckham more and more often."

"Was I?"

They turned into the drive. Celia's heart ached. How often had she ridden along here? She felt awestruck at the sight of the deep blue sky reaching down through the fresh green of the chestnut trees. She noticed there were two or three gaps in the line of trees flanking the drive to the manor house. "They were diseased. We had to fell them," Judy said.

The driver pulled up at the front door. "Oh, look. You've restocked the rose beds. When I left this was still a wartime vegetable patch." Celia was touched to see Bleckham's flowerbeds restored. She let herself out of the car and just stood looking at the house. Judy took care of the children. Celia's eyes rose and lovingly followed the Georgian lines of the manor's high windows. "It's the dearest, sweetest place on earth. How could I ever have left it for so long?" she thought. Slowly, she walked to the front door. As she entered, her hand lightly touched the pillars flanking the front door. The lobby, the hall . . . she knew that tears were not far off.

Then Alistair appeared. "Hello stranger. How are the colonies? All heat, camels and flies, I don't doubt. As you can see, the 'Hôtel des Beaux Americains' has closed for good. You remember the American officers billeted here at the end of the war? I thought you were falling for one of them. What with Caleb being away and all that," he teased. Celia hugged her brother-in-law. The arguments and hurts of the past were long forgotten and forgiven.

The boys stared open-mouthed at the high ceilings and sheer size of the house. Self-confident Yoram found his tongue first. "We'll play chase here," he decided with a leader's spirit.

"No, darling, we don't play chase in the house. There's plenty of room in the garden," Judy dampened his enthusiasm.

"Aren't there Arabs out there?"

"No, darling, there aren't any Arabs around here."

Richard returned from school at half past three, neat, orderly, well kempt – even after a day at school – and polite. The heir to Bleckham welcomed his aunt with poise and dignity. "Welcome to Bleckham Manor, Aunt Cecilia."

His blazer displayed the emblem of the local prep school. He was a prefect and had already been taught that great responsibility goes with great authority. Celia smiled at his boyish good manners and stretched out her hand. "I'm delighted to renew our acquaintance, Richard." Then: "But please promise never to call me Cecilia again. Only my mother does that."

The thought of Lady Norah knotted Celia's stomach immediately. She had done her best to keep in touch with her parents, but their relationship was icy. She had written to tell them about Yoram and Ronit's birth. In reply she had received a brief note of congratulation and a cheque. Nothing more, except . . . a comment that their names were not Christian and sounded quite foreign . . . that "George" or "Elizabeth" would have been much more appropriate . . .

Was she deliberately setting out to embarrass her parents? *"Plus ça change . . ."* thought Celia.

Judy and Alistair were attentive and loving hosts. They did everything they could to make them all feel welcome and at home. But a few days later a roast appeared on the dining table which neither Ruven nor Yoram recognised. *"Ma zeh,* Mamele?" Ruven wanted to know what it was.

Celia felt uncomfortable. "It's roast pork, darling. But we don't have to eat it."

Yoram grabbed himself by the throat and, uttering guttural, mock-strangulation sounds, slid under the table, apparently poisoned. Richard was appalled. "That's perfectly good food. Where're your manners, Yoram?"

Alistair chided him for playing the little professor.

"Anyway, pork isn't food," Ruven said, folding his arms in protest. He knew the Book: pork simply wasn't food any more than frog or snail or horse.

For the next day or two, Celia had to talk her children out of going on hunger strike. What kind of house had Mamele grown up in, they wondered. A home where people ate such revolting things as pork and lobster? They looked at her with suspicion.

Alistair was not too pleased either. He was not impressed by Yoram's constant antics at the table and decided that the younger children should eat upstairs in the nursery. But Celia pleaded – no, insisted – that they should eat with the adults. "Al, in Israel I live in fear for the safety of my children each day. And they spend almost all the time in the nursery or at school. I don't want to be parted from them unless it's absolutely necessary." Alistair graciously gave in.

On their first Shabbat at Bleckham, the children became even more confused. No candles, no *challah* bread, no special dinner, no songs, no prayers? Mamele lit candles with them in her bedroom. Why did she not do it openly, with all the family present, as everybody did in Israel? "Uncle Al and Aunt Judy don't keep Shabbat," she said.

But Ruven was not going to be sidetracked. When the Hornbys returned from church on Sunday and everybody sat down for lunch, Ruven asked, "Aunt Judy, if you are Abba's sister, then you're Jewish, aren't you? Why do you live like a Christian then? Aunt Esti doesn't." He paused for a second. "And Richard and Cynthia must be Jewish too. Just like cousin Shani."

Richard looked at Ruven, troubled. Then at his father. "Father, I am a Christian, aren't I?"

"Of course you are," assured Alistair with a smile.

Ruven was still confused. But he sensed that his questions made Uncle Al and Aunt Judy tense. So he did not ask the other ones that were puzzling him.

The next day, Celia took her children to the Knoll. The view from there was so beautiful. Celia spread out the rug she had brought and sat down. The boys ran off while Ronit played with some twigs and stones. After a while the boys reappeared to recharge their batteries on lemonade and Bakewell tarts.

"Mamele. I am Jewish, aren't I?" Ruven asked suddenly. He looked worried.

"Of course you are, darling." Celia smiled at him and stroked his hair. "Why do you ask?"

"Aunt Judy is a Jewess, but cousin Richard is a Christian. I don't understand . . . Abba is a good Jew, and so are you . . ."

"Sit down, Ruvele. I'll explain." Ruven dropped down on his bottom. "You know the story of Boaz and Rut?" Ruven nodded. This story was read and told every Shavuot. According to Jewish tradition it was the festival where dairy products were served in abundance. A good story and lots of cheesecake: the Jewish people knew how to make their children love the Torah and the traditions. "Well, Rut came from the land of Moab, didn't she? So, do you think she was Jewish?"

Ruven thought. "Probably not . . .?"

"But that didn't stop Boaz, who was a good Jew, from marrying her. Because she loved the God of the Jews, His Torah and His people. God later honoured her by making her the great-grandmother of King David." Celia turned her son's face to her. "Ruven, look at me." Large blue eyes he had inherited from Gertrud looked up at her full of love and trust. "Don't let anyone – Jew or Christian – ever . . . do you understand? . . . ever tell you that you're not Jewish. Is that clear? You're born a Jew and you'll die a Jew."

Ruven nodded obediently. "Aren't you Jewish, then, Mamele?"

"Abba and I are like Boaz and Rut."

Ruven thought for a moment, and then frowned. "So why have you taken us back to Moab, Mamele?"

Celia finally had to admit to herself that coming back to England had been a bad mistake. She had run back to Bleckham as a storm-tossed boat runs for a safe harbour. But she now realised that what had happened in her during the last seven years had taken her past the point of no return. They were changes she had neither asked for nor given her consent to. So many things, like hot baths or good tea – things that had seemed so vital to her – were, she now realised, quite unimportant. Was it a hankering for stability and the familiar that had lured her from Israel and her husband? Was she unwilling to accept the reality of her situation? Or was she simply afraid of further changes, in herself as a person, and in her life? She even wondered, at times, whether she were fighting against God. Did He have a role for her in His eternal plan for His people, Israel?

Her dilemma lay in the fact that, through her marriage to Caleb, her destiny was inseparably linked with the Jewish people and the Land of Israel. She had knowingly and willingly married a Jew. In the fervour of her first love, she had even offered to convert to Judaism. But Caleb had not insisted on this, so she had not actively embraced the religion of Israel. In one sense, she had never had the opportunity to appropriate Rut's promise that "your God shall be my God" as a living reality in her life. Instead she had simply slipped into her role as a support for her husband in his vision and mission. Suddenly she was confronted with the full impact of the promise she had made to Caleb and to God so long ago: "Your people shall be my people; wherever you lodge I will lodge . . ." Deep in her heart, Celia knew what she should do, but she fought fiercely against her avowed destiny. She had been willing to live like a Jew in Eretz – for a season. But actually to become an Israeli, to sacrifice England and her Englishness . . . that was going too far. And why should she, anyway? Thousands of Jews lived happily in Britain. Had not Caleb been born and educated in England? Had he not been more than content to marry an Englishwoman? Why could they not live in England and observe Torah and the traditions here? Many other Jews did. And what about all the Jewish volunteers who had returned to their homelands after the war? Why should her stiff-necked husband insist on staying in Israel and make her suffer? It was not fair.

She found herself trapped by her meandering indecisiveness; she could go neither backwards nor forwards.

~ 37 ~

Bleckham Manor, end of May, 1952

"When are we going home, Mamele? I want to see my friends and tell them all about England." Yoram had started asking the dreaded question Celia could not answer.

They had lived in Israel. Two of the children had been born there. What right had she to uproot them? Had she not insisted that they should be raised as Jews? They should be with their friends, growing up as free and confident Israeli children. What a mess she had made.

Yesterday Judy had persuaded her to come on a courtesy call to meet Brigadier and Mrs Soames. They were new to the village and had just bought the neighbouring estate. Judy wanted to be a good neighbour and help them settle in. The much-travelled brigadier and his wife had been so charming and accommodating. To Judy's immense joy, she discovered they would be attending the same church. While Judy chatted happily, Celia's thoughts wandered.

". . . That's right isn't it, Lady Celia?" Brigadier Soames smiled at her over his teacup.

Celia's mind raced: What was right? "Yes, I absolutely agree." Celia nodded. What on earth had she absolutely agreed to?

The parlour maid appeared and announced more visitors.

"Of course. Show them in, please." Mrs Soames was visibly delighted. More visitors. How nice.

Judy's face drained of colour when Lord Sebastian and his beautiful young wife, Lady Sophia, walked in. Of course, the Soames had no idea of what had once passed between the Honourable Mrs Celia Levine and the Marquess. Celia was ice-cold and unrepentant. An ex-Haganah gun runner was not going to be intimidated by the Twisted Trout of Lenkham Hall.

"Tally-ho, Celia, old girl. My, who'd have thought . . . I'd no idea you were even in the country." Sebastian, who never lost his composure in public, greeted her like an old friend. Celia deliberated as to whether she should take offence at his intimacy or be grateful that he wanted to spare her embarrassment. So she smiled sweetly.

"How do you do, Sebastian? Lady Sophia . . ."

She felt so much older suddenly, so much more worldly-wise than Sebastian. She even looked down a little on sweet Lady Sophia. But she fitted her surroundings flawlessly, with her bottle-blonde hair, immaculate fingernails and fine, delicate hands. Celia usually wore gloves now; her hands looked rather work-worn these days. And her wrists had become too strong to be delicate. When Lady Sophia opened her mouth, her well-modulated voice was adorned with the tactful chimes of polite laughter. Sebastian had chosen well; she was the perfect accessory to his position in society and estate. Watching them interact, it was obvious they were made for each other. And, all of a sudden, Celia's bitterness towards Sebastian and the past evaporated. She felt genuinely pleased for them both and said as much.

Lady Sophia enquired, politely and with some interest, about her "amusing adventures" in the Middle East. Celia said it was nothing; nothing to tell of, really. What could she say? Had her arrest and time in jail been "amusing"? Were mortars exploding around her, and being scared out of her wits, an "adventure"? Hardly. Instead, Celia told about the happy occasions; the celebration over the United Nations' vote on Partition, the Declaration of Independence, the

Jewish festivals, her dairy herd, and weddings at Emek Prachim. She received uncomfortable smiles and "how charming" comments.

"Did you serve in the Middle East, Brigadier?" Sebastian asked.

"Thank God, no. North Africa, Italy and Germany. Barbarous what the Germans did. Especially to the Jews. We could have helped them but didn't lift a finger. If I'd been sent to Palestine, I think I'd have resigned my blessed commission rather than accept an order to catch and re-imprison runaway Jews. People back home just don't seem to realise. The Allies had only just released the poor blighters from their concentration camps. And d'you know what? Before they could say 'Jack Robinson' we're marching them straight back behind barbed wire again. Kept some locked up until 1949. Rotten show, really . . ."

Sebastian cleared his throat and exchanged glances with his wife. Naturally, to the Holsworth-Leighs, the rebellious Jews were the enemies of the Empire. The conversation died.

"Anyone for more tea?" Mrs Soames suggested, hopefully.

Celia was starting to like the brigadier. "You don't happen to know a Major Hickson, by any chance, do you? He served in Palestine."

"I do indeed. Splendid chap. He's a Colonel now. Why d'you ask, Lady Cecilia?"

"Oh, nothing really. We met briefly during the last days of the Mandate. That's all. I wondered what had become of him." Celia's thoughts wandered again, back to Israel and the kibbutz. After three years of wooing, Tsachi had convinced Tsipi that life without him was not worth living: they had got engaged. Celia was about to lose her right hand. Who would replace her, she wondered? And had Leah accepted the post as lecturer at Hebrew University? Who would have thought that the fierce nurse from Austria had a

430

PhD in psychology? She'd kept it quiet all these years. Efrem would be heartbroken if she left. But that would be his own fault. Why didn't he simply tell her what he felt for her? It was obvious to everybody else. Instead he kept his silly *Sabra* mouth tightly shut. And what if Tsachi had delivered the half-dozen unbroken horses he'd threatened her with? Tsachi could sell fridges to the Eskimos. As soon as they got back to Bleckham she'd cable Emek Prachim and put everything on hold until she was back home. Home? Back in Israel? What was she thinking?

Shortly after the visit to the Soames, Celia made a shocking discovery. She was standing by the sideboard in the dining room. She had looked up, straight at the wall and had seen – as if written on the wall by the finger of God – the message, *"Celia, old girl, you don't go with the wallpaper any more."* She had nearly dropped the plate. Then the vision had vanished.

Afraid and confused, she telephoned Barbara and Francis in London. They were now living in the late Lady Agatha's town house. Of course they would be only too delighted to see her and the children. They could all most certainly stay for a week. They took the train to London next day.

The atmosphere there was relaxed. Barbara adored the children. "Your mother has never forgiven me for not producing any offspring, let alone an heir," she confided to Celia.

"Oh, blow Mummy. She barely looked at my three."

The children adored Aunt Babba and got on marvelously with her. Her name reminded them of their father. "Will Abba come and see us?" Ruven asked.

Yoram drew a picture and wrote a little note for Uncle Effi. "Shouldn't you write to Abba first? It'll hurt him if Uncle Effi gets a letter and he doesn't," Celia pointed out. But her heart was aching. So far she had received only one short letter from Caleb. It read as if he had found it difficult to find anything to write about.

"Uncle Effi will be at home for sure. Abba may not be," Yoram replied.

Celia's crisis came to a head when the Glicksmans invited them all to stay for a couple of nights. They arrived and Sarah'le embraced Celia without a word; they understood each other perfectly. Their correspondence over the years, Ben's death, Rosie's remarriage six months ago, Celia's experiences . . . they had formed a deep relationship. Sarah'le's letters had helped Celia understand the complicated ways and mindset of the Jewish people.

Ruven liked Auntie Sarah'le. Auntie Sarah'le was Jewish, and therefore trustworthy. Anyone who was not Jewish might just be an Arab in disguise. It did not take long for a Jewish child to become suspicious of anyone non-Jewish. And at Aunt Judy's, one had to be careful not to shout or even talk too loud, to dress smartly, to mind one's "Pleases" and "Thank yous" and do all sorts of other strange things. Mamele was so much more fussy about his behaviour when they were there, especially when Uncle Al was around. Hopefully they would go home soon, although playing in the woods without Arabs around was great fun. And there was so much greenery and water everywhere . . .

Dani welcomed Celia with a peck on the cheek. The Glicksman household was no longer alien to her. She just slipped into their household routine and felt like family. They enquired after Rosie and the grandchildren, talked about Israel, the peace or absence of it, and her experiences in the Land. Ruven drew pictures of tanks and armed Israeli soldiers. Ronit fell asleep on Sarah'le's lap, and Yoram vied with his brother for Dani's attention. After the children were tucked up in bed and settled, the women did the washing up and talked. Halfway through, Sarah'le stopped and grinned, a saucepan in her hand.

"Why are you smiling?" Celia asked.

"You're drying up more quickly than I can wash. Do you remember the first time you held a tea towel?"

Celia smiled too, but it was a bittersweet smile. "That was a long time ago," she said.

Later she sat with her friends in their little front room, clasping a hot cup of tea between cold hands. With her thoughts far away, she stared at the light-brown brew. Dani lit his pipe and Sarah'le was mending some socks. After a while Sarah'le asked, "Do you think you'll settle in Israel permanently?" She bit off a strand of wool, not looking at Celia.

Celia glared at her hostess.

Dani noticed her look. He took the pipe out of his mouth and lowered his eyes. "Are you happy there? From your letters I got the impression that you'd like to return to England. Have Cal and you talked it through yet?" He inspected his pipe.

"Talked?" Celia's words spurted out like fizzy lemonade from a shaken bottle. "Heavens! What is there to discuss? Israel is my husband's mission. End of story." She made a theatrical gesture to demonstrate her husband's heroic self-denial. "Whenever I broach the subject, he makes me feel utterly selfish and heartless, and we end up having a row. He accuses me of letting him down. Or, to put it more plainly, I hold him back from rebuilding the Jewish State . . . and therefore ruin his life. I'm a millstone around his neck. He seems to think it's up to him, and him alone, to carry the future of Eretz on his shoulders. We don't talk about it any more . . ."

There was a long silence. "How do you feel about it?" Dani probed, cautiously.

"That's quite unimportant. What I think or feel doesn't matter. He has made up our mind and I just have to tag along. It's always been like that. Now I have to decide whether the children and I return to Israel. There we'll live in fear of Arab snipers and war for the rest of our lives. With our marriage in tatters. Or we all come back to England and

Caleb pines away for Israel. With our marriage still in tatters. And what about the children? I vowed to raise them as Jews. They've a right to live in their own Land. You tell me where I go from here. I haven't a clue." Her bitter words sliced through the sweet, smoke-filled air.

Dani knew her deep despair. Sarah'le, shocked, put down her darning. "Oh Celia, is it really so bad between you? We'd guessed it wasn't all rosy, but . . ." She put her warm, rough hand over her friend's clenched icy fist and threw a tough look at Dani. "The things you men take for granted are deplorable," it said.

Dani mumbled an "Oh dear" and puffed hard at his pipe to create a smoke screen.

Celia felt relieved, though. For the first time ever, she had voiced her real feelings. Here she was free; on the kibbutz she was not. To hold back anyone, even your soul mate, from a noble ambition was shameful. And when their goal was Jewish liberation and self-determination, such meanness of spirit was considered doubly shameful, disloyal and close to treason. Every good Jewish wife and mother made all sorts of sacrifices for Eretz, joyfully and without complaint. They marvelled, through their tears, at the awesomeness of their common task. Well, Celia had never felt called to anything, nor was she Jewish. All she had ever known was that she loved Caleb and needed him. But he no longer needed her; he had Israel. In the beginning, their shared vision for the Land had united them. Now it was driving them apart. With Israel, Caleb had no need of her love; without Israel, his love for her would simply die.

Sarah'le squeezed her hand. "You feel cornered, don't you?"

"I should never have married him. He was complicated at the best of times, but now . . . He's changed so much, you'd hardly recognise him. He's become self-reliant, hard-nosed and thick-skinned. Almost like Efrem the Rock: solid, unswerving . . . a great leader of men." Celia's expression moved from desperation to grief, and then settled on sarcasm.

"That's what war does to you . . . We've all lost so many friends . . ." Dani said. He was thinking of Ben.

With tears welling up, Celia continued. "I keep looking for my gentle, loving Caleb, my Caleb who used to make me laugh, whose heart was full of compassion for every living thing. All I find now is an independent, hard, driven, unrelenting . . . male. Sometimes he does try to make an effort to be nice and more attentive. But it's always half-hearted because his head is full of other things. And I feel he only does it to appease his complaining, moody, demanding wife, the one he's chained to, the one with no vision for the greatness of his task. He just makes me feel condemned and guilty all the time."

"I know that you don't really mean what you're saying. But it does a lot of good to vent your anger and resentment when you're with friends whom you can trust," Dani said. What could he do? He prayed for wisdom. It was a poor Jew's only wealth, the only way he could share in the riches of Solomon. He fiddled with his pipe which had at last gone out. "I once knew a young Gentile woman who had bought herself a tallit because she wanted to come under the protection of the God of Israel," Dani mused out loud.

"Just youthful naïveté and enthusiasm," Celia retorted, sarcastically.

"I don't think so. You were very sincere about it. Have you changed your mind over the years?"

"No. I've never stopped trusting God. It was my belief in a good and just God that helped me when I came across the tortured and broken, even demented, Shoah survivors. I trust that, ultimately, He will punish those who did this to them."

"You're absolutely right. We can't lay the problem of faith

435

and life at God's door. That's man's problem. It's a problem called 'sin'."

"Good old-fashioned, Bible-bashing sin . . ."

"Don't mock God, Celia. It doesn't suit you. The Ten Commandments . . ."

"I'm sure I've broken them all in one way or another, at some point . . . Dani, what am I to do?" Celia shook her head. She was hopeless and desperate and needed help. She had reached the end of the road. Before her lay only an endless, merciless, frightening wilderness.

Dani started to sing a song, quietly: "'I heard the voice of Jesus say, "Come unto Me and rest. Lay down, you weary one, lay down your head upon My breast." I came to Jesus as I was, weary, worn and sad. I found in Him a resting place and He has made me glad.'" He stopped singing. "I heard these words fifteen years ago. They were being sung by a Salvation Army street choir. And they've totally transformed my life. What you need is clarity . . . and peace. 'Come unto Me all of you who are burdened and heavy laden, and I will give you rest.' This means more than a friend's arm around your shoulder. It means to unburden yourself of all your pains and worries. And sins: those you've committed in deed, and those you've committed in your heart. Jesus – in Hebrew His name is 'Yeshua' – came to take our burdens away and nailed them to the execution stake."

"What do you mean by 'execution stake'?" Celia asked with raised eyebrows.

Dani shuffled. "The cross. But, as a Jew, it has so many terrible connotations for me that I prefer the term 'execution stake'."

Celia shook her head. "Whatever. The cross is fine when you're a Christian. I don't have that luxury; I believe what Jews believe. Besides, it would cost me everything to accept Jesus . . . my husband, my children . . ."

"But your life is already plummeting towards the rocks, isn't it? You said so yourself. What have you got to lose?"

"It's one thing to go through a legal separation because your marriage has failed. It's quite another to incur your Jewish husband's everlasting wrath and damnation because you believe in . . . What did you say you call him? . . . Yeshua?"

Dani nodded. "Jesus is His English name and along with it come a whole cartload of erroneous Greek and Western ideas and philosophies. And emotive Jewish reactions. The Messiah is Jewish and deserves to be called by His Hebrew name, 'Yeshua'."

At this moment, Celia could not care less about the finer points of theology. "If I became a Christian, Caleb would stop at nothing to get custody of the children. That's what I've got to lose."

"The cost of discipleship is always high. But you know, Celia, it's really a very small price to pay . . . compared with the punishment we actually deserve for our sin . . . and the price – His own life – that Yeshua has already paid for our redemption. Faith isn't really about outward happiness and peace, though that is an important part of it. It's about good-ness and strength of character, and an inner joy and peace with God."

"Hold on, Dani. You're talking just like a Christian. Do you realise that? You haven't become one, have you?" Celia looked hard at her friend, her eyes full of astonishment. "But Dani . . . you're a Jew . . ."

"Is it forbidden for a Jew to believe in the Messiah . . . once he's found Him? Many thousands of Jews believed in Him, in the days when Yeshua lived and taught in Eretz . . . and after His death."

"Well, no, on the contrary, but . . ." Celia slipped a side-ways glance at Sarah'le who was sitting quite still, mending her socks, her eyes down. She was not taking any part in the conversation. Celia wondered what she was thinking.

437

"Yes, Celia. I do believe in the Jewish Messiah that the Scriptures tell us about."

Celia stared at Dani with incredulity. "How on earth did this happen?"

"It started in '35. I was becoming more and more despondent about what was happening to our people. I knew I was powerless to help them. I started to search high and low for a way out. And, being a stiff-necked Jew, I found that the ban against even touching, let alone reading, the 'Christian' New Testament was just too tantalising. So I bought a copy. I read it . . . over and over again. It was totally Jewish and I found that, taboo apart, nothing seemed more natural than for a Jew to believe in Yeshua. I found I was holding, in my very own hands, the evidence that Yeshua was the fulfilment of everything the Scriptures had said about the Messiah. I could no longer deny the truth. So I did the only thing I could: I confessed my sins and asked Yeshua to cleanse and purify me. Oh, what a glorious resurrection it was! Having been dead in my sins for years, Yeshua changed my heart and gave me a new life, an eternal life with Adonai." Dani's face radiated joy.

Sarah'le looked at her husband darkly and pulled harder than necessary on the yarn. Her lips were pressed tightly together. She pricked herself with the needle. "Ouch!"

A burning question arose. "But what about the Torah? Do you believe that Yeshua has done away with the Torah?" Celia asked.

Dani fidgeted. "No. But, sadly, my Christian brothers and sisters don't see it that way. It makes church attendance and sitting through sermons very awkward for me. As far as I can understand, the church has confused the Torah with legalism. Legalism requires that we must achieve and maintain our own salvation by keeping God's commandments perfectly. In large measure, that's what Rabbinic Judaism requires too. But true righteousness, the righteousness imparted by God, is a free gift we receive from Him when we accept His Son, Yeshua, as our Messiah. It is infinitely higher and better than the self-righteousness of man. Legalism or self-righteousness is man trying to reach God by his own efforts; salvation is God reaching down to rescue those who are already irredeemably lost. The Torah is eternal and unchangeable. It's the will of God for all His people; it's part of who and what God is. That means that, when you become a follower of Yeshua, the Torah changes its function: before, its role is to convict us of our sins and point to our need for salvation; afterwards, it becomes our friend who teaches us how to lead a life separated, holy and pleasing to God. You see, the Torah leads a Jewish person to salvation in Yeshua, while Yeshua's salvation leads His followers – Jews and Gentiles – to keep Torah as He kept it. It's really very simple." Dani threw up his arms and smiled.

"If only Caleb could believe that . . ." Celia sighed.

"Never mind about him right now. God has His own plans – good plans – for him. But what about you? You said you believe what Jews believe. I'm a Jew and I believe in the Messiah. *Nu*?"

"Prove to me that Yeshua is the Messiah, and I'll believe."

Sarah'le bade them good night. Celia and Dani talked long into the night. By the small hours of the morning, Celia had run out of excuses and had surrendered, not only herself, but also her sins and shame, to Yeshua. And she had also given her husband and children . . . her life and theirs . . . fully into God's hands.

The Jewish music she had so loved from the moment she had first heard it – with its cadences of joy and sorrow holding hands – was playing in her heart again. But it was also a nerve-wracking time. Should she write to Caleb, or just keep her secret to herself until she next saw him? She could not make up her mind. She had already changed so much; she felt she needed to know herself better before she could tell him what had happened to her. Yeshua had poured love, peace and forgiveness into her life. Now she was sure that she was a full citizen of the Kingdom of God with all its rights and duties. She, the wild olive branch, had been grafted into the cultivated Jewish olive tree. The King of the Jews Himself had done this for her. But she was married to a Jewish man who totally opposed everything to do with Yeshua. What should she do?

In the evenings, she put the children to bed and blessed them. Then she would look into their happy, trusting faces. Their innocent faith that Mamele was best, and knew best, shone out of their eyes. Her heart was torn and bleeding; she pleaded day and night with Yeshua to have pity on her family. If Yeshua were only to reveal Himself to Caleb, then she would do anything He asked of her. Even go back to Israel. If God would only do this one enormous little thing for her . . .

"Ya'akov served fourteen years for Rachel. I'd gladly serve another fourteen if Sarah'le were to acknowledge our Messiah," Dani had confided.

Celia was not convinced that 28 years would be enough to win over Caleb.

~ *38* ~

Emek Prachim, 3rd June 1952

Caleb woke up with a bad hangover. Again. He got up and had a shower, a mug of coffee and two aspirins. It did not make him feel any better. The coffee he had made tasted awful. Ciel's was infinitely better. Mug in hand, he stood in the sun-drenched kitchen. He was bored and depressed. He lifted the lid of the bread bin and looked in. There was only one hard, dried up crust in there. He threw it into the rubbish bin and wandered listlessly around the house. The children's bedroom was deserted. No Ronit escaping from her cot, no Ruvele jumping from the top bunk and no Yori tearing through the house. His and Celia's bedroom was opposite the children's room. He looked in. Her side of the bed was untouched; the sheets were clean and uncrumpled. What would he not have given to see her there, now, hugging her pillow deliciously as she awoke, her limbs in all directions, smiling and purring like a cat. How he missed them all.

But he could not mope about all day, nursing his throbbing head and empty heart. He had a meeting that morning at the Ministry of Defence. Efrem wanted to collect some engine parts and offered him a lift. His own car needed a service, so Caleb accepted the lift gratefully. Half an hour later they were on their way to the city.

For a while they drove along in complete silence. Efrem was angry. Ruchel – he still couldn't bring himself to call her Celia – was a damn fine woman. Almost as good as Leah. Over the years they had grown together, him and Leah and

Ruchel and the kids. Like a family. Yori called him Uncle Effi and followed him around like a dog. He handed him tools when he was under a van and sang like a little bird when he played the accordion. He missed them. Ruchel made a nice cup of tea, too.

He gave Caleb a sideways glance. "They won't be coming back, will they?" Caleb looked away. "You're a fool, Cal, and an idiot. If it would bring back my family, I'd dig to Australia with my bare hands to get them. And you let yours go without even putting up a fight. You don't deserve them. And do you know something else? You're not that important for this country either. You're not irreplaceable, you know. But how will you ever replace Ruchel and the kids if they don't come back?"

Caleb slammed his hand down on the dashboard. "*Da-i!* That's enough! Stop the car. I'm not putting up with that from you." Calmly, Efrem pulled over and Caleb jumped out. "I'll walk."

"It's seven miles to Tel Aviv."

"I know. But right now I feel like walking. It's better than having to listen to your insults all day." Angrily, Caleb slammed the car door.

Efrem shrugged and drove off. He pulled over two miles down the road. He switched off the engine, put his feet up on the dashboard and lit a cigarette. Caleb caught up with him 40 minutes later. Efrem opened the passenger door. Caleb got in. They arrived in Tel Aviv without exchanging another word.

Efrem dropped him off at the corner of Dietzengoff Street. It was hectic in the city. People were scurrying about, sweating, minding their own business. Caleb felt detached, as if it were someone else walking down the street, not him. Then he realised he was late for his meeting and, despite the heat, started to jog through the crowds.

Binim Himmelfarb counted the money in his purse. He had spent more than he could afford, but he was still smiling: it was Erev Shabbat. In his shopping basket lay a tiny, bony chicken, a handful of potatoes, some leeks with limp green leaves, and two shiny red apples. They had been the cause of his financial ruin. But Shabbat is Shabbat; God would provide. He always did. He picked up the basket and tucked a fresh *challah* loaf under his arm. He stepped onto the pavement – without looking left or right. It was a mistake.

Caleb ran straight into him, knocking him down and sending the groceries flying. Caleb just managed to keep his balance, but Binim landed on all fours, his glasses flying off into the road. Caleb rushed to help the elderly stranger. "I'm so sorry! I didn't see you coming out . . . Are you all right?" he asked anxiously.

"Oh, it's me who should be apologising. I was dreaming. I should have looked." Binim brushed the dust off his flimsy trousers.

"No, it was my fault. You shouldn't expect to be run down on the pavement." Caleb picked up the loaf. He hesitated. "At least let me buy you some more bread."

"Oh, no, no. Don't trouble yourself. It's only a little bit of dust. We should be thankful for all our food." Binim reached into his basket to check his apples. They were not too badly bruised. The sleeve of his shirt slipped up to reveal a number tattooed on his arm. Caleb recognised it for what it was.

"Please, I insist. I need some bread anyway," he lied. "Let me have yours and I'll get you a fresh loaf. You've eaten more dirt in your life than I ever will."

Binim looked up. He looked into eyes that were compassionate and sincere. There was something about this man that caught his attention. He studied him for a moment.

"No," Binim said with surprising firmness, "but tonight is Erev Shabbat. If you don't have a family to go to, come to my flat and share my meal with me. And then you can bring a fresh loaf with you. My name is Binyamin, Binyamin Himmelfarb." He spoke with unexpected authority.

"I'd like to, Mr Himmelfarb. I am Caleb Ben-Levi."

"You would?" Now it was Binim's turn to be surprised. The two men did not know what to say next. To break the awkward silence, Binim gave Caleb his address. "So, Caleb . . . I'll see you before sunset then."

Half an hour before the sun had set, Caleb found himself on the pavement outside Binim's house. The staircase had not seen fresh paint for decades and a bare light bulb hung from the ceiling. The house smelled of vegetables and fried fish. Erev Shabbat in Israel. Caleb knocked on a warped and peeling door. He heard shuffling footsteps, and Binyamin opened the door. He was greatly changed: he was wearing a clean white shirt and dark trousers, his eyes sparkled and joy radiated from his face. His flat was filled with the aroma of roasting chicken.

"Come in, come in," he beckoned, "And Shabbat Shalom."

Caleb held out a bag of groceries. "Shabbat Shalom, Mr Himmelfarb. Just a few things I thought might come in useful."

Binim felt ashamed and a little insulted. "I didn't invite you for this. I'm not a *schnorrer*."

Caleb sensed that he had crushed the little self-respect left to a Shoah survivor. "I . . . well, you were taking a chance inviting me. I'm a good eater and . . . I just . . ." The younger man thought, "Oh Binim, God wants to bless you and your pride has got in the way."

Binim sensed that he had embarrassed Caleb. "I'm very ungrateful. Forgive me, my friend. And please call me Binim. My friends used to. Do come through now. I just have to check the meat."

Binim trotted into the kitchen. Then he unpacked Caleb's groceries onto the small kitchen table. At the bottom of the bag he found a bottle of Kiddush wine, that special sweet Jewish reminder of God's blessings and abundance. Binim examined the label. "This is the vintage we drank at home. Purim 1940. After that . . ." He broke off in mid-sentence.

When everything was ready, the two men came to the table to welcome the Sabbath Queen. There was no woman present at the table, so Binim did everything himself. But it was just as meaningful. Caleb thought of Celia and the children. He did not ask after Binim's family.

The chicken was very small, but the meal was well rounded off with the plum compote Caleb had brought. After the glass of Kiddush wine, and some local white that Caleb had also brought, the men felt warm, full and blessed. While Binim cleared the table, Caleb looked round the poorly furnished room. He could smell the damp of winter lingering in the corners. There were no shelves filled with books, no photos, no trinkets. Nothing. Only a Tanach, the Hebrew Bible. A budgie chirped to himself in his cage. A few reproduction paintings, cut from a magazine, were pinned to the bare walls: Van Gogh's bunch of irises and a Monet garden scene.

Caleb got up and had a closer look at the Monet.

"It's my favourite." Binim came in with a tray in his hands. "Everyone knows the Water Lilies and the Bridge, but this one's different. Look at the corner of the house: you can feel the warm evening sun, can't you? Have you seen the original? It's magnificent."

They talked about French impressionists for a while. Then Caleb asked, "Won't you be going to a Motzi Shabbat service?"

"No."

Caleb was taken aback by the curtness of the answer. But again he did not probe further. Unspeakable atrocities had taken place in the camps. They were enough to destroy a man's mind, let alone his faith. Caleb had seen the wretched remnant of God's people creeping, like thieves, up the beaches of Israel from the boats. Sometimes they had escaped the watchful British, often not.

"But let's read the weekly Parashat – the Torah portion – together," suggested Binim.

He fetched his worn Hebrew Bible and put the big book on the table. He chanted the blessings for the Torah reading in fluent Hebrew and read the prescribed portion. Then he passed the book to Caleb to read the Haftorah portion from the Prophets. Binim nodded, satisfied. He adjusted his spectacles and looked intently at his guest. "*Nu?*" he said, "Do you understand what you've just read?"

Caleb felt like a little boy back in his grandfather's study. In the bright light of day, Binim Himmelfarb had seemed a man worthy of compassion, a man to be pitied. Under the ceiling light of his small sitting room, he exuded the grace and wisdom of a Rabbi. Custom required that Caleb submit to his age and wisdom. "I was told this passage speaks of the Messiah."

Binim nodded in the way only a Rabbi could nod. "Do you know what to expect when the Mashiach comes? Would you recognise Him? After all, many false messiahs have come and gone – from Bar-Kochba to Shabbetai Zvi."

"And don't forget our greatest benefactor, Jesus Christ," Caleb added, his voice sarcastic.

Binim turned the pages as if he had not heard. "Our people are deplorably ignorant. We haven't been well taught. We all know about Mashiach Ben-David, but that's only half the story. Let's look at some less well-known passages."

Caleb leant back in his chair and folded his arms. "With all due respect, Binim, I can't believe in the Mashiach. Our Rabbis and sages have been looking for Him forever. And still they can't agree who He is and what He's supposed to do or accomplish. I think the Liberals are right: the Messiah is nothing but an ideal to strive for, that stops us from going *meshugge* as we try to work out our pathetic little lives. Look around you: we've got Eretz back, but look at the trouble we're in. And I don't just mean with the Arabs." He waved his arms dismissively.

"You really don't believe in the Messiah to come?"

"No, not after the Shoah."

"You don't have faith any more?"

"What? After the murder of six million innocents? No." Caleb shook his head vehemently.

"*You* can't believe? *You* can't have faith?" Binim bared his tattoo. "I had a large family, about 50 relatives. They're all gone. I was in the Lodz ghetto. And in Auschwitz. And the forced marches . . . If I told you all the details, they'd drive you insane . . ." Binim's voice was rising. "And, after all that, *you're* telling me *you* don't believe in the Hope of Israel?"

"Why did God not intervene? That's what I want to know. I always trusted God, believed in Him. Before the Shoah. If I sin deliberately, I deserve to be punished. But what about the children? What did they do that was bad enough for them to deserve the Shoah?"

Binim read from the Tanach. "'Arise, cry out in the night: In the beginning of the watches pour out thy heart like water before the face of the Lord: Lift up your hands towards him for the life of your young children' – don't you think we did that as we cowered, ten in a room? – 'our children that faint for hunger at the head of every street.' – as they did in Lodz – 'Young and old lie on the ground in the streets' – I've seen that with my own eyes – 'my virgins and young men are fallen by the sword' – the Warsaw Ghetto Uprising – 'thou hast slain them in the day of thine anger . . . so that that in the day of the Lord's anger none escaped or remained' – except a tiny remnant – 'those that I have cherished and brought up my enemy has consumed.' Can I argue with God? That's what our Prophets told us would happen. Has

447

that never troubled you? Why are you so astonished that what the prophets said would happen has happened? Is it just because these things have come upon us in *our* lifetime? Do you believe the Almighty gave us the last words of Divrei-HaYamin – the Book of Chronicles – and then simply vanished? Why have you lost faith in the days of our adversity? Did you renounce the Messianic Hope because of Massada? Of course not. Or did you say, back in '32, 'I have no faith because of Chmielnicki's massacre in Poland?' Did you? No. Chmielnicki or Hitler . . . What's the difference?"

"The difference is six million murdered Jews," Caleb replied with rising anger.

Binim quoted: " 'He who destroys one life, it is as if he has killed mankind. He who saves one life, it is as if he has saved the world entire.' Hundreds, thousands or millions; a life is a life."

"How often have I wished that God was less faithful to His covenant with Israel. Why can't He pick on a different nation for once?"

"When did you last read the blessings and the curses in Deuteronomy? And take them to heart? And have you noticed that it never occurs to our politicians to let God have a say in the running of our beautiful Land? It is His Land after all, isn't it? He can uproot us again at any time if He so wishes. The Mosaic covenant makes dwelling in the Land in peace and safety conditional upon our obedience to Him. Peace for Israel isn't a right; it's a reward for righteousness. You want Judah to live in peace? Then cleanse your heart from sin and start living Torah as Adonai always meant it to be lived. Life in the Diaspora is a judgement for sin committed in the Land; it's death to us. Always."

Binim's skinny body trembled. The terrors of the concentration camp rose in his mind like poisonous marsh gasses. He started to cry. What could Caleb do or say? He felt at a loss for words. Who could comprehend what these poor people had seen? Who could bring healing to their trauma-tised souls? Who could explain, justify or justly weigh what had befallen them? They were all damaged for life. This was one of the reasons why his fellow countrymen found it so hard to deal with the Shoah survivors. Many Jews had read, sighed, and shaken their heads over the ancient atrocities described in the Book of Lamentations. They had shuddered . . . in the comfort of their German living rooms . . . until they too were swept away in the bloody floodwaters that had crashed through Europe in the last decade. Mashiach – why are you tarrying? Why are you holding back? Why did you not come and do what you promised in the Scriptures? What kind of cruel game are you playing with us?

"Why did Mashiach not come when we most needed him?" Caleb whispered across the table at his aged, memory-tortured tutor.

Binim lifted his bowed head. Caleb watched the glow fade from his eyes, quenched by his memories. "He was there . . . Yes, HaMashiach . . . He was with us in the camps. I am His witness. And thousands of others . . . could have testified . . . if they hadn't been gathered to our Fathers. He never abandoned us, and He never will: He is The Faithful One. But you . . . would you recognise Messiah even if He were staring you in the face? You think He'll come as the glo-rious Ben-David, to deliver us from all our enemies and problems . . . as we continue in our ungodliness and disobe-dience. Can't you see that the real deliverance we need is not from outward oppression? It's from the wickedness within each one of us. The Kingdom of Heaven is not like the king-doms of men. The Kingdom of Heaven begins in the heart. If we don't choose to bow to Adonai's reign in our hearts now . . . if we don't want Him as our King now . . . what hope is there for us as His people? Why should He come to save a people who don't want Him, who have rejected Him in their hearts? First we must change on the inside; then He can

449

affect what's on the outside. The heart of our nation has to be touched first. And the heart of our nation lies in the heart of every Jew. Ben-David cannot deliver us from our enemies out there before we have allowed Him to deliver us from the enemy within each one of us." Binim's tone had mellowed. He was speaking in the soft, gentle way of a Rabbi reasoning with a young Yeshiva student struggling with his lesson.

"So, who can deliver us from this enemy within?"

"A good question. And a good question is as important as a good answer. I can see in your eyes that you've been troubled by this question before. You know that there's something within you that keeps you from leading a Godly life; something that stops you from keeping Torah correctly. Whatever you may say, I don't believe you've totally abandoned the Messianic Hope. You're angry with God because you don't understand His ways. But deep in your heart I can see that you want to understand. You're a true Israelite. And, if you'll listen with your heart, the God of our Fathers will speak to you. God said: 'Sh'mah Yisrael' – 'Hear, O Israel' . . . Remember? Just open the ears of your heart . . . listen, understand, trust . . . and obey."

"Who is this Deliverer then if it's not Ben-David?" Caleb persisted, stubbornly. Binim was keeping him on tenterhooks and he was growing impatient. If there was a real possibility of deliverance for his people, then Binim had a duty to share his revelation.

Instead of answering his question directly, Binim said, "Have you been taught that 'Adonai is the Immersion of Israel'?"

Caleb thought for a moment. "No, I haven't. I've never been a Yeshiva student."

"Here, read this." Binim pushed the Tanach to Caleb and pointed with his bony finger to a verse in *Yirmeyahu* – the Prophet Isaiah – chapter 14.

"*Mikveh yisra'el moshyi'u b'eyt tsarah,*" Caleb read. "O

Lord, the Hope of Yisrael in times of trouble." He was surprised. "But a mikveh is a ritual immersion bath – for our ritual cleansing. So how can Adonai be Israel's 'ritual immersion'?"

"Well, how can He be the Immersion of our Fathers?" Binim asked with a smile. "Here, read this." He pointed to another passage he had turned to while Caleb was talking.

"'U'mikveh avoteynu Adonai.' What? It actually does say that Adonai is the Immersion of our Fathers' . . ."

"Right. Now we'll dig a little deeper: you're a good Jew; you go to the mikveh from time to time. To make yourself ritually clean, you need a ritual immersion, don't you?" Caleb fidgeted. He had not been to a mikveh for years. "But it only ever deals with the external impurities. Do you understand? You're outwardly clean, but what about the inside? Now, look at Yekhezqel (Ezekiel) 36: Adonai promises that He Himself will cleanse us from all our filthiness and idolatry. And look at Yesha'yahu 4:4" – he turned the pages fast – "'When Adonai shall have washed away the filth of the daughters of Zion' . . ." Binim sat back and took a deep breath. Then he continued: "So, if you go to the mikveh you're ritually clean. That's good. But what else do you have to do to be accepted by Adonai?"

Caleb fidgeted. "Keep the commandments?"

"Yes. But how do you deal with the sin you incur when you don't keep the mitzvot?"

"You perform the mitzvot of Tefilah, Teshuvah and Tzedakah – prayer, repentance and charity. You fast on Yom Kippur and hope your name has been written in the Book of Life for another year."

"Yes, you're right again. Anyway, that's what our Rabbis now teach. Rabbinic teaching and Torah interpretation has changed dramatically over the last 2,000 years. Sometimes it has changed so much it has lost touch with what the written Torah text actually says."

Caleb nodded, remembering his arguments with his uncle on this very same issue.

"But let's return to the central point I want to make: can being 'good' or 'observant' – mixed with a shaky hope that it'll be all right in the end – somehow or other – actually atone for our sins? 'Doing good' is what we're meant to do. Yes, of course there is a reward from God for doing good. But the Torah never says that 'doing good' – performing the mitzvot – by itself provides any redemption for our souls. Redemption is needed when we don't 'do good'. So what exactly does the Torah teach?" The question was rhetorical and Binim turned the pages of his Tanach to reveal the answer. "Here. In Vayikra – Leviticus – 17:11 it says that 'blood atones for the soul'. The great Rashi affirms this when he says: 'Let one life be offered to atone for another.'"

Caleb was starting to get confused. "But to offer the sacrifices prescribed in the Torah, you need a Temple, and an altar, Cohanim and Levites; you need to reinstate the whole biblical sacrificial system. That's just ridiculous: we haven't had a Temple for 1,900 years. You know that. And what the Samaritans still do at Pesach on Mount Gerizim isn't Torah either. Since the war, we can't even go to the Western Wall any more . . ." Caleb sighed.

He felt a little depressed. The Western Wall had fallen to the Jordanians in 1948. The Jews had been unable to hold on to it during the War of Independence. Caleb regarded this as a deeply humiliating – almost personal failure. But he wanted to get to the bottom of this issue. "Didn't our Rabbis solve the problem long ago, in Yavne, just after the Temple was destroyed? Didn't they change all the Halachah about the Temple and sacrifices? You know as well as I do that good deeds have replaced the sacrifices, even the ones for sin." He chuckled to himself. "But, Binim, if you want to shed a little blood, you can still swing a chicken on Yom Kippur." He thought back to the time he had watched his

452

grandmother do this in London. "It's messy, though. I'm not sure that's what God wants to see either."

Binim ignored his banter; this was an important issue. "Are you seriously saying that you think the rulings and interpretations of the Rabbis have more weight than the Torah itself? Don't you realise that these are the very words and mitzvot given to Moses by none other than Adonai Himself? And recorded by *Moshe Rabbenu* himself in the written Torah?"

"It's time you were serious, Binim: the Temple was destroyed long ago. So our whole discussion about the sin sacrifice is pointless." Caleb was starting to feel irritated.

"Is seeking atonement for your everlasting soul pointless as well?" Binim asked gently.

"Why do you keep going on about the sin sacrifices and atonement for my soul?" Caleb's irritation was turning to anger.

Binim went on undeterred. "And even if the Temple were still standing, God would no longer accept our sin sacrifices. Do you know that the Talmud records that, after the Yom Kippur sin sacrifice was completed, the Levites used to bind a scarlet thread around the handles of the doors to the inner sanctuary? Why? To know whether their sacrifice had been accepted by Him. And so, in His great mercy, He would miraculously turn the thread white every year. 'Though your sins are like scarlet, they shall be as white as snow (Isaiah 1:18).' However, this miracle stopped in the year 30 of our Common Era and it never happened again. Until the Temple was destroyed in the year 70 CE the thread stayed scarlet. God has no longer accepted the blood of goats and bulls as atonement for our sins since 30 CE. Why? Because, in that year, He Himself provided a sacrificial offering. Just as He had provided one for Avraham to replace his son, Yitzchak, on the altar on Mount Moriah. Avraham Avinu called the place where he was to sacrifice his son 'Adonai Yireh' – 'The-Lord-will-Provide'. And what will the Lord provide? What had God miraculously provided for Avraham? A son and a sacrifice. And what would God provide a second time to Abraham's descendants? Another Son and another Sacrifice. This time, however, the Father who took His Son up to Mount Moriah was given no merciful alternative. The Son became the sacrifice, so that the Scriptures would be fulfilled, 'When you make His soul an offering for sin . . . He bore the sins of many.'"

Binim looked hard at Caleb. His words had reached into the hidden depths of Caleb's soul and awoken old, sleeping traumas. With a cry he jumped up. "You're a Christian! You're trying to convert me. All these trappings . . . pretending to be a Jew . . . were only to trick me into listening seriously to you. This nonsense about blood and water . . . in reality you're talking about Christian baptism and the death of Jesus Christ. You're repulsive! For a moment I really believed you had the answers. May Adonai forgive me for ever having come to this place. You deceived me with your charade of being an honest, God-fearing Jew. I felt sorry for you because you'd been through the Shoah. But it's scum like you who hunt down our people mercilessly . . . not to kill us but to destroy our souls. That's worse than destroying our bodies. What the Nazis didn't manage to do with their whips and poison gas, you'll accomplish with honey-and-death words dripping from your lips."

At the word "Christian", Binim also got up and cried, "What's there left to destroy in a Jew who claims: 'There is no God'? Or in a Jew who's so proud of his piety that he thinks he can command God? Sin alone separates us from God. And our suffering does not unite us with Him. We're separated from Him and therefore suffer because of our sins – our own sins and those of others." He rolled up his sleeve with shaking hands. "Here . . . see this? Do you think I got this mark because I was a Christian? No. It was because I am a Jew. As Jewish as you. So what's the difference? Only that you're stiff-necked, ignorant, faithless and rebellious to the core . . . just as *Moshe Rabbenu* said. You even use the Shoah as an excuse for your disobedience. Did we ever use the Roman occupation and pagan barbarism as a reason for not looking for the Messiah? On the contrary. When He came, thousands of Jews – all zealous for the Torah – flocked to Him. And don't use my sufferings to justify your blindness, disobedience and lack of trust. I was lying half-dead in a mass grave when, miraculously, Allied soldiers pulled me out. If I can still believe in God and His Messiah, so can you."

"You seem to forget that you aren't the only one who has suffered. The German half of my family and Polish relatives died in Auschwitz. My office is full of reports about men and women who work for Israel behind enemy lines. *I* send them there. Sometimes one gets killed. If he's lucky. The unlucky ones die under torture. And those folders sit there in my safe like living nightmares, day and night, like vultures tearing at my heart," Caleb shouted. He wanted to cover his ears.

Binim ignored the interruption. "God – God alone – is just and righteous and holy. He gives to each man according to his deeds . . . and Israel according to her faithfulness. We can blame the Germans, the Nazis, the Allies, the Arabs . . . You can blame us Jews and even blame yourself for what happened . . . But you can never blame the Almighty. When you blame Him, it only shows that you do not know the Holy One, blessed be He, or the Scriptures, or His plan for salvation. If you did, you'd weep over your sins. Then you'd fall at His feet and worship Him for the glorious mercy He's poured out on us for 4,000 years. Instead you . . . Mr perfect, righteous Ben-Levi . . . you mock and insult Him. And now I've had enough of you. Just get out."

And with that – and surprising vigour – Binim pushed Caleb to the door and out of his flat. His voice was shaking with disgust and distress. He slammed the door.

What an end to an Erev Shabbat! For a moment, Caleb stood on the landing, bewildered. Then he shook his head. This would not happen to him again, falling for a Christian disguised as a Jew. In a way he felt sorry. He had liked Binim. His line of reasoning had been so rabbinic and plausible. He put his hand on the banister, ready to go down. A Christian who lived like a Jew? Papa would have loved it . . .

Suddenly, he heard a crash and a loud thud from behind Binim's door. Concerned, he turned back and knocked. There was no reply. He knocked louder. Still no reply.

"Binim! Are you all right?" Caleb banged on the door. A neighbour opened hers instead. "I heard a noise and now Mr Himmelfarb doesn't answer," he said to explain his behaviour. The neighbour came forward and called as well. Still no response.

"Please, step back. I'm going to break the door down." It took Caleb only one attempt and the door flew open. From the floor above a voice called out, "*Oy*, it's Shobbes."

Binim lay unconscious in the narrow hall clutching the tablecloth. Everything on the dresser had crashed to the floor. "Binim!" Caleb felt his pulse. It was very weak. He picked up the frail body and carried Binim into the street. He stopped the next car that came and asked the driver to rush them to hospital.

~ 39 ~

Tel Aviv, 6th June 1952

The nurses' shoes squeaked on the linoleum. The hospital smelled of medicine, antiseptic and floor polish.

While the doctors and nurses fought for Binim Himmelfarb's life, Caleb sat in the hospital corridor mulling over his own. He felt that his life and future were in tatters. And the God he had once believed in . . . Where was He? Had God forgotten him? Or had Caleb simply forgotten God? Binim maintained that God had been with him in the Lodz ghetto. What an absurd claim. But not even the concentration camp had been able to destroy his trust in Him. And what if it were true? And what if God had also been there on the day he and his friends had driven straight into the Arab ambush?

Caleb had lain there, badly wounded, in the scorching sun, feeling his life slowly bleed away. A sky of cloudless blue had expanded above him. It reminded him of the awesomeness of God. Caleb had wanted to pray. But God's Heavenly Throne Room seemed to have been abandoned. Had God finished holding audience with His people? Had He simply packed His bags and left Israel to her own devices? Prayer was only a one-way communication anyway, wasn't it? The Prophets were dead now; God did not speak any more. A prayer might be scribbled on a piece of paper and tucked into the cracks of the Western Wall, but no angel ever came to collect it; no messenger ever left a reply. Prayers were offered in hope, not certainty, weren't they? Caleb had felt forgotten and abandoned; dying on a road of burning stones. Arik's whimpering cries for water had tortured his ears until they stopped. Tears had trickled from his eyes and a terrifying darkness had crept upon him. The next thing he remembered was Celia holding his hand. Now she too was gone.

What a mess, what a waste his whole life was. But did he feel any bitterness towards his Maker? No. God was Supreme and Absolute. He had a right to do as He pleased. It was just the great void in his own soul that he hated. And against that he could do nothing. "It's our sin that separates us from God," Papa had said. "Us from Him," he had stressed. "But He came to us while we were still sinners."

Caleb had hoped that, over time, these unuttered, heart-wrenching questions would resolve themselves. They had not. And, to top it all, he and Celia had drifted apart. She had put thousands of miles between them. The children would grow up as little Englishmen after all. Dammit! And now he sat here, waiting for news about the health of an apostate Jew. Everything in his life was screwed up.

"Mr Ben-Levi?" It was the nurse. "I've got some good news for you. Mr Himmelfarb has regained consciousness. He's asleep now. But you can see him if you come back tomorrow. Are you a relative?"

Caleb looked at her with a tired, cynical smile. "*Chol Yisrael achim,*" he said. All Israel are brothers.

It was late. He went back to Binim's flat to make sure the door was locked and the budgie taken care of. He spent the rest of the night wandering the streets aimlessly. In his hand he was carrying a brown paper bag with two books in it. By dawn, he was in his office.

The brown bag sat on his desk all day. It demanded his attention. Christ was dead and buried. Or was He? Christians said He had risen from the dead and was living in the hearts of His followers, yearning to spread His message of deliverance and salvation through them. But how could Binim live like a good Jew and be a Christian? Impossible. Caleb grabbed the brown bag angrily and left the office.

Binim lay propped up in his hospital bed, resting. He stirred as Caleb approached and opened his eyes. He recognised his visitor. A bright smile lit up his face. "Caleb Ben-Levi! What a most wonderful . . ."

Words failed him, and Caleb too. There was not even a hint of reproach in Binim's greeting, only joy at his visit. Caleb fidgeted. What was he supposed to say to a man he had nearly killed with verbal abuse? And he was now welcoming to him as a father welcomes his son.

"There's a chair. Pull it over and sit down. Or are you in a hurry?" Binim said.

"No, not particularly. How are you?"

"I'm well, thank you. This is a wonderfully comfortable bed. Look how white the sheets are. The food is excellent and plentiful, although I can't eat as much as I'd like. The camps, you know . . . And the friendly young nurses . . . they delight my heart."

Caleb could not help but smile. "Blessed is the man who can give thanks for little things," he thought. "I had to break down your door. But I've made everything secure and your neighbour is looking after your budgie. And I brought you these." He handed the paper bag to Binim who took out the books: a Tanach and a New Testament.

"I'm very grateful. Thank you."

Caleb threw a surreptitious glance at them. Thirteen years ago the title "New Testament"' had blinded him with rage. Now he was resigned. What was wrong with him?

Binim noticed his glance. "Would you like to borrow it?"

"I can't."

"Why not?"

"I'm a Jew."

"So am I. Why do you keep running from the God of our Fathers when He loves you so much?" Binim asked quietly.

But he was not the only one speaking. Caleb's heart had heard, *"I am a Jew. Why do you keep running from Me when I love you so much?"* It was as if God Himself had spoken to him. It was so loud, so clear. It tore at his heart. He left Binim without saying another word.

"God, God," he cried silently as he hurried along the hospital corridors. "If You are calling to me, then show me. I must know." He could not stand it.

Back in his office he asked his sergeant to find him a Tanach. "A Tanach, sir?" The sergeant repeated the request to make sure he had heard right.

"Yes, a Tanach, dammit! What's so unusual about asking for a Hebrew Bible in Israel?"

Later he read a long passage in the Book of the Prophet Yesha'yahu – Isaiah:

He was despised and rejected of men, a man of pains, and acquainted with sickness. And we hid, as it were, our faces from him; he was despised, and we esteemed him not. But in truth he has borne our sicknesses and endured our pains; yet we did esteem him stricken, smitten by God, and afflicted. But he was wounded because of our transgressions, bruised because of our iniquities; his sufferings were that we might have peace, and by his injury we are healed.

All we like sheep have gone astray; we have turned each to his own way; and the Lord has caused the iniquity of us to fall upon him. He was oppressed, but he humbled himself and opened not his mouth; as a lamb that is brought to the slaughter, and as a sheep before her shearers is dumb, so he did not open his mouth. By oppression and false judgment he was taken away, and of his generation who considered? For he was cut out of the land of the living; for the transgression of the people to whom the stroke was due.

For they made his grave among the wicked, and his tomb among the rich; because he had done no violence, neither was any deceit in his mouth. For he said, "Surely, they are my people, children that will not lie": so he was their deliverer. In all their afflictions he was afflicted, and the Angel of His Presence saved them: in his love and in his pity he redeemed them; he bore them, and carried them all the days of old.

But they rebelled and vexed his Holy Spirit: therefore he was turned to be their enemy, and he fought against them. "Behold, thou hast been very angry, and we have sinned. In those ways we remain always: how then shall we be saved? You, O Lord, are our Father; our redeemer from everlasting is your name."

The spirit in Caleb groaned; anguish filled his soul; voices echoed in his heart. "Because you wouldn't recognise Mashiach even if He were staring you in the face," Binim had said. And, "But your iniquities have separated you from your God, and your sins have hidden His face from you."

There he had it, in black on white, these thousands of years. The blood and the water. "With joy we shall draw water from the wells of salvation." Fragments from the Scriptures began to fall together like pieces of a jigsaw. Then suddenly, *"I am a Jew. Why do you keep running from me?"* Again and again these words rang in the ears of Caleb's mind, like the still, small voice of God thundering from on high.

It was already dusk when he arrived at the hospital. He walked straight past the staff nurse's desk, but she blocked his way. "I'm sorry, sir. Visiting times are between three and five each afternoon. You'll have to come back tomorrow. Our patients need their rest."

"Nurse, I need to speak to Binyamin Himmelfarb. It's a matter of national security," Caleb lied with authority. He had never abused his authority as a member of the Israeli intelligence service before. Today was the first time he had used his position to get what he wanted. The nurse relented. After all, what was more important than Israel's security?

The lights were dimmed on the ward. Some patients were

resting, some were reading, others were asleep. Binim was dozing, but awoke as Caleb approached his bed. "Ben-Levi. At this time of night? How did you get past the nurses?" he mumbled sleepily. He pushed himself up on his pillow. Caleb helped him.

"I lied. I said it was a matter of national security."

"It isn't?"

"That depends. Is wanting to know who the Messiah is a matter of national security? Tell me straight: is He the promised Messiah?" However hard he tried, he could still not bring himself to talk about Jesus and the Messiah of Israel in the same breath.

Binim looked at Caleb. He was not taking any prisoners today; he was not going to make it easy for this man. He needed a direct revelation from Adonai, not words from Binyamin Himmelfarb. "I won't tell you. You'll have to find out for yourself."

"But . . . how can I find out whether . . . the evidence . . . that Jesus is . . ." Caleb faltered and thought he was dreaming. Were these words really passing his lips?

Binim let his student struggle. If Ben-Levi were a true seeker then nothing would put him off. What great mercy, what love, what wonderful compassion Adonai showed His people! What amazing grace that He had led a proud Jew at night to the bed of a feeble, sick man in his quest for the Messiah. The ways of God were unfathomable. Binim's heart beat fast as he reached for his New Testament on the bedside cabinet.

He handed the book to Caleb who accepted it reluctantly and with an intense inner struggle. What was going on? Was he really that distraught that he could seriously consider the Christian solution to his lifelong struggle?

"This is the written evidence of what Yeshua Ben-Yossef did. Read it and tell me then if you think He is the Messiah of Israel."

A memory flashed through Caleb's mind. "Yeshua Ben-Yossef, did you say? I've heard that name before."

"The Rabbis used to teach that two Redeemers would come: one, Ben-David the King, and the other, Ben-Yossef the Servant. You don't honestly believe that the actual name of the Messiah of Israel is 'Jesus', do you? HaMashiach is a Jew. So His name is Hebrew. The Messiah's real name is 'Yeshua'."

"But 'Yeshua' means 'salvation' . . ."

"*Adonai yeshuati*. The Lord is my salvation. What did you expect? And salvation comes from the Jews, as Rabbi Shaul of Tarsus taught."

"Rabbi Shaul of Tarsus? You mean 'Saint Paul'."

"No, I mean Rabbi Shaul of Tarsus, who taught in the synagogues on Shabbat. Not the St Paul of the church who some say invented Christianity. Shaul taught what had been revealed to him by Mashiach. He taught the believing communities to keep Messianic Halachah. He was a Jew, a Pharisee of the tribe of Binyamin. Bear that in mind when you read this." He pointed to the New Testament. "Remember, they were all Jews, the men who wrote this book. And it's all about Jews like you and me."

Binim did not see his friend for several days. When Caleb at last returned, he seemed more relaxed. "I'm sorry I didn't visit you earlier. The nurse says you're making excellent progress."

Binim smiled and raised his eyebrows. "And?" He challenged his student for a response to the unuttered question that hung in the air.

"I've read your book. It's not at all what I expected. It's . . . well . . . so Jewish. But I've got lots of questions . . ."

"We can discuss them when I'm out of here. Now, tell me, is Yeshua the Messiah?"

Thrusting his hands deep into his pockets, Caleb went to

the window and looked down at the busy street. Life was so normal, so ordinary out there. People went about their business, made a living, worried about tomorrow, the certainty of the next war . . . Was Yeshua the Messiah? If God had not forgotten His people . . . if Yeshua had indeed risen from the dead . . . then . . . then there was another reality to this soil far beyond what he could humanly conceive. If Yeshua had indeed come to make peace between God and man . . . if He was indeed the *Sar Shalom*, the Prince of Peace . . . He turned to Binim.

"If He is . . . the implications would be enormous. Personally and nationally." His voice wavered. Then he shook his head. "No." He was unable to make that final leap, to betray everything he had ever believed, to join the enemy's camp. "No. I'm not a *meshumad*. I'm not blind to our many shortcomings, but I love my people Israel too much. I'd give my life's blood to save them, but become a Christian . . .? No. I'm sorry, Binim, you're a *mensh*, but you're expecting too much of me."

"But you can never save Israel! Only the Messiah can . . . only Yeshua HaMashiach. Why perish with the rebellious and unrighteous? Will they thank you for dying with them?"

Caleb changed the subject abruptly. "I forgot to bring you your house keys. I'll do that tomorrow." He avoided looking at Binim.

The Shoah survivor watched him leave the ward. Tomorrow he would see Caleb Ben-Levi for the last time. "Caleb!" Binim's appeal was desperate. His eyes were moist.

Caleb kept walking.

Binim's condition deteriorated rapidly and inexplicably over night. The doctors and nurses were baffled. He had made surprisingly good progress so far considering his general poor health. Now he had suddenly relapsed for no apparent reason.

"Any friends or relatives we can contact?" the nurses asked.

Around 3 am, the telephone shrilled. In the darkness, Caleb groped for his rifle, panicked when he could not find it, realised he was at home, and stumbled, only half awake, to the telephone. An hour later he was in the hospital again.

"We don't know what happened. He suddenly took a turn for the worse." The nurse led him to the bed, which was now surrounded by a curtain.

The old man's eyes were closed. His lungs laboured over every breath. This time it looked grim. Had Binim's recovery been only the last struggle before certain death? The fighter, battered by life and war, sat down at the patient's bedside and dropped his head into his hands. Binim had been young once, and in love; he had founded a family and cared for them. Then Nazi horror had torn his life apart. Now one lone Israeli was all he had left. What a wasted life. Around him was the stillness of the fading night. A wall clock above the door ticked away the seconds, minutes and hours of Binim's life. The sound battered at his head. A ward sister sat at her desk. A lamp highlighted her features harshly. Her glasses had slipped to the end of her nose as she concentrated, with a suppressed yawn, on a crossword. A patient groaned, another murmured in his sleep. That Binim was lying here was Caleb's fault alone. But for him, he would probably have lived for another ten years. Why had he not kept quiet about his Messiah?

"You know why this has happened, don't you? What more must I do to make you listen to My voice?" Caleb recognised the Voice.

"But I'm a Jew. I can't possibly . . ."

"I am the Jew you are looking for . . ."

A whispered prayer he would never have thought possible – not from him, not from Caleb Ben-Levi the Jew – started to pour from his lips. He asked God to forgive all his sins and shortcomings because of the sacrificial death and blood shed by Yeshua HaMashiach. He acknowledged that he found it unspeakably hard to make this confession, because he had always mocked Yeshua, blasphemed Him, fought Him, referred to Him as his worst personal enemy, and the enemy of all Jews. Then the tears started to stream, endless tears of shame, grief, remorse and contrition. And his soul crawled to the feet of the One he had once hated and despised. Caleb felt utterly weak and broken. He felt like dying. All his strength, resistance and pride poured out . . . like water onto desert sands. There was nothing left in him, and of him, and to him. Nothing. In his desolation, he cried out to his God for help, for salvation. And the God of Avraham, Yitzchak and Ya'akov answered him in his time of trouble. A wave of love rushed into him, flooding his life; a tenderness and compassion that were not of this world; a love unending, unlimited, unmerited and unconditional. Yeshua's arms of forgiveness and acceptance embraced him tightly. Caleb buried his face in Binim's shoulder. Then he wept and wept. And his Father wept with him . . . and rejoiced: a much-loved son had returned home. A lost sheep of the House of Israel had recognised his Shepherd at last.

Binim gently put his hand on Caleb's head, prayed, and waited patiently. After a long while, Caleb looked up, exhausted – and straight into Binim's open eyes. "It's nice to wake up and find someone with you," the old man whispered.

Caleb took Binim's withered hand in his and spoke the words Binim was longing to hear: "Yeshua is our Messiah."

Binim was shaken. In the ghetto and camps he had told others about Yeshua, giving all he had left to a people fated for destruction. He had faithfully shared the assurance of forgiveness and salvation in Messiah, and the certain hope of a glorious resurrection to eternal life. For this he had been mocked, disowned and reviled by his own people. What a *chutzpah*, what a nerve, to speak of Yeshua and repentance in this living nightmare! Some Jews committed suicide by "going to the wire" and died quickly, a German bullet in their heads. Thousands were collapsing and dying in the streets, diseased and emaciated. Hundreds of thousands were sent to an "unknown destination". And this traitor, this "Christian" dared to speak of repentance! But could Binim deny that Yeshua had paid for the sins of the whole world, even the sins of the death camps? Could he abandon his people in their misery and remain silent? Yeshua had to be with His people now, just as He had once before come to them under Roman oppression. A yet undisclosed number of old and young, men and women, responded. And died reconciled with their Father, their King. Yes, God was in the death camps. And He had sent His messenger, Binim Himmelfarb, to be his mouth, eyes and hands. This was his personal "Great Commission". And now Adonai was rewarding him by allowing him, once again, to watch a fellow Jew receive a circumcised heart from the hands of the God of Israel.

"If you truly believe that Yeshua is our *kapparah*, our sin sacrifice, then you must confess it with your mouth. Tell someone the Truth you have just discovered. Then go and immerse yourself according to the Torah as an outward sign of your repentance and cleansing."

To the amazement of the doctors and nurses, Binim suddenly started to recover rapidly. This time for good.

"Do you believe in miracles, Dr Weichselfisz?" he asked one morning as the doctor was doing his rounds on the ward.

"No, and I never have. But you're a very special case."

Binim smiled. "Doctor, would you recognise a miracle if it spoke to you?"

Caleb's recovery was equally remarkable. For the very first time in his life, he experienced true peace of heart and soul. The permanent presence of his King and Saviour in and around him was so sweet, so wonderful, so amazing, so beyond his wildest dreams. His love and adoration of Yeshua grew day by day. A quiet smile appeared and took up residence on his lips. His friends could not fail to notice it. One asked, mischievously, "*Oy*, Ben-Levi, is your wife expecting again?"

"No," Caleb laughed and answered with a riddle. "'But the virgin was with child and His name is Immanuel.' And do you know who this Immanuel is? No? Then let me tell you . . ."

Efrem took Caleb's joy and peace in an entirely different way. When Caleb was helping him repair a tractor, Efrem suddenly lost his usual self-control. He grabbed his friend, pushed him against the big tyre and pressed his arm against his throat. "Ben-Levi, you son of a proselyte," he growled. "You disgust me." He spat on the ground.

"Efrem," Caleb choked. "What on earth's got into you? What's the matter?"

"What's the matter?" he mimicked. "It's your damn smile that's upsetting me. Ruchel and the children are gone barely three months and you're already having an affair. Your wife stuck with you through thick and thin. But as soon as her back's turned you shack up with some tart."

Caleb put two and two together. "Are you accusing me of adultery?"

"Do you think I haven't noticed your stupid smiles and your chirpiness? What's her name, eh?"

Caleb thought for a second that his friend would really lash out. "Let go of me. I'm not having an affair, you big gorilla."

Efrem let him go. Crossing his arms, legs akimbo, he took up position in front of Caleb, threateningly. "Well then?"

Yes, well. Caleb had been praying that Yeshua would create an opening for him to break the good news to his friends at Emek Prachim. He wanted to say that Messiah had come, but that Israel had not recognised him, that they had missed the time of their First Visitation. But how could he explain this here and now? And especially to the tall, dark and stubborn Efrem? Efrem possessed wonderful qualities, but godliness was not one of them.

"Get the car. I want you to meet someone," Caleb said.

Together they drove to Tel Aviv, where Caleb introduced Efrem to Binim – and to Yeshua. Efrem had been less than delighted.

"Listen, Cal," he warned him. "We've fought together and been through many difficult situations together. But you're on your own with this Yeshua thing. And if you try to stir up trouble at Emek Prachim, the committee won't hesitate to throw you and your family out of the kibbutz. And I'll be the first to support them. For now I won't say anything, because your religious beliefs are your private business. As long as you don't try to destroy our Jewish homeland and our traditions . . ."

Caleb just laughed. "On the contrary, *chaver*, on the contrary . . ."

~ 40 ~

Emek Prachim, 30th June 1952

Celia. How could he explain across the miles what had happened to him? She would just assume, automatically, that he had converted to Christianity. Caleb still wrestled with the idea that he had become a Christian.

Binim vehemently refuted and rejected this notion. "You're a Jew, Caleb, not a Christian. If a Jew has to become a Christian to be saved, then *Moshe Rabbenu* wasn't saved because he wasn't a Christian. And that means that neither Moshe nor Eliyahu met with Yeshua on Mount Tabor. Why not turn the argument on its head and say that a Gentile has to become a Jew to be saved? This false teaching was being propagated by first century religious Judaisers – the so-called 'Circumcision Faction'. Rabbi Shaul killed that argument dead in his letter to the Galatians. A Jew is a Jew; a Gentile is a Gentile; a man is a man and a woman is a woman; some things never change. A Jew who acknowledges Yeshua receives the Ruach haKodesh, the Spirit of God, and keeps the commandments as Yeshua did. He said: 'If you love Me, you will keep My commandments.' So His followers keep kosher, keep the biblical festivals, observe Shabbat and are members of a believing community. I long to see the establishment of a synagogue in Eretz that teaches Torah the way Adonai Yeshua intends us to keep His commandments . . ." Binim sighed.

"You're joking. You'll never see one of those in Eretz . . ."

Binim was very serious. "You don't believe it can

happen? Then think ahead. Be a visionary. As a Zionist it shouldn't be too difficult for you. Be a biblical Zionist. God has restored our nation physically. Let's start praying for its spiritual restoration." Binim's eyes had a sudden sparkle.

Caleb sighed again. "At the moment, I can't think any further ahead than my wife and children. Celia is the most wonderful wife and mother. She's supported me in everything, at great personal cost. I never realised how much I'd taken from her . . . and how little I'd given . . . because I'd made Israel my god. Once Celia wanted to help me by going to look for Messiah. She got so close to the truth. And then I waded in . . . Our kibbutzniks call her Ruchel. She's become so Jewish that you'd almost think she was one of us. Well, our children think she is, and we don't tell them otherwise. And now I've got to tell her that Yeshua is the Messiah after all. That I made a big mistake . . . If I'd only believed at the time – years ago – I think she would have believed too. I pulled her away from God. If she won't come to Yeshua now then I'm the one to blame . . ." Caleb was terrified to think about the consequences of his rebellion.

Binim reassured him. "God knows whose names are written into the Book of Life. He's outside of time. He knows the end of our lives before we were conceived. He alone knows which way we'll turn. Now it's between Him and your Celia. God alone can save her. Not you. Not me. We're commanded to warn mankind and to lead them to The Way. But in the end, every person is responsible for his or her own sin, and his or her own decisions. And your wife is responsible for hers. Yeshua has predestined love and peace for her too. Believe it and trust God. Pray for her, and your children."

* * *

Bleckham Manor, 4th July 1952

The postman delivered a rather strange but wonderful letter from Caleb. Something tremendous and amazing had happened, he wrote, something he could not explain or put in writing. He wanted to tell her personally. He would do all he could to come as soon as possible. She was not to worry; everything would be all right. Celia's first thought was that he had resigned from the Mossad. Did he want to surprise her? Other things he had written were very personal. They melted her heart and increased her agony. Ruven noticed his mother's fretfulness and thought of his father. He had noticed that "Abba" and "upset for Mamele" were always linked.

Then Caleb sent a telegram announcing his imminent arrival. Celia's hands started to tremble as she read the message. She simply did not know how to tell him. His last letters had been so sweet, so funny, so loving. They had touched her deeply. Now she would have to tell him that she believed in Adonai Yeshua. She could no longer avoid the issue.

Celia arrived at the station a quarter of an hour before Caleb's train was due. She sat on a bench outside the stationmaster's office. She was nervous, and tense enough to snap. She had prepared herself carefully, what to say and how to say it. Still, she kept rearranging sentences, throwing them out, starting again . . . it was useless. But she just had to tell him. "If you confess with your mouth, 'Yeshua is Adonai,' and believe in your heart that God raised Him from the dead, you will be saved." There was no way around it; she had to tell him. Yeshua had acknowledged her before His Father. How could she not acknowledge Him before her husband? She braced herself as the train – steaming, huffing and puffing – came into earshot, then into sight. Her hands turned cold and clammy in the warm summer sunshine. With shrieking brakes, the train ground to a halt, hissing and clanking. She saw Caleb get off at the far end of the platform. He looked out for her, but people got in the way. He got his bags from the carriage. What should she do? Run away? Then he turned again and saw her. Oh, Caleb, my love . . . Celia flew towards him. They flung their arms around each other. Caleb was still her place of refuge in times of trouble. But how could he know the torment he was causing her at this moment? He was both her shelter and her storm. He kissed Celia on the forehead as he had always done. She closed her eyes.

"How are you, my beautiful *sarai*?" he enquired tenderly. "Are you all right? And the children?" He searched her face.

Celia avoided his eyes. With her conscience crying out, she replied, "We're fine."

"You look much thinner. Are you sure you're well? You haven't been ill?"

"No . . . Let's get a porter for your suitcases. You've brought rather a lot. How long can you stay?"

"That depends. I'm on leave and have made it clear that I'm not to be contacted unless there is an emergency. I left Bleckham's number with the embassy in London. I hope that'll be all right with Alistair and Judy."

Caleb had changed beyond recognition. He looked happy and at peace. Maybe it had been the right decision for her to leave in order to save her marriage . . . only to destroy it now. What bitter irony.

They drove back to the manor in near total silence. Caleb grew worried and gave her a sideways glance. Had Celia decided to stay in England? Was that the problem? Or, worse still, was she about to ask for a separation?

In her anxiety, Celia was perspiring visibly; she knew she had to tell him. The sooner the better. She pulled over into a farm track, stopped the car and clutched the steering wheel with both hands. She could no longer control their shaking. "There's something I've got to tell you, Caleb. It has to be now. Otherwise every moment together will be a lie." Celia's voice trembled. She started to stammer, "Caleb, I believe in Yeshua of Nazret. He is the Messiah you've been waiting for. I'm so sorry. I know I promised but . . . please don't divorce me . . . but I can't deny Him. It's the truth. God help me."

It was the hardest confession she was ever to make. Her legs were shaking uncontrollably. She closed her eyes and thought of Lady Anne. This was how she must have felt as they put the torch to the tinder beneath her. Fearful, yet resigned, she waited for Caleb's judgement to fall on her. Seconds seemed to turn to hours. Her nerves snapped and she started to sob.

Caleb sat stunned as the news sank in. Thousands of miles away he had been praying with anguish in his heart that his wife . . . while she wrestled in England not knowing how to tell him . . . God, what wonders and miracles You do perform. How can words describe the amazing ways in which You deal with man? How much higher are Your ways than ours. You arrange all things beautifully, in Your wonderful wisdom, love and understanding of the human heart.

Very tenderly, so as not to frighten her, Caleb put his hand on Celia's shoulder and caressed it soothingly. "Celia. Celia, my love. Please listen. I've found Yeshua too. Or rather, He's found *me*. He literally stepped into my path and I fell over Him . . . and into His arms. Celia, I too believe."

Judy and Alistair could hardly grasp the wonderful news. They were full of joy and praised Jesus together for this miraculous conversion. Caleb and Celia had become Christians at last. Praise the Lord.

Caleb laughed as he watched them. He could now understand what they had been trying to tell him all those years. But then he became serious.

"Alistair, Judy, listen to me, please. This is important and it needs to be said. I am a Jew and believe in Yeshua. My children are Jewish and we shall raise them as Jews. My wife is a Gentile believer in the Jewish Messiah. We shall continue to live as God commands us in the Torah He gave us through His servant Moshe. We shall live out the fullness of the Torah as Yeshua HaMashiach lived it, and as He taught His disciples to live it. There will be no room in our home for Christian teachings and traditions that are rooted in Greek philosophy and pagan religions. Nor will we be bound by Rabbinic Judaism or Christianity. We'll continue to eat kosher as the Bible teaches. We'll keep the biblical festivals with joy and gladness. We'll celebrate the historical Jewish feasts, such as Purim and Chanukah, which Yeshua also celebrated. We will be living a biblical life; the life God always intended for all His people. We believing Jews – Messianic Jews – are the righteous remnant of Israel that Rabbi Shaul spoke of. We have an important role to play in God's plan for the salvation of the world. We intend to be obedient to Him, and to His revelation to us, and to His plan for us. Now more than ever. *Am Yisrael chai*: The people of Israel live!"

Judy and Alistair were shocked, confused, hurt and even angry. "But . . . if you believe in Jesus you're Christians . . . you must not forego the Christian festivals in favour of the Jewish ones . . . only the devil doesn't want you to celebrate Easter . . . you mustn't rebuild the wall of separation that Jesus destroyed on the cross . . . you mustn't separate yourself from the church . . . only the church can teach you about life in Jesus . . . you must be humble . . . you can learn so much from Christianity . . ."

Caleb sighed. Their differences would continue, it seemed. But at least they were now all one in Yeshua – even if they called Him "Jesus". His heart was light. Yeshua had searched out and found his family. And Yeshua was a Jew. End of story.

He smiled at Alistair. "Let's discuss this another time, shall we?"

Holding hands, Caleb and Celia Ben-Levi went for long walks along the beaches of Norfolk. They sat, silently, arm in arm. They ate cucumber sandwiches and drank tea from a Thermos flask. They were in love again. Celia had never looked lovelier than now. Her quiet, womanly smile said, "I know exactly what you're like. And I *still* love you."

Caleb mused as they walked: "You know, *sarai*, alone, I'm not perfect; alone, you're not perfect; but together, we're both perfect for each other, because God made us fit together perfectly." He drew her into his arms and kissed her.

They talked, poured out their hearts, and cried together. They started to reclaim those fourteen years that the wars had eaten up. Like desert flowers, withered by long years of drought, they burst into bloom with the coming of the rains.

Celia looked up into his smiling face. "You know, Caleb, the only time we ever truly had to ourselves was our honeymoon and then those few weeks before Papa died. After that, world events just took over and swept us along. And I know that, deep down, I've been a bad, selfish wife. I married a Jew, but however much my lips professed loyalty, in the end it was only you I wanted – not your people, not your calling, not your Torah, and not your Land. Not really, not deep down. And I didn't know the true faithfulness of God. I was deceiving myself and that caused my jealousy, confusion and rebellion. God had betrothed you to Himself by eternal covenant. I didn't understand that. I still wanted to lure you away and claim you, just for myself. Deep down, I only wanted you if I could have you on my own terms. I'm glad now that you didn't listen to me. Please forgive me for trying to drag you away from the path God had chosen for you."

Caleb took her hands in his. "Your loyalty was so deep that you put your life on the line for me, for us, for Israel. I know you made a lot of sacrifices – more than I would have been willing to make in your place. And it could have cost you your salvation if you had always listened to me."

It was still early in the morning when Celia got up. She opened the curtains and window wide, flooding the bedroom with sunlight. Contentedly, she surveyed the peaceful English country landscape. Dani had once said: "The Lord does not choose the equipped, but He equips the chosen, lest we trust in our own strength. That way, all the glory goes to Him . . . where it belongs." Celia knew now that God would continue to equip her to live and work in the Land that He had given her . . . after she had truly left her home and her country behind. At last she was really free. She no longer had to cling to the past because she was afraid to let go, or wrestle with a future she could not predict or control. Their lives were in God's hands; He knew all of their days. Whatever might befall them, they could now live in the revelation that Yeshua was walking ahead of them and beside them, protecting their backs. His plans for them were for love and peace, not pain and destruction.

Celia turned and leant back against the windowsill as she watched her sleeping spouse. He stirred and blinked in the sunshine. He saw her silhouetted against the window and stretched out an arm towards her. "*Matzah ishah matzah tovah* – He who's found a wife has found a good thing," was all he needed to say.

Celia reflected his loving smile back at him. "Time to get up and move on, my love. I've wasted enough of God's time. And I've a promise to keep . . . I've got a beef herd to raise. And I need to teach our people all I know about farming. By the way, do you think it's kosher to breed beef and dairy cattle on the same kibbutz?" She grinned irreverently.

Caleb rolled on his back and covered his face with his hands. "*Oy*! It's only six in the morning and my wife wants to revolutionise Rabbinic-Jewish agriculture."

Celia explained her idea while he half-listened, sleepily. Then she said, seriously, "If they throw us off the kibbutz because of Yeshua, maybe we can buy or build our own farm and take it from there. Employ our own workers and run it according to Messianic Torah. Tell the labourers – Jews *and* Arabs – about Yeshua . . . 'There's so much to do, the exiles are returning . . .'" She smiled as she quoted her husband's well-used phrase. "Let's go home, Caleb. Let's go back to Israel right away. *Eyn li eretz acheret*."

I have no other homeland.